PRAISE FOR *THE*

"Alastair Luft has made a major contribution to our knowledge of PTSD by putting a personal face on 'the battle within,' which will serve both soldier and citizen alike."

—Lieutenant General Michael K. Jeffery (retd.), former chief of the Land Staff, Canadian Armed Forces

"Although this book is a work of fiction, it shines a searing light on the real-life challenges and sometimes tragic consequences of PTSD."

—General Raymond Henault (retd.), former chief of Defence Staff, Canadian Armed Forces

"Anyone who wishes to understand the silent curse of PTSD, no matter what their background, would benefit from reading this compelling story."

—Major General Lewis MacKenzie (retd.), Canadian Armed Forces

"A must-read—a raw and real account of the harsh battle that rages on all fronts for many soldiers upon returning home from deployment. These shared soldiers' perspectives in Luft's words draw you into the daily struggles and challenges our finest face when dealing with PTSD as a result of their service, with the highest price of all often paid by their loved ones. Hard lessons that we tragically seem destined to learn over and over again."

—the Honourable Peter MacKay, PC, former Canadian minister of National Defence

THE
BATTLE
WITHIN

THE BATTLE WITHIN

ALASTAIR LUFT

INKSHARES

Published by Inkshares, Inc., San Francisco, California
www.inkshares.com

Edited and designed by Girl Friday Productions
www.girlfridayproductions.com
Cover design by Alban Fischer

ISBN: 9781942645498
e-ISBN: 9781942645504
Library of Congress Control Number: 2016945702

For Tabatha,
My favorite person in the whole world.
And in space.

A true war story is never moral. It does not instruct, nor encourage virtue, nor suggest models of proper human behavior, nor restrain men from doing the things that men have always done. If a story seems moral, do not believe it. If at the end of a war story you feel uplifted, or if you feel that some small bit of rectitude has been salvaged from the larger waste, then you have been made the victim of a very old and terrible lie.

—Tim O'Brien

If you're gonna fight with monsters, you'd better be ready to do some monstrous things.

—Daryl Robertson

CHAPTER 1

Major Hugh Dégaré bolted upright, blinking in the abyss-like darkness. Adrenaline pumped through his body as he raced from deep sleep to full throttle, thanks to years of practice. The familiar sights of his bedroom came into focus, everything tinted silver from the moonlight streaming through the window. A sound from across the room pulled his gaze. His wife sat shuddering on the floor in the corner, making herself even smaller by clutching her legs against her chest.

He threw off the covers and jumped out of bed. Sure-footed as a leopard, he crossed the distance to her in two purposeful steps.

"Elizabeth, are you all right?"

She cowered, clutching herself tighter. "Stay away."

Kneeling, he reached out to caress her leg. She shrank from his touch.

"What is it?"

She wiped her eyes and stared at him, her eyes reflecting the moonlight. "You hit me."

He shook his head. *That can't be true.* Reaching out again, he moved to stroke her leg. "Was it a nightmare?"

She swatted away his hand. "You hit me," she said deliberately, heat rising in her voice as she pronounced each word like she was speaking a foreign language. Even in the dark, the set of her jaw was unmistakable.

A knot grew in his stomach, and he shook his head slowly, grappling with the information. "I would never do that."

"Look!" Her hand jerked up, pointing to her face.

A tone in her voice made him hesitate, and he stared at her a moment longer, then stood and turned on the light. He squinted as darkness fled the room. Elizabeth's blonde hair hung in her face as she looked up at him, her dark-blue eyes a turbulent sea of emotion. On her cheek, an angry welt the size of a fist was already forming. The knot in his stomach grew. Moving closer, he held out his arm. *Where to begin?*

"How?" It was all he could get out.

She cast him a penetrating look, then stood and walked slowly toward the bed, never turning her back to him.

"You were dreaming, flailing around," she said, voice trembling. "I reached out for you, and when I did, you hit me. You were about to hit me again when I screamed."

That can't be true, can it? He turned away, unable to meet the unspoken answer in her eyes.

"What were you dreaming of?" she said.

He opened his mouth, but nothing came out. Something touched his arm, and he flinched as if burned. For an instant, he'd thought he might still be dreaming, but it was only Elizabeth reaching out to him. As her hand settled on his shoulder, he focused on the two misshapen fingers on her left hand, souvenirs from a car accident in college that had landed her in the ICU for a week and ended a promising career as a swimmer. Focusing on her fingers, he willed the remnants of his nightmare from his head.

"Was it the same one?" she said, her voice growing softer.

He slowly nodded, then looked away. "But different, too," he said. "More vivid."

She stepped closer, enveloping his chest with her arms and resting her head on his back. His own hands came up and covered hers, and for a while, they simply stood together.

"I'm sorry," she said.

Tears welled in his eyes, and he clamped his lips tightly together. "I'm the one who's sorry."

She softly cried. Moments later, she asked, "Do you want to talk about it?"

He shook his head. Even if he wanted to talk about it, could he? The wrenching in his stomach suggested otherwise.

"It's getting worse," she said.

He stiffened. It was true. The dreams had gradually been getting more intense since they'd started two years ago—following his third deployment to Afghanistan—but he'd never hit her before.

"I know," he said finally. In a flash, he thought of everything he'd fought for in a long career of serving his country, his hope of maybe commanding a battalion someday. It was all on a razor's edge. "I can handle it."

She gently turned him to face her. The top of her head barely came to his nose, yet he felt strangely cowed, as if she drew strength from some hidden reservoir that he couldn't match.

"It's okay to ask for help," she said.

"I'll lose everything I've worked for, everything we wanted."

"Oh, my brave soldier," she said, whispering softly. "You've got nothing to prove to anybody." She caressed his face, tracing a finger along the network of crow's-feet that had not been noticeable until recently. "Besides, you can't save the world by yourself. There's no shame, you know that."

He slowly pulled her hands from his face. "That's what they say," he said. "But I've seen how people get treated. Like they're contagious."

"Just think about it," she said, radiant eyes shining at him. "Please?"

He met her gaze. But the sight of the swelling on her face overwhelmed him, and he dropped his eyes, instead focusing on the tattoo of St. Michael that covered the outside of his bicep and shoulder. The ink-black archangel wore a breastplate imprinted with a set of scales and clutched a fiery sword in one hand and a large shield emblazoned with a cross in the other. Along with the angel were the words, words he couldn't see but that traced a grim trail from the inside of his bicep down and along his forearm: *Sancte Michael Archangele, defende nos in proelio, contra nequitiam et insidias diaboli esto praesidium.* Saint Michael the Archangel, defend us in battle, be our defense against the wickedness and snares of the devil.

Whatever was going on with him, it was starting to feel more and more like he was in a battle right now—one he'd never trained for. With the weight of Elizabeth's gaze still on him, he nodded, almost imperceptibly. "Okay," he said, then pulled her close.

After several minutes, they separated and he turned out the light. Crawling back under the covers, he cradled her until her breathing grew rhythmic and deep. Then he let go and rolled onto his back, folding his hands across his chest like a corpse. As he stared numbly up at the ceiling, the darkness of the room closed in with a physical presence. He shut his eyes and wished for sleep, shuddering slightly as an image of the dream returned.

Was this what it felt like to go crazy?

CHAPTER 2

Hugh sat on the upper level of a double-decker bus headed into downtown Ottawa, staring listlessly at windows covered in thick frost. At six thirty sharp, just like every morning, the bus left the Eagleson park and ride on the first leg of its thirty-minute commute. As it lurched forward, he pulled out his BlackBerry. The harder he tried to concentrate on his inbox, the more insistently the images came to mind of Elizabeth cowering from him, the welt rising on her face.

His uninspiring inbox didn't help his mood, mostly e-mails reminding him about National Non-Smoking Week or warnings about upcoming network outages. How could anyone enjoy working at National Defence Headquarters? Letting the BlackBerry flop into his lap, he scanned the bus, jammed with people. Nobody ever talked, or even really looked around. Still, today he was glad for the silence. Closing his eyes, he leaned his forehead against the icy window, savoring the coldness.

A vibrating in his lap drew his attention back to his phone. A text from Elizabeth.

Thought you might like the contact information for
the therapist my friend told me about. He's really
good. Nobody at work has to know. Think about it.
Dr. John Taylor, www.johntaylorcounselling.com
Love,
E xxoo

Sighing, he closed the text and stared blankly to his front.

What had happened to him? Less than a year earlier, he couldn't have imagined doing anything other than being in the army. Since he'd joined in 1992, he'd worked his way through the ranks from private to major, deploying on five operations and receiving recognition for valor multiple times. Plus, he had a wonderful wife who was willing to follow him around the country. Bottom line, his future had looked bright.

Then he'd been posted to defense headquarters to see how the military worked at the national level, something his career manager had said was important if he ever wanted to get promoted to lieutenant colonel and command a battalion. Ever since, the most soldierly thing he did was put on his uniform.

He'd known working in the headquarters would be challenging—he'd heard all the stories—but it was something more than just the work that made it so, some intangible soul-eroding element. Lately, he was always irritable, maybe because he hadn't slept a whole night in what seemed like forever. People increasingly annoyed him, especially crowds, and since his thirty-ninth birthday three months ago, his jet-black hair had begun showing the first flecks of gray. Whatever was bothering him, he needed to sort it out ASAP so he could get back to normal.

His stop was coming up, so he grabbed his bag and headed for the stairs. Hunching under the short roof, he stumbled down the narrow steps, eager to escape the air of resignation wafting off the other commuters. Then the bus stopped and spewed its contents into the dull cold of downtown Ottawa. As he walked to the entrance of National Defence Headquarters—NDHQ—his breath condensed in the cold air. He imagined it mingling with that of other people, tiny pockets of mist forming a dense fog.

NDHQ was built from the same gray concrete as almost every other government building in Ottawa, distinguished only by twin north and south towers at either end of a main center block. After clearing through security at the main entrance of the north tower—the one closest to the bus stop—he navigated a labyrinthine arrangement of cubicles to get to his workspace on the ninth floor of the south tower.

Even after six months, the drabness of the building still bothered him, everyone arranged like broiler chickens in battery cages. With their five-foot-high walls in bureaucratic blue or gray, the cubicles provided enough space to give the illusion of privacy, but not enough to actually conceal anything. He paused briefly to take in the sole distinguishing feature of his designated space, a nameplate that read, MAJOR HUGH DÉGARÉ, INFORMATION COORDINATOR.

When they'd moved to Ottawa the previous summer, Elizabeth had been supportive enough to act impressed with his new title, saying that information coordinator sounded much more important than Company 2IC. He'd quickly corrected her.

While he did manage some of the information flow in his directorate, it was mostly nonessential administrative issues that probably would've sorted themselves on their own. In fact, for what was supposed to be a step up, he'd probably had more responsibility in his previous position—not exactly fodder for a motivational poster. Hell, in the big scheme of things, getting shot at would probably be better than working in the headquarters. At least in a combat zone, he could shoot back. And at least he wouldn't die of boredom.

He pulled a makeshift curtain across the entrance of his cubicle and began shedding his civilian clothes to put on his uniform. There was a rule against changing in the cubicles since the walls weren't high enough to prevent most people from seeing over the top, leading to the potential for embarrassment or offense. Since the locker room was on the fifth floor of the north tower, almost everyone ignored the rule. Still, few people came to work this early, so it was normally safe.

On this morning, Lieutenant Colonel Dan Williams, his supervisor, made a rare early appearance, walking down the corridor just as Hugh was donning his pastel-green service dress shirt.

"Morning, sir. You're here early," Hugh said, hastily doing up buttons, but it was useless. Although Williams couldn't see anything improper, Hugh was obviously dressing, so the damage was done.

"Lots to do," Williams said, businesslike as always. The man had a personality like a rock. "Maybe find the locker room next time?"

He grimaced as Williams's head, shaved bald to compensate for his thinning hair, bobbed away over the tops of the cubicle walls. Williams had an enormous capacity for paperwork. Whether drafting instructions about the completion of annual personnel evaluations or preparing presentations on quarterly budget reporting, Williams embodied the industrious staff officer in the eyes of many people. Hugh wasn't so convinced. In Hugh's experience, Williams seemed to either simply repeat work that had already been done elsewhere in the chain of command or add redundant procedural steps to interject himself, almost like a self-licking ice-cream cone.

Still, doing paperwork was probably the best employment for the man. Williams looked like he'd collapse from holding a rifle, never mind shooting one. It really was easy to become lazy in a headquarters. In fact, Hugh had missed his own workouts for almost a week. Vowing to hit the gym later that morning, he finished straightening up, then went for a coffee.

When he returned, he sat down on the exercise ball he'd bought to replace the cheap rolling chair in his cubicle. He pulled out a tin of chewing tobacco, grabbed a pinch, and stuffed it in his lower lip, relishing the shiver that came with the harsh taste. He'd tried quitting—even switched from berry-flavored Skoal to Copenhagen straight, hoping the foul taste would drive him away—but he felt naked without a dip in his mouth. Spitting into an empty cup, he logged on to his computer.

The first thing he did was check out Dr. Taylor. From his website, Hugh learned that Dr. Taylor primarily used cognitive behavioral therapy—whatever that was—and specialized in about twenty other disciplines, including post-traumatic stress disorder, PTSD.

A brick formed in his stomach. Was he really considering seeing a psychologist? Even with the events from last night still fresh in his mind, he wasn't convinced therapy would help. What was sitting around talking about dreams going to do? Especially with a guy who probably knew nothing about the military.

He scrolled down the page until he found Dr. Taylor's hours. The clinic didn't open until ten o'clock. He spat tobacco juice into the cup on his desk, then brought up a memorandum he needed to finish.

A light rapping came from behind him, and he glanced over his shoulder. Major Bill Roach from the administration section occupied what passed for a door to his cubicle, his uniform so disheveled he might possibly have slept in it.

"Dégaré, I need that floor plan," Roach said.

He swiveled on the ball, athletic body ramrod straight. Even sitting, his head came to Roach's slumped shoulders. He blinked once, slowly. Why did Roach insist on calling him by his last name? It had been a long time since he was a recruit.

"I finished that weeks ago."

About a month ago, Lieutenant Colonel Williams had tasked him with reorganizing the section's individual cubicles into a single open area, or a bullpen, to promote better workplace collaboration. But since everyone worked on different things, Hugh figured the only thing the bullpen would likely promote was aggravation. But if his boss wanted to give him make-work projects—even a goat rodeo like this one—that was his prerogative.

Roach shrugged, and as he did, the fabric of his shirt tightened against his plump stomach. Hugh's eyes narrowed. *Sad.*

"The template changed. You need to submit the paperwork again, this time in the new format," Roach said. He leaned closer, as if sharing a secret. "Take some advice, less time in the gym, more time working. You're not in a field unit anymore."

"Nobody told me it needed more work."

"It came up at last week's coordination meeting."

"The one I missed?" He willed his face to remain blank.

"I did my part, can't help it if the system misfired," Roach said, eyes sliding around the cubicle. "You don't have much in here." He took an invasive step forward. "What's that?"

He followed Roach's gaze to a three-foot-long midnight-black shillelagh on his desk. Mitchell had given it to him the last time they'd seen each other. Two months later, Mitchell's body was being flown home from Afghanistan.

During this brief reminiscence, Roach had shouldered past and snatched up the shillelagh, swinging it around like he meant to take a trial hit. Hugh jumped up and placed a meathook hand on the club's shaft, arresting its motion as abruptly as a vise. Their eyes locked.

"That was a gift," he said, plucking the shillelagh from Roach's grasp. He cradled the weapon briefly before setting it gently back in its stand. He turned to Roach, adjusted his large frame. The small cubicle suddenly seemed even smaller.

Roach met his gaze for a second. Then he began edging toward the entrance, taking shuffle steps to traverse where Hugh stood like some mythical Titan.

"Yeah, well, it's a nice club, Dégaré." Slouching out of the cubicle, he glanced back, eyes going to Hugh's nameplate. "Hey, I always forget, what did you say your name meant?"

Hugh sat on the exercise ball, his back to Roach in dismissal.

"It means strayed or lost." He should never have told Roach, but it had seemed like an innocent enough question at the time and he hadn't yet realized that the man was a waste of rations. Thank God he hadn't added that his parents had named him Hugh, meaning man with spirit, to offset the negative connotation of his last name.

Roach snorted. "That's right. So make sure that floor plan doesn't get lost, too. Williams is busting my balls to get contractors in, and I can't do anything until you get it in the new format," he said, then turned and walked away.

Hugh closed his eyes, breathed deeply, and counted to ten. If Roach spent as much time doing work as trying to get out of it, he'd be the most productive person on the floor. Thankfully, the man was an outlier in the department in that regard, although lately he personified the increasingly pointless disruptions that burglarized Hugh's time. And Roach hadn't even told him what new format he was supposed to follow. He shook his head.

Adding the floor plan back to his to-do list, he returned to the memorandum with renewed determination. In a way, it was like filling sandbags—keep shoveling until one was full, then get a new one. Except sandbags were more useful. A rueful grin broke over his face, and he took a last breath, then emptied his mind to focus on the task at hand.

The hours dragged on, then suddenly it was sixteen thirty, and he was one of the last people there, as always. He did a last scan of his inbox, then smacked his forehead. *Damn.* He'd done nothing with Elizabeth's text.

With an impatient glance at his watch, he brought up Dr. Taylor's website again and stared at it. What should he do? As troubled as he'd been this morning, work had calmed his nerves. Last night seemed distant, like it was months ago. Surely a few nights of good sleep would sort him out. Even as he thought this, the image of the welt on Elizabeth's face returned to him, and he tensed. He picked up the phone.

"What are you working on?" Lieutenant Colonel Williams's voice sounded right behind his ear.

He jerked his head around, then hung up the phone. "Just personal stuff, sir," he said, ears burning. Why did it feel like he'd been caught doing something he shouldn't?

"Well, if there's nothing to do, don't do it here. Remember, it's a marathon, not a sprint," Williams said. He rapped his knuckles on the edge of a cubicle wall and pointed at Hugh. "See you tomorrow."

"Good night, sir," he said, watching Williams retreat to his office. From experience, he knew he didn't want to be told twice. If Williams saw him again, he'd be just as likely to give him more work as to force him to leave. Plus, he'd met his quota of motivational clichés for one day.

Once Williams was out of eyesight, Hugh got changed. He really did feel much better than when the day had started. Then again, nighttime worries always seemed less urgent in the light of day. Maybe it was a good thing he hadn't called the psychologist. A waste of time and money. With a last scan of his cubicle to make sure he hadn't forgotten anything, he grabbed his backpack and headed to the lobby.

❧ ❧ ❧

Heavy snowfall during the day made the commute home torturous, with snarled traffic and buses jammed with frustrated travelers. But it had been the oblivious man on the bus, engrossed in the bass beat emanating from his headphones—who had spilled coffee on him—who had tipped the scales. Hugh couldn't handle crowds anymore. By the time he got to his truck at the park and ride, he was seething. The drive home did little to calm his nerves.

"Elizabeth?" He walked into the kitchen, but the only answer was the tinny echo of his voice. They always tried to eat dinner together. Then he remembered: Tuesday. Yoga. He glanced at the microwave clock. Considering the traffic, she could be a while.

He could start supper, but tonight was only leftovers, which he'd warm up when she got home. Grabbing an apple, he strode to the mudroom and into the garage. The aroma of sawdust hit him like a wave, and he stood for a second on the landing, holding the door open and inhaling deeply.

Flicking on the light, he descended the bare wooden steps into the garage, crunching away at the apple. Under the fluorescent lighting, which he'd installed himself, he scanned the workbench paralleling one wall. Working with his hands always helped him relax, but just being in the shop made him feel better.

He tossed the apple core into a garbage can, then opened a mini fridge and pulled out a beer. Bottle in hand, he rummaged through a nearby drawer for a bottle opener when the grumbling of a car engine and the crunching of tires on snow came through the garage door. She was home.

The front door slammed shut as he continued to search in the drawer, the frustration from his drive home returning. Using his whole hand, he shifted the clutter around, forcing it from one side of the drawer to the other as he tried to spy the metal opener. Seconds later, the door to the mudroom opened and he glanced up. Elizabeth was there, snowflakes still melting on the shoulders of her coat.

"Glad you made it home safely," she said, gliding down the stairs and hugging him. "The roads are terrible."

He set the beer on the counter. "How was yoga?"

"Cold," she said, shivering. "The room was drafty, and the heater was broken. I haven't been warm since I left home." She stepped back, trailing a finger onto his shoulder. "What are you looking for?"

"Bottle opener."

"Can I help?"

"I got it."

"One of those days?"

"Every day is one of those days," he said. Suddenly, there was a sharp jab in his finger, and he hissed in pain, yanking his hand out of the drawer. Elizabeth leaned in to look over his shoulder, and he tensed, hand balled into a fist. He opened his fist slowly, expecting to see blood trickling from his injured finger, but it seemed fine.

"Are you okay?" she said, reaching for his hand. "Let me see."

"Mm-hm," he said, raising his finger to his mouth.

"What do I know? I'm only a nurse," she said, watching him suck on his finger. "So, did you call?"

"Call who?" he said, returning to the drawer with a vengeance.

"Dr. Taylor. Remember?"

He exhaled sharply, closing his eyes. "I totally forgot," he said, turning around to peer dejectedly at her face. He raised a hand to her cheek. "How is it?" At first, he could barely make anything out. She looked flushed from yoga, but the unforgiving garage lights highlighted the sheen of cover-up.

"You said you would call."

He felt trapped, not knowing what to say. He moved to brush aside a strand of hair that had fallen across her face, but she flicked her head back, out of his reach.

"Don't try to distract me," she said, eyes flashing. Sometimes she knew him better than he did himself. "Did you even look into it?"

He studied her face for a second longer, then abruptly turned back to the drawer, pulling out tools and laying them on the counter. "Things got busy."

She moved beside him. "This is important, honey. I worry about you," she said. "You could tell your boss you—"

"It's under control," he said, forcing his voice to remain calm. "And talking to my chain of command won't help. It'll just make work even more awkward."

She placed a hand on his shoulder. At her touch, he flinched, his elbow knocking the beer bottle off the counter. It tumbled to the ground, striking the concrete floor in an area not covered by the rubber matting he'd painstakingly laid down. With a sharp crash, the bottle shattered. He slammed the drawer shut with both hands and reached for a roll of shop towels.

"Let me help," she said, moving to pick up the roll at the same time.

He grabbed her wrist without thinking. "I don't need your help," he said, voice almost shaking. He spoke his next words slowly, emphasizing each point. "I don't need any help."

"What are you doing?" She squirmed in his grip, trying to draw back. "Hugh, you're scaring me . . ."

He pulled her closer, opening his mouth to speak, then stopped, mouth half-open. This close, the dark-blue mark flowering on her cheek underneath the cover-up was unmistakable. The fury that had come over him so suddenly departed in a flash, leaving him feeling sick, spent. He released her arm abruptly. What the hell was he doing?

Silence descended over the garage. Then she slapped him, her palm striking his cheek like a crack of lightning. With her backhand, she struck him again, across his other cheek. He stood penitently, embracing the sting of her hand. If only whatever was wrong with him could be so easily solved.

"You have no right," she said, her voice trembling. Tears welled in her eyes, but she made no move to wipe them. "I love you, but if you ever raise a hand to me again, it will be the last time."

His eyes stung as they watered up. "I'm so sorry, Elizabeth—"

"Stop," she said, clutching her arms across her chest. "If you were sorry, you'd get help." She glared at him a moment longer, then turned and moved toward the stairs.

"I'm scared," he said to her back.

She stopped in midstride, her body erect and proud.

"I don't know what's happening to me."

She paused, then faced him, her brow furrowed in concern. "You should be scared, Hugh. I love you, but you need help, the kind I can't give you. And I won't live like this. I deserve better."

He hung his head as she climbed the stairs and entered the mudroom. As much as she'd always told him he was the only one for her, even saying she'd never marry again if anything ever happened to him, he didn't doubt her threat for a second. The decision to call the shrink had just become incredibly easy. Still, what kind of soldier couldn't handle a few bad dreams?

CHAPTER 3

Hugh paused in the doorway. Scanning the room, he quickly took in the tufted leather furniture, the full-length bookcase, and the rich rug that looked like many he'd seen in Afghanistan. He sniffed the air, half expecting the fragrance of pipe smoke, only to be disappointed at what was probably the smell of some New Age aromatherapy diffuser.

"Mr. Dégaré? Please come in."

His gaze settled on the speaker, a man with thick, wavy hair and a full beard flecked with gray, features Hugh didn't see often among soldiers. His new therapist sat writing in a journal at an oversize wooden desk like a parody of the perfect psychologist.

It had been two weeks since his argument with Elizabeth. Loath as he was to admit it, she was right—he needed professional help. But would this man be able to give it to him?

Maybe he should reconsider this whole thing. His eyes narrowed as he studied Dr. Taylor and his wire-frame glasses. Hesitating, Hugh looked back at the waiting room. Thinking of

Elizabeth, he sighed, then turned back and slowly crossed the threshold of the doorway.

Dr. John Taylor did not speak again for several minutes. Hugh felt like he'd been sent to the principal's office. Finally Dr. Taylor arose and offered his hand. They shook, and then Dr. Taylor settled himself in the chair opposite him.

"So, Mr. Dégaré, or would you prefer to be called Major?" Dr. Taylor sat with one leg crossed, hands folded in his lap like some Victorian manor lord.

His brow furrowed. Could this man possibly understand what it was like to be a soldier? "Hugh is fine," he said, sitting rigidly on the couch.

"Hugh then," Dr. Taylor said. "What is it you would like to discuss, Hugh?"

He paused, the words stuck in his throat. Best to tackle this head-on. "I think I have PTSD."

"I see," Dr. Taylor said, opening a notepad. "And you think that because . . . ?"

"Uh, a variety of reasons," he said, stammering. He prided himself on his ability to communicate clearly, but when it came time to discuss feelings, he may as well have just crawled out of a cave. "I have trouble sleeping, bad dreams, I'm irritable, that type of thing."

Dr. Taylor looked up from his notes. "All right, Hugh," he said. "Why don't we start with a few generic questions."

He nodded. Dr. Taylor flipped to a new page.

"Try to answer as honestly as possible," Dr. Taylor said. "How would you describe your general attitude, positive or negative?"

"It depends, I guess," he said.

"Well, are you mostly happy during the day or not?"

"Not," he said, lips tightening. He looked over to where the door signaled escape.

"Do you have feelings of anger?"

"Yes."

"How frequently?"

"Every day."

"How intense are they?"

He shrugged. "Sometimes just mild annoyance, I'd say that's pretty common. Other times, it's like I'm the Hulk. I just get angrier and angrier."

"How about feelings of sadness?"

Hugh looked down, twisting his wedding band. "Sometimes."

"How often?"

"More than I used to."

"Do you have feelings of anxiety?"

"Sometimes."

"Have you noticed any specific things that trigger your anxiety?"

He thought back to the last time he and Elizabeth had visited a shopping mall. "Crowds of people, loud noises." He'd had to go sit in his truck to get away, and the mall hadn't even been that busy.

"How is your sleep? Broken or solid?"

"Poor, maybe five or six hours a night. And it's broken."

"And you said you had disturbing dreams?"

Hugh nodded.

Dr. Taylor flipped to a new page. "Recurring dreams? Or aspects of your dreams that repeat?"

He ran his tongue around his suddenly parched mouth and simply nodded.

Dr. Taylor looked up, made a note, then continued. "What are your energy levels?"

"I generally feel tired, but I always have enough energy to get through the day, sometimes with a bit of help."

One of Dr. Taylor's eyebrows rose up. "Help such as?"

"Caffeine and nicotine."

"You smoke?"

"Chew."

Dr. Taylor glanced at him. "Pardon me?"

His mouth broke into a small smile. "I chew, or dip."

When the furrow in Dr. Taylor's brow grew deeper, Hugh pulled out a can of Copenhagen to show him. The therapist looked briefly, then returned to his notes. Hugh's smile disappeared.

"Do you use any other stimulants? Alcohol or drugs?"

"A beer every now and then."

"How is your performance at work?"

"Fine," he said. "Work actually helps me take my mind off things."

"So you like your work?"

"No," he said, surprising himself with the blunt answer. He was normally more diplomatic. "But it gives me something to focus on."

Hugh briefly recalled a mock interrogation he'd undergone during an advanced reconnaissance course he'd taken several years ago. It had been late November, and his simulated patrol had been captured behind enemy lines. Hooded, they'd been taken to a cinder-block hut, enough shelter to stop the wind and snow, but not the cold, which penetrated the concrete bricks and leached warmth from anything they touched. After trading their winter uniforms for threadbare coveralls, they'd been forced into stress positions, leaning forward with hands braced high on a wall or sitting cross-legged on the bare floor with hands laced behind their heads. All the while, recordings of babies crying or white noise played loudly in the background. Then the questions had started: Were there other patrols? Was an attack planned? It had gone on for twenty-four hours, but as bad as it had been, he'd give almost anything to be doing that now instead of this. He checked his watch.

"Almost there," Dr. Taylor said, studying his notepad for a moment longer before closing it. "I think it's time I explained my treatment philosophy."

Hugh settled onto the couch. Finally, a break from talking.

"In my practice, I adhere to the concept of Dr. Judith Herman's three stages of recovery. Stage one is about the safety and self-care of the patient. Especially with post-traumatic stress, the patient must realize that they are not alone. It's very common for patients to be embarrassed by their feelings, but it's important to remember this is a normal reaction to being exposed to an abnormal situation. When those feelings are shared with other people who suffer from PTSD, they can be used as a powerful bond from which to draw strength."

"Like the bond shared by soldiers in combat," Hugh said, eyes growing distant.

"I suppose so," Dr. Taylor said, smiling. "Now, stage two is basically mourning, or working through your memories and any grief associated with them. Lastly, stage three is reconnecting across a variety of fronts, most obviously with people, but also with your own ideals and beliefs."

He held up a hand, and Dr. Taylor paused.

"So, it's basically like building a house," Hugh said. "Focus on a good foundation first, then worry about the upper levels and what's inside after that."

"Exactly," Taylor said, waving a finger in the air. "Now, within this overall treatment concept, I employ cognitive behavioral therapy. Have you heard of it?"

He nodded. "I saw it on your website, and I Googled a couple of explanations, but to be honest, it seems like jargon to me."

Dr. Taylor smiled. "Fair enough." He paused and held the tip of his pen to his lips, then sat up. "Let's just say that assuming you do have post-traumatic stress, my approach would be to figure out who you were before the inciting incidents that triggered your symptoms. After that, we would seek to bring that person into harmony with your current self. Understand?"

His lips tightened, but he said nothing, and Dr. Taylor kept speaking.

"Another technique I like to use is habituation. Are you familiar with that?"

He shook his head. The only thing that came to mind was habits, like chewing tobacco, which he was pretty sure Dr. Taylor wasn't talking about.

"Habituation, or desensitization, is a decrease in responsiveness to a recurrent stimulus," Dr. Taylor said. "You're aware of the idea that the best way to overcome your fears is to confront them?"

He nodded.

"Habituation is simply the academic term for it. The more someone is exposed to their fears, the more they come to understand that there's nothing to fear."

"Makes sense. We do the same in the military."

"Good, good," Dr. Taylor said, pulling out the notepad and opening it. "Do you like to write, Hugh?"

"Not particularly," he said. As an officer, he'd been obligated to get a university degree, but his BA in military history was more of a check in the box than anything else.

"Well, keeping a journal is a key part of the habituation process. We use the journal entries as a basis for session discussions," Dr. Taylor said. "So for instance, in your case, to help you deal with whatever is causing your nightmares, I would have you keep a journal in which you document the incidents you dream about. In turn, those entries would be used as a map to guide our discussions and begin the process of desensitizing you to your fears."

"Okay," Hugh said, more from a need to say something than because he understood. What had he gotten himself into?

Dr. Taylor glanced at his watch, then closed Hugh's file and held it in his lap. "I think that's it for today, Hugh, assuming you believe I'm a good fit for you. But before we finish, I do have one question for you, if you don't mind."

He nodded.

"I noticed this was a direct booking as opposed to a referral from the military system," Dr. Taylor said. "I've worked with soldiers before, but rarely without a referral, which leads me to suspect that you haven't told your superiors. Would that be correct?"

He nodded, his cheeks growing hot.

"And may I ask why?"

He took a long breath. Why hadn't he mentioned anything at work? Williams wasn't the most personable guy, but he'd understand something like this, wouldn't he? Finally, he answered.

"I'm worried about what would happen if I did," he said, his voice thoughtful, as if explaining it to himself at the same time. "To my career, with my peers. I'd like to handle this on my own, that's always been my way." He looked down. "Besides, it'd take forever to get help through the military system."

Dr. Taylor leaned back and folded his arms across his chest. "I understand that your position is a not-uncommon one among soldiers," he said. "I'm obviously bound by confidentiality, unless of course I assess there's a risk to someone's safety. Other than that, we can handle this according to your wishes."

Dr. Taylor leaned forward and rested both elbows on his knees. "Now, before we finish, do you have any questions for me?"

There was only one question he wanted to ask, but the words caught in his throat. He fingered his ring again. "Do you think I've got PTSD?"

Dr. Taylor studied him for a moment, the silence in the room palpable. "Normally, I wouldn't be so blunt with somebody on the first session, but my sense is that you'd appreciate a straightforward answer." The therapist paused, then sighed. "So yes, Hugh, I think there's a good chance you've got PTSD based on the symptoms you've described."

His heart sank. He massaged his temples with a thumb and forefinger.

"That being said, I must say I have no idea how serious it is. It's something we'll of course have to explore."

"But you can fix it, right?" he said, his words catching. "You can make me better? Back to what I was like before?"

Dr. Taylor sat back and steepled his fingers together. "Hugh, I—"

"Don't answer," he said, dropping his hand to his lap. "I should know better than to ask you that." He stood and began walking robotically to the door.

"It depends, Hugh," Dr. Taylor said from behind him. "Everyone is different, different strengths, different situations. Given an honest effort, though, we should be able to make some headway." He stood up and came to Hugh's side. "But I'm willing to work with you on it if you are." Dr. Taylor held out his hand.

Hugh stared at the outstretched hand, numb. Until this moment, he might have been able to pretend everything was under control, but now, he didn't know what to do. Faces of soldiers he'd known with PTSD flashed through his head, proud men reduced to shells of their former selves. Could this man really help him? This man with his soft hands and highfalutin language? Hesitantly, he took Dr. Taylor's hand, pleased at least to feel strength in the grip.

"I look forward to our next meeting. Good evening, Hugh," Dr. Taylor said, shaking his hand warmly. The therapist held open the office door, then closed it behind Hugh, the sound resonating through the hallway with a sense of finality.

Hugh took several deep breaths while he collected himself. Once ready, he walked into the lobby to make another appointment. He stammered nervously as he made the booking, and then it struck him that the receptionist who took his details, she did this every day, all day—made appointments for people to talk to a shrink. Maybe he wasn't so crazy, so alone, after all. The thought consoled him slightly. Then he opened the door and stepped out into the lonely winter cold.

❤ ❤ ❤

When Hugh arrived home, he made no move to turn on the foyer light, just remained rooted to the floor with his eyes closed, trying to recover a sense of himself while white flecks of snow slowly melted on his coat.

Footsteps approached from the kitchen. Elizabeth flicked on the light. The harsh glare made him squint. Then she came over and wrapped her arms around him. "How was it?"

"Oh, you know," he said, staring over her head. "Dr. Taylor's probably smoking a pipe right now, marveling with his therapist buddies at what a Neanderthal I am."

She smiled and giggled. When was the last time he'd heard that beautiful noise?

"Do you want to talk about it?"

He shook his head. "Not right now. Maybe I'll head to the basement for a bit, unwind a little."

She nodded, then took his coat, hanging it in the closet as he kicked off his boots. In silence, she followed him to the stairs leading to the second floor, waiting at the landing as he walked up. Minutes later, he returned wearing shorts and a ratty T-shirt tinged with the faintly cloying smell of sweat, no matter how many times it was washed.

When he opened the door leading to the basement, she stood on her tiptoes and gave him a small peck on the cheek. "Take as much time as you need."

His lips tightened briefly in what he hoped was a smile, and then he walked down to the basement, the wooden stairs creaking under his weight. At the bottom, he flicked on the lights, and several bare incandescent bulbs sparked to life. Moving boxes were stacked almost to the ceiling in one corner—things they hadn't yet unpacked—along with odd pieces of furniture. He moved past these things to the other side of the room, where his barbells, dumbbells, and a weight bench had been arranged.

He set up the bar for a bench press, then sat down. On the ground beside him was a small piece of white chalk, which he picked up and ground into his hands.

With a few sharp breaths, he shimmied underneath the weight, gripped the bar, and pushed it up. He held the weight in the air for a moment, letting its heaviness sink down through his arms and press him into the bench, then slowly lowered the bar until it almost touched his chest. Holding it until his arms started to shake, he finally exploded the weight up, forcing the remaining air out of his lungs. Already feeling his forehead grow damp, he racked the weight and sat up.

When he felt ready, he repeated the exercise, then moved on to others, his body falling into a well-trained routine. But his brain raced with what Dr. Taylor had told him and what might be coming.

And what was coming? Dr. Taylor had said he had PTSD, but that could mean many things. Some soldiers had PTSD and nobody even knew. Still, the soldiers he'd known with PTSD who'd spoken up had all seemed to permanently disappear into support units to supposedly focus on getting better. There was Laliberte, the sniper whose team had single-handedly killed the equivalent of a Taliban platoon on Operation Medusa, and Dwyer, the bin rat who'd never been the same after surviving an ambush on a resupply convoy. So many, most never heard from again, unless they showed up on the evening news. There was even a term for it—taking the crazy train—although the chain of command frowned on such talk. If only there were someone he could talk to, someone who'd gone through this already and knew what it was like.

He lay back down and lowered the weight onto his chest once more, heart racing. The muscles in his arms tensed, but this time, the weight didn't budge. Panic shot through him. Breathing in and out rapidly, he threw himself into the bar with every last effort, the small of his back arching off the bench as the weight slowly rose, trembling every inch that it traveled. A primal groan escaped his mouth, ringing off the exposed metal support beams. With a final gasp, the bar rattled back into place.

He sat up, his T-shirt clinging wetly to his trembling body. Elizabeth was standing at the bottom of the landing, her forehead furrowed in concern.

"Are you all right?" she asked.

"I tried to do too much," he said, head hung sheepishly. His lips parted in a small smile. "Guess I'm not as strong as I thought I was."

She returned his smile. "Well, let me know if you need me to help," she said, then turned and put a hand on the bannister. "I'll be upstairs with my book."

He swallowed. "What are you reading?" he asked, his voice stopping her with one foot on the bottom step.

"It's a fantasy," she said, "about a dragon and a prophecy."

"I see," he said, wrestling with what he was trying to say. "Not one of those Amish romances?" It was her guilty secret.

"Of course not," she said, her smile in her voice. "I'm on a waiting list for the next one at the library." The steps creaked as she began to climb.

"Dr. Taylor thinks I've got PTSD," he said.

She stopped and studied him over her shoulder. "What do you think?"

He opened his mouth to speak, but his answer was cut off as his body suddenly convulsed in sobs, his shoulders heaving. Then she was beside him, her arms holding him tightly. Reaching up with his hands, he clung to her, riding out the storm. He couldn't have said how much time passed, but eventually he regained control, at least enough to talk.

"Sorry," he said, sniffling.

"For what?" she said, gently brushing away a tear on his cheek. "It's not your fault. We'll get through this."

He held her hand, drawing strength from her touch. "It just feels so unreal. I almost can't believe it," he said. "I mean, I've seen some bad things, but PTSD is something that happens to someone else, not me. I don't even know where to start."

She sat on his lap, her legs straddling him as she cradled his head to her chest. "What did Dr. Taylor say? Is there anything I can do?"

He smiled wanly and shook his head. "We didn't get into much about treatment or coping," he said. "Dr. Taylor seems good, but I'm worried he won't get the whole military context."

"Is there someone else you can talk to? Me?"

He stammered until she interrupted him with a smile, warmth in her eyes.

"I know, you need someone who's been there," she said. Her eyes brightened. "What about Daryl? You were always such good friends; maybe talking to him could be good. And it might be nice to reconnect."

Daryl Robertson had been his best friend since they'd done basic training together in 1992, one of the last courses to go through Canadian Forces Base Cornwallis. After basic, they'd been assigned to the same battalion, and when Hugh had taken his commission and gone off for several years of study at the Royal Military College, Daryl had stayed in the unit. Despite their different paths, they'd stayed friends, even with Daryl's new arsenal of officer-related insults with which to torment his friend, like offering to carry Hugh's junior general kit or claiming Hugh's parents had never worked for a living. That was what made the army great; getting teased meant everything was fine.

On Daryl's last tour in Afghanistan—a bad one, 2008 maybe—his vehicle had struck an IED. Nobody died, but Daryl lost both legs below the knee. He'd fought to stay in the military as long as he could, but it was obvious to everyone except him that it was only a matter of time. Even with two state-of-the-art prosthetic legs, he'd been deemed to have a long-term disability that precluded him deploying on future operations.

When Daryl was finally kicked out in 2011—the official phrase was transitioned to civilian life—he'd severed ties with most of his military friends. It was understandable in a way; having lost the only thing he'd ever wanted to do, why would he want the reminder of what he was missing every time he met a friend? Despite half-hearted attempts, Hugh hadn't talked to him since arriving in Ottawa, even though he only lived a few hours away in Kingston.

"I'm not sure he'd want to talk to me." The last thing he needed right now was to be rejected.

"What do you have to lose?" she asked.

He slowly nodded, mulling it over. "Good point," he said. And honestly, who else was there? "I'll give him a call."

"Thank you. For seeing Dr. Taylor. For trying to figure this out," she said, holding his face in her hands and staring into his eyes. "Whatever you need, I'm here for you." Leaning in, she kissed him.

He returned the kiss, tensing slightly at the soft probing of her tongue. She drew back, but he leaned into her, suddenly conscious of the warmth of her body. Her eyes opened with an unspoken question, and he pulled her close.

One of her fingers traced the line of his triceps, stirring him. He relaxed, feeling something he hadn't even realized was missing. When they'd first met all those years ago in Kingston— he a cadet at RMC, she a nursing student at Queen's—they couldn't keep their hands off each other. Now he couldn't even remember the last time they'd been together. Then all he could think of was her mouth on his.

Still straddling him, she lifted his shirt over his head. Bathed in the yellowish glow of the basement lighting, she traced her fingers across the black lines etched on his shoulder, smoky spirals that extended from the wings of the shadowy St. Michael. She'd always been fascinated by the story, how proud Hugh had been to receive his St. Michael's medallion when he qualified as a paratrooper, and then how he'd gotten the saint imprinted on his body.

"It's like he's always watching over you," she'd said the first time she'd seen it. They'd been in her room, a simple upper-level space in a house shared with two other girls, tinged with the aroma of rose incense.

"It's just a tattoo," he'd said and pulled her into his embrace. "I was just a dumb kid when I got it." But it was much more than that. He'd jumped from the air and conquered his fear, joining an illustrious brethren of men apart.

"I like it," she'd said. "I'll pray that he always protects you." Then her lips had met his.

Now, as then, Hugh's body tingled in response to her touch. She leaned forward and kissed him again, her blonde hair falling over his face and obscuring anything else. His body ached for her.

But something felt wrong, like he was a silent observer. As much as his body reacted, he was empty. He willed himself to perform, stripping off the rest of his clothes and hers and sitting back on the weight bench while she straddled him again, guiding him into her.

A pang of alarm rocked through him. Was he going soft? To counter the feeling, he stood up aggressively, clutching her to him, then turned around and set her down on the bench, never breaking contact. Still inside her, he pumped fiercely, mechanically as she moaned. He watched her, studying her expressions detachedly. Was she enjoying it? Could she tell it was all he could do to finish?

She climaxed, and for a time, he wondered if he would be able to finish. His cheeks grew hot at the thought, and he doubled down, thrusting as if possessed. Then he was done, not with ecstasy or even satisfaction, but simply relief that it was over. He stayed motionless inside her until he noticed her eyes were open, staring at him.

"Everything all right?" she said.

"Sure," he said, forcing a smile. "It's just been a while."

She sat up and wrapped her arms around him, drawing him close.

He tried to relax, but couldn't. With a chill in the air, he stood and began pulling on his clothes. In silence, she joined him.

Both dressed, he pulled her into an embrace, holding her tight. They'd used to stand like this all the time, but again, he couldn't remember the last time. Relaxing his hold, he gazed down at her, then gently wiped away tears from the corners of her eyes.

"What is it?" he said.

"I don't want to lose you," she said, sniffling. "We've been through so much, I don't know what I'd do without you."

He buried his face in her hair, treasuring the familiar smell that brought memories of lazy days of watching movies and cuddling in sleeping bags. In their first year of dating, on their first vacation, they'd gone on a three-day trail ride in a remote area of the Rocky Mountains. Each night, crisp and cool as only a summer night in the mountains can be, they'd lie staring up at the midnight sky, every inch sparkling with stars that could only be seen miles away from the mad lights of civilization. That last night, holding each other for warmth, he'd told her he loved her, the first time. In return, she'd said she was going to marry him.

"My friends all told me I was stupid," she'd told him three years later when he'd proposed, the confidence in her voice awing him. "They told me I was too young to know, only twenty-four with my whole life ahead of me. But I knew you were the one. Underneath all the bravado, you have a caring heart."

"Don't let that get out," he said, smiling. "I'd never hear the end of it if the troops found out."

The warmth of her breath had sent tingles down his spine. "Joke all you want," she said, kissing him. "But we were meant for each other. We've made it against all odds—you deploying, me volunteering in Peru—we'll make it through anything."

Then he'd lost himself in her kiss and everything had gone dark.

But it hadn't felt dark, or cold, not like how the basement now felt as he gazed sadly into her eyes. The sparkle he loved so much was still there, but was there something else there now, too? A sadness of his own creation that threatened to drive her away?

She said nothing, only hugged him tighter, so close, yet at the same time so distant. He buried his head in her hair and clenched shut his eyes.

CHAPTER 4

Hugh drove his tuxedo-black F-150 SVT Raptor truck to the Italian restaurant in Kingston where he'd agreed to meet Daryl, swerving to avoid a large pothole in the parking lot. The lot was dimly lit, much like the surrounding neighborhood, with falling-apart houses crouching on the sidewalks in the wintry gloom.

He wedged the truck into a space that was almost too small and climbed out. He'd driven by the restaurant twice before deciding it was the place. On his first two passes, the place had looked closed down; the decaying brick facade, poor lighting, and parking lot with more potholes than spaces seemed to indicate as much. On his third time around, a flickering neon sign by the main door had persuaded him to give the place a try, but he still wasn't convinced he had the right address.

He scanned the lot, hoping to see Daryl and Laura. He'd called Daryl a few days after Elizabeth's suggestion and was promptly surprised when Daryl had invited him for supper in Kingston that weekend. Elizabeth had been invited, too, but she'd had to work. She had taken a job at the National Arts

Centre as an usher while she continued to look for an opening for an ER nurse. Being an usher didn't pay well, but it got her out of the house, and she was happy for the excuse to rekindle her love of symphonies and the theater, something she'd enjoyed so much growing up but that hadn't been part of her life with Hugh.

Standing near the restaurant's door in the lonely cold, hands jammed in the pockets of his peacoat, he wished she were there. He didn't know how this would go, and she had a knack for enlivening conversations. People always seemed to confide in her. Daryl had sounded steady enough on the phone, but the man had shut him out for years.

Just then, a rickety Volkswagen Golf drove into the lot, the screeching of metal scraping on pavement growing louder until it parked. A couple got out, arguing. As they walked, the woman's hands flew at the man, coming close but never touching him. The man, portly and hunched, absorbed the tirade as he shuffled toward the entrance, taking aggressive drags on a cigarette, which he periodically thrust at the woman whenever her hands got too close.

Hugh turned away, studiously ignoring the couple. He hated being around other people when they argued; it was like he was spying on something private. As they got closer, accompanied by the smell of stale smoke, he moved a few steps to the side, making room for them to get by.

When the couple reached the door, their faces turned toward him, as if they'd only now realized he was there. The man took a last puff on the cigarette, flicked the butt into the parking lot, and stepped toward Hugh, two tree-trunk arms coming up to encircle him in a hug. Hugh backed away uncomfortably, smiling politely, then paused, wondering what to make of the confusion written on the other man's face.

"Still afraid of hugs, eh?" the man said, arms suspended in the air.

Hugh peered closer. This man, with his scraggly beard covering pudgy jowls and a sallow complexion, could this be Daryl? His gaze flicked to the woman, who was averting her eyes. Her flaming-red hair stood out even in the dimness of the parking lot. Definitely Laura's hair. With a start, Hugh looked back at the man, recognition dawning.

A smile broke awkwardly across his face, which was getting hotter by the second. "Do I ever feel stupid. You must think I'm the worst friend."

"Hardly," Daryl said, enveloping him in a tight bear hug and lifting him off the ground. "I've got much worse friends, believe me." He set Hugh down on the concrete landing and backed away, moving unsteadily.

"Still pretty solid under there," he said, glad to be out of Daryl's crushing embrace. Despite the evident atrophy, Daryl had clearly retained much of his strength from his days as a power lifter.

"Not quite a brick shit house anymore, but close," Daryl said, a thin smile appearing on his face.

"Forgive me?" he said, turning to Laura. As he reached out to hug her, her perfume filled his nose with hints of rose petals and black tea. She returned the hug stiffly, saying nothing, and he quickly released her. Had he offended her?

"Let's get some food," Daryl said, yanking the door open.

Moving from the dingy lobby into the main dining room, Hugh stopped and stared. The large open room was warmly lit by chandeliers and wall sconces, which were themselves interspersed between alcove booths lining the exterior walls. At the other end of the room, the plush flower-patterned carpet gave way to a black-and-white-tiled dance floor before an elevated stage. It was like he'd walked onto the set of a mafia movie. Blinking rapidly, he walked dumbly behind Laura and Daryl.

When Daryl stumbled while sitting down, Hugh shot out an arm to stabilize his friend. Saying nothing, Daryl brusquely shrugged him off, then leaned heavily on the table before slowly lowering himself into the chair.

Hugh glanced under the table for whatever Daryl had tripped on, then froze. The cuffs of Daryl's jogging pants had risen up, and his twin prosthetic legs were clearly visible, the metallic tubes gleaming where they rose up out of a pair of white sneakers.

"Why don't you take a picture?" Daryl said. "It'll last longer."

He flushed and jerked his eyes up, but Daryl wasn't talking to him. Instead, he was glaring at the hostess, who was also staring at Daryl's hardware.

The girl—probably no more than sixteen—looked like she wanted to crawl into a hole. "Excuse me," she mumbled, her face turning bright red. As Laura and Hugh sat down, she hurriedly filled glasses, almost spilling water on Laura. With a rush, she tossed their menus down. "Your server will be by shortly." Then she was gone.

"You forgot our drink order," Daryl called after her. Not waiting for a response, he picked up his water and sipped loudly. "Why do we come here?"

Laura said nothing, simply glaring at her husband as awkward silence descended on the table.

Not knowing what else to say, he gestured toward Daryl's legs. "How are the legs working out?" he said. "Your balance seems pretty good." Aside from the stumble and a somewhat stiff-legged gait, he wasn't sure he'd have been able to tell that Daryl had dual prosthetic limbs.

Daryl's eyes stayed focused on his menu. "I get around."

"So, no more dancing?" he said, trying a smile.

It seemed like eons ago, but when Daryl had first started dating Laura, he'd tried to impress her by taking ballroom dancing lessons. When Hugh found out, Daryl had sworn him to secrecy.

Daryl grunted, then took a loud sip of water.

"I guess I got thrown by the dance floor," Hugh said, nodding toward the checkerboard-tiled floor. He'd get a smile from Daryl if it killed him. "How did you guys even find this place? From the outside it looks abandoned." He glanced over his shoulder at the waitress who'd come up behind him and grimaced apologetically. "No offense."

The waitress placed a basket of bread on the table and smiled politely, then took their order and left.

"Daryl's family is from Kingston," Laura said in a distant voice when the waitress had gone. "We thought you and Elizabeth might like it. Sorry she couldn't make it."

"She's sorry, too," he said.

Laura cast a glance over the dining room, her eyes lingering on the dance floor. "We tried it out when we first moved here, even tried dancing again once he got a little more used to his new legs." Her gaze flickered to Daryl, then back to Hugh. "It didn't turn out well."

The waitress returned with their drinks, red wine for Laura, beer for Hugh, and a double rye and Coke for Daryl. As she set down the glasses, Daryl glared at her, dark shark eyes absorbing the light from the room.

"Don't get our drinks mixed up," he warned.

The server paused, drawing back from Daryl, who had a small smirk on his face. Attempting a short laugh, she hurriedly left.

Hugh grinned in spite of the waitress's discomfort. Finally, the old Daryl was poking through.

Laura looked at him, the puzzlement on her face growing more intense. "What are you two laughing at?"

"Don't tell me you haven't heard that story," Hugh said.

Taking a sip of her wine, Laura shook her head.

"When we were in Afghanistan in 2002, we got sent to Bagram Airfield to stage for a major operation, what was supposed to be taking out the last Taliban defense in the Shah-i-Kot Valley," he said.

"Supposed to be," Daryl said, lowering his drink from his mouth just enough to speak, his voice echoing in the glass. "All we ended up doing was chasing shadows."

"While we waited to deploy," Hugh continued, "we were all bunking together in these old modular tents." He nodded toward Daryl. "Ol' charming over there and I had cots beside each other. Since the situation was pretty dynamic and there was only so much we could do to get ready, we ended up spending a lot of time racked out in the tent while waiting for the chain of command to figure out what was going on."

"Hurry up and wait," Daryl said, swirling the ice around his glass. "That's what being a soldier is all about, long periods of boredom mixed with moments of sheer terror."

Hugh nodded. "One morning we were just hanging out, shooting the shit. I was chewing and spitting in a plastic water bottle that I had beside my cot."

"Right beside my bottle of grape Kool-Aid," Daryl said, "from all those care packages you sent."

"I remember you asking for juice crystals in your care packages," Laura added.

"Yeah, we didn't have much," he said, smiling. They'd even had to burn their own shit in barrels full of diesel. "I didn't have a real shower for almost the first month. We took bird baths and used an old camping shower once a week or so. But we had a lot of bottled water, so juice crystals were handy."

"By the end of the tour, that stuff was like currency," Daryl said. "The month before we left, you could trade for almost anything with juice crystals—that or chew, or cigarettes."

"Why did juice crystals get more valuable at the end of the tour?" Laura said, focusing on Hugh.

"At the start, we got supplied with plastic water bottles. Pallets of the stuff," he said. "Not too environmentally friendly, but that was pretty much the last thing on our minds."

"Then they brought in that fucking ROWPU," Daryl said, grabbing a piece of bread and stuffing it into his mouth.

"Reverse osmosis water purification unit—ROWPU," Hugh said, turning to Laura. "It's a machine that purifies water. They brought one in halfway through the tour, which on the one hand was great because we had tons of water—"

"Which tasted like shit," Daryl said. "Some guys started buying their water at the PX instead of drinking that garbage."

"It was pretty bad," Hugh said, pretending to gag. "The only way most guys could drink it was to use juice crystals to make it bearable. So if you remember basic supply and demand, when the PX ran out of juice crystals, they became like currency."

"Once I traded a tub of grape Kool-Aid for a flip-up sight for my rifle," Daryl said, holding his head up. "Only man in the company to have one."

He stared at Daryl, glad he was getting involved in the conversation. His friend had always been rough around the edges, but never taciturn. And it was true, Daryl had been the consummate infantryman in so many ways, with scrounging and bartering being particular strengths, not to mention fighting. Basically, everything that was really important to an infanteer. Maybe that's why he'd always sought Daryl's advice, including now.

"So how does all this relate to cots and chewing?" Laura said, pulling Hugh back.

He started to speak, then stopped as the waitress appeared with their meals. After she'd set the plates down and left, he carried on. "It's probably been a while since you chewed."

"Please, that's disgusting," Laura said.

But was she chuckling a little? Hugh smiled and gave an apologetic shrug. "Well, in that case, I guess you can be forgiven for not remembering that tobacco spit is pretty dark and brown."

Daryl paused, a forkful of spaghetti halfway into his mouth. "Kind of like grape Kool-Aid."

"Only if you weren't paying attention," Hugh said, his tone defensive.

Laura's face grew pale, and she put down her fork.

"Like hell I wasn't paying attention," Daryl said.

Laura held a finger to her lips and closed her eyes. "So he drank your spit? Your tobacco spit?"

Hugh chuckled. "He did. And like a trooper, he didn't even get sick."

Her face scrunched together. "That's revolting," she said. Definitely no chuckling this time.

Hugh's laughter faltered. Why did revulsion fit Laura's face so well? He tried to lighten the mood again. "I like to think it brought us closer, tightened our friendship."

"How do you figure?" Daryl said.

"I don't share bodily fluids with just anyone," he said in mock seriousness.

Laura snorted, choking on the wine she'd been drinking, and Daryl smiled.

As she wiped her face with her napkin, Laura spoke, her voice hoarse and broken as she continued to cough. "Elizabeth would be jealous."

Daryl rested an elbow on the table and pointed at Hugh. "Don't bother mentioning how that makes me your bitch, either."

Hugh burst out laughing, then threw up his hands. "Hey, we were using different bottles, how was I to know you'd be so careless? One man, one kit, remember?"

Laura laughed, and Daryl even appeared to be chuckling.

"My ass," Daryl said, shaking his head while his shoulders bucked up and down in mirth. Laura continued to laugh as well, tears appearing in her eyes, until gripped by another fit of coughing.

Hugh's laughter tapered off, and he looked at Laura, one hand reaching out to pat her on the back. What was wrong with her? It hadn't been that funny, and she was practically in hysterics.

She wiped her eyes. "It's been a long time since I laughed like that."

Daryl said nothing, although the smile on his face tightened.

"Maybe not quite supper conversation, but too late now," Laura said, sipping from her wine.

"It's like shit in your pants," Hugh said. "Once it's there, you can't put it back."

Daryl coughed, and wine sprayed out of Laura's mouth as they were again gripped by laughter. Laura drew an imaginary line on the table with her finger. "Honey, if this was the line, you're way over here," she said to Hugh, pointing to the other side of the room. She met his eyes, a twinkle in them for the first time that evening. "You always were the funniest man I knew, underneath that professional exterior of yours."

Daryl snorted, but said nothing. When Hugh looked at him, he just shook his head and returned to eating.

At least he'd gotten them to smile; it was a start. For the rest of the meal, they caught up, Laura talking about her banking job and Daryl explaining how his physiotherapy had gotten him to the point he could do practically everything he did before.

The meal passed quickly, and he became fully absorbed in Laura's and Daryl's lives. If only there were more people he could be himself around. He didn't make friends easily, and when Daryl had shut him out, there hadn't really been anyone else. At work or in the officers' mess, he was always Major Dégaré; how long had it been since he'd allowed himself to just be Hugh?

As they were finishing their desserts, Daryl turned to Hugh. "Why don't you come over after we're done, have a few drinks? Even stay the night, if you want."

"He probably wants to get home," Laura said, her face suddenly as strained as when she'd first arrived. "Elizabeth will be worried."

"Liz isn't waiting up for me," Hugh said, looking apologetically at Laura. "And considering she suggested I call in the first place, I'm sure she wouldn't mind."

"It's settled then," Daryl said loudly, draining what must have been his fifth drink.

He looked up as the waitress appeared, the bill in her hands. Hugh glanced at Daryl, who was intensely ignoring the waitress. Hugh reached out. "I've got it."

"No, we invited you," Laura said quickly, her face growing red as she glared at Daryl, who sat impassively. "We'll pay."

"Don't even think about it," he said, extending his credit card to the waitress.

Laura reached out to intercept his hand, and he jerked it away, smiling. "Laura, it's okay, I got it." When the waitress took his card, silence descended on the table. Hugh tried to restart a conversation, but failed. As he followed Daryl and Laura out, it was like an invisible cloud had descended over them. Hopefully he wasn't making a mistake by going over to their place.

After a short, winding drive following behind their VW, he arrived at Laura and Daryl's house. He could hardly believe his friends had chosen this place as their retirement home. The entry was dominated by a set of crumbling concrete steps leading to a tiny front porch with a wobbly railing. Two plastic patio chairs sat on the porch, looking like they'd break if someone sat in them, and the patio door was ready to fall off its hinges.

He tore his gaze from the house to where Daryl and Laura were exiting their car, their voices piercingly loud in the cold, clear night. He tried smiling as they walked up, but Laura ignored him, brushing past and up the steps. In one fluid motion, she opened the door and entered, the patio door slamming behind her. He looked at Daryl.

"Everything all right?" he asked. He still wanted a heart-to-heart with Daryl, but maybe this was a bad idea.

Daryl grunted. "She's all worked up about you coming over. Says the place embarrasses her." He grabbed a railing and began working his way up the stairs.

The thin metal swayed under Daryl's weight, and Hugh stepped closer, poised to catch his friend should he fall. "I could come back some other time. I don't want to cause you grief."

Daryl paused halfway up the stairs and looked over his shoulder. "You're not causing me any grief. Come in, don't insult my hospitality." Turning, he resumed plodding up the stairs.

He looked wistfully at his truck, then at the house, where Daryl was holding the door open. After being cut off from his friend all these years, how could he refuse? He walked up and entered, crinkling his nose as an invasive smell of dog assaulted him. Looking around the foyer, with its tattered carpet and cracked linoleum, there was so much clutter there didn't seem to be anywhere he could put his boots.

"Just toss 'em anywhere," Daryl said. "Come on." Opening a creaky wooden door, he began descending into the basement, taking care with his footing on the bare wooden planks that made up the steps.

Just before following, Hugh spied Laura at the kitchen table, illuminated by a sickly yellow glow. One of her arms was crossed over her chest, and in her free hand, she held a cigarette near her lips, the smoke curling lazily up to join a haze near the ceiling. Their eyes met, and she pursed her lips, then took a drag and looked away. By the light of a single incandescent bulb in the stairwell, Hugh braced himself on the exposed wall studs and slowly followed Daryl.

Daryl's basement was only half finished, with a hodgepodge of drywall and sporadic pieces of carpet crisscrossing the floor. Hugh looked around at the detritus of a military career, all jammed into green duffel bags and barracks boxes and continued into what looked to be the sole finished room. He stopped and stared, a low whistle escaping his lips.

"Nice, eh?" Daryl said, clapping him on the shoulder. "I did most of this myself, except the track lighting. I had to get somebody in for that."

The room was impressive, a true man cave, with modern lighting and a gray stone wall dominating the far end of the room. Digging his toes into the plush carpet, so soft after the cold concrete in the rest of the basement, he took his time taking everything in, especially the oversize chairs, projector system, and mini bar standing in one corner.

"Grab a seat," Daryl said, moving to the bar and pulling down a bottle and some glasses.

Hugh noticed a number of framed papers hanging prominently on one wall. He slowly walked the perimeter of the room to get a closer look.

The first frame held a certificate stating that Private Daryl Robertson had graduated as top candidate on his basic infantryman course. On a mantel near the mini bar rested a cherry-stained box that housed Daryl's medals, a rack that would have extended past his shoulder if he'd been wearing them on his chest. Alongside the medals was a scroll Daryl had received on being presented with the Star of Military Valour, a decoration only a handful of Canadian soldiers had ever received.

Catching movement in his periphery, Hugh started, surprised to see Daryl standing beside him, a glass filled with amber liquid proffered in an outstretched hand. With an appreciative nod, he took the glass, then nodded toward the mantel. "The only thing that's missing is the flag and certificate signed by the prime minister you got when you retired."

"I sent them back," Daryl said, standing beside him and staring at the medals.

His mouth dropped. "You did what?"

"I got forced out against my will, so I sent them back. If the prime minister really appreciated my service, he could've found me a job," Daryl said. "Cheers."

He clinked his glass against Daryl's, then drank. As warmth spread down his throat and into his chest, he moved toward one of the chairs and sat down. Daryl sat in the other chair, grabbed a remote, and turned on the television.

"So, how're things really going?" Daryl said, pulling a pack of cigarettes from his shirt pocket. He offered the smokes to Hugh, who put up a hand and shook his head.

"Well, like we were talking about at supper—"

"You mean that shit you were feeding Laura?" Daryl said, shaking a cigarette from the pack and gripping the end between his lips.

"It wasn't shit."

"Come on, man, don't snow the snowman," Daryl said around the cigarette. "You were totally fluffing her. Anybody can see there's more going on with you than meets the eye, so why don't you just come out with it?"

He ran a hand over his scalp. "Things could be better," he finally said.

"Oh yeah? Does Ottawa suck that bad?"

"No, no, the city is nice," he said. Not exactly a ringing endorsement. "It's got everything a city should have, and there's tons to do outdoors, good restaurants. I've heard the nightlife could be better, but I'm not exactly a bar star now, so that's not really a big deal."

"So?"

Hugh grimaced. "The job sucks."

"You can't tell me you didn't know it would suck. It's a head-quarters," Daryl said, digging into his pocket for his lighter.

"I know, I know, but it's like knowing you're going to be cold, versus being cold," he said. "The real thing is always worse."

Daryl snorted, a harsh, bitter sound. "Yeah, or like knowing you're going to get kicked in the balls versus actually getting kicked in the balls."

He grinned into his drink, watching the whiskey cling to the frosted glass as he swirled it in his hand. This was more the Daryl he remembered.

"Things okay with Liz?" Daryl said as he lit his cigarette.

He nodded. "She's fine," he said. "She likes Ottawa, too, but hasn't been able to find a job yet. To be honest, she probably won't."

"You don't think so?"

"Maybe," he said, shrugging. "It's doubtful a hospital would pick her up knowing they're going to lose her in a year and a half when we move again."

"She doesn't have to tell them you're going to get posted."

Hugh smiled. "You don't know Liz well enough. Still, she likes this usher job she's doing with the NAC. Her family is nearby, too, which is nice."

"Really?"

"Nice for her, that is," Hugh said, his smile growing broader. "Not sure if you remember me telling you, but her dad takes some getting used to. The rest of her family aren't much better. I think I'm the only soldier any of them have ever met." He sipped his drink. "How about you and Laura?"

"We're fine."

"Really? Supper seemed a little tense."

Daryl raised his glass. "It is what it is."

Silence filled the room, and Hugh took the opportunity to look around again. Why had Daryl put so much effort into this room, but left the remainder of the house so run-down?

"You going to level with me or not?" Daryl asked.

Hugh thought for a couple of seconds before answering. "Things are rough," he said. Why couldn't he just spit it out? He pulled out a tin of Copenhagen and showed it to Daryl. "Mind if I dip?"

Daryl shrugged. "Go ahead," he said. "Grab a spit cup from the cupboard."

Standing, he grabbed a battered coffee mug from near the mini bar then came back to the chair. Taking a large pinch of tobacco, he stuffed it into his lower lip, then laid the tin on the table. "I think I've got PTSD."

"Finally, we get to it."

He spat in the coffee mug. "I needed someone to talk to who's been through it."

Daryl scoffed as he threw back the rest of his drink. "Well, I guess I fit that bill." He pulled out another cigarette and lit it from the dying embers of the first one, then stood and moved to the mini bar. "Have you talked to a doc?"

"Last week," he said. "I had my first therapy session, more like an intro."

"And what did he say? I'm assuming it's a he?"

He nodded. "He's pretty sure I've got PTSD, although he had lots of caveats that it was a first meeting and all."

"Doctors do that," Daryl said, returning to his chair with a whiskey bottle that he thunked down on the coffee table. "So what sort of problems are you having?"

He hesitated, then spoke slowly, as if searching for the right words. "Trouble sleeping," he said. "I keep thinking about things I've seen, things I've done."

"You tell your chain of command?"

He shook his head.

"Why not?"

He fidgeted in his chair. "I thought I could handle it myself."

"And?" Daryl said, refilling his glass.

"And . . . we'll see."

Daryl stared at him, saying nothing.

His shoulders slumped. He'd do well to remember that for all Daryl's disheveled appearance, a razor-sharp mind lurked behind those flat black eyes. "I guess I'm worried about what happens if I tell anybody at work."

Daryl gave him a hard look, then lifted his glass to drink, his eyes never leaving Hugh's face. When he did speak, his glass held to his lips so that his voice echoed hollowly in the room, it was as if he were giving a proclamation. "You're right to worry. They'd fuck it up."

Hugh stood and paced between his chair and the mini bar. "You're probably right," he said. "The military is so backward, it's actually impressive. It's the only organization I know that always talks about how much it cares for you, then screws it up when they try to do anything."

Daryl snorted. "You really think the military cares what happens to you?"

He turned and faced his friend. The intensity in his friend's eyes was like a red aiming laser. So they were going to get into it—well, wasn't that what he'd wanted? He set his jaw and nodded.

Daryl sneered, then reached for the bottle. Dispensing with his glass entirely, he raised the bottle to his lips.

"So lemme see if I understand. You think the military cares about you because it says people are its most important asset. Am I right?" Daryl drank, then lowered the bottle and wiped his lips with the back of his other hand. "You know what that line of reasoning also implies? That we're all just numbers, resources. The military doesn't care about you, not really, except when they need a narrative, like when they're recruiting or when you die." Daryl took another drink. "You're just a fucking resource to them, to be used as they see fit."

"I don't believe that. And neither do you, or at least you didn't," he said. "And even if it was true, it doesn't matter. We're a profession. We might have to consider soldiers as resources sometimes, but we still care about them." He pointed at Daryl. "Look at me and tell me the senior leadership doesn't care about the soldiers. You can't. Sure, there might be some idiots in the senior ranks who don't get it, but by and large they really do care."

Daryl rolled his eyes. "Can you hear yourself? Can you hear how stupid you sound?" he said. "Sure, some leaders might give a fuck, but the military as an institution doesn't care, nor should it. That's where you're wrong."

"I'm not wrong."

"You are. You're fucking designed to be replaced, because you have to be." Daryl rubbed his eyes. "Listen, I'll speak slowly so you'll be sure to follow, all right? The whole nature of war is that soldiers get killed. When they do, someone else fills their spot. It has to be that way if an army wants to take casualties and still win. You can't cry yourself to sleep every time someone bites the dust. You forget about 'em, fill the blank file, and get back into the fight. Bottom line, you're old news once you're gone."

Daryl took a deep breath and held out his hands, as if explaining a rudimentary concept. "Leaving aside the inconsistency where you say the chain of command cares, but then don't trust them enough to tell them about your problem, let me ask you this. You always believed in the military, so how does your view that the military cares for you hold up against the perspective that the needs of the organization outweigh the needs of the individual?"

Hugh sat down, cradling his glass in his lap. Staring at the copper liquid, he kept his voice steady. "You know the answer as much as I do." He raised his eyes, shooting Daryl a penetrating glance, searching for the same man he'd done basic infantry training with almost twenty-one years ago. "Those aren't either-or propositions, they can both be true." He pointed at Daryl. "And you once believed, too, if I remember."

Daryl laughed once, a harsh bark. Swinging his legs up onto the coffee table, he pointed to the two prosthetic limbs attached to his legs below the knees, hiking his pants up so the steel tubes were clearly visible. "That worked out really well for me," he said. "Look where duty and loyalty got me."

He stared at Daryl's prosthetics. He couldn't help it; the sight unnerved him. *There but for the grace of God.* Ripping his eyes away, he tightened his grip on his glass. His reply was quieter this time, almost a whisper. "That's not the military's fault."

Daryl moved his legs back under the table, a gleam of satisfaction appearing in his eyes. "No, I guess not," he said. "I did my duty, and the military did theirs. They treated me like the collateral damage that I was."

Hugh dropped his head slightly and massaged his temples. "They did everything they could."

"Did they?"

He looked up suddenly, his brow furrowing. "You know they did," he said. "You couldn't meet the physical standards, simple as that."

Daryl slammed the bottle on the table, liquid spurting out the top. "I never got a chance," he said. "I passed all the physical tests with these things, got better scores than some of the pieces of shit still in uniform."

The two of them locked eyes, neither speaking. Hugh dropped his gaze first. "You know that's not how it works," he said. "There are rules, and we don't get to pick and choose which ones we follow."

"Oh, the rules are clear," Daryl said. "Like I said before, we're all just resources. Everybody can be replaced." He gestured at Hugh with the bottle. "Including you, my friend."

His spine tingled with cold, like someone was behind him. His eyes flicked to Daryl, searching his face. "What does that mean?"

"Just that it's easy to be the company man when you're inside looking out," Daryl said. "You might be singing a different tune if your situation ever changed. Which, from what you've told me, it probably has. So I say again, you're right to worry about telling your chain of command."

He leaned back into his chair and massaged his eyes with the palms of his hands. How long had it been since he'd had more than a beer at one sitting? He wasn't exactly setting himself up for success in poking holes in Daryl's argument.

Daryl grabbed another cigarette and lit it.

"I can't believe you can afford to chain-smoke," Hugh said, shaking his head and smiling slightly. "And you're like the only guy who still smokes, you know that, right?"

Daryl took another deep drag, then blew the smoke out his nostrils. A wispy gray haze filled the room. "I don't really care," he said. "A man's got to have some vices."

They sat quietly. Hugh ran his tongue over the wad of tobacco in his lip, staring at his friend. Would this be him in five years? Less?

"So how bad is it?" Daryl said, butting his cigarette in the ashtray.

Hugh pressed his lips together. Daryl's PTSD had been made worse by the explosive-induced brain injuries that had accompanied the attack that took his legs. How could they even begin to compare symptoms?

"I'm still functioning," he said. "Mostly it's insomnia. I get angry a lot, or at least more than I used to."

"Well, it must be pretty bad if you're talking about it," Daryl said. "I only knew you to speak up when it was really bad. Like that time on course when you had cellulitis in your knee. That was gross, man."

"My knee was so swollen it was like I had on a knee pad." Hugh chuckled. "I remember the doctor who saw me told me I'd have to be hospitalized with an IV. I couldn't handle not finishing the course, so I told him to just give me some pills and I'd tough it out. He looked at me like I had a dick growing out of my forehead."

Daryl laughed, too, a welcome break. "You always were hard."

Hugh held up his glass, enjoying the faint aroma of caramel and spices of the whiskey. "If you're going to be stupid, you better be hard."

They both raised their glasses in a toast, and then silence descended once again. Hugh fidgeted in his chair. What exactly had he been expecting from this conversation with Daryl? Sympathy? Advice?

"Spit it out," Daryl said, interrupting his reverie.

Hugh looked up.

"I can see the gears turning in there, always could, so just say whatever you're thinking," Daryl said. "You'll find the doctors encourage talking, by the way, so you should probably get used to it."

He stared at his glass. "I guess . . . ," he said, hesitating. What was it exactly? He started talking in a quiet voice. "Sometimes I have these second thoughts about things that we did, that I did, and I want to know that I did them for a reason. That they meant something." A bitter sting attacked his eyes, and he coughed. There was no way he'd be crying in front of Daryl. "Sometimes it feels like nobody cares." Could he blame them, though? Why would anyone care about someone who'd killed women and children? But he hadn't done anything wrong.

Daryl reached across the table with the bottle and refilled Hugh's glass. When he spoke, his voice was surprisingly gentle, a tone Hugh had only heard once or twice before. "Bad news, bud. Nobody does care, not really. Except other soldiers of course." The glass full, he settled back into his chair.

Hugh glanced up, brow furrowed. "I'm serious," he said. "On some missions we were judge, jury, and executioner, all at once. We made mistakes sometimes, we're only human." He shook his head. "Add to that the people we lost, good people, and it had to have been for something."

Daryl nodded. "Sure we did," he said, then burped. "But we lost some shit pumps, too. Or did you forget the guys that were less than the angels they were made out to be by the media? The guys who were cheating on their wives, or were selling drugs? The guys who died because they were stupid?" Daryl held his glass in front of his mouth, shaking his head. "Besides, whether they were good or bad is missing the point."

"And what is the point?" he said, spitting out the words.

"Good soldier or bad soldier, either way you're just a tool of the government. And what all governments really want, regardless if it's a dictatorship or a democracy or whatever, is to stay in power," Daryl said. "The only difference is what that government does to stay in power."

"Where are you going with this?"

"Just listen and I'll get there," Daryl said. "A government that depends on being elected is going to do things it thinks will get it elected, or reelected, as the case may be. It's like an investment. They'll invest in things that will get them elected, and they won't invest in things that won't get them elected. You follow?"

Hugh nodded.

"So let's take Afghanistan," Daryl said. "Afghanistan started out a good investment. Canadians died in 9/11, global war on terror, blah, blah, blah, people loved it. But somewhere along the way, it soured. Who knows when, maybe when body bags started coming home. In the end, the government decided it was a bad investment. So they stopped throwing good money after bad, and we pulled out, regardless of whether we accomplished anything, good or bad. The government only cared about Afghanistan because they could use it to get elected. Just like every other issue." Daryl pointed at Hugh. "And this isn't one party or another, remember that. All of them would do the same, because they want to take power and keep it."

Hugh shook his head. "That's a pretty narrow view."

"You think so, eh? You think Aunt Sally in butt-fuck Manitoba gives two flying fucks about a shithole like Afghanistan? Beyond the five minutes she might think about it when she sees a story on the news?" Daryl said. "Then it's back to bitching about the wireless Internet being slow or how long it's been since the Leafs were a contender. No, unless it's touched them personally, and I'm talking about seeing their kid or husband in a casket or short a leg here and there, people don't give a rat's ass about what happened in Afghanistan, or, by extension, you."

Daryl sat forward, a fever pitch in his eyes.

"That's how you explain the shitty way veterans get treated," Daryl said. "Taking care of veterans because they served their country? How quaint. It's not about that at all. It's about balancing the books so the government can get elected. The question the government really asks is what's the minimum amount they need to shell out to keep veterans quiet, while at the same time not pissing off another constituency. It's not about looking after veterans, it's about owning an election issue. God knows I can speak to that."

"Stop," he said, needing to stem the bombardment. "With all due respect, you're biased."

"Open your eyes," Daryl said, slapping the table. "All these so-called veterans' initiatives? They're nothing but ways to cut corners and save money."

"No, they're about delivering benefits more efficiently," he said. "I suppose you think it's just the government trying to screw us over?"

"You still don't get it, do you?" Daryl said, shaking his head. "I'm not blaming the government. Hell, they're only doing what everyone in the same position would do, hedging their bets to stay in power."

"So what is it then?" Hugh said, growing frustrated. Sure, Daryl had been through some hard times lately, but this was getting to be too much.

Daryl leaned back, silent for a moment. "The problem isn't the government, but the people," he said. "People should be holding the government to account, but they don't because most have it so fucking good they couldn't conceive of sacrificing something for the greater good, even thirty minutes of their time. And you're looking for someone to tell you it all meant something?" He grabbed the bottle and took a swig, then stared hard at Hugh. "It didn't matter. People don't care. And the quicker you accept that, the quicker you'll come to terms with whatever's eating you."

"Well, that's really inspiring," he said, licking his suddenly dry lips. "Thanks for the pep talk."

"Well, I am admittedly a bitter ex-soldier with no legs, so maybe not the most objective opinion," Daryl said, chuckling grimly. "Or biased, as you would say. Asshole."

Hugh couldn't help but laugh, too, feeling a bit better. They sat in silence again, sipping whiskey. After a few minutes, Daryl stood up, teetering so badly Hugh thought he would fall over.

"Maybe that's enough for tonight, eh?" Daryl said, taking the bottle back to the mini bar. "I'm going to hit the sack. You okay sleeping down here?"

Hugh nodded, and they mumbled good nights. He watched Daryl stumble upstairs, amazed the man could walk given how much he'd drunk. He lay down but hardly felt tired. Thoughts swirled through his head.

Service before self was supposed to embody a soldier's life, service predicated upon special trust placed in members of the military profession to execute their duties responsibly on behalf of society. Killing was, after all, a hell of a thing. But didn't trust go both ways? Shouldn't soldiers be able to expect that society would take care of them after the sacrifices they'd made in service to their country?

Was he just a resource? Damaged goods to be thrown away the minute he couldn't perform his duties? He knew well enough how Daryl had fought against his release, pointing out the numerous jobs he could still do without legs. And it was true, there were many things he could have done where his years of experience would have been put to good use, like teach in a school or get units ready to deploy. So if Daryl was the example of what could happen to a proud and decorated soldier, then where did that leave Hugh?

He flipped around on the couch, unable to get comfortable. Daryl was an outlier. He had to be.

Still tossing, he willed sleep to take him.

❧ ❧ ❧

Hugh's eyes blinked open. He sat up abruptly, then just as quickly hunched over, nausea gripping his stomach. He tried again, more slowly this time, then looked around. His neck ached, and it was only by turning his entire torso that he could look left and right. What an idiot he was.

Cursing, he leaned forward, braced his elbows on his knees, and checked his watch. Eight o'clock, almost six hours after he'd called it quits with Daryl, although it felt like he'd just lain down. He rubbed his eyes, then remembered he'd told Elizabeth he'd be back by lunch. Time to get going.

He stood up and folded the blanket Daryl had given him, willing his stomach to stop churning. It didn't help that his head felt one second behind whatever he was doing. He tossed the blanket on a chair and went upstairs.

In the kitchen, he found Laura wearing one of Daryl's old regimental sweatshirts and snow pants. She stood near the sink, sipping coffee and fiddling with an edge of the vinyl countertop that was lifting from the counter. Beside her sat a massive dog, its head coming to her waist. He said good morning, then sat down at a simple wooden table that had seen better days.

"You boys must have hit the bottle pretty hard," she said, pouring the remains of her coffee down the sink.

"Yeah, not sure if we solved any problems or just created more. I feel terrible."

"You look terrible. You're welcome to sleep more, if you want," she said. She tousled one of the dog's black ears, then ran her hand down the white markings on its snout.

"I wish I could," he said, rubbing his eyes. "But I need to get home by lunch."

"Have something before you go," she said, gesturing around the Spartan kitchen. "There's coffee on, and you should be able to find some cereal or toast or something. I've got to take Turbo for a walk."

"Do you want some company?" he said. Maybe the fresh air would do him some good.

"If you want," she said coolly. When she walked past him, Bernese mountain dog in tow, he stood and followed.

He got dressed and went outside into the blinding white glare of sun reflecting off snow and ice. Coughing in the cold air, he quickly fell behind Laura's blistering pace, almost like she was trying to lose him. He tried making conversation, getting only curt answers in response. At a snow-covered park, they stopped, and Laura unhitched Turbo's leash. Free, the big dog bounded into the snow.

While Laura watched the dog play, he studied her. She'd always been so full of life; what had happened? Under the bright sunlight, he spied something on her cheek, a slight discoloration. He took a few steps forward to examine her from a different angle. Had that been there last night?

Laura's eyes flickered to him, then back to the dog. "Turbo," she said, stamping her feet. "Time to get back."

As she bent to greet the dog, he spied the discoloration again. "What happened to your face?"

"Nothing."

"No, there's definitely something on your cheek," he said, pointing generally in the direction of her face. "I know it's rude to point, but I thought you'd want to know."

"Leave it, Hugh," she said, straightening. She turned on her heel and aggressively jerked Turbo's leash. "I don't want to talk about it."

"I'm sorry," he said. "If I didn't know better, I'd have said someone hit you."

She stopped and cast a furtive look over her shoulder, then yanked on the leash and resumed walking, almost trotting. He reached out to grab her elbow—she was practically running from him now—when Turbo turned and growled at him, fangs barely concealed.

"Did Daryl do that?"

Laura dropped a mitten-clad hand to Turbo's head, calming the dog. She did not reply.

"He did, didn't he?" he said, the cold forgotten.

Laura's shoulders slumped. She brought one hand up to her face.

"Was it an accident?" he asked, stammering. "He'd never do something like that on purpose."

Laura turned, her bottom lip quivering. "Never say never," she said, as if repeating some tragic mantra. "The man you used to know might not have done that, but not the man he is now. I don't even know who this man is." She mopped an eye with the back of a hand, then stroked Turbo's broad head. "I used to hope the man he was, the one I fell in love with, would come back, but I've stopped kidding myself."

Hugh stood rooted to the ground. What should he do? He reached out a hand to offer her comfort, but as he neared, she recoiled.

"Don't," she said, positioning Turbo between herself and Hugh. "Just don't."

His mouth opened and closed silently. What right did he have to say anything? His hand dropped limply to his side. "He's seen some pretty bad stuff," he said, blurting out the first thing that came to his mind. "Probably worse than me and—"

Her head snapped up, eyes blazing. "Don't make excuses for him," she said. "Don't you dare justify what he's done."

She advanced toward him as if possessed, her hand driving like a piston into his chest while Turbo stalked along beside her, growling. He reflexively backed up, hoping he didn't trip as his eyes darted between Laura's face and Turbo's teeth.

"You all come home thinking you had it rough wherever you were when you all knew what you were getting into," she said, her voice trembling. "Or you should have known, if you weren't just a bunch of stupid overgrown boys. What did you think being a soldier was all about?"

He stumbled in the deep snow and brought his hands up to ward off Laura.

"You go off to play silly bugger, leaving us at home to sort everything out, waiting for you, trying to keep families together," she said, her voice lashing him. "Then you get hurt somehow, because that's what happens to soldiers, and you come home expecting us to take care of you. But who takes care of me?" Flecks of spit landed on his face. "You're so quick to talk of sacrifice—well what about my sacrifices, what I gave up? All this support that's supposed to help him, what about me? Where's my support? My life changed, too, and I never even got a say. When do I get to grieve?"

She glared at him, daring him to say something. Then her eyes dulled and she half turned from him, wiping a hand across her face.

"Part of me wishes he would just kill himself," she said. Her chest heaved with a single, heartrending sob. "The other part hates me for thinking that." She took a deep, shuddering breath. "But it doesn't disagree."

His mouth dropped, as if she'd just punched him in the solar plexus.

She wiped her eyes. "I'm sorry," she said. "You didn't need to hear that."

He looked up slowly, still processing what he'd heard. "No, I'm the one who should apologize," he said. "I didn't mean to pry. Maybe I could help?"

"You can't."

They walked back to the house in silence. At the foot of the driveway, he stopped by his truck while she kept walking toward the door. When she noticed he'd lagged behind, she turned.

"I should go," he said.

"At least have breakfast," she said, sniffling.

Jamming his hands into his coat, he curled his frozen toes, trying to generate warmth. "I'm not hungry," he said, wanting nothing more than to leave. Looking back at Laura, framed in front of the run-down house, he felt he was seeing her for the first time. She looked small, trapped.

A lump formed in his throat. "I'd better hit the road before it gets too busy."

She stepped closer and leaned in, giving him a polite peck on the cheek. "I'll tell him you said good-bye."

"I'll call," he said. "Good-bye, Laura. Thanks for letting me stay." He turned, digging out his keys. He paused and looked over his shoulder. "For what it's worth, I'm sorry."

"Me, too," she said, her voice full of resignation. With a small wave, she turned and entered the house, the cheap metal door slamming harshly in the frigid air.

CHAPTER 5

"Today, Hugh, I'd like to discuss your work history so we can better understand how you've come to be where you are," Dr. Taylor said. "I'd also like to touch on support networks so we can make sure that we're promoting patient self-care. Any questions before we begin?"

Hugh shook his head firmly. He'd done a lot of soul-searching in the days since he'd visited Daryl. Tragically, his friend was probably a textbook example of how an injury, PTSD or otherwise, could be mishandled. He wouldn't end up the same. From here on in, he'd own his problem. "Let's do this."

"Good," Dr. Taylor said. "So when did you join the army?"

For most of the next hour, they dissected Hugh's career. At sixteen, the ink still fresh on his driver's license, he'd signed up as an infantry reservist. He'd gotten his mom's permission—in a rare moment when he could get her attention—and it would be the last thing he'd ever ask from her. When he graduated high school in 1992, he bolted into the full-time army as an infantry private, the quickest route to escape the default careers of forestry or mining.

"I've heard the training was harsher back then," Dr. Taylor said.

He chuckled. "It wasn't all bad," he said. "Although if I had a quarter for every time my section commander called me an asshole, I could have retired long ago."

Service in an infantry battalion came next, an exhilarating life for a young man in great shape and unafraid to work hard or party hard. To his excitement, his unit had been selected to deploy to Bosnia in the early nineties.

"Was it the experience you had hoped it would be?" Dr. Taylor asked, looking up from his notepad.

"Not exactly," he said. "Looking back, we were unprepared, although other countries were just as bad off. Then again, we learned a lot, especially about things like rules of engagement."

"How so?"

"They were confusing," he said. "Guys didn't know if, or when, they could shoot, even in self-defense. As a result, the chain of command kind of made things up along the way. Considering the ROE we later had in Afghanistan and how detailed those were, we've come a long way."

"Anything else?"

He whistled. "Peacekeeping is hard, there's no getting around it," he said, leaning forward and resting his elbows on his knees. "I mean, it's cliché to talk about how Canadians love their peacekeeping, but I don't think people realize what a dog's breakfast it can be to enforce peace or prevent crimes when you don't even know what force you can use."

"What kind of crimes?"

"You name it," he said, his chest tightening. "Rape, murder, ethnic cleansing. Both sides did it, playing the peace process, and us, for time. And they were better equipped than us, so they could do what they wanted."

"So you were being ordered to do something you didn't have the resources to do?"

"Absolutely."

"How did that make you feel?"

Hugh paused, blinking rapidly. "Angry. Embarrassed. We were supposed to be helping people, and we could barely help ourselves." *Scared, too, why not mention that?* He shook his head slightly, as if a bug had flown by his ear. No, that wasn't something he'd tell a man he barely knew.

"It sounds almost like a betrayal in some respects," Dr. Taylor said, head buried in the journal as he scribbled furiously. "The violation of moral conventions or social values can be as big a psychological stressor as scenes of violence, if not more. People feel like their trust has been betrayed, that what's right has been betrayed. Would you agree with that?"

He nodded, his hands trembling. He clasped them together in his lap, trying to still them.

"We'll explore this theme more," the therapist continued, "but let's finish your work history first. What happened next?"

After that tour, he'd had a few years mostly spent in training, but in the late nineties, he'd deployed back to Bosnia to find a far different mission, one largely more concerned with the rest-and-relaxation program than achieving any sort of military objective.

When that deployment finished, he'd toyed with getting out of the military, especially since peacekeeping was the flavor of the day. In the end, he'd stayed in, mostly because he couldn't think of anything else he'd rather do. He entertained the idea of taking his commission, even took several part-time university courses, but by and large, he was bored. Then 9/11 happened and everything changed.

"I deployed to Afghanistan in 2002 on the first Canadian mission," he said.

"And how was it?"

"Incredible," he said. "I mean, people forget that when 9/11 happened, Canadians died, too. Getting a chance to take the fight back to the enemy was, well, let's just say we were the envy of every other soldier in the Canadian army. In fact, it's probably not a stretch to say that I'd have gotten out of the military if 9/11 hadn't happened." *Maybe that would have been for the best.* He coughed. Where had that thought come from?

"Then what happened?"

"After the tour, I took my commission and got promoted to the lofty rank of officer cadet," he said, smiling. "Then I went to the Royal Military College for three years to get all edumacated."

Dr. Taylor glanced up. "Pardon?"

"To get a degree," he said, still smiling. "Edumacated means I got smart."

"Only three years?"

"I was able to get a year shaved off through equivalencies, thank God," he said, nodding. "Because I finished early, I got back to battalion in the fall of 2005 and was slotted as a platoon commander for a deployment to Afghanistan in 2006. I deployed again in 2009." Had it been that long? Some of the memories seemed like they'd just happened a week ago. Like the time—

"—on that deployment?"

He started, turning to focus on Dr. Taylor. "Excuse me?"

"What did you do on that deployment?"

"Uh, in 2009?" he said, blinking. "I was a staff officer in the operations cell of a brigade group. Busy times." He shook his head. "Anyways, that's more or less it for deployments. I got promoted to major in spring of 2012 and was posted to Ottawa that summer."

"So you've been in Ottawa less than a year?" Dr. Taylor said, eyebrows rising. "Do you like it?"

"It's nice," he said. "My wife's family lives outside Toronto, so it's nice to be close to them."

"And your family? Brothers or sisters?"

He rubbed the back of his neck. "Elizabeth is really my only family," he said. "My dad died in a mining accident when I was eleven, and my mom hooked up with some real losers shortly after. I'm an only child, so I got away from all that as soon as I could. I guess the army was my family until I met Elizabeth."

"And when did you meet her?"

"When I was at RMC," he said. Looking back, three of the best years of his life, studying the profession of arms, challenging his mind, and, of course, meeting Elizabeth. "She was taking nursing at Queen's, and a mutual friend set us up for the Christmas Ball." The annual formal dance was a Cinderella-like event, the one time of year an RMC cadet was guaranteed a date.

"You would have been much older than her, weren't you?"

"A bit—I was twenty-eight, she was twenty-three." He shrugged. How to explain? "Elizabeth was in a bad car accident when she was twenty, she almost died. She was on track to go into law school, follow in her dad's footsteps, but she had to take a year off to recover. She said the recovery changed her, made her realize she wanted to do more with her life than just make money. So yeah, there was an age difference, but she was pretty mature for her age." Probably more mature than he.

"I see. And do you have any kids?"

He shook his head. "Elizabeth wants kids—she says she wants three or four—but I've been away so much it never seemed like the right time. We were hoping this job would give us the stability so we could start, but it hasn't worked out that way." His voice trailed off as he looked at his wedding ring, its matte-gray finish making it look tattooed to his finger. When was the last time they'd talked about kids? "She's only thirty-four though, so we've still got a bit of time." Would there ever be a good time?

"What about you? You said Elizabeth wants to have kids. Do you?"

He cleared his throat. "I do, I just . . . have a hard time seeing myself as a dad."

"I see," Dr. Taylor said, scanning his notes, then peering over his glasses. "I'm amazed how much you've been sent overseas. Is that typical?"

He shrugged. "I've deployed a lot, maybe more than others, but it's not out of the ordinary," he said. "Mostly right time, right place."

Dr. Taylor pulled off his glasses. Holding them by one of the arms, he peered up at the ceiling. "Most of what I've heard about Afghanistan is from the news, and I've rarely had the opportunity to talk with someone who's been there so much," he said. "What is it like?"

"Where should I start?" he said, snorting. "Every time was different. In 2002, it was straightforward. Most Afghans were happy we were there and the Taliban wasn't. That feeling was still there later on, but I think people were getting impatient. I mean, there was progress, but it was so slow. Then around 2005, it became a counterinsurgency, although we didn't figure that out until much later." He shook his head. "After all this time, I'm still not convinced we understood even the basics of Afghan society, much less everything we would have needed to successfully apply a counterinsurgency strategy."

"Such as?"

He bit his lip and looked at the ceiling. "Oh, even basics like tribal dynamics," he said. "I think most people in the West would find it odd that a modern country could still be governed through tribes, but that's a big deal over there." He leaned forward and pointed at Dr. Taylor. "Or something simpler, like farming at night." He remained still, finger extended and mouth opened as if to speak, not making a sound. Gradually, he sank back into the couch.

"Why do they farm at night?"

He began toying with his wedding band. "It's simple, really. It's too hot in the summer to work during the day," he said, his voice growing quieter. He looked up abruptly. "Did you know a farmer digging in a field beside a road at night looks a lot like an insurgent digging in an IED? Especially through a video feed." Looking away, he cleared his throat.

"And what does it look like?"

He put a finger to his lips for several seconds as he contemplated the question. "One night we called in a strike on an insurgent digging beside a road. There were a lot of improvised explosive devices—IEDs—on that route. Hell, over the previous week alone, two of our patrols had been attacked within half a mile of that same spot. We watched him for a while, got the assessment from the intelligence guys that he was digging something in, checked our ROEs, then finally got approval to drop a bomb on him."

He closed his eyes. It was still so vivid, after all this time. The sudden flash and instant dust cloud of the explosion captured in perfect black-and-white clarity on a high-definition television screen. How many times had he seen something like that? Why was this one any different? He took a deep breath.

"That pilot must have dropped three bombs on that guy, not small ones, either, but big ones, five hundred pounders, I think." He shook his head. "When the dust cleared from the first drop, the guy got up after a minute or so and walked away, stumbling all over the place, but still moving. A couple minutes later, there was another bomb. Boom!" He brought his fist up and rapidly opened it, miming an explosion.

Dr. Taylor started. "Then what?"

He stared at his hand, the fingers open, but losing tension. "He got up again. So he got another bomb dropped on him." He glanced up, emphasizing his next words. "And he got up again. It was unbelievable. We were all cheering, everyone in the TOC, like we were watching *Rocky* or something." Except it wasn't a movie; it was real life. He leaned forward, elbows on his knees. "Then an A-10 strafed him." He paused, bringing his hands to his lips. "He didn't get up after that."

Dr. Taylor reached onto his desk for a box of Kleenex, which he gently set on the table near Hugh.

Hugh inhaled deeply. "You know, nobody ever questioned that engagement. And we didn't get attacked in that area for the rest of the tour." He closed his eyes. "But when we dropped that bomb, we didn't know the Afghans farmed at night."

"Do you have second thoughts?"

"Not really," he said, blinking rapidly, then looking down. "Maybe, I don't know." He sighed, rubbing his eyes. "It's so surreal."

Dr. Taylor placed his notepad on the table beside his chair. "It sounds like you had to make some very hard decisions."

He exhaled sharply. "Tell me about it," he said, slumping into the couch. "I wouldn't say we were playing with people's lives, but we reached out and killed that guy in an instant, like it was a video game. People were cheering, for Christ's sake."

"It's natural to feel empathy toward a fellow person," Dr. Taylor said, speaking as if he might spook a wild animal. "In fact, that's one definition of PTSD, a normal reaction to an abnormal situation."

"Well, I'm not sure sympathizing with the enemy is a great quality in a soldier," he said. "I guess it's that I don't know for certain. Maybe we got the right guy. Or maybe we just scared off the guy that was actually emplacing IEDs by killing some farmer. But I do know the last moments of the guy we killed were terrible. At least if I knew for certain we'd killed the right guy, maybe I'd feel a little better."

Dr. Taylor studied him a moment, then picked up his notepad. "All right, Hugh, I'd like to explore this more, but before we get to the end of this session, I'd like to talk briefly about support networks."

He nodded slightly, then wiped a hand across his damp forehead. Would every session be like this?

"In the interest of your self-care, I want to make sure you have people you can turn to, if and when you're ready," Dr. Taylor said, punctuating his words with movements of his pen. "I'd also like you to think about whether there's someone who can be honest with you, who's strong enough to take action for you, should that be necessary. Is there anyone that springs to mind?"

"My wife, Elizabeth," he said immediately. "She knows me better than I do most times."

Dr. Taylor jotted some notes. "Do you share everything with her?"

He shook his head. "We don't talk about what happens on deployments. And I haven't really talked about the details of my nightmares, only that I've had them."

"Why is that?"

"What happens overseas should stay overseas," he said. "I'm not being glib, there's a security aspect—it shouldn't be in the open."

Dr. Taylor grunted acknowledgment.

"More importantly, I don't want to talk to her about people blowing themselves up, firefights, and all the shitty things people do to each other."

"You don't think she could handle it?"

"No, that's not it. She supports what I do completely, and I think her faith would keep her grounded," he said, fidgeting.

"Is she religious?"

"I wouldn't say that, it's not like she goes to church. But is she spiritual? I'd say so."

"And are you spiritual or religious?"

He snorted. "No."

"Not even a little? I thought everybody became a believer in the trenches."

He looked up, eyes like laser beams. "Sure, I've prayed to God. Prayed to Allah, too, for that matter, and Buddha. I'd have prayed to the devil if I thought it would make a difference, but I'd probably have been better off praying to Lockheed Martin or whoever makes our munitions." He shook his head. "Everyone with their different gods, they might as well argue about whose imaginary friend is bigger."

"How does that affect your relationship with Elizabeth?"

"It's the only part about her I can't understand," he said, shaking his head. "I can't understand her faith, how whatever she believes could possibly justify people treating each other the way they do, like they're no better than animals." He closed his eyes and took a deep breath, hating the wetness pooling in his eyes. "If there is a God, He doesn't care about us." How could He care? All the terrible things in the world—sometimes done in His name, for fuck's sake—how could He not even give people a sign? No, the prisoners were running the jail and no help was coming.

The silence in the room grew heavy.

Cursing under his breath, he snatched a tissue from the box of Kleenex and blew his nose. "I also don't talk to her about this stuff because I don't want her to think the worst about me." Bad enough he was crying in front of some man he barely knew—what would Elizabeth think?

"Would she? If her faith is as strong as you say?"

"Why take the chance?" he said, dabbing his eyes. "And it was never an issue before."

"Is there someone else you could talk to?"

He sighed. "I have a friend, Daryl," he said after a few seconds. "We joined at the same time, but he's out now. I can talk to him about pretty much anything, although he's a little hot and cold these days."

"Why is that?"

"It's complicated." Is that what it was? Complicated was what described Daryl's unplaced bitterness and his small, trapped wife with her bruised face? When Dr. Taylor looked up, eyebrows raised, he continued. "He got hit by an IED and lost both his legs. He was medically released against his will, and he's a little bitter." What else could he say?

"I see," Dr. Taylor said, turning back to his notepad. "Well, is there anyone at your work?"

He hesitated, then shook his head. "I don't get close to people at work much, not since my second tour in Afghanistan."

"What happened?"

"I needed distance," he said. "I loved the people I worked with, but as a commander, sometimes you've got to send them into situations where they might die. It was getting hard for me to do that, so I started putting space between me and everyone else."

"That must have been difficult," Dr. Taylor said. "Cutting yourself off from others?"

"In the army, it's called the burden of command," he said, looking down. The army was good at making shitty things sound noble, wasn't it? "I didn't even realize it was happening until one day I realized I wasn't working with anyone I considered my friend."

"Other family? Are you in touch with your mother perhaps?"

His mom? Who'd never shown an interest in the military except as a way to keep Hugh occupied? "She wouldn't understand."

"Other friends?"

He silently ticked off his options. Mitchell was in the ground, Daryl was damaged goods, and Elizabeth was, well, his wife. There was Steve Richardson, who'd been at RMC at the same time, but Steve was deployed for a year in Africa. Was he that big a loser? No, he couldn't be. He had friends—there were lots of guys he could get a beer with—but there was a difference between sharing a drink and sharing the contents of your soul. His body suddenly felt very heavy. He shook his head no.

"Well, in that case I guess your wife and Daryl will have to do," Dr. Taylor said, referring to his notes. Shaking his head, he looked up, eyebrows crinkled above his nose. "The last thing I'd like to discuss is your journal entries."

He glanced at the clock behind Dr. Taylor's desk.

"Nothing fancy, Hugh, but you need to start keeping a journal. Write about your dreams, things that happened overseas, things that bother you. We'll use them to guide some of our future discussions. Any questions?"

He shook his head.

"You should be aware that the journal may open the floodgates, so to speak." Dr. Taylor frowned. "It's not unusual for patients to have repressed many things, and the act of journaling can sometimes bring those memories to the surface, often unpredictably. It's part of the habituation process, but it can be overwhelming."

"What are you saying?"

Dr. Taylor's lips formed a thin line as he pressed them together. "It could make your symptoms worse."

CHAPTER 6

Hugh stood in line at the NDHQ cafeteria, waiting to pay for lunch and staring at the tables around him like they were a surrounding minefield. He held a white takeout box containing a greasy BLT and fries; he'd forgotten his lunch. It was probably on the counter in his kitchen, maybe even in the same spot he'd left his building pass yesterday.

He sighed. The way his memory was going, by next week, he wouldn't remember his name. At least he'd remembered his wallet. Now all he needed to do was get through the cafeteria without seeing someone he knew so he wouldn't have to pretend everything was good to go.

He reached the pay station and handed over his money. While the cashier dug for change, he turned his head and glared at the air force officer behind him who'd been jostling him with a meal tray. He opened his mouth to speak just as the cashier held out his money. Snapping his mouth shut, he took his change and headed for the exit.

Probably better he hadn't said anything. Every little thing was setting him off today. His heart had already sped up as his anger fought to escape. *Please let me get through the day.* Things would be better tomorrow; they had to be.

"Dégaré!"

It was Roach, of course, down here brownnosing with Lieutenant Colonel Williams over lunch. He pretended not to hear. As he neared the exit, he spied where they were sitting. Shit, he'd have to walk right by them.

"Dégaré!" Roach called again, louder this time.

He grimaced. There was no way he could pretend he hadn't heard this time. He stopped walking and feigned looking around, exaggerating his surprise when he inevitably met Roach's gaze.

"Grab a seat," Roach said, waving him over.

He walked nearer. "I was going to eat in my cubicle," he said, holding up the Styrofoam box as proof. "Lot of work to do."

"I'm sure your boss will understand," Williams said.

Well, that settled that. He sat opposite Roach and opened the box.

Roach gestured toward a television hanging from the ceiling. "You hear about what's happening in Pet?"

He shook his head as he bit into his sandwich.

"There's some master corporal in a standoff with the military police."

"What?" he said, twisting to look at the screen.

The news anchor was discussing another story, but the ticker tape at the bottom of the screen described an armed standoff between a soldier and military police at Canadian Forces Base Petawawa.

"What happened?" he asked.

"Apparently this guy came home last night and beat up his old lady," Roach said. "The neighbors complained and called nine-one-one, and when the meatheads showed up, the guy fired some shots in the air, then locked himself in his house with his kids."

Williams nodded. "I was just telling Bill that my buddy's the base commander there. I spoke to him this morning."

Roach rested his forearms on the table, fawning over the more senior officer. "How badly does the media have it wrong, sir?"

"They're not too far off," Williams said, shrugging. "The master corporal came home last night, assaulted his wife, and dumped her on the front lawn. When the police showed up, the guy met them at the front door with a shotgun. It was touch and go for a half hour or so, but he eventually let them call an ambulance, then barricaded himself in the house."

"The media is saying he's got their two kids with him, sir," Roach said.

"That's right," Williams said.

"What a piece of shit," Roach said. "He should kill himself and get it over with."

Williams coughed. "Well, hopefully it won't come to that."

"Do they know what triggered him?" Hugh said. People didn't get into a standoff for nothing.

"What does it matter?" Roach said, glancing dismissively at Hugh, then turning back to Williams.

"It might help the police defuse the situation," he said through gritted teeth. "Maybe it's a cry for help."

"What are you, Dégaré, a shrink?" Roach said, sneering. "You defending a guy who takes his family hostage?"

"No, but clearly something else is going on. Maybe he's got PTSD like that reserve corporal who killed himself on Monday," he said, warmth blooming in his cheeks.

The story had been all over the news earlier in the week about a reservist shooting himself in Edmonton, reportedly because of PTSD.

"Oh please, the guy who deployed once and couldn't hack it?" Roach said. "PTSD doesn't even exist. It's like having a sore back. Nobody can prove it."

Hugh clenched his jaw and fought the urge to smash Roach's face into the table. With a shaking hand, he dropped an uneaten fry to the pile, then closed his eyes and willed the image to leave him.

Williams glanced at his watch. "This is riveting, but I've got a meeting in ten minutes," he said, standing up. "Have a good afternoon, gentlemen."

When his boss had departed, Hugh turned to his meal with a vengeance.

"You get your posting message for next year?" Roach asked.

Hugh shook his head as he jammed fries into his mouth. If he was lucky, by next summer, he'd be back in battalion, freshly appointed as a company commander tasked with training and leading one hundred soldiers on operations, potentially involving combat. Even if he'd probably be slightly more removed from the action than during his previous deployments, it would still be a huge step up—and away—from here.

"I got mine," Roach said, pushing his tray away. "Posted to army headquarters."

"Are you happy with that?" he said in a flat voice.

Roach frowned. "It'll be better than here, but not what I wanted."

Hugh stuffed the last bit of his sandwich in his mouth, saying nothing.

"I should be a commanding officer now, that's what all my peers are doing," Roach said. "But I need a top-tier job to get promoted, and my next job won't do that. Now it's another year of marking time."

He wiped his mouth. "The job's probably still important. And not everybody gets to be a commanding officer. There just aren't enough spots."

"Easy for you to say," Roach said. "You commissioned from the ranks, so nobody expects you to make lieutenant colonel anyways. Besides, you'll be posted out of here next summer to take a company, so you still have a shot. Me on the other hand, if I don't make light colonel, I'll never hear the end of it."

"Why?"

"You never met my dad. He was a full colonel back in the day. Had three boys, wanted all of us to go into the army," Roach said, crossing his arms. "My brothers both already made lieutenant colonel, and I'm the oldest. The old man never misses a chance to bring it up."

Hugh slowly folded up his empty takeout box. That explained a lot. Too bad Roach would never get promoted again since he'd been fired from a previous command billet three years ago. "I'm sure your time will come, just keep soldiering," he said as politely as he could muster. "Excuse me, I'm going back upstairs."

Roach grunted. "You want a coffee?"

He shook his head and stood up.

"See you later then," Roach said, making no move to leave.

When he got back to his cubicle, he sat down on the exercise ball and logged on to his computer. Instead of working on his current assignment—vetting a series of documents for sensitive information as part of a media request—he searched for stories about the situation in Petawawa.

Most of what he found only confirmed what he'd already heard, although he did find an updated article on the suicide from earlier in the week. The corporal's parents were claiming their son was being forced to retire because of an injury he'd received while serving in Afghanistan, but because he didn't have the minimum years needed to receive his pension, he'd been incredibly distraught, made worse by his PTSD.

He rolled around on the ball, mulling over the story. Service pensions had been in the media a lot lately, especially for injured members who were being forced out. Maybe he should get smart on the subject. Ever since he'd joined, his pension was simply something that was there, something to benefit him when he was older. He'd already qualified for his pension, so the only remaining question was how much it would be. Could that change if he was diagnosed with post-traumatic stress?

He checked his watch, then minimized the Internet and got to work. Several hours later, Roach's animated voice pierced his concentration. Stretching, he stood up and walked over to Roach's cubicle, where he and Lieutenant Colonel Williams were staring at the computer screen. They both glanced over as he knocked on the cubicle frame.

"Things are wrapping up in Petawawa," Williams said, turning back to the screen.

"How did it turn out?" Hugh said.

"Shot himself," Roach said.

Hugh sighed. Whatever had happened, this was somebody's life, and Roach may as well have been talking about making photocopies.

Williams straightened, still peering over Roach's shoulder. "Maybe a bit hasty, but probably the simplest explanation." He turned to face Hugh. "The master corporal released the kids sometime after lunch. Once the kids were out, he locked himself back in the house, and a few minutes later, there was a gunshot. The police went in, but the news isn't saying what happened, only that the guy is dead."

"What a loser," Roach said.

Hugh's mouth dropped.

"Well, come on," Roach said, holding up his hands. "What kind of guy kills himself with his kids right there? It's selfish."

Hugh began to speak, then stopped. It was actually a good point.

"Who knows what he was going through," Williams said. "He must have had some serious problems for suicide to seem like the easy way out." He shuffled out of the cubicle.

"This PTSD crowd, what a scam," Roach said, shaking his head and turning back to the computer screen. "Soldiers are weaker today than they used to be. We should never have gotten rid of the old training. That would have toughened these guys up."

"That's harsh," he said, crossing his arms. "And having gone through some of that training, I'm not sure how much it would help."

Roach swiveled in his chair, leaned back, and put his hands behind his head. "You're missing the bigger picture here, Dégaré," he said. "These guys killing themselves, it's not just about them and whatever problems they think they have. It goes against everything the military stands for."

"How's that?"

"The world is chaotic, and the only way we can do our jobs is to impose order on that chaos," Roach said, staring at the ceiling. "All those baloney tasks we make the troops do, painting rocks, digging holes and filling them back in, that's all about creating order, getting troops to do something they normally wouldn't so they'll obey orders under fire." He pointed at Hugh. "And getting people to do something they normally wouldn't is the definition of leadership."

And you wonder why you won't get command of a battalion. Hugh said nothing.

"When these guys kill themselves, what kind of message does that send? It undermines the very order the military tries to instill. It's a symptom of mental weakness. Believe me, a soldier who'd kill themselves over a made-up reason like PTSD should never have been let into the military in the first place."

"So what's your solution?" Hugh forced the words out while he stared at Roach's gut, jutting out as he reclined in his chair. A perfect target.

Roach's eyes narrowed as if the answer were obvious. "Redirect all the money that goes into treating PTSD to the recruitment budget. Pick the right people at the start, and we wouldn't have these types of issues. Problem solved."

He opened his mouth to respond—tell Roach what an idiot he was—then shook his head and walked away. Where would he even start? Besides, the more they talked, the harder it was getting to not smash Roach's teeth down his throat. When he got back to his cubicle, he tried to work, but Roach's words kept echoing in his head. How could someone not even believe in the possibility of PTSD? And Dr. Taylor wondered why he didn't want to talk to anyone at work.

Finally, he pushed away from his desk in resignation. It didn't look like he'd be getting any more work done that day.

It was twilight when he rolled into the driveway. As he entered the house, Elizabeth met him at the door with a kiss.

"Were you watching the news today?" she said, taking his coat and hanging it up.

"You mean the standoff?" he said. "Of course, everybody was following it."

"So tragic," she said. "If only someone had been able to help him."

He followed her into the kitchen. "Maybe he tried to get help and it wasn't there," he said, opening the fridge.

Elizabeth turned on the faucet and began rinsing the Tupperware she'd brought home from work. "I'm not saying he didn't try, just—"

"Then what are you saying?" he asked, closing the fridge and turning around.

Elizabeth paused, and for a few seconds, the only sound was the faucet running. When she did respond, her voice was quiet. "Only that whatever help he needed he hadn't got yet." She picked up a container and resumed washing.

"So that's his fault?" he said, then cringed inside. Why was he being so hard on her?

"Are you upset because it's a PTSD case?" she said, turning off the water and staring at him. "Do you agree with what he did?"

"No, of course not," he said quickly. "I'm sorry, honey, it's been a long day." She was right; he was overreacting. Or was he? What exactly was a normal reaction after being told he had an imaginary disease that could cause him to kill himself? "I'm not saying what he did was right, I just think people are being quick to judge this guy."

"His wife's in a coma," she said. "His kids don't have a dad. How could people not judge him?"

"I know, but there's another side," he said, moving toward her. "This guy served his country and probably saw some terrible things. He gets messed up and can't handle it, and somehow that's his fault?"

She reached up and caressed his cheek.

"I know it's a tragedy, but nobody seems to care about him," he said.

"People care deeply about soldiers," she said. "You've seen it yourself."

"Then why doesn't somebody do something?" he said, pulling her hand from his cheek. "It's all over the news, but by next week, everyone will have forgotten. Until the next time."

"That's not true, what about all the services that are in place? Or even self-help, like you're doing?"

"You mean the ones with huge waiting lists that are frowned upon for using because you're letting the team down?" He shook his head. "Come on, Liz, people only want to do the absolute minimum needed to make this problem go away. Nobody cares, not really. So while I'm not defending him, I can understand why he might have thought suicide was his only solution."

Elizabeth looked piercingly at him. "Would you ever do something like that?"

"No, of course not. Never," he said, too quickly. He felt a twinge of doubt deep inside him. He pulled her close. "But you can't train somebody for war, send them off to fight, and then be all upset when they use violence to solve their personal problems. The country creates these soldiers. It needs to look after them when they come back." He stroked her hair. "Not make them feel like they can't take a knee when they need help."

"You'll be all right," she said, wrapping her arms around him.

"Sure," he said. She still didn't get it. How could he make her see?

"You know that book, *On Killing*? It says there's three types of people in this world—sheep, wolves, and sheepdogs," he said. "Most people are sheep, they don't want to hurt anyone, they just want to live their lives. But there are others who don't mind hurting people, they see them as prey. Those are the wolves. Then there are the sheepdogs."

"I know this one," she said drily.

"Then you know soldiers and police are the sheepdogs, they protect the flock. Do you know how the sheep feels about the sheepdog?"

"They probably appreciate them, think they're sexy."

"You're not a sheep, honey, believe me," he said, chuckling. "The sheep fear the sheepdog because they remind the sheep of the wolf. They look similar, have sharp teeth, fur. And they're a constant reminder that wolves are out there, which scares the sheep."

She frowned. "What about when a wolf comes around?"

"Then the sheep love the sheepdog," he said, face growing serious. "But as soon as the wolf is gone, the sheep go back to trying to forget about the sheepdog because in their heart, the dog isn't much better than the wolf." He gazed into her eyes. "That's what I'm worried is happening here. There's no wolf for most people. In fact, they've never been safer in their lives. So why should they care about what happens to worn-out sheepdogs?"

And why not mention what happens when a sheepdog gets the taste of blood in its mouth? He shivered. The only thing to do then was kill it. He pulled Elizabeth tighter.

CHAPTER 7

"You look tired, Hugh," Dr. Taylor said, opening Hugh's file. "How are you sleeping?"

"I've slept better," Hugh said, only too aware of the bags under his eyes. His dreams had intensified, cutting into his already-diminished sleep. "But I've got a week off as of tomorrow, so I'm hoping to catch up." If he could wait that long—Dr. Taylor's couch was comfortable.

"Has something changed?"

He frowned. "I've been having a new dream, a pretty intense one, and it's been keeping me up."

"Shall we talk about it?"

The prospect of discussing his dream woke him as effectively as a jolt of caffeine. Well, wasn't that the point of this therapy? He rubbed his hands together, then pulled out his journal and opened it to a recent entry. He hesitated and glanced up at Dr. Taylor. "Never done this before."

"It's all right," Dr. Taylor said, as if this happened all the time. "Whenever you're ready."

Hugh cleared his throat. "It starts with me fishing," he said. "I'm standing in the water, in a sort of swampy lake I'd normally never fish in. There's all these bulrushes around, rising over my head, so I can't see my surroundings very well. The water's dark, almost maroon, like when a pond forms upstream from a beaver dam." He could almost smell it now, the stagnant marsh, thick with decay.

"What happens then?" Dr. Taylor said, gazing intently at Hugh.

He started and glanced up. The dream was still so intense, like he'd just woken up. He shook his head, then went on.

"I walk deeper into the lake, bulldozing through the mud. It's tough going, and I sink with every step. It's dark out, not night, just cloudy. I want to turn around and go back, but I keep going." He paused and wiped a hand over his mouth. "I get to a spot that's a little more open, and I know this is what I've been looking for. I dip my leader, set up my hook, and then cast out into the open water. There's no sound. It's completely still, and the hook just hangs in the air until it plops down." He shivered.

"And then?"

He took a deep breath. "I'm standing there, waiting, when something brushes my legs. I look down, but I can't see anything. I feel something again, and I start getting anxious, so I start reeling in my line. Then something grabs my leg. I stumble back, but the mud is so thick I lose my balance." He wiped a hand across the moisture beading on his forehead. "Excuse me, it's hot in here."

"Take your time," Dr. Taylor said, his eyes glued to Hugh.

"I . . . keep staggering back, and then the hook catches," he said. "There's a jerk on the line, and I yank it, by instinct. And there's something big there, I can tell." He rubbed his neck. "Part of me doesn't want to know what's there, but I pull on the rod anyways—I can't help myself. I fight with it a bit, then I give another yank and . . ."

Dr. Taylor waited a few seconds, then spoke softly. "And what, Hugh?"

"It's a hand. All bloated and gray. I freeze. The hand grabs the line and pulls, jerks the rod out of my hands. So I turn and run, but I'm so slow." He closed his mouth, inhaling deeply through his nose, then exhaled and continued. "I'm stumbling now, the swamp is closing in around me, and I'm brushing reeds out of the way as I run. I get to another clearing, but I can feel something behind me. Then I see something, some sort of mound."

"What is it?"

"It's a carcass," he said, revulsion seeping into his voice. "A big stag, waterlogged and rotten. The rack is huge, most of the horns are still out of the water, and I can smell death on it, dank and putrid. I keep running. When I reach the other side, I hear someone call my name, but I don't want to stop. Then I hear it again, so I turn and . . . there's somebody on top of the carcass."

"Do you recognize who it is?"

He brought a hand to his mouth. In silence, he dug his teeth into a knuckle, grounding himself in the sharp pain. At the metallic taste of blood, he pulled his hand away and went on. "An old platoon warrant of mine," he said, eyes dropping. "Kevin Mitchell."

"And what happens next?"

He closed his eyes only to find the scene tattooed to his eyelids. "His head is missing from the forehead up, where his helmet got blown off. He asks me not to leave him." His eyes opened, moist in the corners. "Only he doesn't say it, the words just kind of come to me. I mean, his mouth is opening and closing like a fish breathing, but there's no sound. I want to go to him, but I don't, I'm scared. I turn around. And then I run."

He leaned forward and buried his head in his hands. The silence in the office was broken only by the scratching of Dr. Taylor's pen, then even that stopped.

"Then what, Hugh?"

"I'm sorry," he said, hating himself for breaking down in front of the therapist. What kind of man could handle combat, then cry at a simple dream? "I'm just really tired."

"Do you want to talk about something else?"

"No, I can do this." He sighed. "So I leave him there, and I keep running. I reach the edge of the swamp, and the reeds give way. There's something behind me, I know it, but I don't want to turn. Then I'm at the bank, only it's steep and I can't get out. I keep slipping back, and then I feel whatever's been chasing me right behind my back. I turn around, I can't stop myself." He looked into his lap and absently twisted his wedding ring.

"And?"

"It's a little girl. I recognize her from Afghanistan. We killed her at a vehicle checkpoint. She was in a car that wouldn't stop, and we thought it was a suicide bomb. But it wasn't. Just a little girl with her parents in a car that wouldn't stop." He reached for a tissue, appearances forgotten, and blew his nose. "She's missing half her face, and her clothes are covered in blood, just like we found her."

Silence hung heavy in the room.

Hugh stopped playing with his ring and looked up. "There are others with her, all dead. I knew them all," he said, staring past Dr. Taylor at some faraway point on the wall where the bodies from his dream were assuming corporeal form. When next he spoke, his voice seemed to come from that same place, outside him. "Some are charred, some have bones sticking out, some have hands dangling from wrists, held on by skin too tough to snap. Some Afghans, some of us. All dead."

"What do they do?"

"They come for me." He spoke as if the answer were obvious. "They reach out, surround me, start pulling me under. I fight back, but I can't escape," he said. The Afghan girl clung to him like a lover even as he threw hammer fists into the remnants of her face. All the while, cold, clammy hands dragged him into the dank blackness. "As I go under, there's a whisper. It's the girl. She says they miss me, that I should come home." He could hear her now, telling him she loved him. What kind of a sick fuck was he? "I scream, then the water closes over my head, filling my mouth, and then I wake up." He blinked, then forced his gaze on the therapist, silently willing his eyes back under control while sweat trickled down his cheeks. Sleep was now the furthest thing from his mind.

After a minute, Dr. Taylor looked up from his note taking. "How did this dream make you feel?"

He scowled. "How do you think?" he snapped, then closed his eyes and took a deep breath. "I'm sorry. It's just so vivid, even now."

"It's all right, Hugh, I should have prefaced my question," Dr. Taylor said. "A dream can be interpreted in different ways based on what a person is feeling when they experience it. I obviously have a sense of how you were feeling at the time, but I wanted to explore it more."

He hesitated. "I feel . . . everything," he said. "Scared, nervous, angry, guilty. I feel like I'm in hell."

Dr. Taylor's pen flashed across the page, then he stopped and reviewed something he'd written. "Who is the person on the deer? You said his name was Mitchell?"

He nodded. "Kevin Mitchell, my first platoon warrant." Seeing a furrow appear in Dr. Taylor's brow, he continued. "The platoon warrant is second in command."

Dr. Taylor nodded, as if understanding, but he probably didn't. It was always so frustrating explaining concepts like this to civilians. How best to explain it? The pairing of a new officer with an experienced noncommissioned officer as the second in command was a long tradition that worked. The officer was in charge, but the platoon warrant normally had much more experience, which they used to mentor their typically younger counterpart. It was a dynamic relationship and normally worked well, but occasionally disaster resulted. Hugh and Kevin had been so close the soldiers in their platoon had called them Mom and Dad. Mom and Dad need some time alone. Mom and Dad aren't talking right now. Did words even exist that could express that type of bond?

"Where is he now?" Dr. Taylor said, interrupting his musing.

He involuntarily tensed. "He's dead," he said. "He died in an ambush in 2009."

"I'm sorry," Dr. Taylor said, looking up and removing his glasses. "Why do you think he would be in your dream?"

"It's stupid, I know, but I feel responsible for his death." He drew a shuddering breath. "Or at least like I could have prevented it."

"Why would you say that?" Dr. Taylor said. He put down his pen, lowered the journal, and stared at Hugh intently.

He looked down. "We were supposed to deploy together in '09, but I got rotated out because I'd had my chance to be a platoon commander. So a new guy came in, inexperienced," he said. Tendons stood out on his cheeks as he clenched his jaw. "You see, the army isn't about fielding the best team, it's about giving everyone a chance to tick their box. If I'd been there, we'd have never gone into that ambush. But instead of leaving an experienced guy in charge, they had to give some new guy a chance."

"That seems strange."

"That's how it works in the army," Hugh said. "Put a team together, then tear it apart just before you need it. It's a tradition of sorts."

"I see," Dr. Taylor said. He slowly replaced his glasses and scanned his notes. "And who is the girl you mentioned? She clearly means something to you."

Silence filled the office again until Hugh finally spoke. "During that tour in 2009, I deployed with the brigade headquarters, knowing I'd never leave the base. As it turned out, some friends in the frontline units began inviting me on missions to break up the routine. My boss was pretty supportive, so whenever I could manage it, I'd ride along on short missions." He took a breath. "Sometimes I felt like some flopper out for combat tourism, but I always told myself it wouldn't hurt having an extra rifle along. Many of those missions were vehicle checkpoints."

"What exactly happens on a vehicle checkpoint mission?" Dr. Taylor asked.

"They're pretty self-explanatory. Pick a spot on a road, then stop traffic so you can question people and search their vehicles for explosives or weapons," Hugh said. "On this one, we set up on the main highway west of Kandahar City midmorning, stayed there until midafternoon, then headed back to Kandahar Airfield. About as straightforward as you could get." He leaned forward, using his hands to explain his next points. "We had six vehicles, all light armored vehicles, which is a lot of firepower for the sort of threats we were expecting. Some Afghan police also came with us."

"What would those threats have been?"

"Well, the intelligence guys used to say that vehicle-borne IEDs were the biggest threat." He snorted. "I can't even remember how many threat reports I saw about white Toyota Hiluxes or Corollas being used as suicide bombs. Too bad that was about fifty percent of the cars on the road. But we took every report seriously."

"So what happened?"

"Everything started out well," he said. "No problems setting up, and we stopped traffic throughout the morning with no issues." He looked up. "By then I think most Afghans knew the drill, stop far out from the checkpoint, drive up slowly when told, keep your hands in sight. It was actually pretty boring until just after lunch, right when we were getting ready to shut down." His voice trailed off.

God it had been hot, so hot he'd needed gloves to hold his rifle. He'd been baking underneath his body armor, Kevlar helmet, protective glasses, radio, and chest rig, and he didn't even have special gear, like a grenade launcher. Technology was supposed to lighten a soldier's load, but in practice, that meant more gear could be carried.

"We knew right away something was wrong, because the car didn't slow down, not like the others," he said. The car was white, just like in the intelligence reports, its image shimmering in the heat radiating from the road. "And it looked like it was running heavy."

Although it had been difficult to tell. The hundred days of wind had begun, and fine sand had been thick in the air, moondust that caked flesh, glasses, sights on the weapons, everything.

"Running heavy?" Dr. Taylor said. "Why would that have been significant?"

"A car rigged as a bomb will sometimes run low on its axles from the weight of the explosives," he said. "Unless the suspension has been reinforced, but that's pretty sophisticated. As this car got closer, it looked weighted down, but we couldn't see inside because of all the shiny stuff Afghans decorate their cars with." He took a sip of water. His mouth had been dry then, too, like it was made from the same blasted landscape. Strange what stood out after all this time. "At this point, everyone's aiming their weapons at the car and signaling for the driver to slow down." Why hadn't it slowed down?

He'd been standing with the platoon commander, teasing him about how badly he smelled. The platoon had been aggressively patrolling for weeks, even forsaking the isolated operating posts by living out of their vehicles. To a soldier they'd stunk, their uniforms so absolutely filthy they probably would have stood up by themselves.

"Then what?"

He glanced up, startled. "Someone fired a warning shot, and the car swerved a couple of times, but it didn't stop. Everyone was pretty frantic, wondering what to do, should they shoot? Time was running out, it wasn't slowing down," he said. If anything it had sped up. Hadn't it? "I asked the platoon commander what he was waiting for. He was so pale, even under the dirt." Tinny voices had broadcast urgency across the platoon's radios, vehicle commanders looking for direction.

Dr. Taylor leaned forward, notebook perched precariously on his lap. "So what did you do?"

"We fired," he said softly. "Everyone fired, and the car stopped. It was so close." The air exploded as the LAVs engaged with their 25-mm chain guns, the concussions alone jarring the body. Then it was over, silence but for the ringing in his ears and the reek of gunpowder. "We all got under cover, expecting it to blow, but it just sat there. After a few minutes, one of the Afghans went up. We yelled at him to stop, but he ignored us, just walked up and pulled open the driver's door. Nothing happened." He swallowed. "Then a body toppled out, a man, his head smacking the road and just sitting there at a crazy angle. Then the Afghan waved us up."

"What did you find?"

He blinked repeatedly. "No bomb," he said. "Just a family. Dad up front, mom and a little girl in the back. All shredded. The girl was the worst, probably only eight or ten. It's hard to tell ages there, life's so harsh, people age before their time." He drew a shuddering breath. "Half the girl's head was red mist all over the backseat and rear window. Of course there wasn't a weapon or explosive anywhere to be found, just a car with a shitty suspension." And the coppery smell of blood, mixed with burning plastic, an acrid odor he could almost taste. The blood had run from the man's body, staining the massive concrete slabs that formed the highway.

The silence in the office grew oppressive. Dr. Taylor pushed the Kleenex box closer to Hugh.

"We told the guys they did the right thing, they'd stuck to the drill and executed it to the letter. There was an investigation, too, and it came to the same conclusion—we were well within our authorized use of force. It was us or them." He sat back and folded his hands in his lap, then spoke in a deep, authoritative voice. "We were told what we'd done was preferable to the scenario where we didn't open fire and it really was a suicide bomb."

"Do you believe that?" Dr. Taylor said.

His lips tightened. "We didn't have a choice," he said, his normal voice returning. Then why was he here? "I keep asking myself why they didn't stop. Why the fuck did they not stop?" He massaged his temples. "Do you remember the other session when we talked about religion?"

"I do."

"Well, I might have lied a little when I said I didn't believe." He closed his eyes and rested his forehead on his hands. "I must believe in something, because I'm absolutely sure I'll have to answer for killing that little girl one day."

He grew silent again. While Dr. Taylor reviewed his notes, Hugh listlessly gazed around.

The office, so typical of what he'd expected when he started therapy, stood out in a new light. The first time he'd sat down, the books, faux plants, and comfortable furniture had been mere stage props, artifacts that were a part of the psychological profession just as saluting and uniforms were totems of the military profession. But that was only part of it. This room was more like a gym, only for his brain—maybe even his heart. How silly was that? It had to be true, though. It was the only explanation for why he was so exhausted. He sank deeper into the couch.

"I'd like to bring this back to the dream," Dr. Taylor said, snapping him out of his reverie. "In light of what you've told me about your friend Kevin and this little girl, what do you think the dream means?"

He slowly looked at Dr. Taylor. "Aren't you supposed to tell me that?"

The therapist smiled politely. "Perhaps. But dreams are intensely personal. Any interpretation I give will still only be my opinion, so I thought you might like to offer your view first. Thoughts?"

He quietly groaned, then glanced at his watch. *Almost done, hang in there.* He sat up. "Well, clearly I'm still bothered by what happened with that girl, and also with Mitch, that seems obvious."

"All right," Dr. Taylor said, his tone suggesting a five-year-old could have made the same observations. "Anything else? Perhaps something deeper?"

He crossed his arms and shook his head.

"Are you familiar with the meaning of water in dreams, Hugh?"

He shook his head again. This was getting tiresome.

"Normally, water represents the subconscious."

"Okay."

"Objects within the water can be viewed as things inside the dreamer's subconscious, like memories," Dr. Taylor said, waving his hands in the air. "The act of fishing could imply you're trying to come to terms with your suppressed memories." He paused, waiting for a response from Hugh, who remained silent. "When these memories catch up with you at the end of the dream, you fight them, which could imply that they remain unresolved. The little girl may only be the first, several others could come as well. As much as this dream bothers you, I'd say it's a good sign, as it suggests the habituation process is under way."

"Great," he said in a dead voice. "Does that mean I'm getting better?" Facing this memory was bad enough; how was he going to cope with additional ones?

Dr. Taylor shifted in his chair. "It does, but there's still a lot of work to do. Not only do we need to examine any other memories—which may not be ready to reveal themselves at this time—we also need to revisit these current memories so they lose their hold over you."

"Can you give me a time estimate, though? How much longer will this take?" Every time he closed his eyes, the little girl was seared to the inside of his eyelids.

"That depends on a number of circumstances," Dr. Taylor said, closing Hugh's file. "Months, maybe years."

Had he heard right? "Is there some way to speed things up?" Could he make it through years of treatment?

"We're making progress," Dr. Taylor said, folding his hands. "We could medicate of course, but to be honest, that will only make the symptoms more bearable. It won't treat the root causes."

He shifted, hands fidgeting in his lap. "So what if we stopped treatment? Left things that don't want to be found alone. Would I go back to what I was before all this?" It was a Hail Mary, but as bad as it had been only months ago, it was still a cakewalk compared to the last few weeks.

"It's possible, I suppose, anything is, but in my professional opinion, that outcome is extremely doubtful," Dr. Taylor said. He breathed deeply, then spoke in a patient tone. "Hugh, you should know that some people never fully escape their symptoms. Recovery becomes more a question of learning to live with their condition than anything else. But as I said, we're making progress, and I have no reason to suspect you can't make a full recovery. As hard as it is, I believe continuing treatment is your best option."

He looked down, limbs growing heavy. What choice did he really have?

Dr. Taylor glanced at the clock. "Unfortunately our time is up."

With effort, Hugh stood up, as if gravity itself were fighting him. He mumbled a good-bye, then walked to the door, oblivious to Dr. Taylor's response. If only the Pandora's box inside his brain had never been opened.

CHAPTER 8

"Your Majesty," Hugh said, bracing open the hotel room door.

Pausing in the doorway, Elizabeth rose up on her tiptoes and kissed him on the cheek. "I could stay here forever."

He followed her into the room and let the door swing shut. A deluxe by the Château Laurier's already high standards, the room's nontraditional layout felt cozy, with a small nook containing a writing desk and windows overlooking the city's downtown.

"Which one should we stay in next?" he said, sitting down on the king-size bed, its soft white duvet already turned down. It had been so nice to see Elizabeth enjoying herself today— even with the annoying cold she was fighting—almost like before they'd moved to Ottawa.

"How about the Château Montebello?" she said, her voice coming from the bathroom. "I've heard a lot about that one, and it's close."

"Done," he said. "I'm glad you're so easy to please."

She laughed. "Easy, but not cheap. You've spoiled me."

He smiled. After they'd both finished university, he'd gone to battalion and she'd volunteered for a year as a nurse in Peru. She'd visited him a couple of times, and on her second trip, he'd arranged for a weekend in the Rocky Mountain resort town of Banff. He'd been trying to impress her, to convince her she should move near him when her year in Peru was up. They'd stayed at the luxurious Fairmont Banff Springs Hotel and had such an amazing time they'd sworn to stay in all the Fairmont hotels, a joke at first, but not after she moved to be near him.

"There's Mont Tremblant as well," he said, pulling aside the thick drapes to reveal a well-crafted window frame better suited to an old house, a refreshing change from the modern high-security windows in most hotels. In the slowly fading late-afternoon light, he gazed out over the city.

To the west, not much farther than a stone's throw away, was the terminus of the Rideau Canal, still frozen beneath a light dusting of snow. The Commissariat Building, where the canal joined the Ottawa River, was a squat throwback to another era with stone walls and oversize arched access points, all boarded up for the winter. Across the waterway, dense trees peppered a steep slope that culminated with Parliament Hill, where stately buildings formed a cutout skyline against the setting sun. The East Block, Centre Block, and Library of Parliament crouched atop the hill like Gothic monuments.

A noise came from behind him, and he turned to catch Elizabeth exiting the bathroom. She had a skirt and blouse in hand, which she tossed onto the bed. She smiled.

"What are you looking at?" she said.

"My beautiful wife," he said, pretending to bow.

She giggled. "No, out the window."

"Just sightseeing," he said. "I thought you'd be able to see the inside of Parliament Hill from here, but you can't. The East

THE BATTLE WITHIN 109

Block is in the way." He looked north into Major's Hill Park, barren under a blanket of snow. "And the park looks cold."

Indeed, in the lengthening shadows, the trees bordering the park's southern and northern edges were skeletal and gray, their summer foliage only a memory. To the east, the massive brick-shaped building that housed the American embassy loomed over the park with an Orwellian air.

Hands snuck under his arms, wrapping around his chest. He involuntarily tensed.

"And?" Elizabeth said. "How's the view?"

"I like it," he said. "Probably a great spot to watch Canada Day celebrations. The trees might block the view a bit in summer, but maybe not."

"That's a great idea, honey," she said, peering over his shoulder. "We should stay downtown and enjoy the holiday this summer without having to worry about going home."

He shivered. Downtown would be crawling with people on Canada Day. Good thing he wasn't a cop, it must be a security nightmare.

She released him, then walked over to a mirror, gazing into it as she changed her earrings.

He continued staring out the window, his professional curiosity piqued. This position would make a fine vantage point if somebody wanted to attack a crowd. How did the police deal with something like this?

"Are you getting ready?" she said, fiddling with the clasp of a necklace.

Tearing himself from the window, he walked back into the room. He was changing into a pair of chinos when he looked up and saw Elizabeth standing in the foyer with her arms crossed and a studious look on her face.

"I just wanted to say thank you," she said, her face flushing. "For this weekend." She looked away briefly, then met his eyes.

Speechless, he stood teetering with one leg in his pants.

"I know you're under a lot of stress, but I really appreciate you making the effort," she said, then scrunched up her face. "If I didn't have this flu, or cold, or whatever, it would be the perfect weekend."

His face grew warm, and he cleared his throat. "I've had fun, too, even with you being sick." He finished pulling up his pants, then cast about for his dress shirt. "Do you ever miss staying in places like this?"

"We stay in places like this whenever we can."

"No, I mean when you were growing up. This is the type of hotel your family must have stayed in when you went anywhere."

Her eyes flickered to him, then back to the mirror. "We didn't take many vacations."

"Still, if you hadn't been in that car accident, you'd have probably finished law school and be hanging out in hotels like this all the time," he said, shrugging into his shirt. "You ever think about it?"

"I don't need to. I'm staying here right now," she said. "I have everything I need."

"No, I mean . . ." What did he mean? That a life of luxury might somehow be preferable to lonely nights wondering if he'd return safely from a combat zone? "I mean if we'd never met."

She turned to face him. "What are you getting at?"

"I don't know," he said, pausing with his shirt half buttoned. "You gave up a lot to be with me. Do you ever wonder if it was worth it?"

"Meeting you was the best thing that ever happened to me," she said, walking toward him. "The second best was giving up law to become a nurse, but I'd made that decision before we met. Even still, I'm not sure I would have stuck with it if I hadn't met you."

"Yeah, well, no need to thank me," he said, cheeks growing hot. "You know I'd do anything for us."

"I believe you," she said, her full lips parting in an uncertain smile. "That's why I love you. Even when you're away, I know you still think about us."

He placed his hands on her arms. "I'd rather deploy a hundred times than have our kids need to deploy ever, you know that."

"I know," she said softly, blinking back tears. "What you do is so important. I worry about you."

"Don't," he said, pulling her to him. But this is what he'd been talking about—was this better than whatever her alternative would have been?

"I can't help it," she said, resting her head on his chest. "Today when we were out on the canal, you were so jumpy. There were too many people, right?"

They'd rented skates and stopped for BeaverTails along the frozen Rideau Canal, taking in an Ottawa winter tradition. He stiffened. "You noticed?"

She nodded. "A couple times I thought you were going to dive on the ground. Like when those hockey players were yelling."

There hadn't even really been many people—what would it be like in the summer, with tourists crawling everywhere? He stroked her blonde hair. "I'll get things back on track."

"Maybe it doesn't have to go back to how it was," she said, sniffling.

"I'll never get command like this."

"Maybe you don't need to."

He pulled away from her. "What do you mean?"

"Nothing," she said, then looked up at him. "Only that there's lots of other things you could do."

"What would I do if I wasn't a soldier?"

"I'm not saying you should stop being a soldier," she said, reaching up to caress his cheek. "You could stay in the army, but do something else. Something less intense." She glanced away. "I just thought maybe your environment could be aggravating your stress, that's all."

He softly took her hand and held it away from his face. "You think I'm getting worse."

"No," she said too quickly, then hesitated, studying him before speaking again. "I don't know. What do you think? Is seeing Dr. Taylor helping?"

Now it was his turn to hesitate. He'd been so focused on getting help he'd never stopped to consider if the therapy was actually working. Was it? It had only been a month and a half, but the longer he mulled over the answer, the more his heart grew heavy. "It might be getting worse," he admitted. "Dr. Taylor says that's part of the process."

"Do you feel like talking about it?"

"I want to." The words caught in his throat. Did he really, or was he only saying that? "But I've always tried to keep work separate from our personal lives. Plus, it's hard talking about this stuff, even with you. And I don't want you to think less of me."

She pulled herself slightly away. "I would never think less of you."

He raised a finger to her lips. "You don't know some of the things I've seen, things I've done."

"Don't shoulder this yourself," she said, gently brushing aside his hand. "I'm a good listener."

"I don't know," he said, making a show of checking his watch. "Our reservation is in twenty minutes, and the show starts at eight. That's not much time."

"Honey," she said, "I work at the NAC. I'm pretty sure I can get us in if we're late."

Hadn't Dr. Taylor said that sharing was an important part of getting over his problems? If he couldn't share with his own wife, who could he talk to? He glanced at his bag, where his journal was safely stored. "I've been keeping a diary of various memories," he said uncertainly. His heart raced like a schoolboy about to ask his first crush out on a date. "Do you want to hear one?"

"Of course," she said. She released him and sat down pertly on the bed, her feet dangling over the edge. "I promise to listen, that's it."

He paused and looked at her, then slowly walked over to his bag and pulled out his journal gingerly, like it was a grenade that might accidentally be set off. He sat beside her and flipped through the pages, looking for a suitable entry, his writing harsh and childlike to his eyes.

"This is awkward," he said, tensing to stand up. "Let's forget it." His palms were sweaty.

"Sit," she said, placing her hand in the crook of his elbow and gently dragging him down. "It's okay."

He kept scanning, finally settling on one of his first entries. "This one's pretty straightforward."

She nodded. The care in her eyes was almost more than he could bear. Would it still be there when he'd finished? *Only one way to find out.* He cleared his throat and began reading.

"February tenth, two thousand and thirteen," he said in a formal voice, then glanced up.

She sat attentively, hanging on his words.

He sighed. "In 1994, I was in Srebrenica on a peacekeeping operation. One day, we received a mission to patrol into a local village—one we went to all the time—to check out reports of violence in the area and show our presence.

"Our convoy ran into a Serbian roadblock just outside the village, as usual. We were allowed to go there, but the Serb soldiers had more weapons and better equipment than us, so there wasn't much we could do. Our commander argued with their commander, but they wouldn't let us go.

"Things got heated. We tried to force our way through, inching the vehicles up, but the Serbs trained their weapons on us. They were shouting a lot, waving their guns around. I found out later they'd threatened to take our equipment, which they could have done. The older soldiers in my vehicle coached us through our basic drills. In case shooting began. It seemed like we were there forever, but it was probably only a half hour or so. At some point, the Serb commander got a phone call, and when he finished, he waved us through, smiling."

He paused, eyes frozen on the next sentences while his jaw clenched and unclenched. When something touched his leg, he started, but it was only Elizabeth's hand. Inhaling deeply, he continued.

"The village was completely destroyed. Some buildings were still on fire, most were just scorched shells. Some stray dogs were nosing around the ashes. Not knowing what to do, we drove to the mayor's house.

"The mayor's house was still smoldering, with only some pillars holding up a blackened roof. Outside the front door were four charred corpses, three big and one small, almost unrecognizable as people, their clothes burned into their skin. They were still warm, with tendrils of smoke rising up. I threw up."

He closed his eyes. Elizabeth's hand on his leg—even her presence beside him—was momentarily forgotten, replaced with memories of the pungent odor of cooked meat that had hung in the air, mixed with wood smoke. It had been so out of place, so wrong. His heart was pounding in his chest, and he popped open his eyes, dreading the images that he knew were coming. He glanced at Elizabeth, motionless beside him. *And you wonder why I don't like to barbeque.* Turning back to the journal, he summoned his courage.

"We found the same scene repeated in the rest of the village, over and over. Behind the town, on a big hill, we found a large swath of overturned dirt, almost a hundred yards long. It had been dug up, then put back down, and the grass was flat and blackened, moist, like the earth itself was bleeding. Glittering amid the clods of dirt were hundreds of empty bullet casings, so many they clinked under your feet. It was a mass grave. We reported it, but got no direction. After an hour or so, we were ordered back to camp. So we left, just like that."

The smell of death had followed them away, lingering on his uniform and amplified by the heater in the back of the cramped M113 personnel carrier. He'd almost been sick again.

"The Serbs that had stopped us on the way to the village were in the same spot as we drove away. They didn't stop us this time. They just laughed, some telling us to go home in their thick Slavic accents. I remember crying, feeling so ashamed. My section commander cried, too. He said it was all right, that there was no shame in it. But it wasn't all right.

"I see those corpses in my dreams. They reach for me, charred hands cracking, pleading with me to do something, but I do nothing. I run, just like then."

He turned the page and pulled out a piece of paper that had been wedged into the journal. "Dr. Taylor had me do a thought chart for this entry," he said, pointing to a table with headings like situation, mood, and hot thought. His finger traced the entries he'd written in each column.

"Whenever someone mentions peacekeeping, I think of that village. I feel angry and guilty and helpless. I wish we had attacked the Serbs, even knowing professionally that we were outgunned and outnumbered. Better to die trying to do the right thing than live with the guilt of having done nothing. I want to yell at people who believe in peacekeeping, even though I know they won't listen. They never listen."

He stopped and stared at where his writing trailed off. His throat was raw, a soreness that thirsted for the biting warmth of hard liquor. Coughing softly, more to break the silence than anything else, he looked up.

Elizabeth's hands covered her mouth, but couldn't hide her pale face. Tears welled in her eyes.

He sprang up, the taste of vomit in the back of his mouth. "I'm sorry, I should have stopped. I got caught up," he said, words gushing out.

She clasped her arms tightly to her chest, her bare skin covered in prickly gooseflesh. "That was horrible."

Air rushed out of his lungs. The walls pressed in, crushing him, and his eyes flitted about like a trapped animal looking for an escape. When his gaze settled on the door, he pitched headlong toward it, grabbing his coat on the way.

"Wait," she said, standing up. "I didn't mean it like that, don't go."

He yanked open the door. "I need some air."

She was coming, reaching for him, but it was like his dream, and he couldn't bear it, not now, not here, even if he knew he'd heard her wrong. He was suffocating, no matter how quickly he gasped for breath, and he needed to get out of this room, so threatening with its unfamiliarity.

He stormed into the hallway, almost bowling over a portly housekeeper who clung to her cart to steady herself. Muttering an apology, he kept walking, almost jogging, throwing on his coat as he left. He looked back once, locking eyes with Elizabeth, who was standing in the doorway to their room, one hand holding on to the frame as if afraid she'd be sucked into whatever vortex was whisking him off. Then he turned and hurried away.

❧ ❧ ❧

Hugh returned a few minutes before midnight, frozen hands fumbling with the key card as he glanced at the lonely remnants of a meal on a room-service tray. After a brief struggle, he got the door open, revealing a room shrouded in darkness save for the weak efforts of a desk lamp. Sighing, he walked in, then eased the door shut.

He padded into the bathroom and closed the door, then cranked the shower as hot as he could. Teetering on feet numb from hours walking the cold downtown sidewalks, he clumsily shed his clothes, then stepped under the showerhead. The water seared him, but he willed himself to endure the scalding heat. Within seconds, his skin reddened, then grew numb, matching the deadness inside.

When he exited the bathroom, a plume of steam escaped with him, condensing on the mirror in the foyer. Tossing the towel onto the floor, he turned out the light and got into bed as quietly as he could. He took deep breaths, slowly counting to ten, willing each part of his body to relax. Suddenly Elizabeth spoke.

"What I said came out wrong," she said. "I'm sorry."

He flinched, his breathing faltering as he lost count.

"I never meant to upset you. I just didn't know what to say."

"It's okay," he said. "We've never talked about these things before." *And we won't, ever again.*

"I kept reading," she said.

"You did what?" he said, half sitting up.

"I wanted to know more, and your journal was just sitting there. I couldn't help myself," she said, turning toward him. "I want to understand what you're going through."

He lay back down, cautiously resting his head on the pillow. "And?"

She sniffled. "I'm so sorry," she said. "I had no idea. You shouldn't have had to bear those things alone."

The silence grew thick, save for a couple of loud, slurred voices in the hallway. How wonderful to be so carefree, never suspecting things could change in a moment.

"I thought I could handle it," he said, his voice barely more than a whisper. "I wanted to protect you."

She reached out and gently pulled his face toward her. "But what about you?"

He placed his hand on top of hers and caressed her forearm. "I'm supposed to be strong enough for both of us." He pulled her close, taking comfort in her warmth. "Sometimes all I feel is anger," he said. "I can't even describe it—it's a doom loop where everything just makes me madder. Every little thing makes it worse, even knowing how stupid it is. It takes everything in me to ride it out."

She stroked his cheek, fingers lingering over the stubble of his beard. "I know," she said. "When you're angry, the vein on the side of your head sticks out. When that happens, I leave you alone."

He smiled sadly in the dark. How could he do this without her? If only there was something he could give back. "The worst part is not knowing if what I did mattered," he said. "Most of the time it seems so senseless. What was the point of it all?"

"You're a good person, honey, you did what you had to do," she said. "None of it was your fault. We'll get through this, whatever it takes."

"Whatever it takes," he said. Was that true—was he a good person? It must have been true at some point or Elizabeth would never have married him. But now? "We used to say that sometimes, before missions. Whatever it takes to win." He held a hand in front of his face, not able to see it in the dark, but knowing all the same that it was shaking. Did good people do bad things? "Then I discovered I was enjoying some of the things we had to do." Was it okay to do bad things to bad people?

She rested her chin on his chest, and her breath grew quiet.

"You've got so much power when you're deployed," he said, swallowing. "You can break into people's homes, order them off the road, almost anything. And for every bad thing about war, it's also awe inspiring, as magnificent as it is terrifying. The firepower at your fingertips—nothing else compares. An artillery barrage can make even the best fireworks show seem like a hillbilly fair." Explosions so loud they weren't even heard, but felt in the bones, and heat blasts that could sear paint. Even now his heart was racing, his body priming itself at the mere thought. "Combat's addictive. So addictive you can forget you're supposed to be protecting people. There's even an Afghan saying for it, how in a war between the bulls it's the sheep that get trampled." Ah, but to be a bull.

She laid her head down on his chest. "I'm sure you did your best. You always do."

"Don't be too quick to give me a pass," he said, laughing bitterly. His best, yes, but that didn't mean he was a good person. "I've taken satisfaction from people getting hurt."

His unit had rescued a dog once, a half-fed, mangy survivor, Afghani in so many ways. They'd found it in the middle of a firefight, and it became their mascot. Its balls were so large they called it Testicles, like some Greek hero. In the small world of their area of operations, the troops grew to love the dog, and they'd made fantastic plans to bring it home to Canada, dreaming ways around army rules and policies. They even got dog tags for him.

One scorching summer day, an Afghan police officer gouged out Testicles's eyes. There was no explanation, just another random act of violence that characterized the country better than any other metric. Hugh's soldiers were livid, mostly at the callousness of the whole thing, but doubly so at the indifference the Afghan police showed when they were confronted. It was all he could do to protect the police when they departed the small outpost to return to their isolated police substation.

The next day, that same police detachment was attacked by the Taliban. They called for reinforcements, and his unit got tasked to provide backup. They deployed in almost record time, but were still too late, arriving to find all the Afghans dead. Their bodies had been mutilated, their remains scattered among the filthy piles of discarded boxes, cans, and moldy food. The police officer they'd suspected of maiming Testicles was found on the sandbagged front steps, his penis in his mouth.

"Fuck 'em," one soldier said, spitting on the ground. Another replied, "Guess he got what he deserved."

It was wrong, unprofessional, and he should have chastised them, but he'd said nothing. And he'd never lost a second of sleep over the matter, even now. Was that his truth? Someone who felt more remorse at the death of an animal than a human being was no better than an animal themselves. It was impossible to believe he was a good person because he wasn't. He was a monster, no better than the enemy he'd fought.

Elizabeth caressed his cheek, and he started, the heat of her hand pulling his attention back to the room. "You must have had a good reason," she said.

He turned onto his side and cradled her in his arms, even while hoping not to contaminate her with his touch. Her breath evened out quickly, and he released her soon after, rolling onto his back. Sleep would be a long time coming.

CHAPTER 9

"What does being a soldier mean to you?" Dr. Taylor asked.

Hugh leaned back on the couch and looked out the office window while he pondered his answer. Outside, the parking lot was a mess, full of gray slop as a beautiful spring day melted the snow, tugging at him to be outside breathing fresh air, not stuck navel-gazing in this office. He'd been discussing journal entries for the past forty minutes, and he was running out of juice.

"Almost everything," he said carefully, like the words might betray him. Dr. Taylor always found hidden meanings in his words.

"Almost? How do you mean?"

His head bobbed slowly from side to side. "I wouldn't sacrifice my marriage to be a soldier, but I can't think of anything else I'd rather do," he said. "And to be honest, a younger version of me would have—and did—choose soldiering over family. I think I've changed on that now."

"Why is being a soldier so important to you?" Dr. Taylor said, leafing through his notes.

He sighed. That question was on his mind a lot these days. "I can make a difference," he said. "When I look at myself in the mirror at the end of the day and ask if I helped make the world a better place, most days the answer is yes." He shrugged. "Some days it's no, but most of the time, I feel I've helped at least a little. I don't think anything else would give me that gratification."

"Even now?" Dr. Taylor asked. "It seems like you don't much care for your current job."

"True," he said, "but it's not like that in a frontline unit."

"But as a soldier, your stock-in-trade is violence, is it not?" Dr. Taylor said. "Isn't it ironic that you're making the world a better place through violence, which is normally considered bad?"

"You could say violence never really solves anything, but sometimes it's absolutely necessary. That's why it's such a great responsibility to have the authority to use violence on behalf of the country, if and when it's required."

"Has your identification with being a soldier ever caused you problems?"

Hugh drummed his fingers on his leg. "Sometimes, I guess."

Dr. Taylor motioned for him to continue. Of course he wouldn't get off that easy.

"Sure, I've felt alienated from society, but it's not rocket science to figure out why." His chin jutted out as he spoke, daring the therapist to disagree. "I don't think most people know how well they have it. Sometimes it doesn't go over well when I share my opinion."

Dr. Taylor smiled. "Most people would have no context whatsoever to even begin understanding some of what you've been through, Hugh."

He pressed his lips together. Was that supposed to make him feel better?

"Do you have a specific example of a time you felt at odds with society?"

He hesitated. There were so many, where to start? "On my first deployment to Afghanistan, we lost some soldiers to friendly fire. An American pilot mistook our position for an enemy and dropped a bomb on us, killing some and wounding a bunch of others."

"That must have been difficult," Dr. Taylor said as he scribbled.

Hugh clenched his jaw. Did Dr. Taylor have any idea what *difficult* meant, or was he just using an active-listening technique?

"It was, but not how you'd probably think," he said. "Don't get me wrong, the bombing was a real tragedy, but it wasn't like the pilot did it on purpose. People make mistakes, and there's not a lot of room for error in what we do, so when mistakes happen, the results normally aren't good." He closed his eyes. "What was hard was the reaction from home. Completely over the top."

"That would be understandable, wouldn't it?"

"To a point," he said. How to explain without seeming callous? "Everyone was so upset, almost personally insulted, like they were there. They didn't have the first clue what it was like. I remember getting an e-mail from my aunt saying how sorry she was. She closed out her note by writing that she wished our men hadn't died on a mission that meant nothing."

"How did you react?"

He ground his teeth. "Not well," he said. "I smashed the keyboard, which was a problem since there were only two Internet stations for a hundred guys. But everyone cooled off when I explained what happened, because they all got it. I've never spoken to that aunt since."

"Why did it make you so angry?"

"Isn't it obvious?" he said, his brow furrowing. "We're in Afghanistan, only a few months after 9/11, on a United Nations–approved mission with a coalition of all countries, living in shit conditions, and she thought it didn't mean anything? I've had people tell me that our boys and girls shouldn't be shedding their blood in some faraway land. But if not there, where? We made a difference in Afghanistan, and maybe it didn't get a lot of coverage, but only because the good stuff we did wasn't sexy compared to suicide bombs or body bags." He took a deep breath, then exhaled. "No, it meant something then, and it means something now. And I'd do it all over again if I had to."

"Even with your family?"

His lips tightened. "My wife understands."

Dr. Taylor brought his pen to his mouth and began chewing on the end. "Hugh, what's more important to you, your family or being a soldier?"

He began to reply, then fell silent. This should be easy, why was he hesitating? "I already answered this question." So why didn't he just answer it again?

"Yes, you said you wouldn't sacrifice your marriage to be a soldier. But you also mentioned your wife understands why you have to do what you do. What if she didn't understand and you had to choose? Your family or being a soldier? What's more important?"

"That's not the case," he said, shifting on the couch. "I don't have to choose."

"What if you did, though? Humor me, please."

He frowned. "I'm sorry, I don't like these what-if questions."

"But you must deal with what-if scenarios at work, don't you?"

"Yes, but at some point, they're not helpful. Besides, you can't think of every scenario." Sighing, he rubbed his face. Why was he making this so difficult? "It's like, what if Superman flew down and jizzed in your face? It doesn't matter because it'll never happen, so there's no point talking about it."

"But this is not an unlikely scenario," Dr. Taylor said, folding his hands in his lap. "People leave their spouses all the time because they can't choose between work and—"

"What I do isn't work," he snapped. "It's a profession, a calling."

"I see."

Hugh inhaled deeply and stared at the floor. "I love my wife," he said, deliberately choosing each word. "But being a soldier gives meaning to my life." He closed his eyes. "They're both important."

Dr. Taylor closed Hugh's file and gently placed it on the table beside him. "Are you familiar with the legend of Achilles?"

He nodded cautiously. "Mightiest Greek warrior at Troy, led the Myrmidons, killed Hector." Where was this going?

"That's right," Dr. Taylor said, steepling his fingers in front of him. "Do you remember the two choices that were presented to Achilles for how his life would turn out?"

He shook his head.

"On the one hand, he could forego the war and live a long, peaceful life, yet die in obscurity. On the other, he could fight at Troy, where he would die young, but win eternal glory. What do you think about that choice? How does it make you feel?"

He sighed and held his head in his hands. This was the stuff he hated, word games that showcased his shortcomings. Why couldn't Dr. Taylor cut to the chase? "Are you saying that my choosing between family and work parallels Achilles's choice?" he said, shifting on the couch. "That if I keep pursuing my career as a soldier, I'll potentially risk my family? That's a stretch." Besides, what self-respecting soldier wouldn't want to be like Achilles?

Dr. Taylor crossed a leg. "Not what I asked, but a fair linkage." The therapist looked up briefly, finger to his lips. Then his mouth parted suddenly, like something had just occurred to him. "Did you know Achilles had PTSD?"

Hugh's face contracted. "Say that again? Greatest warrior ever had PTSD?"

Dr. Taylor held up his hands as if apologizing. "Odysseus, too," he said. "At least according to Dr. Jonathan Shay."

"Who?"

Dr. Taylor picked up a book from his desk and passed it to Hugh. The title was *Achilles in Vietnam*, by Dr. Jonathan Shay. "He wrote two books documenting how Vietnam veterans suffering from PTSD could be understood through the main characters of *The Iliad* and *The Odyssey*, or Achilles and Odysseus."

"They both had PTSD?" he said, his brow scrunched up.

"Exactly," Dr. Taylor said, his hands coming to rest on the arms of his chair. "Dr. Shay makes a compelling argument. His book on Achilles deals with PTSD in combat, while the one on Odysseus addresses veterans with PTSD after leaving a combat zone, such as reintegrating into civilian life. But that's only partially my point."

Half listening, Hugh flipped the book in his hands and read the back cover.

"If you accept Dr. Shay's argument, then Achilles and Odysseus give us two different examples of soldiers suffering from PTSD." Dr. Taylor held up an index finger. "Of course, this can partially be explained by the huge differences between the two men."

"Like what?"

The therapist paused, stroking his graying beard. "Well, as you pointed out, Achilles was more or less the consummate Greek warrior. He was also a superb leader."

A whisper of high school English studies was coming back. "Didn't he represent honor, loyalty, and courage?" he said. Those same values were enshrined in the Canadian military ethos—probably why he identified with Achilles so much.

"Yes, but also care for others. He had great empathy both for his own men and for civilians," Dr. Taylor said. "By contrast, while Odysseus was also a well-regarded warrior, he is known more for his guile and intellect, his use of the Trojan horse being the most obvious example. Not that those qualities are necessarily wrong, only different."

Hugh nodded. "Militarily speaking, deceptions and feints are very important, although we pay them lip service most of the time."

"But Odysseus was also deeply flawed," Dr. Taylor said. "In *The Iliad*, he's mostly a staff officer, really no better than one of Agamemnon's yes-men, and during his return home in *The Odyssey*, he proves to be a terrible leader, with almost callous disregard for his men." The therapist waved a hand dismissively. "At any rate, it's interesting from a classical literature point of view, but there's a more valuable lesson."

"Which is?"

Dr. Taylor leaned forward. "Each man responds differently to combat stress."

Hugh shifted uneasily on the couch. "I'm not sure I follow."

Dr. Taylor sat back and ran a hand through his thick hair. "Both men had post-traumatic stress, but their responses were dramatically different," he said. "Like a burning star, Achilles was consumed by rage, and ended up dying in battle. Odysseus, however, made it to the end of the war, but then encountered all sorts of problems associated with returning to his normal life. The analogy, of course, is that the ten years it takes for him to make it home could be describing a mental journey as much as a physical one. Even when he does return, he still has problems to solve."

"But he does make it home," he said tentatively.

"At great cost," Dr. Taylor said. "He loses all his men, all his ships, and provokes an uprising in his own lands by slaughtering Penelope's suitors. But in the end, yes, he does make it home, which tells us one important thing."

"And that is?"

Dr. Taylor slapped his palm on his knee. "It can be done, Hugh," he said. "It is possible to overcome the challenges associated with combat stress, and to me, that is the real difference between Achilles and Odysseus. Achilles gives in to his rage, kills Hector and desecrates his body, and becomes a shell of the man he was. But Odysseus overcomes it. Or perhaps it is better to say he learns to live with it."

What to think? It was intriguing, sure. PTSD had been around forever, called shell shock or soldier's heart or any number of labels, but he'd never heard of *The Iliad* or *The Odyssey* as studies in combat stress. Still, if anybody knew anything about battle, surely the ancient Greeks did. But what did this story have to do with him? "That's a great story, really, but I'm not tracking how this affects me."

A small smile appeared on the psychologist's face. "It means you have a choice," he said. "Will you be Achilles? A hero in every way who dies a tragic death? Or will you be like Odysseus, who undertakes a perilous journey, but ultimately salvages that which was most precious to him? Which will you be?"

He sank into the couch, understanding beyond his grasp. "Okay, I get it, I have a choice," he said in irritation. "I'm sorry, Dr. Taylor, I'm still not sure what you're trying to say."

Dr. Taylor leaned his elbows on his knees. "Ultimately, Hugh, I'm saying you need to figure out what's important to you."

"So I can choose between being a model soldier who dies and a cowardly trickster who blunders around but survives? What kind of choice is that?"

The therapist shuffled in his chair. "It's just an illustration—"

"Can't I have both?"

"I'm not suggesting—"

"I want to be a good soldier who's also beaten PTSD," he said, scooting forward to the edge of the couch. What good was learning to live with PTSD if it meant he was a poor soldier? He'd be no better than Roach. He opened his mouth to speak.

"Hugh," Dr. Taylor said, his voice loud and firm as he held up a hand. "It's an example I thought might help give you a different perspective. Maybe I should have thought more about its relevance." He pulled off his glasses and rubbed the bridge of his nose. "The question I'm trying to help you with is what does a life worth living look like to you? Knowing that, I think, will help provide you focus in dealing with some of the challenges you're facing." He replaced his glasses. "Either way, I think that sooner rather than later, you're going to have to face the fact that if you're really serious about dealing with your PTSD, you need to at least consider the possibility of making changes in your life. If you're not even open to the discussion . . . well, I'm not sure how much more progress you'll make."

This was progress?

Dr. Taylor glanced at the clock. "And unfortunately, we'll have to continue this discussion next week. Until next time," he said, standing.

Hugh stood and walked to the door, moving robotically. What the hell was he supposed to do now?

CHAPTER 10

Hugh jerked; someone's hand was on his shoulder, pulling him back onto the sidewalk. Seconds later, a car whizzed by with its horn blaring, the momentum pulling him in its wake. He could see the driver leaning across the passenger seat, shaking his fist and yelling. Then the car was gone, leaving Hugh with his heart thumping against the walls of his chest.

"Where's your head, Dégaré?" Bill Roach said, releasing his shoulder. "You almost got yourself run over!"

He turned and stared dumbly at Roach. "Thanks. I must have zoned out for a second," he said weakly. "I haven't been sleeping well." In truth, he'd been sleeping three hours a night max. On good nights, he woke up in a cold sweat; on bad ones, he woke up screaming.

Roach sniffed. "Probably the change in humidity."

Hugh blinked. "What?"

"You know, the change in weather with spring coming. Humidity. That's probably why you can't sleep."

He nodded robotically. "Of course."

"Anyways, like I was saying before you almost got yourself killed, I have no idea why there hasn't been a serious terrorist attack in Ottawa. The place is a complete shit show," Roach said. The crosswalk light changed from stop to walk, and he boldly strode into the intersection without looking either way.

Hugh remained on the street corner, rubbing his eyes.

"You good?" Lieutenant Colonel Williams asked. The three of them were walking together to a restaurant for a small retirement ceremony being held for a member of their directorate.

He nodded, then followed Williams into the intersection, catching up with Roach in the middle of his ongoing diatribe.

"Look over there," Roach said, pointing to a series of squat, multistoried buildings bordering the street on his left. To Roach's right was the black wrought-iron fence that nominally barricaded off Parliament Hill, beyond which was the wide expanse of the inner courtyard lawn. "There's so many buildings you could shoot from, it'd be like fish in a barrel."

"Too bad they're all government buildings with controlled access twenty-four hours a day, seven days a week," Williams said. His tone was clipped, as if he'd had this conversation before.

"Guarded by the Commissionaires? The same guys who sleep while they're supposed to be escorting noncleared personnel around NDHQ?" Roach said. "Some of them are so fat it's easier to jump over them than walk around them. They're not a security force, they're a make-work program for ex-military."

Hugh smiled to himself even though he was only half listening. *The pot just called the kettle black.*

"Most of those buildings are also pass controlled," Williams said.

Hugh studied Williams as they walked. His boss probably deserved to know what was going on, but what would he say? That he felt like he was losing his mind? He shivered in the warm afternoon sun. And what would Williams do with the information?

"What about the Château Laurier?" Roach said. "That must have a good vantage point onto the Hill."

Was he still talking about attacking Parliament Hill?

"You can only see the backside of the buildings from the Laurier," Hugh said instinctively.

Both Roach and Williams glanced back at him, seemingly having forgotten he was there.

He shrugged. "Liz and I stayed there over March break."

"The Laurier does have great views into Major's Hill Park," Williams said, holding up his index finger.

Roach scoffed. "So what?"

Hugh mulled Williams's words over. What was he getting at?

"Tons of people go there for big events," Williams said. "Canada Day, for instance. If I wanted an easy target, that's what I'd pick."

"Good thinking, sir," Roach said eagerly as the men stopped at a crosswalk.

He gritted his teeth. *What a brownnoser.*

Williams continued as they crossed the street and began looking for the restaurant.

"Even better would be to run straight into Parliament itself, guns blazing," Williams said. "The different security organizations in and around the Hill would be so disorganized a person could probably get pretty far."

"Don't the RCMP have that locked down pretty tight?" Hugh said, puzzled.

Williams glanced over his shoulder, always happiest with an audience. "There's three, maybe four groups responsible for security over less than a square mile of space around Parliament Hill," he said, speaking as if he knew everyone in the security details by name. "Ottawa City Police, the RCMP, and the

Parliamentary Security Services, which I think have separate Senate and House of Commons groups."

"But that must be a nightmare for command and control, sir," Hugh said.

"I've heard it's pretty dysfunctional. I don't even think they have one unified command center, to be honest."

Hugh's pace faltered, but he was enjoying the look of confusion on Roach's face. Would the man keep his mouth shut or open it and confirm he was a fool? He turned his attention back to Williams as they approached the restaurant. "How do they relay information to each other? They must have compatible radios at least."

Williams shook his head as he held open the restaurant door. "I wouldn't be surprised if they don't." He shrugged. "Let's just say we're lucky that nobody's tried anything."

Hugh was speechless. He and Williams and Roach entered the restaurant, and the hostess directed them to a small meeting room on the second floor, where some other uniformed members had gathered for the ceremony.

He barely knew the retiring member, some major with thirty-five years under his belt. Truth be told, Hugh was only here because attendance was obligatory. He sipped water and checked his watch as various speeches and presentations droned on, all things he'd seen maybe twenty or thirty times before.

Hugh was still wondering if or what to tell Lieutenant Colonel Williams. He wiped his sweaty hands on his pants and scanned the crowd for his boss, finding him standing a couple of people away. Williams had been in Ottawa a long time; if nothing else, surely the man would have advice on what resources were available for Hugh to draw on. God only knew that Hugh could barely figure out the shuttle system to get to base supply when he needed to exchange anything for his uniform. Plus, there was the whole integrity thing—didn't he owe it to his boss to tell him he had an issue? Hugh would expect nothing less from one of his own subordinates.

But Williams could also just as easily marginalize him. He sipped again, his mouth still dry. There had to be a way to feel out Williams's intentions before telling him everything. But how?

When the last speech finished, Hugh waited another fifteen minutes, then walked up to the retiree and offered some token best wishes on a happy retirement. Then he made a beeline down the stairs and for the exit. He was standing just inside the door, shaping his beret on his head, when Lieutenant Colonel Williams appeared beside him.

"Heading back?" Williams said.

"Yes, sir, I've still got some work to do."

"Mind if I join you?"

He gestured up the stairs. "Don't you need to stay and show the colors?"

"I've also got work," Williams said, pulling out his own beret and putting it on. It was poorly formed to his bald head, making the man look more like a painter than a soldier. "After you."

Williams set a brisk pace, and within a few minutes, sweat was trickling down Hugh's forehead. God, he was out of shape. Roach probably would have fallen behind within ten seconds. A small smile appeared on his face.

"Something funny?" Williams said.

He glanced at his boss and shook his head. "Just nice to get some fresh air."

"Yes, it is," Williams said. "What did you say you needed to work on?"

"I'm still working on the bull pen, sir," he said, face heating up. "I know that was supposed to be done a month ago, but it keeps getting pushed aside."

The plan had actually been approved a week ago, but the construction contractor had said work couldn't begin for months since he was missing the walls in the height called for in the original floor plan. Hugh had suggested using lower-height walls, which the contractor both agreed to and had in stock, only to have Roach decree that before the change could be approved, the existing floor plan needed to be amended to account for the use of low-height walls instead of medium-height walls. In the interim, the actual work was stalled.

"Okay, keep on top of that," Williams said.

There was a moment of silence as they crossed a street, then kept walking with the Parliament buildings on their left. At this rate, they'd be back in NDHQ in five minutes. He looked at Williams out of the corner of his eye. Should he tell him now? Time was running out.

He opened his mouth to speak.

"Hugh, is everything all right?" Williams said.

His words caught in his throat. Where had that come from? "I'm fine, sir, why do you ask?"

Williams grimaced. "You haven't seemed yourself the last few weeks."

Hugh shook his head slowly. "No, everything's good." What was wrong? This was his chance. But something seemed off. It was like Williams felt he had to do this as a supervisor, but wanted to finish it as soon as possible.

"And your wife? How is she?" Williams said as they passed the National War Memorial, its slate-gray arch towering over a squad of soldiers bedecked in trench coats and First World War–era Mark I helmets.

"Liz is fine," he said absently. "She's been sick a lot the last few weeks."

"It's that season," Williams said. He looked squarely at Hugh. "And you're sure you're good?"

Time to see where Williams was coming from. "Honestly, sir, things haven't been that great," he said. "I haven't been sleeping well the past month or so, and it's starting to catch up with me." He looked up and smiled wanly. "Also, working in NDHQ leaves a bit to be desired."

Williams pressed his lips together. "It's tough, but a great experience. All officers should come to Ottawa in their careers, the earlier the better."

As Williams launched into an explanation of the virtues of working in NDHQ, he silently berated himself. How could he have forgotten? Of course Williams would think it was a good thing; he'd worked in the army's equivalent of human resources as a career manager for years, more commonly known as a career mangler. His boss had no doubt been advising people that NDHQ was a great place to work for years.

He stayed quiet while Williams walked and talked, nodding at the right places and offering the occasional "Yes, sir." As they reached the main entrance to NDHQ, his boss finally paused, evidently satisfied at having set a subordinate straight.

They cleared through the main entrance to NDHQ, getting separated due to the continual outflow of people exiting at the same time. They caught up just inside the main foyer and walked to the elevators.

Hugh gestured to the crowd heading toward the exit. "Just after three o'clock, time for the daily exodus."

Williams smiled. "Tumbleweeds are probably already blowing in our corridors."

The ringing of a bell announced the arrival of an elevator, which they boarded. Williams hit the button for their floor, then stared at Hugh.

"So, just to confirm, everything's all right at home?"

He nodded. In comparison to Dr. Taylor, talking with his boss was like pulling out his own teeth. Had he actually thought about confiding in this man? "Like I said, sir, I've just been having a hard time sleeping for some reason."

"Try NeoCitran," Williams said, watching the ascending numbers as the elevator climbed floors. "It always works for me."

"I'll try that," he said. He'd tried NeoCitran weeks ago, then spent the night peeing every hour. He'd be damned if he'd go through that again.

The elevator arrived at their floor, and Williams stepped onto the landing with its grayish-blue walls covered in bilingually approved and utterly bland posters that supposedly improved morale. "Well, glad to hear it's just sleep problems," he said.

"Nothing a few good nights of sleep won't take care of," he said, putting on his best brave face. *You've got the check in the box now, feel free to go back to your work.*

"Let me know how it turns out," Williams said. "If you ever need to talk, my door is always open."

"Thanks, sir, I'll remember that."

"I'm glad," Williams said as he moved off toward his office. "And good luck with that floor plan."

He stared at his boss disappearing down the artificial corridor, the walls crushing in on him. Things would have to get a lot worse before he'd turn to anyone from work for help.

$$\boxed{\text{\Yleftvert \; \Yleftvert \; \Yleftvert}}$$

Hugh got home around five o'clock. The sun was still out, and although some snow still dusted the ground, the air had a freshness that teased him with its promise of renewal. Winter was over.

He stood for a moment on the front step, breathing deeply, then tried the door, which was locked. He decided to sweep out his workshop until Elizabeth returned.

A fair amount of grime had accumulated over the winter, and clouds of brown sediment quickly filled the air like fog as he swept dirt out the open garage door. Yet even through the haze, hints of spring snuck through the thick, musty odor, and before long, he was whistling, absorbed in pushing piles of gunk around the floor matting.

Something caught his peripheral vision, and he looked down the sidewalk. Elizabeth was strolling toward the house, framed in the late-afternoon sun, with strands of hair wafting around her face in the light April wind. When she met his gaze, her eyes reflecting the sun and full of life, the small smile fixed to her face broadened. How had he gotten so lucky?

"You're home early," she said when she reached the end of their driveway.

"Taking advantage of the nice weather," he said, smirking while he made an exaggerated show of wiping his brow. "Besides, I saved the world enough for one day and thought it was time to clean out the garage. Feeling better?"

"Great," she said, wrapping her arms around him and planting a kiss on his cheek.

He kissed her forehead in return, then waited for her to let go. When she didn't, he looked down. Her smile had shrunk, but was still there, along with a sparkle in her eye.

"What is it?" he said.

"We're pregnant," she said in a quiet voice.

He involuntarily tensed. "I'm sorry?" He drew back from her, looked her fully in the face.

"We're pregnant."

"What . . . how?"

"How do you think?"

Stammering, he looked away, then took a deep breath. A lingering cloud of dust wafted into his face, and he coughed.

Elizabeth placed a hand in the small of his back as he set down the broom. They walked farther out the driveway where the air was clearer. "I'm sorry, I know it's a surprise."

Tears in his eyes, he spoke, his voice hoarse. "I thought you were on the pill." This couldn't be happening, not now.

"I stopped in the fall," she said, a small frown joining her smile. "Remember?"

"I didn't think we'd actually decided," he said, dredging his mind for the conversation. The specifics wouldn't come to him.

"We agreed this would be the year we tried," she said. "We talked about it before we moved and—"

"Right," he said, forcing a smile on his face. "I'm sorry, it's just a surprise."

"It's okay, honey," she said, placing one of her hands in his. "It was a surprise for me, too. We hadn't been . . . you know . . . in a while. Then there was that one night a couple months ago." Her cheeks bloomed with color.

He pulled her to him, resting his head on top of hers. The softness of her hair tickled his chin, and stray strands drifted up into his nose. "And you're sure?" Could there have been a worse time for this to happen?

She looked up at him, sad eyes contrasting against a small smile. "You know that's the only time we've had sex in months."

"No, about being pregnant," he said, face growing hot. *Don't be an ass.* "I heard those kits aren't always accurate." He put his hands on her shoulders. Suddenly he was sixteen again, hands on his girlfriend's shoulders, and she was telling him she'd missed her period. That pregnancy had resulted in her parents forcing her to get an abortion, against his wishes; how would this one turn out?

"I just came back from the doctor. They confirmed the pregnancy."

His vision was darkening at the edges, slowly constricting his view. He blinked rapidly. "Well, that's . . . that's great," he said, picking a point on her face and staring at it. *Keep a grip, man, don't faint.* This was supposed to be happy news.

She held a hand up to his cheek. "I know it's bad timing," she said tenderly. "But things happen for a reason. This could be good for us."

He buried his face in her shoulder, shifting his focus to a point on the pavement. *Tell her.*

"Talk to me, honey," she said as she stroked the back of his head. "This is going to be tough, I know, so we need to talk to each other."

The blackness in his vision had stopped closing in, leaving a small hole he could see through, like he was holding a roll of toilet paper to his eyes. "I'm worried about us," he said, his voice muffled. "I'm . . . I'm happy, but you're right. It doesn't seem like the right time." How many times had he heard stories about kids bringing people together? Not many, and by not many, he meant none. And what about the kid? Growing up with a crazy dad in an even crazier world? What kind of life would that be? He needed to say something to reassure her, but what? He swallowed. "I just . . . being a dad is a big responsibility."

"You'll be a wonderful father," she said. "Don't worry. We'll make it work, somehow. We don't exactly have a choice, do we?"

Don't we? He clenched his jaw as a wave of nausea gripped him. *What kind of person thinks that, picks themselves over their children?* He tightened his eyes, willing away the threatening tears. His world shrank as he warred to regain control. Finally, the blackness in his vision began to recede.

He lifted his head and gave her a small, wistful smile. *Say something.* "Are you sure it's mine?" he said, making sure his tone was light. She was right, the pregnancy was happening, and this was no time to bring up parenthood fears.

"I'm sure," she said, her eyes regaining the sparkle they'd had when she'd arrived home.

"Sorry," he said, burying his face back into her shoulder. "I love you." So why did she feel further away from him than ever?

"I love you, too," she said.

They stood for a couple of minutes, holding each other while the sun sank beneath the skyline, slowly muting the crisp spring colors to gray in the advancing twilight.

He shivered, the freshness in the air turning to cold with the lengthening shadows. He relaxed his grip on Elizabeth, who stepped toward the house. "I guess we'll have to make some changes around the house," he said as her fingertips trailed off his.

"I know, it's exciting," she said, then tittered. "I hope it's a girl."

Numbness shot through his body, his mind jumping to the only little girl he could ever think of, her ragged clothes hanging from her shredded body. "As long as it's healthy," he said, through cold lips.

She stopped suddenly, then whirled to face him. "Speaking of family, please don't say anything when we're at my parents'. I want to let some more time go by before we start telling people."

He forced a groan through his lips, focused every thought on playing his part so she didn't ask what was wrong. "I forgot," he said, his face scrunched in a mockery of pleading. "Do we have to go? Wouldn't the easiest way to not tell them be if we didn't go?"

"We have to be there. This was the only time everyone was available around Easter," she said, taking his hand. "Besides, we haven't seen them since Christmas, and they're only a four-hour drive away. Before we were in Ottawa, there was a reason, but now . . . I need to make the effort."

"What about me?"

Her lips tightened, but the smile didn't disappear. "You know you don't. I know my family can be a lot to deal with, especially my dad," she said, looking at him with eyes he could never refuse. "But they're my family. It would mean a lot to me."

He sighed. How could he say no? "We go late and leave early," he said in resignation.

"Thank you," she said, her face brightening. She turned to go into the house. "I'll see you inside."

He watched her enter the house, then took a deep breath and picked up the broom. In silence, he returned to sweeping. The shadows had grown long, and he shivered again in the cooling air.

CHAPTER 11

Saturday came far too fast for Hugh. It wasn't that his in-laws weren't good people, even though they probably would never have talked with him if he wasn't married to their daughter. If anything, he was humbled by them, both in their material accomplishments and in their tight family bonds. So what was it that bothered him so much?

He racked his brain for an answer as he pulled into the long tree-lined driveway of his in-laws' sprawling lakefront house in Oakville, a stately neighborhood where the houses were probably worth more than he'd make in his lifetime. By rights, they should have at least some common ground, like with her brother, Conrad, who was an investment banker, or her uncle Bob, who owned some sort of real-estate business. At previous family events, he'd mentioned the similarities between military strategy and business strategy, or enemy analysis and market analysis, but he'd never gotten more than a polite acknowledgment. It was almost as if he were a kid being humored. *Look at the cute soldier; he knows about supply chain management, isn't that simply adorable?* Whatever it was, he'd need a whole lot of discipline to make it through the night.

He turned off the truck and checked his watch. Just after four o'clock, which meant at least three hours to go. He could do it. His lips pressed together, and he looked up, then noticed Elizabeth studying him.

She reached over, placing a hand on his thigh, probably to reassure him. It didn't work, but he smiled anyways to give the impression that it had.

"Thank you for coming," she said, giving him a smile of encouragement. "You'll be fine."

"We leave right after supper?" he said, knuckles turning white on the steering wheel.

"Sure thing," she said, rubbing his leg, then hopping out.

"That means without staying to help with dishes."

She looked at him over the passenger seat, only her head and shoulders visible. "We're staying for dishes," she said, then closed the door.

He sighed, then got out and followed her up the flagstone driveway like a dog being dragged to the vet. As they passed the three-car garage with two levels and chalet-style windows—a decent house for an average person—his eyes were inevitably drawn to the main residence, an impressive English-manor-style home. He shook his head.

"It always amazes me you grew up here," he said.

"Only since I was ten," Elizabeth said, squeezing his hand. "Our house in Montreal was much smaller."

"Why was it you moved again? Your dad got sick of sticking it to Anglo-Quebecois and wanted to try his hand on Anglo-Ontarians?"

"Hardly," she said. "Daddy'd had enough talk about separation and the referendum." She grabbed his hand, bringing him to a stop at the bottom of the stairs. "He means well. He's just very competitive. Are you ready?"

He nodded. Time to get on with it.

They climbed the front steps, and Elizabeth knocked on the double wooden doors. Instead of waiting, she opened the left door and entered, leaving it ajar. The sound of multiple conversations, a television, and music all washed over him as he stood rooted to the front step, like he was about to dive into ice-cold water. Grimacing, he took a deep breath and followed.

Compared to the outside of the house, the foyer was relatively small, although still twice the size of the foyer in his house. Immediately inside was a small landing, where Elizabeth was hugging her father, after which the floor dropped three steps to an immaculately finished atrium complete with glass-inlaid doors leading to the main part of the house.

Elizabeth's father released her and pulled the massive wooden door shut. He then extended a hand to Hugh. "Been a long time, Hugh." George Kerr—even now, Hugh always thought of him as Mr. Kerr—never ceased to look every bit the aging corporate lawyer that he was, all slicked-back graying hair and too-soft skin.

Hugh shook his hand and gave him a polite smile. "Only since Christmas."

"You should bring my daughter down more often," her dad said, wrapping his arm around Elizabeth. He was smiling, but it seemed to stop short of his eyes.

Hugh nodded. *You could come visit us, for once.* But why would they start now? It had been that way ever since he and Elizabeth had started dating.

Elizabeth hugged her older sister, Joanne, impeccably dressed as usual, a wizened and bitter, albeit more fashionable, version of Elizabeth. At the bottom of the landing stood Elizabeth's brother, Conrad, then two cousins, Marissa and

Melissa. Wait, Marissa was a cousin, Melissa was married to a cousin. Or was it the other way around? And what were the names of their husbands? He forgot as Joanne leaned in to hug him. He angled to kiss her on the cheek, then hesitated. Which one was he supposed to kiss first, left or right? Was it both sides or just one? He wavered, and their lips almost brushed. His face grew hot—what was wrong with a simple hug? Then Joanne moved on, and Conrad was shaking his hand, pulling him awkwardly closer and bumping shoulders. The next moment, Marissa was kissing him, no, it was Melissa, then the other one, then any one of a number of cousins, aunts, uncles, and random friends who'd happened to have been invited. He cast about for Elizabeth, spotting her near the entrance to the dining room, and tried to move toward her, slipping two steps away for every step he got closer.

His shirt was clinging to him, and between shaking hands or hugging people whose names he'd forgotten—never mind the people he hadn't yet met—he dried his palms on his pants. When he'd started seeing Elizabeth in 2003, he'd gotten her to quiz him on family names prior to big functions so he could remember everyone. But Kingston had been close, so they'd visited at least once a month, much more often than the once a year they'd averaged later when he was in battalion. He'd also cared back then, as a keen RMC cadet—even if Elizabeth's dad seemed to think he was second-class for having started out in the ranks. All considered, today the quiz had been too much effort. He knew his place, and it wasn't among them. Hugh checked his watch. Only fifteen minutes had gone by. He silently groaned.

When the introductions and greetings were finally over, he found himself alone in one of the large common rooms, a spacious area with a high vaulted ceiling and rich hardwood floors. He'd almost reached Elizabeth, only to have her drawn off by a cousin to talk about an upcoming wedding. In her absence, he gravitated to a corner where he could at least watch television while pretending to listen to a nearby conversation. He'd gotten a beer from somewhere, and he took small sips, not wanting to assume any risk of getting too drunk to drive home.

God, it's hot. He unbuttoned the cuffs of his shirt and rolled up the sleeves, then looked around to see if there was a space with fewer people, somewhere less confining. He took two steps toward the dining room, which appeared to be more deserted, when one of Elizabeth's uncles—was it Uncle Bob?—caught his eye. *Great.*

"General," Uncle Bob said, his voice gravelly from too much smoking. He had an old man's bulbous nose, crisscrossed with blue veins and set between two droopy, bloodshot eyes. Jamming the stub of an unlit cigar into his mouth, Uncle Bob put out his hand. "How goes the battle?"

He shook the man's hand, annoyed at remembering too late that Uncle Bob always tugged slightly when shaking hands, hoping to pull the other person off balance. "Good, but Major is fine," he said, stumbling slightly forward and inwardly cursing. Why did he even bother? Uncle Bob was just going to keep calling him General. "And you?"

"Fine, fine," Uncle Bob said. "And how are things at National Defence? I keep reading about what a mess you fellas have made out of procurement." He leaned in conspiratorially. "Soldiers should stick to fighting wars and leave the financials to the professionals."

"I guess," he said, sipping from his beer to cut off a retort. Hugh only ever saw Uncle Bob at bigger family functions, maybe once or twice a year at best, but it was often enough to know that the man always started out conversations by pointing out something National Defence had done wrong. The best answer was to feign ignorance. "I don't have much to do with that. All I know is pretty much what's in the news."

Uncle Bob frowned, although whether from disappointment or scorn wasn't clear. He looked away, gazing out one of the several sets of patio doors that lined one wall of the living room. "And what is it, exactly, that you do these days?" Bob said, switching the cigar from one side of his mouth to the other.

Hugh stared at the self-satisfied old fool. *That's how you want to play it? Get ready for milspeak.* "I'm the info coord," he said, speaking in his most earnest voice. "I work in the HQ and handle admin and fin issues in support of the COS. I'm also the OPI of our admin SOPs, like processing PERs, so that keeps me busy. Basically, I keep the wheels on the machine greased."

"I see," Uncle Bob said, a glazed look spreading over his face. He reached up and pulled the cigar from his mouth, studying the unlit tip. "I keep reading about military anniversaries and such. Do you have anything to do with that?"

Smiling politely, he adopted his best shit-eating voice. "Sure," he said, dragging out the word and raising the pitch in the middle. "There's been lots of planning for important anniversaries of great battles. As you know"—which Bob probably didn't, but would never admit—"this year is the two hundredth anniversary of the War of 1812, and the hundredth anniversary of the First World War is coming soon, so there's lots to do to prepare."

"Our tax dollars at good work," Uncle Bob said, putting the cigar back in his dour mouth. "And how would you go about commemorating the War of 1812 anyways?"

He hesitated. This wasn't actually his file, and all that came to mind was a small diamond-shaped pin everyone had been ordered to wear on the left breast pocket of their uniform. But that would only invite another comment about money wasting.

Taking a slow sip of his warm, now vaguely skunky beer, the answer came to him. "Parades," he said, lowering the bottle. "We have parades to mark significant events of the war, like the Battle of Queenston Heights. There's a parade in Toronto, you should think about going."

Uncle Bob grunted and glanced at him out of the corner of his eye. "Don't soldiers have anything better to do than march around?"

What was that look on Bob's face? Not quite contempt, but close. And was that a no to attending the parade? "Probably," he said. "But I don't make those decisions. Frankly, I'd prefer to do almost anything else besides be on parade, but I don't have much choice in the matter."

Uncle Bob looked at him blankly, saying nothing.

Hugh returned silence with silence. What had Bob expected anyways?

After a few moments of awkward silence, Elizabeth appeared and saved him. She reached an arm around Hugh's waist and gripped him close, then gave her uncle a small peck on the cheek.

He snaked an arm around Elizabeth's back, silently thanking her with a quick look. "Just updating your uncle on work."

She flashed a smile. "Hugh's job is quite interesting."

"Yes," Uncle Bob said, glancing dismissively at Hugh, then back to Elizabeth. "Henry has an interesting job, too, did you know that? I still keep in touch with him."

Christ, not this again. Henry was the rich douchebag who'd been seeing Elizabeth in her first year of university, who'd caused the accident that ended her swimming career, and who was now an investment banker who could buy and sell Hugh ten times over, at least if Uncle Bob could be believed. He clenched his jaw and counted to ten. If it wasn't so enraging, it would make a great drinking game—how many times in a night would a member of Elizabeth's family mention her ex-boyfriend? He'd be loaded before supper. He glanced at Elizabeth, whose face was scarlet. *Keep a grip, for her sake.*

Thankfully, supper was announced while Elizabeth was waffling through a response. Family and invited friends, at least thirty if not more, migrated into the dining room, where two large tables had been set up end to end. Elizabeth's mother rang a bell, then invited everyone to help themselves to a buffet line in the kitchen. Hugh drifted to the back, delaying as much as possible before sitting down. When he did sit, he found himself seated near the foot of the two tables, Elizabeth to one side, her cousin Annabelle to the other.

At least the food was good. Not just good, it was great. His stomach rumbled after one bite of the moist turkey, and he aggressively tucked into the meal. Conversation went on around him, but Elizabeth did most of the talking for them. It was mostly small-talk catching up anyways, and after a few minutes, he tuned out and focused on his meal.

It was always the same at these events; repeat the same story over and over to each subsequent family member not seen since whatever previous event they'd all been at. Since none of them understood the military, they'd smile vapidly at all the right spots, then ask polite questions about how the army worked and which he'd probably already answered the last time they'd spoken. It was like being a fireman in a room full of people who'd only seen fires on the news. *Honey, Hugh here says that fire gets hot—can you imagine?* It was so tiresome.

He finished his first plate and helped himself to another, which he ate more slowly, but somehow he still ended up done before everyone else. Laying his knife and fork together on the plate, he began paying closer attention to the conversation, which had now turned to politics.

Beside him, Annabelle was ranting about the federal government. She was in her midtwenties, enrolled in some philosophy or politics program at the University of Toronto. Petite and strawberry blonde, Roach probably would have described her as good from afar, but far from good. Unable to control the smile forming on his face, he wiped his mouth with a napkin and focused on what Annabelle was saying, some nonsense about the government suppressing voters and turning Canada into a dictatorship.

"These tricks they're playing are unconstitutional and misleading voters," she said, waving her glass of wine around. "They're undermining democracy and need to be stopped."

His mouth opened of its own accord to respond when Elizabeth put a hand on his lap and squeezed his leg. Startled, he glanced at her, then shut his mouth. Thank God she was here.

"That's not unique to this government," Elizabeth said. "Any of the parties would do the same thing. It's what they have to do to stay in power."

An aunt—was it Doris?—reinforced Elizabeth's point, suggesting voter apathy was the real problem. Annabelle ignored this comment and rounded on Elizabeth.

"I totally disagree," she said, leaning across Hugh. "This government is fascist, and they rule through censorship and authoritarianism. The prime minister runs the country like it's his personal fiefdom, which is what it will become if they're not defeated in the next election. The longer they're in power, the more big business is empowered and the more the middle class is oppressed." Annabelle sat back and drank from her wine, a contented look on her face.

He couldn't bite his tongue any longer. "I'm no politics major, but I do follow a bit of history, and it doesn't sound like any sort of fascist government to me."

Annabelle's body tensed slightly, and a rush of satisfaction swelled through him, even as he registered other family members turning to watch the conversation.

"I also don't see any Blackshirts or Brownshirts around. I could be wrong, though." He held a hand up apologetically, oblivious to the tightening of Elizabeth's hand on his leg.

Annabelle set her glass on the table, wine sloshing over the sides, and swung toward him, scarlet blooming in her cheeks. "That's a simplistic perspective," she said. "And it doesn't mean they're not using the same antidemocratic tactics Mussolini or Hitler used while they consolidated power. Voter suppression, treating Parliament with contempt, doing whatever they can to sidestep the electorate, these are all signs they don't respect democracy. They don't even represent a majority of Canadians, only the few that actually voted. I could go on and on."

He set his hand on the table—it had begun to tremble— and stared at a candle. His heart was racing, and he took a deep breath, staring at the flickering orange flame and willing himself to see a man who was able to keep control. Hopefully it was him.

"For starters, what is this voter suppression you keep talking about? Robocalls?" he said. "I don't think a few annoying phone calls supposedly misleading people about locations of voting stations really constitutes voter suppression, at least in terms of what's normally meant by fascism. And proroguing the House is a centuries-old tradition that's been used by all governments. It's called politics."

The redness in Annabelle's face was spreading, working its way up her cheeks to her glaring eyes. "Well, as you said, you're no politics major, just a representative of the governing regime, and one of the military class at that," she said, her voice dripping with sarcasm. "We all know where the military's loyalties were in the fascist regimes you seem to know so much about." She turned away from him and sipped her wine.

Annabelle may as well have waved a red flag.

"I may be a soldier, but to make the mental leap that I support fascism because I wear a uniform is utter bullshit," he said. The room suddenly became quiet, but all he could hear was a rushing in his ears. "It might surprise you to know there aren't many professions that get the same degree of training in ethics and moral responsibility as the military does, certainly not the bankers and business elites who dragged the global economy into recession and got away with no punishment whatsoever. And unlike someone who's only seen the world through a university classroom, I've actually had to make difficult ethical choices through the course of my life."

The words were spilling out as if from a burst dam, and he kept going, his hand punctuating each point with a sharp chop like he was cutting a pie. "Are you so simple that you think because a government pulls a few political tricks that it's all of a sudden a dictatorship? When there's a system in place to investigate every one of those supposed tricks?" He smacked his forehead with the palm of his hand. "Wait, that's right, in your world, the other branches of government are beholden to the executive, so any investigations are phony baloney because . . . well, just because, right?"

Annabelle drew away from him, like she'd suddenly realized she'd sat beside a poisonous creature.

"You want to talk about voter suppression? Here's what real voter suppression is like," he said. "Real voter suppression is when you threaten to cut off people's fingers who vote, like the Taliban do. Then when people actually vote—which you can tell from the ink on their fingers—you cut those fingers off."

"That's different—" Annabelle said.

"Will you stop talking and listen for once?" he said, spittle flying from his mouth. "Voter suppression is when you cut off a young girl's nose because she had the audacity to accompany her parents to a voting station. Better yet, voter suppression is when you saw some farmer in half with barbed wire because he had the gall to think he could take part in an election, that he had a right to air his opinion. Then string up the two halves near the voting booth. No need to mislead people on polling stations then. That's voter suppression."

The whites of Annabelle's eyes were showing. A new voice spoke across the table, and Hugh turned to see who was speaking.

"Hugh, you're talking about Afghanistan. This is Canada," Joanne said. "And none of what you've seen there takes anything away from the seriousness of problems here."

He nodded. "I never said it did, only that it doesn't make the current government a fascist one."

"But you have to admit, voter apathy is at all-new highs," Conrad said. "I think it's fair to say much of that is linked to the behavior of the government. Say what you will, but they don't represent most people. The stats from the last election prove it. And a government that doesn't truly represent the people doesn't really have the authority to govern, does it?"

Hugh looked down at his plate, shaking his head. "Are you really suggesting that voter apathy is solely the fault of the current government?" he said. "When that problem exists in most Western democracies? At every political level?"

"How would you explain it then?" Conrad said, a smug expression on his face.

"I'd say people take for granted what they get too easily," he said, looking at Conrad, but speaking to the room. "People care more about a sale on new gadgets than in taking part in any political process. They need to step up and accept some responsibility, not wait for it to be spoon-fed to them." He gazed around the table. "As shitty as it is in Afghanistan, in some ways it's refreshing. Afghanis understand they're exercising their rights by voting and risk their life to do so. Did you know that in the last election, the Taliban attacked voting stations and people just kept right on coming after the attacks were done and the bodies were cleared away? You think that would happen here?" He gestured around him. "You think people would risk their lives to vote? People have given up that right, and the only thing that will get them to take it seriously again is to take it away completely."

Tendons stood out on Conrad's neck, and Joanne looked like she'd just eaten a lemon.

"Of all the simple-minded arguments—" Joanne said, slamming a hand on the table.

"That'll do," Mr. Kerr said.

All heads swiveled to where he sat at the head of the table, a look of infinite patience on his face.

The silence in the room pressed in upon Hugh, finally overcoming the blood rushing through his ears and broken only by the sounds of the light jazz music. Around the table was a mixture of faces covered in thinly veiled disgust, not so thinly veiled in some cases. He willed himself to look at his father-in-law, while his face positively boiled. How could he so lose control like that?

"Hugh's had some . . . unique . . . experiences," Elizabeth's father said in an even voice that carried throughout the entire room. "Clearly those experiences color his views, which is understandable. And no doubt those experiences bring him and our armed forces, which we're all proud of and support, great perspective. Sometimes we might wish their missions were better thought out, but we can hardly blame the troops for that, can we?"

Elizabeth's elbow dug him in the ribs, and the knuckles of her hand were white where she gripped his leg. He glanced at her, saw the silent pleading in her eyes, then looked back at her father.

"But let's not forget ourselves, shall we?" his father-in-law continued, eyes glued to Hugh. "There's a time and place for everything, and perhaps right now we might all be better served being thankful for the presence of our loved ones."

Hugh looked at the table, willing himself to remain seated while every fiber of his body strained to upend the table. Elizabeth's hand burning into his leg was his lifeline, and he focused on the pressure of her nails digging into his flesh. *Be strong for her.* He bit down hard on the inside of his cheek, savoring the salty blood blossoming in his mouth, diverting his attention from the rage threatening to erupt.

Across the table, Joanne rose, her chair scraping along the wooden floor. "Excuse me, Daddy," she said, eyes boring into Hugh. "I seem to have lost my appetite." Tossing her silk napkin on her chair, she turned and stormed away.

Her husband—whatever his name was—threw an accusing glance at Hugh, then ran after her. Annabelle stood up next, almost upending her chair, and left without a word.

He set his elbows on the table, clasped his hands together, and rested his chin on his intertwined fingers. He glanced at Conrad, who was the next to stand.

"You outdid yourself this time, Hugh," Conrad said. "Way to go."

"That will be all, Conrad, thank you," Elizabeth's dad said.

Conrad continued to glare at Hugh, then his eyes flickered to his dad. Shooting Hugh a last look, he, too, huffed out of the room.

Those remaining returned to picking at their meals in silence. After a few minutes, Elizabeth's mother stood up, mumbling something about dessert.

Beside him, Elizabeth's body tensed as her gaze followed her departing mother, and then she looked at Hugh and settled into her seat. Throughout, Elizabeth's father unceasingly stared at him.

When Elizabeth's mother returned with a cherry cheesecake and a blueberry pie, smatterings of conversation began, at least near the head of the table. At the foot of the table, near Hugh, people picked at their desserts and avoided eye contact, despite Elizabeth's best efforts to get people talking. While coffee and tea went around, which most people declined, Elizabeth's mother wolfed down her pie, then abruptly stood up and went into the kitchen. Other family members soon followed, and within minutes only Elizabeth, her dad, and Hugh were left.

He looked at Elizabeth, who was squirming in her chair, her eyes darting between the kitchen, her father, and Hugh. He sighed, then nodded toward the kitchen. "Go on, I'll be all right."

"Do you want to go now?" she said quietly, placing a hand on his arm.

He shook his head. "I'll go get some air," he said. "I don't think I'll be missed." He slowly pushed back his chair and stood up, then grabbed his coffee and moved toward the front door.

Elizabeth rose as well, following him into the foyer, where she held on to his shoulder, gently turning him to face her. "Wait," she said. "It's not like that. My family just has different priorities." She leaned close to hug him, and he stiffened. Slowly, she drew away, trailing her fingers on his sleeve before crossing her arms.

He turned and opened the door. "I get it," he said. Different priorities? That was one way to describe worshipping on the altar of the almighty dollar. "You'd think I'd be used to it by now." He stepped out and walked down the driveway.

Elizabeth stood framed in the doorway for a moment, then quietly closed the heavy wooden door.

As he walked, he pulled out his Copenhagen and put in a dip. He let down the tailgate on his truck and sat down, feet dangling in the air while he sipped coffee and periodically spewed out streams of black juice onto the asphalt driveway. The air was crisp, clearing his head.

Supper had been bad, maybe even the worst, but not by a big margin. There'd been the time he'd gotten into it with Joanne over the United Nations and Canada's peacekeeping tradition, and the time he'd unfortunately found himself explaining what happens during a suicide bombing and how the bomber's head is normally always recovered intact. People had cleared the room that time, too. And of course, there'd been the time Conrad had asked if Hugh had ever killed anyone, right after Afghanistan in '09. At that point, he'd still been in control of his thoughts. He'd pushed aside the times he'd seen a person through the scope of his rifle and explained how killing people was something every soldier was trained for, yet hoped they'd never have to do, all while sweat had poured from his body. Had that been around when the dreams had first started? Maybe. He couldn't remember.

He swallowed the last of the coffee and pulled out his Copenhagen. Still, dinner could've been worse. At least nobody had mentioned the wedding, a grievance he was sure Elizabeth's mother would carry to her grave. But it wasn't like he'd had a choice, not after being selected at the last minute for the deployment in '09. It hadn't been his fault the deployment dates erased all the work he and Elizabeth had already spent planning their marriage. When predeployment training had been factored in—the tour before the tour—it was either a destination wedding at the last minute or postpone everything until after he returned. Even then, there would've been no guarantee; there never was. As it turned out, he'd gone on his qualification course to be promoted to major shortly after redeploying, so the last-minute wedding prior to deploying had been the right call, even if only a few guests had been able to make it. Elizabeth's family would never understand how the military's operational tempo controlled Hugh's life, the notion of service before self. He shook his head and took a pinch of tobacco.

The sound of the front door slamming echoed down the driveway, the dull thud carrying in the early evening air. Hugh paused and cocked an ear toward the house, small flecks of tobacco slipping between his fingers. As the footsteps got louder, he hurriedly stuffed the tobacco into his mouth and wiped his hands on his pants, then turned. Elizabeth's dad was ambling down the drive.

"Mind if I join you?" Mr. Kerr said, hands jammed into the pockets of a tan polo jacket.

He shuffled farther along the tailgate, saying nothing.

"I'd like to apologize for the argument at supper," Mr. Kerr said. "Our family can be very passionate."

He studied his father-in-law's face. Was this a genuine apology, or was he being baited? But the man's face was as impassive as ever. "Thanks."

"I meant what I said about supporting the troops."

What was this? Had he been misjudging Mr. Kerr all this time?

"You've got a hard job that's not for everyone, and I'm personally glad someone like you is doing it," Mr. Kerr said. He paused and pursed his lips, then drew them back, briefly baring his teeth. "But just because you're a good soldier doesn't mean you're good for my daughter."

His heart was suddenly racing. Had he heard right?

"You're damaged goods, Hugh," Mr. Kerr said as matter-of-factly as if he'd been discussing the weather. "And you don't fit in here. You've clearly been exposed to some terrible things while serving your country, and for what it's worth, I'm sorry for that. But I know what happens to soldiers with experiences like yours, and it's rarely a good news story." He hesitated, then leaned closer and spoke in a slightly quieter voice that somehow carried more conviction. "In the end, the safety of my family is my primary concern. If you hurt my daughter, you will regret it."

His vision filled with red, and he shot off the tailgate, landing on his feet and closing the distance to Mr. Kerr in two steps. He glowered down at his father-in-law, their faces only inches apart. "You call this an apology?"

A small frown appeared on Mr. Kerr's face. "This is exactly my point," he said, holding his hands out at his sides as if to illustrate his argument. "You're incapable of dealing with problems other than through violence and threats. That's great in a soldier, but it is unacceptable here, in my family. You think it's unreasonable for me to assume that you would harm my daughter?" He nodded at Hugh's clenched fists. "For God's sake, look at yourself. You're about to hit me."

He ground his teeth, nostrils flaring as he sucked in air. Images of his fist smashing into Mr. Kerr's mouth morphed into Mr. Kerr cowering beside his truck, which in turn became Elizabeth cowering in the corner of their room. He gasped and staggered back.

Shaking his head, Mr. Kerr lowered his jacket zipper, reaching inside to pull out his wallet. "How much would it take for you to leave Elizabeth?"

"What?" he said, swooning.

"Come, Hugh, you're not stupid," Mr. Kerr said. "I asked how much it would take to get you to leave Elizabeth. Twenty thousand? Thirty? I can't give all that to you now, but you could have a couple thousand to start." As he talked, he pulled out a wad of hundred-dollar bills.

He leaned heavily on the truck's tailgate with one hand. This could not be happening.

"More, Hugh? It can be arranged. Take this for now," he said, reaching out to jam the bills into Hugh's breast pocket.

As the money brushed his chest, he snapped his hand up, grabbing his father-in-law's arm at the wrist. "Don't touch me," he said. Animal rage filled him, stoked by the first glimpse of uncertainty in Mr. Kerr's eyes.

"Daddy? Hugh? Are you two all right?"

They both froze, rooted to the ground as Elizabeth's voice interrupted them. They glanced toward the house as one. She was stepping down the front steps and heading their way.

"Fine, just fine," her dad said, eyes returning to Hugh's face. "We'll be in shortly."

Her footsteps faltered, then kept coming, her pace slower. Her dad's eyes flickered between her and Hugh, until he snatched his hand from Hugh's grip. As she neared the front of the truck, he stuffed both hands into the pockets of his jacket, then leaned close to Hugh.

"Think about it," he said quietly. "No shame in making the most out of a bad situation."

"Is everything all right?" Elizabeth asked.

Her dad leaned over and gave her a peck on the cheek. "Perfect, sweetie. I was just apologizing for supper. Hugh was actually telling me he thought it might be time to leave." He looked pointedly at Hugh. "Isn't that right, Hugh?"

He stood speechless, hands shaking as fury rose in him like magma beneath a caldera. How could that bastard be so two-faced? He blinked away a vision of smashing Mr. Kerr's head into his tailgate, all while forcing his lips into a rigid grin. Suddenly, his rage solidified, and calmness spread over him.

"That's okay, Mr. Kerr, no need to cover for me," he said, reaching out to take Elizabeth's hand. "I'd asked your dad not to mention I'd said you were pregnant, but he shouldn't have to lie on my account."

"Hugh," Elizabeth said, turning to him with a frown on her face. "I said not to tell anybody."

If possible, Mr. Kerr's eyes became even harder. "Yes, congratulations are in order," he said in an unwavering voice. The man could have put trained killers to shame.

Elizabeth turned to her dad, a hand on Hugh's chest as if to restrain him. "Daddy, please don't tell anybody. Hugh should never have told you, it's still early."

"Don't worry, sweetie, I promise," Mr. Kerr said, his voice emotionless.

Hugh feigned a yawn. "Your dad's right, though, it's a long drive back to Ottawa. Maybe leaving isn't such a bad idea," he said. "Are you ready to go?"

Elizabeth looked from her dad to Hugh, then back again. "I'm sorry, Daddy," she said, removing her hand from Hugh and folding her arms across her chest. "I think it's best if we go." Moving closer to her dad, she pecked him lightly on the cheek, then stepped back. "Before we do any more damage." Turning to scowl at Hugh, she began walking toward the house. "I have to get my coat."

As her footsteps faded, he and his father-in-law watched each other silently, gauging each other like fighters circling.

"Found your tongue, eh?" Mr. Kerr said. "Well, my offer stands."

He turned his back and headed for the driver's side door.

"If you so much as touch a hair on her head"—Mr. Kerr's voice followed him—"I'll make sure you never see her, or your child-to-be, again."

He whirled around and rushed his father-in-law, grabbing him at the lapels and corkscrewing his hands into the man's chest so that he had hold of his jacket, his shirt, and likely the skin of his chest by the way Mr. Kerr raised up on his toes. "You son of a bitch."

Mr. Kerr smirked, the only emotion he'd shown all night. "Not exactly alleviating my concerns, Hugh," he said, his voice betraying no trace of pain or discomfort. "Or is that irony lost on you? And did you notice my daughter seems none too taken with you at the moment? The best thing you could do is get out of her life."

Time slowed to a crawl while he warred with the demon that had taken over his body, all while Mr. Kerr simply met his eyes, offering nothing. *You bastard.* He clenched his hands tighter.

The sound of the front door closing brought him back. Shaking his head, he shoved his father-in-law backward, releasing him. How close had he come? Too close. With a final glare, he turned on his heel and walked around the truck, reaching the door as Elizabeth appeared. After giving her dad a hug and kiss good-bye, Elizabeth got in the truck, the air in the cab almost cooling as she stared stonily out the side window.

Let her be angry; at least they were leaving. He'd probably get along better with a frontline Taliban soldier than with this Potemkin family. He cranked the key, and the engine roared to life, a deep-throated rumble ominously filling the air. Slamming the truck into gear, he glanced in the rearview mirror. Mr. Kerr was still there, staring at him. Hugh stomped on the accelerator and roared out of the driveway.

CHAPTER 12

"If you don't mind me saying, Hugh, you don't look so good," Dr. Taylor said, brow furrowed in concern. "And it's been almost three weeks since our last session. How have you been?"

Hugh lethargically looked up from the depths of the leather couch. "I haven't been avoiding you," he said, his voice emotionless. "Things kept coming up." He reached up and absently rubbed his neck. Where to start? The disastrous weekend at his in-laws'? Elizabeth barely talking to him?

He started, glancing up at the therapist, who must have asked him something. "Pardon?"

"How are you sleeping?"

He snorted. "Hit and miss."

"But getting worse, I take it?"

His head seesawed. "Yes and no. I sleep less—max two or three hours a night—but at least it's uninterrupted." He sank farther into the couch, tiredness oozing from his very bones.

"When did that start?"

"A few weeks ago," he said, staring at his wedding band and twisting it between the thumb and index finger of his right hand. "After visiting my in-laws."

"Did something happen?"

He raised his eyebrows. "You could say that." Talking took so much effort.

Dr. Taylor waited, staring at him while he played with his ring. In the silence, the ticking of the clock on the wall filled the room.

With a sigh, Dr. Taylor uncrossed his legs. "Hugh, I know you know this, but this only works if you talk."

"I know," he said, releasing his ring and rubbing his face. "A few weeks ago, right after our last session, Elizabeth's family had a big dinner at their place in Oakville."

"I remember you mentioning that."

"There was an argument at supper. A bad one."

"What makes you say it was bad?"

"Half her family walked out."

"Ah, I see." Dr. Taylor nodded.

"After supper, Elizabeth's dad tried to pay me to leave her."

"Pardon me?" The therapist stopped writing and peered at him over his glasses.

Hugh returned the stare, nodding. "I know, crazy, right?" He shrugged. "I said no."

"Did you . . ."

"Did I what?" he said. "Did I hit him?" He leaned forward, elbows on his knees, hands clasped. "No, but I wanted to. I wanted to beat the living hell out of him, but somehow I didn't." He raised a hand and massaged his temples. "But I had to do something, so I told him Elizabeth was pregnant. Unfortunately, she was beside me."

"I had no idea," Dr. Taylor said. "Is she?"

Hugh nodded, his lips pressed tightly together. "She's in the first trimester."

"I see. And I take it she wasn't ready to tell her parents." The therapist whistled. "And you? How are you feeling about the pregnancy?"

"I have no idea," he said with a sigh. Ever since she'd told him, her pregnancy had been like a weight on his back, getting heavier with every picture of a stroller or car seat or crib that Elizabeth was already showing him. "It feels like the straw that's going to break the camel's back."

"What is it that bothers you most?"

He was getting better at these questions, especially when he was tired. Just say the first thing that came into his head. "The cycle continuing."

"What do you mean by that?"

Now the hard part. What exactly was he worried about? He looked around. "What if I do something that messes them up? What if I . . . what if I hurt them?" He clamped his jaw shut, willing his emotions back into control. "I don't want another human being to be punished because of me."

Dr. Taylor's voice was soft. "Hugh, you haven't done anything wrong. And even if you had, children don't bear responsibility for things their parents have done."

"Sure they don't," he said. *Try telling that to the kids of the master corporal who killed himself in Petawawa.* "Can we talk about something else?"

Dr. Taylor paused, seemed almost ready to pursue the question further. "As you wish, Hugh, but I'd like to revisit this later," he said. "Getting back to the dinner, how did Elizabeth react when you told her dad?"

"How do you think?" he snapped, then sighed. "She's still not really talking to me."

"And your sleeping? That's when it started getting worse?"

He nodded. "She didn't speak to me the whole ride back from Oakville. When we went to bed, I couldn't sleep, there was too much anger coming off her, like she was radiating heat. So I got up and walked around."

"An effective coping mechanism," Dr. Taylor said. "Focusing on a different activity sometimes helps. The body will naturally sleep once it reaches exhaustion."

Snorting, he settled back into the couch. "Not sure about that. For me, it was more like I had to walk around, like someone was watching me and I had to check it out." He closed his eyes, envisioning the now-nightly routine. "I checked the alarm, checked all the windows and doors, even scanned outside the house to make sure everything was good. When I went back upstairs, Liz was asleep, but then I felt I needed to walk around again. So I did."

"Did it help?" Dr. Taylor said.

"Halfway through the night, I fell asleep in the living room," he said. "I was watching the patio door and dozed off, but I got a couple of hours. When I woke, I had the urge to check things out again, and when that was done, it was time to go to work. Every night since has been more or less the same."

"Persistent mobilization," Dr. Taylor said. "Not uncommon in combat stress cases, although somewhat unusual this symptom didn't present earlier." He glanced up. "Medication might help."

He shook his head. "Not unless there's no other choice," he said. "I've seen too many guys start taking pills and never stop."

Dr. Taylor referred to his notes. "All right. Has this type of behavior ever occurred before?"

"Once," he said. "On my second tour in Afghanistan in '06."

"What were the circumstances?"

He paused, staring between his legs. "We were escorting a psyops team around," he said, then glanced up. "Sorry, psychological operations. They broadcast messages, tell the people how awesome we are and tell the enemy how they don't want to fight us. It's called winning the hearts and minds." *Or two in the heart, one in the mind.* At least that's what the psyops team commander had joked about while he'd mimed shooting a rifle.

Dr. Taylor motioned for him to continue.

"We were out patrolling in the boonies when we got attacked," he said. "It was touch and go for a while. Some enemy fighters got pretty close, but they finally let up around evening prayer time. Even still, we could hear them making plans to attack again during the night."

"How was that possible?" Dr. Taylor asked.

"The psyops team had Icom radios on the same frequencies as the ones the insurgents were using. They also had a guy who could speak Pashtu and he would translate," he said. "Sometimes the psyops guys would fuck with them, sorry, mess with them by saying stuff on their net, misleading information or even insults. Anyways, the insurgents wanted to recover their dead and were planning to attack, so we knew we had to be ready."

Shuddering, he closed his eyes. The ticking of the clock gave way to the sound of static breaking on the handheld radios, the excited voices of the enemy speaking Pashtu or Dari or gibberish for all he knew. While the enemy prepared, the sun had dipped below the mountains, advancing the shadows over their position like skeletal claws reaching from the ground to claim them. He blinked the vision away.

"While I was working on getting air support, those idiot psyops guys decided to burn some of the enemy bodies," he said, staring at a design on the carpet. Concentric blue and red diamonds began bleeding into one another. They seemed to flicker as they blurred, like the flames that had consumed the dead Taliban fighters, ablaze within minutes while the acrid smell of diesel permeated the air. "I lost my shit, but by then we had no way to put out the fires."

"What had they hoped to accomplish?" Dr. Taylor said, face scrunched in distaste.

"Get them angry so they'd make a mistake," he said, glancing up. "The Taliban like to gather their dead at the end of the day for burial, it's a Muslim thing. But when the psyops team burned the bodies, that wasn't possible." His voice grew quiet. "Then those idiots broadcast it."

"What?"

"Psyops vehicles have big speakers so they can broadcast messages. Once the bodies were burning, the team taunted the enemy through the loudspeakers, saying they were cowards, too afraid to stop us." His shoulders slumped. "I didn't even find out what they'd been doing until halfway through the night. They didn't bother telling me until the terp took a bullet." And only after the Taliban's first attempt to recover the bodies, when they'd fought like they were possessed.

"Terp?"

"Interpreter," he said, then took a deep breath. "Needless to say, their plan didn't work. We got attacked most of the night, almost got overrun."

"But you made it through?"

"We did." *Barely.* In the end, he'd called in fire virtually on their own position. The rounds had fallen so close the explosions had lifted him off the ground. "For about a week after, I couldn't sleep without double- or triple-checking everything around me."

Dr. Taylor pushed his glasses up and briefly massaged the bridge of his nose. "You know, Hugh, some would say we're losing," he said quietly. Then he reset his glasses, picked up his pen, and resumed jotting notes.

Hugh's head snapped up. "What did you say?"

Dr. Taylor stopped writing and studied him. "Does it bother you to hear me say that some people feel we're losing the war?"

"We're not losing," he said, emphasizing the first word while pointing at himself.

Dr. Taylor pressed his lips together. "All right, but with the coalition pulling out and the Taliban still there . . . well, the problem isn't really solved, is it? Would you call that winning?"

The two men locked eyes. Hugh opened his mouth, and Dr. Taylor held up a hand. "I'm going to push you on this, Hugh, because it's important. Are you arguing from an emotional or intellectual standpoint?"

"From a professional standpoint," he said, spitting out the words. "And as a professional soldier, I can tell you the military didn't lose jack shit in Afghanistan. Every time we fought the Taliban, we handed them their asses." He pointed at Dr. Taylor. "You want to talk about losing the war, then talk about the loss of political will, the total failure of politicians and the public to think about anything but themselves. We were winning."

Dr. Taylor removed his glasses. "I understand," he said. "But what of everything that remains broken? You may have won all the engagements, but that doesn't mean you won the war. The same was said of Vietnam, after all."

He leaned forward. "What about the schools we built? Roads we constructed? Medical clinics we ran?" he said. "Too bad stuff like the model village approach to counterinsurgency isn't front-page material like a dead soldier or a suicide bomber."

"Is it not a little more complex than that?"

"You're fucking right it is," he said, voice shaking. "You want to know who lost the fucking war? Go ask your local politician. We were supposed to buy time, and we did. Every second purchased with flesh and blood, over and over. We brought security so the international community could help the Afghans sort their shit out, but did that happen? No fucking way. Because our country didn't really give a fuck about some shithole on the other side of the world, only that our army was off making us proud." He sprang to his feet and began pacing.

Dr. Taylor held up a hand, shifting in his chair. "It sounds like you feel betrayed."

He whirled around. "You fucking armchair generals are all the same, you never listen," he said, shaking his head. "You say you support the troops but have no fucking clue what that means. Instead, you follow whatever the media says like a bunch of sheep. But to have the balls to sit there and tell me we lost? Like I threw in the towel? That's fucking bullshit."

"I know this is hard—"

He growled through clenched teeth. "What do you know about hard?"

Dr. Taylor spread his hands. "Hugh, I—"

"Let me tell you about hard," he said, punctuating his words with jabs of a finger. "Hard is driving a known ambush route every day wondering if it's your turn. Hard is picking up body parts after an explosion, or lining up outside a hospital to give blood so the docs can work on some guy who's bleeding out. Hard is—no forget it. We're done." He stormed toward the door.

"You're right," Dr. Taylor said to his retreating back. "I don't know about those things, but I can listen. I'm good at that."

He flung open the door and paused briefly on the threshold. He glanced back at Dr. Taylor, who was standing, one hand held out. It was like the guy thought he could save Hugh, if only he would take his hand.

"I didn't mean any offense," Dr. Taylor said. "I felt you were ready to be challenged as part of the treatment process."

He remained motionless, one foot out the door.

"I'm human, Hugh, I make mistakes," Dr. Taylor said, edging closer. "But I can help you, I know I can. Come back, please." He motioned to the couch.

He rubbed his face. *More talk, great.* He balled his hands into fists. All these words, never making anything better, only worse. His heart pounded, trying to jackhammer its way out of his chest. Was it going to give out? Maybe. So hard to concentrate with the fury raging. Soon he'd be like a runaway gun, firing by itself and too hot to control. And how did a good soldier handle that situation? Point the gun in a safe direction and break the ammo belt. No, more talking wouldn't help, not now. He had to break the link. Get out. Now.

Saying nothing, he abruptly turned and strode into the lobby, grabbing his coat and blowing out the door.

❯ ❯ ❯

Hugh gunned his truck, tires spinning as he fishtailed onto the road and squealed away from Dr. Taylor's office. There weren't many cars out, but light rain was causing the ones that were on the road to drive slowly, forcing him to hit the brakes hard and often. Good thing the meeting had been for seven o'clock. Sitting in rush-hour traffic would have been a bridge too far.

He was being ridiculous. Dr. Taylor had been apologizing; it was only some stupid technique. Still, that was logic. Right now, logic only inflamed his rage. The primal, reptilian part of his brain was on the verge of taking over, and his best option was to get away, deprive it of targets upon which it could vent. Let the wrath consume itself, then he'd think about Taylor's words. And try to forget this was happening more often. He took the next on-ramp, headlights reflecting off the wet asphalt, obscuring the white lines dividing the road lanes. Suppressing an interior plea for caution, he accelerated into the turn, forcing the pedal to the floor as a surge of horsepower pressed him into his seat. When the road straightened, he jerked the steering wheel sharply to the left without looking, wedging his way into traffic. Engine roaring, he spared a glance in the rear-view mirror. Behind, a blue car swerved, projector headlights swinging side to side as the driver struggled for control. His lips tightened, then he looked to the road.

Sorry, bud. Muttering, he reached for his backpack on the passenger seat, rummaging blindly until his hand wrapped around the comforting tin of Copenhagen. He removed the tin, cupping it in his hands while he braced the steering wheel with a knee. Pinching a large wad of tobacco, he stuffed it into his lip, then replaced the lid and tossed the puck into the center console. Trembling slightly as the nicotine penetrated his gums, he grabbed an empty bottle, raised it to his lips and sent a stream of black, viscous liquid running down the inside. *Better.*

He wedged the bottle between his legs and cast a look in the rearview mirror. Out of the sea of headlights, one set of brighter beams was growing bigger, causing him to squint. Was that the vehicle he'd cut off? Checking his speed—over 100 mph and climbing—he eased off the accelerator, then cranked the radio, catching the start of the hourly news. He focused on the broadcast, anything to drown out Dr. Taylor's voice. There'd been another shooting rampage somewhere, same story as always: some disgruntled person killing inno-cents with a high-powered rifle until turning the weapon on themselves. *Not exactly helping.*

"What makes somebody think that's the answer?" he said distractedly, attention on the fast-approaching headlights in his rearview mirror. As the vehicle moved onto his left and pulled even with him, he glanced over. It was a blue Subaru WRX, quite possibly the same car he'd cut off. Well, the guy had a reason to be pissed, but so what? He couldn't do much about it now.

He shifted his gaze back to the road. When the Subaru continued to pace him, he looked over again. The driver, barely visible through lightly tinted windows, was holding his right arm extended toward Hugh, fist clenched and giving a thumbs-up. *What the hell?* As he watched, the driver retracted his hand and dragged his outstretched thumb across his neck, mimicking the slitting of his own throat.

"You need help," Hugh said. *Trust me.* The embers of anger he'd been smothering began to fan up, and he looked away, reaching for the spit bottle. In his periphery, the Subaru accelerated, overtaking him. *Good riddance.* He looked down, unscrewed the lid from the bottle, and brought it to his lips. A flicker of movement drew his eyes back to the road; the Subaru was veering in front of him. A tingle ran up his spine. "What—"

The Subaru's brake lights flashed bright red at the same time bluish-black smoke appeared at the car's rear tires.

"Fuck," he said, slamming on the brakes and grabbing the steering wheel with both hands, the open spit bottle dropping into his lap. Tires shrieked as he wrestled to control the truck, whose back end threatened to come to the front. For one nausea-inducing second, he was weightless, and then he was spinning the steering wheel, somehow keeping all four wheels on the road.

When the truck steadied, he scanned for the Subaru, spying it drawing away ahead. He reached for the gas, foot kicking the spit bottle and spewing tarry liquid over his boot. "Goddamn it!" He snatched up the bottle and jammed it in a cup holder, stringy spit covering his fingers. Wiping his hands on his pants, he floored the accelerator, and the engine roared to life. In seconds, the distance between the two vehicles began to narrow.

"Let's see what you've got," he said, eyes glued to the Subaru like a heat-seeking missile. As the distance closed, the blue car began weaving through traffic, sending ripples of red brake lights among nearby cars. He followed, throwing around the truck's greater size and forcing other drivers to make room, overtaking them at will, even on the inside shoulder, gray concrete slabs whistling by, inches from his side mirror. Only a few car lengths separated hunter and hunted.

The Subaru's brake lights flashed for an instant, harsh red in the darkening night. *Not this time.* He gripped the steering wheel tighter, leaving the accelerator on the mat. As the distance vanished, there was a slight shudder when the front bumper of the Raptor nudged the Subaru's rear. Lips pressed into a grim smile, he eased off the pedal, holding position a car length or two behind. *Had enough?*

Around them, traffic slowed as more vehicles appeared, taillights shining like a field of neon poppies. The Subaru lurched to the right, swerving across three lanes toward an upcoming off-ramp. He followed, tossing the truck after his quarry like he was possessed. As the left tire dug in, the truck's center of balance shifted sickeningly and the weightless sensation returned, but again, he kept control, by some miracle making the exit.

The Subaru was nearly three hundred feet in front, approaching the green traffic lights of a major intersection, when the brake lights came on.

What's he doing? Hugh eased off the pedal and scanned the road in front. An orange hand blinked beside a countdown timer; the tricky bastard was going to slow roll the light and let traffic separate them. He shook his head and sped up, hands tightening on the steering wheel.

As the light turned yellow, the Subaru sped through the intersection, making it across at the same time the light changed to red. On the cross streets, cars paused, then slowly began to roll forward. Gritting his teeth, Hugh flashed his headlights on and off and sailed into the gap. To each side, cars screeched to a halt and horns blared all around him, but the noise quickly faded as he gained on the Subaru.

He played cat and mouse with the Subaru for the next five minutes, and then the car turned onto a nearly deserted side street. Hugh glanced at the street sign as he followed. A cul-de-sac. *Perfect.* A surge of satisfaction rushed through him, the thrill of seeing one's enemy walk unsuspecting into a kill zone.

In the fading twilight, the Subaru drove on, the skeletons of half-constructed houses watching from under the yellowish-orange glow of streetlights. In the light rain, the street had become a morass of mud and dirt. Hugh slowed. What would the other driver do? He didn't wait long for an answer.

When the street widened into a circle, the Subaru's brake lights illuminated and the front wheels cranked to the left, spinning in the muck and sending up rooster tails of mud. Instead of turning the vehicle, the wheels plowed straight forward, unable to find traction. The brake lights flickered on and off, and then the front wheels hit the curb and the car shuddered to a stop.

Hugh closed the distance, bumper touching bumper as the Subaru's white reversing lights came on. Seconds later, the lights extinguished. Smiling, he put the truck in park and placed both hands on the steering wheel, breathing deeply. *What a rush!* His heart was racing, thumping in his ears. After a few breaths, panic stabbed him in the gut. *Holy shit—that was stupid.* His hand fell to the gear selector, searching for reverse, when the driver's door of the Subaru opened and a man got out.

The man was tall, at least six and a half feet, although the dim light and his slouching posture made it difficult to be sure.

He wore a loose hoodie that shrouded his face. He stalked to the front of the vehicle, examining where it had hit the curb, then strutted toward Hugh, shoulders swaying bizarrely from side to side.

Hugh frowned. Was this supposed to be intimidating? Despite the man's height, his pencil-thin frame couldn't have weighed more than 180 pounds soaking wet. He put the truck in reverse and looked over his shoulder. Then a slight tremor shook the truck, and his eyes shot forward.

"Did you just kick my truck?" Hugh said. The tendrils of doubt that had been urging him to leave shriveled on the vine as his smoldering anger fanned up. This punk needed to be put in his place.

The man kicked the truck again and puffed out his chest.

Hugh removed his hand from the gearshift and got out.

"The fuck's your problem?" the man said.

Hugh deliberately shut the door while he took stock of the man, whom he'd designated as Hoodie. Under the flat brim of Hoodie's baseball cap, a frowning face covered in a thin beard glared back, lips pursed. Hoodie played a good game, but something was missing. What? Hugh stepped forward, boots splashing in the muck.

"I said, what the fuck is your problem?"

Hugh kept walking. Hoodie paused for a moment, then retreated, jamming his hands in the pockets of his hoodie and jutting his right hand forward.

Time slowed as Hugh oriented on the threat, the smell of wet wood and mud drifting from a nearby construction site. The pitter-patter of raindrops falling on the hood of the truck filled his ears as he took in Hoodie's stance, the way he held his body, his right hand, even the frown on his face. His body screamed for action. Now. If Hoodie had a weapon, he needed to move fast, gain the element of surprise. But something didn't add up. He needed more time to assess.

"Why don't you calm down?" Hugh said, holding up his hands with palms forward even as he relentlessly edged closer. *Get him talking.*

"Why don't you go fuck yourself?" Hoodie said, taking two quick steps back. "Stay away from me." He jabbed his right hand again.

Hugh turned slightly and spat, then zeroed in on Hoodie while he continued forward, step after step. Hoodie's posturing had disappeared—no puffed-up chest now—but it was Hoodie's eyes that drew Hugh's attention, rolling in their sockets. They said there was no threat. They weren't killer's eyes, not like some of the Afghani mujahideen, men with eyes so black and emotionless—abysses instead of windows. This man, a kid really, would've been eaten for lunch by men like those.

"You can still get out of this without getting hurt," he said calmly. *Fat chance.*

"Fuck you, man, you cut me—" Hoodie said, then the heel of his still-retreating right foot caught against the curb. An O appeared on his lips, and then he was stumbling backward, arms windmilling through the air.

Hugh pounced. He jammed his knee into Hoodie's solar plexus, then ground the man down into the muddy gutter. Hoodie gasped, and his head jerked up only to be met by a sharp jab from Hugh's right hand, crumpling his nose. As Hoodie fell back, Hugh grabbed his shoulder, flipping him on his side and applying an arm bar along the way. Now seated astride Hoodie, Hugh wedged a heel into the man's throat, increasing the pressure until Hoodie gagged.

"Show me your hand," Hugh said. When there was no response, he applied more pressure to the arm bar. "I won't ask again."

Hoodie's feet thrashed as he flopped about until his free arm extended in front of him on the ground, palm empty. His hat had come off, and his face was covered in mud.

Gritting his teeth, Hugh tightened the arm bar even more. "Now stop moving, or I'll break it. Then the other one."

Hoodie froze.

"Good."

Reaching into Hoodie's pockets, Hugh recovered a chocolate bar from one side and a wallet from the other. A wave of relief flooded through him, and he briefly relaxed the arm hold. Just as quickly, the wave subsided, replaced by the ever-present anger. Snarling, he pulled his boot off Hoodie's throat, then reached down and grabbed the man by the lapels, lifting his torso off the muddy ground.

"A chocolate bar?" he said, his voice shaking. "You threatened me with a chocolate bar?"

"Fuck you, you piece of shit," Hoodie said in a raspy voice. With a grunt, he flailed with one arm, trying to hit Hugh's face, but only succeeding in cuffing an ear.

Hugh drove a knee downward into one of Hoodie's thighs, and the man went rigid, his hands grabbing Hugh's wrists as he gasped against the pain. Still holding the lapels, Hugh dragged Hoodie to his feet, jammed his fingers into the other man's neck and made a fist around Hoodie's windpipe. Was this why he'd risked his life for his country? Guttural hacking came from Hoodie's throat, and his eyes began rolling back in their sockets. Hugh blinked, then shook his head. What was he doing? Summoning all his effort, he forced his hands open.

Hoodie slumped. "You're crazy, man," he said, hands rubbing his throat.

"Shut up," Hugh said, stalking forward, driving Hoodie before him. His blood boiled. *Smash him. Destroy him.* He took a few more steps, then stopped, glancing behind Hoodie. *Get a grip.*

Hoodie stumbled and fell, then twisted to look behind, finally seeing the edge of an open basement excavation, nearly ten feet to the bottom. He collapsed to his knees at the edge of the pit.

Hugh clenched his jaw and retracted his lips. "Get up."

"No," Hoodie said, the words almost a whisper. Snot running down his face, Hoodie tucked himself into the fetal position in the mud.

Hugh stared at him like he was an insect, then sent a stream of tobacco juice onto Hoodie's face. "I said, get up."

Instead, Hoodie crawled away from the edge of the hole into a spot of dim orange light from a nearby street lamp. Hugh paused. What the hell was he doing? Hoodie was only a boy, hardly more than a teen. And what if someone came by, what if even right now some unseen observer was calling the police? Shivering, he took two slow steps backward, nausea coming across him. He walked faster, retreating toward his truck.

When he reached his truck, Hugh doubled over and vomited, noxious green bile flecked with black tobacco that sprayed his boots. Wiping his mouth, he took a last look at where Hoodie lay, a dark shape against the muddy ground. What had he been about to do? Nausea gripped him again, and he dry heaved, then spat and got into the truck. He started the engine, turned around, then sped off, mud and dirt spraying behind him.

As he drove, he couldn't stop checking the rearview mirror. *Please get up.* No movement. Emptiness formed in his stomach, and he looked back at the road, steering out of the cul-de-sac and toward the highway. The longer he drove, the more the emptiness grew, threatening to overwhelm him.

He stood on the brakes, stopping the truck so fast his body thrust forward against the locked seat belt. Reaching up, he grabbed the rearview mirror and turned it on himself, pressing his face close so all he could see was his own eyes. Turning his head from side to side, he stared. Whose eyes were those looking back at him? Shuddering, he let his foot off the brake and drove away. He wasn't sure anymore.

CHAPTER 13

"Loser buys drinks?" Daryl asked. He was standing on the firing line clutching his Glock pistol in front of his chest.

"Sure," Hugh said, smiling. *I missed this.*

Daryl had called the day after his run-in with Hoodie, inviting him for a day on the range at a shooting club outside Kingston. He'd leaped at the opportunity. He'd had a few reservations—the whole issue with Laura bothered him—but the chance to hold a gun again was too good to pass up. As it turned out, aside from the summerlike heat forcing sweat to drip into his eyes, it was the perfect day. He looked at his friend. "Ready?"

Daryl nodded back, the pistol held like a natural extension of his arm, then wiped his brow and looked downrange, all business. Crouching slightly, he inhaled deeply, then exhaled under control, air hissing between his lips as he leaned forward into a shooting stance, wobbling slightly on his prosthetic limbs.

"Up!" Hugh ordered from his own firing position about ten feet away. Ignoring Daryl, he raised his own pistol, a Sig Sauer

P226 Daryl had loaned him, took a sight picture on the target ten yards to his front, and squeezed the trigger. When the pistol went off, it surprised him; he'd been concentrating on his trigger manipulation. After a small pause, he carefully reset his shooting position, digging his feet into the gravel, then focused on his next engagement, repeating the process. As he fired, holes appeared like magic in the paper target, two cartoonish zombies reaching for a small boy clutching a teddy bear.

Beside him, Daryl shot without pause, the concussions making a staccato rhythm as precise as a metronome.

He concentrated on his target. *Forget Daryl.* After fifteen rounds, the pistol's slide stuck to the rear, and he checked the chamber—out of bullets. He unloaded the magazine and performed a safety check, then inserted the pistol into the holster on his right hip. When he looked up, Daryl was staring at him, pistol already holstered. Removing his ear protection, Hugh started walking toward the targets, gravel crunching under his boots.

"If this was the real thing, you wouldn't have time for deliberate shots like that," Daryl said, following him downrange. "Better to get more rounds off. Fill 'em so full of lead they drop under the weight."

"They won't drop if you don't hit them," he said, pointing at Daryl's target. "Hope you brought your wallet."

Daryl looked at his target. "Shit." Holes were everywhere, including one in the child's teddy bear. By contrast, all of Hugh's shots were generally in the right area, even if not all of them had hit the zombies. Spitting, Daryl grabbed a new target, this one a group of zombies reaching for a buxom young woman, and began stapling it over the old target.

Hugh chuckled quietly, then grabbed a new target for himself and waited for Daryl to finish with the stapler. When fresh targets were up, they headed back to the firing line.

At the ten-yard point, Daryl turned to face the targets. "Even a shitty day on the range . . ."

"Beats a day in garrison," he finished, grinning beside him. "You miss it much?"

"Every day," Daryl said as he stared downrange, focusing on some point far beyond where the targets stood. "Even this kind of sucks, to be honest. Only reminds me what I lost."

Hugh's grin melted away, and he looked down, fiddling with his magazines. What did one say to someone who couldn't do what they loved? Even worse, wasn't he in the same boat as Daryl? He shook his head. His current job wasn't great, but he still had the option of going back to a unit—even if chances looked slimmer every day.

Beside him, Daryl blinked, and then his eyes hardened, crow's-feet deepening as his face tightened. He coughed, then looked at Hugh. "Enough about me, what about you? This helping your treatment?"

"Not sure, but I'll take it," he said, staring at the ground. He sighed. "You know, I'd hoped things would be sorted out by now, but they seem to be getting worse."

"PTSD tends to do that."

Hugh looked earnestly at Daryl. "I just want things back to normal. Get my life back, you know?"

"Yeah." Daryl held Hugh's gaze. "I felt that way when I lost my legs."

"You never told me that story."

"You never asked."

A lone gust of wind blew down the firing line, stirring up a tiny dust devil that veered drunkenly toward the targets before hitting a patch of grass and falling apart.

"I remember waking up in the hospital. Some nurse was running off at the mouth about the surgery, technical terms that didn't tell me shit." Daryl tugged on his shooting gloves, flexing his fingers to get a better fit. "I asked if my balls were still there, and she turned red. I thought she was going to pass out. So I asked if I still had my legs, and some doctor jumped in, told me they'd had to amputate—below the knees, thank Christ—but my package was safe and sound." He grabbed his groin, giving it a small tug. "At least the doc gave it to me cut-and-dry, though. Bad news don't get better with time."

"Damn," Hugh said. What else could he say? He grabbed a fresh magazine from the holster at his hip.

"I still feel them sometimes, mostly late at night," Daryl said, lifting a foot off the ground and staring at the metal appendage visible above the white running shoe. "Like it was a bad dream and I could jump out of bed and walk around like anybody else." He looked a second longer, then stomped on the ground, a small cloud of dust forming around his foot. "But I can't. And neither can you."

Hugh paused, magazine in one hand, pistol in the other. "What do you mean?"

"What I mean is, there's no going back to normal."

Hugh cocked his head to the side. "Come again?"

"That normal life you want back so badly," Daryl said, drawing his pistol, "it's gone." He loaded a magazine and pulled back the slide, holding it to the rear. "Full recovery is impossible. It's a sci-un-tif-ic fact." He released the slide, and it slid forward with a smooth, mechanical chunk.

Hugh shook his head and returned to seating the magazine on his gun. "That's not true," he said. "Lots of guys recover." But hadn't Dr. Taylor told him the exact same thing? His grip tightened on the pistol, and he fumbled the magazine.

"Lots of guys learn to cope," Daryl said, his tone that of an instructor correcting a pupil. "Nobody fully recovers, not from serious PTSD."

"Is that right?" he said, spitting out the words. The magazine dropped, and he stooped to pick it up, swearing. When he stood, he went back to loading. Finally, the magazine slid home, and he jammed the gun in its holster, then settled his hands on his hips. "So why are you telling me this? You think you're doing me some kind of favor?"

"Now those," Daryl said, his voice patronizing, "are great questions." He turned to Hugh. "See, your problem is you still think you can be the guy you were. But you can't."

"Oh yeah?" Hugh said, his chin jutting out. *Enough.* "Is that what you tell yourself when you beat up your wife?"

"Why? Thinking about using it for when you're beating up Liz?"

He stiffened. "That's different."

"Is it?" Daryl said, curling his bottom lip. "We always hurt the ones we love, don't we?" His face hardened. "But you of all people should know how useless it is to fight the anger. When it comes, you can't resist. That only makes it worse."

"Shut up," he said, his voice a whisper. Daryl was right; he was no different.

Daryl's eyes narrowed. "See, once you accept your old life is gone, you can get on with replacing what you used to live for with something new. It's called transference. Maybe your therapist guy mentioned it?" He paused. "Take that rage and focus it someplace else, make it useful."

"Is that what you did?"

"In a way," Daryl said. He gestured at his prosthetic limbs with the barrel of the Sig Sauer. "I decided to make the people who did this to me pay."

He threw his hands up. "Good luck. The insurgents who did that are probably dead already."

"You don't get it, do you?" Daryl said, crouching into a shooting stance. "I never said insurgents. They never did this to me, not really. They were following orders, like me. No, some-body else is responsible." With one hand, he reached up and dropped his ear defenders into position, then raised his pistol.

Hugh hurriedly pulled down his own ear defenders, almost missing Daryl's next words.

"I'm talking about the people who sent us to war." Then Daryl was squeezing the trigger, the sharp cracks echoing off the berms of the shooting range. When he was done, he hol-stered his pistol and looked at Hugh. As if on cue, they lifted their ear defenders at the same time.

"You missed again," he said, nodding downrange, where all Daryl's rounds had hit the paper woman fleeing the zombies.

"Did I?" Daryl said, eyes never leaving Hugh's.

He glanced from the target to Daryl. What the hell was he talking about? Had he aimed for the civilian? The blood drained from his face.

Daryl laughed. "Stop," he said. "I'm not talking about kill-ing anybody, I'm talking about targeting people through pro-test. Civil disobedience. Political noncooperation. Veterans in this country have a voice, it's time they used it."

"That's subversion," he said. "And it's illegal."

"It's retribution," Daryl snapped, eyes flashing. "People think harder about what type of phone to buy than about send-ing soldiers to war. They want to make the hard decisions, but accept none of the consequences. That needs to change."

"And who's going to change it? You?" he said. "How do you plan to do that?"

"Fucked if I know," Daryl said, ripping off his baseball hat and throwing it on the ground. They faced off in the heat, the sun beating down relentlessly. "You got a better idea?"

Hugh's breath came in angry gasps as he glared at Daryl. His friend's cheeks were scarlet, red veins crisscrossed his nose, and his loose shirt, damp and clingy in the sweltering heat, highlighted a gut straining over the top of his pants. Had he really looked at Daryl since they'd been here? The man was in bad shape. His breathing slowed with the revelation, his heart going out for his friend.

"Thing is, most days I'm so angry it's all I can do to control it," Daryl said. He stooped awkwardly and grabbed his hat, then straightened. He slapped the hat against his leg, raising a small cloud of dust. "Sometimes I can't. I'm not proud of that, but that's reality. That's why I need to focus on something else, something bigger. If I didn't, I don't know what I'd do. Probably kill myself." He snorted, then replaced the hat on his head. "Shit, enough of this heart-to-heart crap. We good?"

He nodded. "We're good."

"Sweet. Let's break out the heavy artillery."

They replaced the targets, then walked to the three-hundred-yard line, where a corrugated steel shooting canopy covered the firing point, offering welcome shade. Hugh sat down at a picnic table beneath the metal cover, and Daryl went to his car, returning with an Armalite AR-15 carbine.

He whistled. "What's that?"

Daryl sat across from him, smiling. "Bought it as a present to myself when I got kicked out." He cradled the weapon like a child. "It's got all the bells and whistles. Nightforce four-by-twenty-four scope, front pistol grip, collapsible stock, even some ten-round magazines."

"Aren't those illegal?"

"Yeah, it was tough, but I did it. Don't ask me how," Daryl said.

"I probably don't want to know anyways."

Daryl smiled wider and handed over the rifle. "Take a look."

He whistled again as he turned the weapon over in his hands. "It's nice. How does it fire?"

"Like a dream," Daryl said with a proud smile. "No kick at all. Want to try it out?"

"Absolutely."

Grabbing a couple of boxes of ammunition, he accompanied Daryl to the hundred-yard firing line. Daryl fired first, going through two magazines; then he passed the rifle to Hugh for a turn.

"It fires nice," he said after his second go-round. He grabbed one of the empty magazines and helped Daryl reload.

"I know," Daryl said. "Want to see who can get the best grouping? Might be unfair . . ."

Hugh smiled. "You're on."

An hour and several competitions later, they ran dry on ammunition.

"Let's take a break," Daryl said, standing up after losing a competition to Hugh. "We need more ammo anyways." He did a safety check on the AR-15, then turned and began walking back to the shooting canopy at the three-hundred-yard line. Hugh followed.

He wiped his brow as he walked, drinking in the smell of brass and gunpowder on his fingers. When had being tired last felt so good?

At the three-hundred-yard line, Daryl laid the AR-15 down on the picnic table, then opened a small cooler. From inside he removed two Cokes, tiny droplets of melting ice glistening on the cans. Tossing a can to Hugh, he briefly held his own to his forehead, then popped the lid and took a long mouthful.

Hugh followed suit, drinking deeply. "That hits the spot," he said, exhaling in satisfaction.

"Smoke 'em if you got 'em," Daryl said as he fished for a pack of cigarettes from his shirt pocket. Pulling one out, he flipped it end over end on the picnic table, sliding the white dart between his thumb and index finger, then repeating.

Hugh glanced over, smirking. "You can't smoke here, dip-shit," he said, voice artificially deep as he imitated a sergeant they'd served under as young privates. "Too close to the ammu-nition point, don't you know that?"

"So charge me," Daryl said, his voice emotionless as the cigarette continued making rotations between his fingers.

Hugh pulled out his Copenhagen and took a pinch of tobacco, then jammed it in his lip.

"Remember that kid? Burnsy?" Daryl said abruptly, study-ing the cigarette as he slowly flipped it, running his fingers from the filter to the tobacco end. "He was in our platoon in 2002?"

"Sure," he said, spitting in the gravel between his feet, his saliva long and stringy and clinging to his lip. "Good kid, tried hard, not too smart. Why do you ask?"

Daryl didn't answer right away. "I always think of him this time of year," he said. "It's been five years, can you believe it?"

Shit. How could he have forgotten? "I'm sorry," he said. "I should have remembered." Burnsy—Corporal Derek Burns—had been one of Daryl's subordinates when he'd been killed by friendly fire around this time five years ago. A red flush crept up his neck into his cheeks.

"That's all right," Daryl said. He lit the cigarette and took a deep drag. "Listen, I think I'm done for the day. You good?"

"Sure," he said, nodding.

"We can clean up when I'm done with this smoke."

"No worries," he said. "What are you doing the rest of the day?"

"Supposed to meet Laura."

"When?"

Daryl checked his watch. "Ten minutes ago."

He sat forward. "What? Why didn't you say something?"

Daryl shrugged and took another drag. "I don't really care if I'm late," he said. "I'd rather be shooting anyways. Not sure when I'll get another chance."

"Yeah, but Laura's going to be pissed," he said, gulping the rest of his drink. "You get out of here, I'll clean up." He started to stand.

"Laura's leaving me," Daryl said in a monotone voice.

"What?" he said, half standing.

"Said she wants a trial separation or some fucking thing. That's what we're supposed to be talking about," Daryl said, butting his cigarette on the sole of his boot and immediately lighting another.

"I'm sorry."

Daryl coughed, then looked at the ground. "Yeah, well, it's not like I don't deserve it."

"You want to talk about it?"

"Not really," Daryl said. "It is what it is." He sat silently until his second cigarette was done, then butted it out on the table. "Might as well clean up."

Working together, he and Daryl stripped the targets and gathered the empty brass casings from each place they'd fired. Within twenty minutes, the cleanup was done. While Daryl smoked another cigarette beside the vehicles, Hugh policed under the shooting canopy one last time.

"I think that's everything," he said, tossing a sandbag of brass into the bed of his truck. "I'll drop this off at the range hut on the way out." He looked at Daryl, whose eyes were blood-shot. "What's wrong?"

Daryl took a nervous drag from his cigarette. "I need a favor," he said, exhaling smoke through his nostrils.

"Anything," Hugh said, concern in his voice.

"I wouldn't ask if it wasn't important."

"I know, what can I do?"

"You gotta take my guns."

Hugh swallowed. "What?" he said, forcing out the question.

"You gotta take 'em," Daryl said, taking a last drag and flicking the butt. "I don't trust myself around them."

"What does that mean?" The last thing he needed was guns around the house. *Elizabeth'll kill me.* "You said you didn't want to hurt anyone."

"I can't have them around, not with Laura leaving me," Daryl said, his voice shaking. "She was always the one to calm me down."

He stared at Daryl. What could he do? The thought of taking the guns made him cold all over, but Daryl looked like a beaten puppy. What kind of friend would refuse? But if it was the right thing to do, why did he have goose bumps? "All right," he said quietly. "I'll hold them for you. Only until you're ready to take them back."

After a few seconds, Daryl nodded slightly. "Thanks." He pulled the AR-15 from the backseat of his car and handed it over.

"Where's the carrying case?" Hugh asked, looking into the AR-15's chamber to perform a safety check.

"About that," Daryl said, his face strained. "I've only got a case for the Sig." He smiled in a rare apology. "I sold the others about a year ago."

"What?" he said, looking uncomprehendingly from Daryl to the guns. "Seriously?" That could be a problem.

"I know what you're thinking," Daryl said. "And you're right. It's a great big shit sandwich. Put as much mustard on it as you want, it'll still taste like shit. Sorry man."

He sighed. Was there another solution? Not really. He carefully laid the AR-15 on the floor of his truck behind the driver's seat, covering it with a ratty gray fire blanket. The Sig Sauer got packed in its carrying case and placed on the passenger-side floor, while the other pistol, the Glock, went in the glove compartment underneath the vehicle manual. The magazines and leftover ammunition went into the center console, under the seat, wherever he could put it where it wouldn't stand out. He didn't know what he'd do when he got home—Elizabeth hated guns—but he'd think of something on the drive.

When he was done, he turned to look at Daryl. "I'll take good care of them," he said, then cleared his throat. "You'll probably reconsider before I even get off the range."

"I don't think so."

"It'll be okay." *This is wrong, on all sorts of levels.*

"We'll see." Daryl clasped his hand and pulled him close, wrapping his free arm around Hugh's back. "Thanks for coming. I mean it."

He blinked rapidly, eyes suddenly moist, then released Daryl and took a step back. He looked at the sky, the ground, anywhere but at his friend. "Listen, you need anything else? Want me to come with you?"

Daryl shook his head. "No, I'm good," he said. "You've already done enough. Besides, Liz is gonna flip if she sees you with those guns. Feel free to blame me."

"Don't worry, I will," he said, unable to stop a sad smile from appearing. "Good luck with Laura. You guys will work things out."

"We won't," Daryl said, hobbling to his car. "Like I said, it is what it is." He leaned heavily on the roof of his car, then maneuvered his bulky frame into the driver's seat. Pulling the door shut, he fumbled with his keys before finally getting the car started. He put the car in gear, glanced at Hugh, and gave a small wave before slowly rolling away, dust kicking up as he drove off.

Hugh waited until Daryl's car had disappeared down the winding road that led away from the range. When the car was out of sight, he stirred, reaching into a pocket for his keys. Stepping onto the truck's running board, he paused, then turned his head to scan through the back window. Everything was good, the fire blanket covered the entire back floor in undulating mounds. *This is no big deal.* So why the tightness in his chest?

❦ ❦ ❦

"Goddamn it," Hugh said, smacking the steering wheel. He'd been stuck behind the same four vehicles for a half hour, led by a rusty blue pickup truck pulling a horse trailer that struggled to make the posted speed limit. There'd been few chances to overtake on the twisting single-lane highway cutting through the Canadian Shield, and the times he'd tried, there was always a car coming from the opposite direction.

"There's no rush," he said, taking a deep breath. And it was true. Until he'd gotten jammed in this impromptu convoy, it had been a nice drive through old-growth forest, cozy farms, and peaceful villages, like a real-life car commercial. Besides, the last thing he needed was to get pulled over for speeding.

He glanced at the center console then back at the road. He couldn't see the guns, but they were there all the same. The sooner they were out of his truck, the better, even if his plan to get them into the house was mostly based on the hope that Elizabeth wasn't there when he got home. If he could get them into the garage, he'd be okay. Still, the first thing he needed to do was drive carefully and not do anything stupid. He repeated the thought like a mantra. But the longer he stared at the bumper of the silver Toyota Corolla a car length in front, the more it mocked him. "Someone, please, pass that goddamn truck," he pleaded under his breath, but nobody had so far, despite numerous chances.

The highway straightened, and he pressed on the accelerator, edging into the center of the road to scan ahead. He had a small window, but the cars in front were packed end to end behind the blue pickup. He'd either have to pass them all or risk getting caught halfway up. *Screw it.* Stomping on the pedal, he veered into the opposing lane, the truck's engine roaring as it dropped gears. No sooner had he pulled even with the rear of the Corolla than a pair of yellow headlights crested a hill in the distance, shimmering in the heat radiating off the highway.

"Shit," he said, slamming on the brakes and pulling back in behind the Corolla. This was getting ridiculous.

Coming round the next corner, a sign with a dual-pronged arrow appeared on the side of the road. Finally, a passing lane. His heart pumped faster as the pickup truck leading the convoy reached the point where the lanes divided, but his elation was short-lived. As each subsequent vehicle hit the dual lanes, they pulled into the inside, including the silver Corolla.

"You've got to be kidding me," he said, tailgating the Corolla so close there was barely any space between their bumpers. When the silver car abruptly pulled into the outside lane, he accelerated, glaring at the driver as he raced past. He looked back at the road in time to jam on the brakes and prevent a collision with the next car, a blue Volkswagen Golf that was passing the horse trailer.

"Come on," he said, hands tightening on the steering wheel, knuckles turning white. The road was running out, and he wanted, needed, to get past that damned pickup.

Slowly, the Golf overtook the pickup, then pulled into the outside lane as the road entered a gentle curve. Halfway through the turn, a sign warned the passing lane would end in less than a quarter mile.

"Now or never," he said and accelerated, a surge of power pressing him into his seat. On the console, the speedometer steadily moved around the dial with no signs of slowing. In seconds, he'd passed the truck and the Golf. The next car, a red MINI Cooper, was within striking distance. After that, the road would be free and clear. Adrenaline rocked through him as he kept the pedal floored. This is what the truck had been made for.

He caught the MINI as the dual lanes began to converge, hugging the center of the highway and overtaking the tiny vehicle like it was parked. A whoop of joy escaped him as he burned past, swerving back into his lane to narrowly avoid an oncoming car. He glanced in the rearview mirror, where the vehicles were rapidly getting smaller, then let off the pedal, the roar of the engine giving way to a soft rumbling. Was it his imagination, or did the truck sound disappointed? Smiling, he revved the engine, hugging the outside of the road into the next turn. Then the road straightened, lengthening his sight line. About half a mile up, parked perpendicular to the road, was a dark-blue sedan. *Shit.*

He hit the brakes, and the seat belt locked up, digging into his chest. Too late; he was still way over the speed limit when he passed the car, unmistakably an unmarked police cruiser. His heart sank. A flash of light in the rearview mirror drew his attention. Behind, blue and red lights.

He craned around to look in the backseat, confirming the blanket was still in place atop the AR-15. It was there—screaming that a rifle was underneath—but there wasn't much he could do now. He checked behind him, where other drivers were pulling onto the small gravel shoulder, letting the patrol car pass. His eyes flitted back to the road. A turnoff was coming up; maybe he could outrun the cop on the back roads. *No way.* The cop probably knew these roads better than he did. Besides, he was out of time; the patrol car was right behind him.

With a sinking desperation in his stomach, he slowed and tucked one wheel onto the shoulder, like he was making room for the car to pass. Slim chance, but maybe the cop was after someone else. No such luck; the patrol car closed and stayed behind him.

At the next clear stretch of road, he pulled over and stopped. The police car followed. Moments later, all the cars he'd overtaken drove by, passengers gawking. *Sanctimonious fucks.* He pressed his lips together and waited, watching in the rearview mirror. When the policeman exited his car, he placed his hands on the steering wheel.

The cop was a beast, bigger even than Hugh's own six foot three, and he was fully geared up in a midnight-blue uniform, complete with bulletproof vest and a cobalt-blue Stetson. He remained beside his car for a couple of seconds, then closed the door and adjusted his hat so the brim was exactly perpendicular to his face. Apparently satisfied, he hitched his utility belt and started walking forward, thumbs hooked behind his buckle.

Great, it's John Fucking Wayne. He closed his eyes and breathed deeply. *Just stay calm.* A small rapping came from his window, and he looked over. The police officer's hulking form occupied most of the window. Keeping one hand on the steering wheel, he slowly moved the other hand to the power control and dropped the window.

"Good afternoon, Officer," he said, flashing a polite smile.

The officer did not smile in return, nor even alter his expression from what could be seen around his mirrored aviator sunglasses. "License and registration, please."

"Sure thing, Officer," he said. *Keep cool.* "My license is in my wallet, which is in my pocket, and my registration is in the glove compartment. I'm going to get them now, okay?" He waited for the police officer to nod, then fished out his wallet, fumbling inside for his license. It wouldn't come. He yanked, but the plastic card still wouldn't come. Hands trembling, he flashed an apologetic look at the officer, then tugged again, pulling out two cards and shoving both of them out the window.

"You can keep that one," the officer said, plucking the pale-blue driver's license from Hugh's fingers.

He retracted his hand and stared dumbly at his military ID, then stuffed it back into his wallet and reached for the glove compartment. Fingers brushing the latch, he stopped. The Glock was in there. Would it be visible?

"Everything all right?"

His head jerked over, and he smiled reflexively. "Absolutely." He hooked his fingers under the glove compartment's latch, gingerly lifted it, then slowly let down the box. Inside, the black faux leather pouch holding the driver's manual covered most of the space. *So far, so good.* But his registration was somewhere underneath that, which meant underneath the Glock.

He swallowed, then leaned across, putting his torso between the console and what the cop could probably see. Digging into the compartment, the cold metal of the Glock rubbed the back of his hand, clunking against the plastic as he rustled around. His heart skipped a beat, but he said nothing, only kept rummaging. Finally, the small plastic auto insurance holder surfaced, and he pulled it out, slamming the glove compartment closed. A tight smile on his face, he gave the package to the officer.

"Any idea why I stopped you?" the officer said, Hugh's documents held up to his face.

To admire all the guns? Crazy laughter threatened to escape, and he looked straight to the front. "No, sir."

"You were speeding," the officer said. "Know how fast you were going?"

He clenched his jaw, willing the giggles trying to break free to disappear. *Light speed?* He coughed, then glanced at the officer, focusing on his name tag: P. MacInnis. "No, sir."

"Eighty," Officer MacInnis said. "Do you know what the speed limit is?"

"Fifty."

"That's right, fifty," Officer MacInnis said. He leaned forward, peering into the truck. "Where were you going in such a hurry?"

"Ottawa," he said, his body trembling. Thirty over the speed limit? What had he been thinking? "I guess I got carried away in the passing lane back there." *Stop talking, for Christ's sake.* That was the problem; he hadn't been thinking, had just been on autopilot.

"I guess so," Officer MacInnis said, half turning to walk away. Pausing, he leaned back. "I see from your other card that you're in the military. What do you do?"

"I'm an infantry officer," he said reflexively. "I'm working a desk job in Defence Headquarters right now."

"Sorry to hear that." Officer MacInnis smiled, his slightly parted lips revealing coffee-stained teeth. "Paperwork is no fun. I'm sure you'd rather be blowing away terrorists."

Did people really talk like that? "You don't know the half of it."

MacInnis nodded, then the smile disappeared, and he returned to his car.

Hugh's stomach twisted into knots. His driving record was clear, but this would be a hefty fine for sure, if not a court date. Just what he needed. Closing his eyes, he attempted a deep breath, but stopped when a maniacal urge to repeatedly smash his face into the steering wheel came over him. This was getting out of control. When he opened his eyes, they were drawn to the glove compartment, the knot in his stomach doubling upon itself. Ironically, right now the guns were the only thing keeping him from losing his cool. He wiped his clammy hands on his pants, then turned to watch MacInnis in the side mirror.

Scenarios raced through his head. Would MacInnis impound the vehicle? If so, the weapons would be confiscated for sure; how would he explain to Daryl? He wiped a hand over his sweaty face. A voice inside his head railed that Daryl should have kept the carrying cases, only to be rebutted by another voice pointing out that Daryl had other things to worry about, like not killing himself. *Good point.* Maybe it would be best if MacInnis confiscated the weapons. Good? It would be awesome—they'd been unsettling ever since he loaded them in the truck.

His thoughts were disrupted when Officer MacInnis started walking back to the truck. When he reached the window, he handed over Hugh's license and registration, holding back a piece of paper in his hand.

"You been over there?" MacInnis said.

Must be talking about Afghanistan. He nodded. "Couple times."

"Well, I'd like to thank you for what you do," MacInnis said, tipping his hat. "On behalf of the nation, we appreciate your service."

Hugh's words caught in his throat. "Thank you," he mumbled.

MacInnis handed over the slip of paper, and Hugh snatched it, impatient to see the damage. A wave of relief surged through him; the fine was only for fifteen over the speed limit, a huge difference. He looked up, eyes wide. "Thank you," he said in someone else's voice.

"Anybody who fights for their country deserves a second chance on a speeding ticket," MacInnis said. He grabbed an arm of his sunglasses and lowered them, revealing two pene-tratingly green eyes. "As long as it's not a habit."

He nodded dumbly. "Sure thing," he said, the words coming automatically.

MacInnis leaned one forearm on the windowsill. "Where did you say you were coming from, anyways?"

"A shooting range near Kingston," he said distractedly, the words popping out. *Dumbass.* He clenched his jaw, forcing himself to relax. *Hold on a little longer.* He focused on his license and registration still clutched stiffly in his hand. *Put them away, and not in the glove compartment.* He wouldn't make that mistake again. That left the center console. He reached beside him.

"Nice day for the range," MacInnis said. "What were you shooting?"

"Pistol," he said, opening the console cover beside him and lifting it up to deposit his registration. As the lid popped open, he froze, midnight-black magazines gleaming up at him. *Keep talking.* "Rifle, too." *On second thought, stop talking.* He slowly deposited the registration in the console, then closed the lid and turned back to MacInnis.

"Something wrong?" MacInnis said. "You're all pale."

"I'm fine," he said, forcing a smile onto his face. "Will there be anything else, Officer?"

MacInnis stared at him for what seemed like a minute. "I guess not," he said, then slapped his hand on the door. "You have a nice day." He turned.

Hugh's hand inched toward the ignition.

"You know, I have to ask one other thing," MacInnis said, stopping and looking over his shoulder. "If you were on the range today, can I assume you've got weapons with you?"

The ground dropped out from under him. He slowly looked at Officer MacInnis, one hand halfway to the ignition as he struggled to keep the smile on his face. "I've got a pistol," he said, nodding to the black plastic box on the floor of the passenger side of the truck. "That's it on the floor in its carrying case."

MacInnis gazed in, then leaned over and looked into the rear window, hands lowering his sunglasses. "That so?" The police officer took a step back from the truck and placed his hands on the buckle of his equipment belt. "You wouldn't have anything bigger with you, would you?"

Did he nod toward the backseat? "No, Officer," he said, meeting the police officer's gaze while the late-day humidity rolled through the open truck window. A drop of sweat trickled down the side of his face, but he made no move to wipe it away.

MacInnis paused, as if sizing him up. "Well, if you did have something bigger, I'd tell you to make damn sure you were transporting it properly," MacInnis said, leaning closer. "Not every officer might be so willing to give a second chance. You read me?"

"Loud and clear, Officer." This could not be happening.

MacInnis stared at him a little while longer, then tipped his hat one last time. "Drive carefully, sir," he said, then turned and walked back to his car.

His brain was fried. It took all his willpower to sit and watch in silence as Officer MacInnis got into his car. After a few minutes, the patrol car moved forward, pulling onto the road and slowly passing him with Officer MacInnis staring at him through the window as he drove past. When MacInnis's car had disappeared, he reached for the ignition and turned the key. Immediately, the truck fired to life. Had MacInnis seen something? He turned around, peeking into the backseat. The fire blanket was still in place, even if it didn't seem all that effective. But it must have worked. Whatever MacInnis had suspected, he still had Daryl's guns, and that was a good thing. Right?

CHAPTER 14

"Elizabeth?" Hugh called as he walked in the front door. "We need to talk." He cocked an ear for her response while hanging up the olive-drab cotton-lined field coat he'd been wearing, much too heavy for mid-May, but a good indicator of how his brain was working these days.

Nothing.

"Liz?" *I can't do this on my own.* He stood awkwardly in the foyer, but silence was his only answer.

Today had been rough. He'd thought seeing Daryl would have refreshed him, but in little over a week since their day on the range, the opposite seemed to have happened, perhaps best embodied by the shouting match he'd gotten into with Roach that afternoon. When it was over, he'd had to hide in the bathroom, sitting in a stall until he'd regained some composure.

"Liz?" he repeated.

Who was he trying to convince anyways? He knew what she'd say. Maybe he needed to hear the words, get the extra push to smash through whatever self-made obstacles were preventing him from getting help. Still, enough was enough, and at least he'd finally decided. He moved onto the main landing toward the kitchen.

"Liz?"

The quiet was thick, like the house was full of hiding animals watching him, waiting for him to leave. Still nothing. On the kitchen table was a cup half full of green tea and a book with a crow on the front. *She's here, but where?*

He checked the living room next, squinting in the bright sun shining through the west-facing windows. The heat in the room was stifling.

"Liz?" Nearing the windows, he reached out to draw the curtains, then paused as a warm draft blew on his face through the half-open patio door. Sliding open the screen door, he poked his head outside, shielding his eyes with a hand against the late-afternoon light.

She was seated on one of the chocolate-colored rattan chairs they'd purchased last summer, eyes closed while she basked in the sun.

"There you are," he said, stepping onto the patio and closing the screen door behind him. "Why didn't you answer?" He sat down opposite her.

"I didn't hear you," she said, stirring sluggishly, almost drunkenly. Turning her head, she stared at him through unfocused eyes, as if looking through fog. It took several seconds before a semblance of recognition appeared in her face. "Hi."

"Are you all right?" he said, his own problems forgotten. "You don't look so good."

"I'm fine," she said, her voice listless as she looked over their backyard, as if unsure how she'd come to be there.

"You don't sound fine," he said. "I'm kind of an expert."

With a grunt, she leaned forward, muscles clenching in her lithe legs as she prepared to stand.

"Wait a minute," he said, taking her hand and pulling her gently back into the chair. "Talk to me. What's going on?"

Sighing, she leaned back, arms crossed over her chest, and mumbled something too low to hear.

"What was that?" he said, heart in his throat.

"We're losing the baby."

What? "Say that again, please?"

Then she was staring at him, her eyes suddenly completely focused and offering a glimpse of a pain that took his breath away. "We're losing the baby," she said, then frowned at her stomach. "Or whatever it is."

His chest tightened, but from relief or distress? "Who told you that? What do you mean?" he asked, forcing himself to draw a steady breath.

"Dr. Sloan told me," she said. "I had an appointment today, remember?"

He looked away. "Shit," he said, face burning. "I was supposed to get time off."

"Did you even ask?" she said, eyes flashing. Inhaling deeply, she closed her eyes. "It doesn't matter."

He hung his head, inwardly cursing himself. She'd reminded him every day for the last week to check with his boss, but organizing his thoughts was like herding cats.

"It does matter," he said. "I forgot, I'm sorry." If this wasn't proof he needed help, what was? Still, now wouldn't be the time to take sick leave; he had to be strong for her. "I thought it was a routine checkup."

"It was with the obstetrician, and yes, it was supposed to be routine," she said, her voice lined with an icy edge. "We were going to review the ultrasound from my last appointment. You missed that, too."

"I'm sorry," he said, rubbing his temples. "I have a lot going on."

"I needed you," she said, voice shaking. "It wasn't routine."

He looked up, expecting the coldness in her voice to be matched by an accusation on her face. *Let it.* He deserved it. But her eyelids remained closed, eyebrows furrowed as if in pain. A tear slowly traced a path down her cheek, momentarily hanging motionless on the ridge of her cheekbone before racing to the corner of her mouth. *Let me bear this pain, not her.* But it was too late for that.

"What did they say?"

"The ultrasound showed something wrong, a snowstorm pattern, or that's what Dr. Sloan called it. He said it's a molar pregnancy."

"Have you heard of that before?"

"I'm an ER nurse, not an obstetrician, Hugh." She sighed, her lips forming a thin line. "But yes. Sometimes a fertilized egg develops wrong. Instead of becoming a fetus, it turns into a mass of loose cells."

He scrunched his face. "But won't the baby sort itself out over time?" This was like discussing rocket science.

She shook her head. "Don't think of it as a baby," she said. "There's nothing that could survive."

"I thought it was the size of a fig," he said quietly. Each day for the past month, she'd showed him pictures estimating the baby's size.

"It's not," she said, sobbing once and bringing a fist to her mouth. "That was just a stupid website."

He took her hand in his and held it on his knee. "But you've been throwing up," he said.

"It's also a sign of a molar pregnancy," she said, sniffling. "My body thinks it's pregnant, but eventually it will reject the thing inside me."

"Could they have made a mistake?" Was he asking out of sadness or hope? A knot lodged itself in his stomach.

She squeezed his hand. "Maybe," she said. "But Dr. Sloan doesn't think so."

"So what's next?"

She absently tucked a loose piece of hair behind her ear. "The next thing was to get some blood work done, which I did after my appointment. Now, we wait." The ice had disappeared from her voice, replaced with a clinical detachment. The coldness had almost been better.

"And then?" He hated being at the mercy of doctors, having to take their word for what would happen.

"Assuming it confirms a molar pregnancy, I'll get a D and C as soon as possible."

He looked at her blankly. "A D and C?"

"Dilation and curettage," she said in a monotone voice. She met his gaze, the dullness in her eyes wrenching his heart. "They go in and suck out the tissue."

His heart skipped a beat. "An abortion? Isn't that dangerous?"

"It's not the same thing," she said. "But it's not like I have a choice. I either get this done or it will come out on its own."

He shook his head. "Wouldn't that be more natural?" he said. "Safer?"

Her face hardened. "The D and C is safer. If it comes out on its own, I could bleed to death."

Part of him wanted to run, get into his truck, and drive, but he was frozen, unable to move from the patio chair. *Coward.* It was true; losing her would be worse than the world ending. Anything could happen to him, or even to the baby, but not her. The thought broke his paralysis, and he moved beside her, wrapping her in his arms while perching on the edge of the chair.

She stiffened at his touch, then gradually relaxed, letting her head rest against his chest. After a moment, she began to shake, the heaving of her shoulders heartbreakingly spastic.

Be strong. What hadn't he thought about? "What happens if they're wrong about this?" If only his brain were working like it used to.

"They're not." Her voice was muffled, her mouth buried under his arms. "I can feel it."

"But what if they are?"

She paused, drew a sniffling breath. "Then it's something else, and we'll still lose the bab—lose it."

He clenched shut his eyes and clung to her until her trembling stilled. Relaxing his hold, he looked into her eyes. "We'll be all right." He'd been stupid to think of getting help now; no matter how bad it got, now wasn't the time.

She smiled weakly, then looked away. The tears, which had stopped, welled up again. "There's more," she said, voice wavering.

"More?" He held his breath.

She nodded, head barely moving. "We'll have to wait at least six months before trying again."

"Okay," he said, exhaling in relief. That might be for the best. "It's all right, we've got time." But did she feel that way? *You're thinking of yourself again.* His face grew hot, and he looked away. "Why six months?"

"There's a chance it could become cancerous," she said in a hush, lips quivering. "They need to observe my hormone levels to make sure they go back to normal."

"Cancer?" His chest tightened. "What? How?"

She crumbled into tears. "I don't know, Hugh, I don't know," she said, burying her face against his chest. "I'm so scared. I wish we'd never gotten pregnant."

"Hush, you don't mean that," he said, holding her to him. "You've always wanted kids."

"I do mean it," she said, spitting out the words. "I should give up, be like my brother and be more concerned with money."

"That's not who you are," he said, cupping her cheeks. "You could have lived that life. You chose not to."

"Maybe I was wrong."

"And what about all the people you've helped? The lives you've saved?" He pressed his forehead to hers. "Besides, your brother's an asshole."

She snorted, spittle spraying from her lips as sad laughter fought against her tears. "But caring hurts so bad," she said, the tears winning out. "I just wanted a family, our own baby I could love and introduce to the world. Is that too much to ask?"

"It's not," he said, her words rending his heart. "Someday we'll be there."

"We won't," she said, wiping an eye. "The world slaps you when you care too much. Look at you. You cared about helping others and the world made you experience all those terrible things."

He pulled back from her and stared into her eyes. "Liz, this has nothing to do with me." Didn't it? Maybe he'd brought this on them through his anxiety about being a father, his reluctance to expose a baby to his PTSD. Maybe his seed had sabotaged the pregnancy from the start. He swallowed, forcing himself to go on. "We have to care, or we lose whatever it is that makes us human, become no better than animals."

"It's just . . ." The tears came again and he pulled her close. "I feel like I'm losing you and now this."

"Everything will be all right," he said. "We'll get through this." If only the words didn't feel so hollow.

ꙮ ꙮ ꙮ

Hugh pushed back from his desk and stretched, looking away from the three-page briefing note that had been mocking him all morning. Reviewing the note was his only task for the day, yet after reading the opening page over ten times, he still couldn't grasp the subject. Stifling a yawn, he sluggishly checked his watch. *Only ten thirty.* Sighing, he grabbed his mug and left for his third coffee, two more than he used to drink all day.

Would Elizabeth call? Dr. Sloan had confirmed the molar pregnancy last Friday and had said he'd call again on Monday with details for the D and C. Now that it was Monday, he couldn't stop checking the time, wondering if Elizabeth had gotten an appointment.

This would be so much more bearable if he were sleeping properly. How long had it been? Months if it was a day. *Remember I used to worry I'd fall asleep at work?* He smiled. Now he'd welcome the disciplinary action if it meant an hour of uninterrupted slumber. And as much as Elizabeth's pregnancy worried him, it barely registered against the purgatory-like existence of his sleep-deprived waking life. Sometimes he almost anticipated the night, despite the hours of tossing and turning. At least at night he felt something. During the day, he was walking dead, feeding on nicotine and caffeine instead of brains.

The hiss of the coffee maker signaled the end of the brew cycle, and he grabbed his cup, then returned to his cubicle. Setting the coffee on his desk, he pulled out his Copenhagen, grabbed a large pinch, and stuffed it into his mouth, wincing slightly. He'd been chewing so much the inside of his lower lip was like sandpaper. Still, nobody liked a quitter. He spat in an empty cup, then picked up his coffee.

"Chewing? Again?"

He started, spilling coffee down the front of his uniform. "Shit," he said, setting the dripping cup on his desk. Wiping his shirt, he turned to find Lieutenant Colonel Williams frowning down at him.

"How many times do I have to remind you that chewing isn't suited to an office environment?" Williams said, his voice heavy with disapproval.

"Yes, sir," he said automatically. What else could he say? Williams had gone over the antichewing rule a hundred times, but what other option was there? Caffeine alone wasn't cutting it.

Williams continued to stare at him. "You look terrible," he said after several seconds.

"I'm fine, sir," he said, his mouth filling with tobacco-induced saliva. "Just didn't sleep much last night."

Williams pursed his lips. "You want to spit that out? You sound like you have a cock in your mouth."

He flushed, hurriedly spitting the black lump of tobacco into his spit cup.

"You don't shave anymore?"

His hand shot to his face, rubbing the thick stubble on his cheek. "Shit."

"Forget it," Williams said, his face suggesting the issue was anything but forgotten. He nodded toward Hugh's desk. "Are you done with that?"

Spinning, he reached for the briefing note. "Almost, sir, it's right . . ." He paused, his arm half stretched out.

"Under the coffee?"

He nodded, then slowly removed his coffee mug to reveal a damp brownish ring on top of the papers. *That was the only copy.*

"Clean that up and come see me when you're done," Williams snapped. "We need to talk."

"Yes, sir."

Williams lingered a moment in the cubicle entranceway, then shook his head and walked away.

Hugh picked up the coffee-stained papers and sighed. *Back to the beginning.* Two hours later, he knocked on Lieutenant Colonel Williams's office door. Glancing up from his desk, Williams gestured to an open chair. He entered, closed the door, then sat down across from his boss. The office was small, barely bigger than his cubicle, but at least it had full walls, a faded light blue that complemented the faded dark blue of the thirty-year-old carpet.

Williams waited until he was settled, then leaned forward and picked up some papers. "Hugh, the purpose of this meeting is to counsel you on adverse performance," he said, eyes flicking between Hugh and his notes. "Your work has been steadily getting worse, and the past few weeks have been especially disappointing. I want to make a course correction so we can nip this in the bud. Roger so far?"

He nodded, biting his tongue at Williams's speech. Why did military geeks always think that clichés made them sound professional?

"I know this is your first time in Ottawa, so you're short on experience, but you started out strong," Williams said. "You quickly figured things out, and you've done well on several big files, like coordinating our management action plans. The audit on contracted support was also very well done. But lately, there's been a real drop in your performance. Do you know what I'm talking about?"

"Yes, sir," he said in a quiet voice.

Williams traced his finger along several bullet points in his notes. "Late to work, poor dress and deportment, continually disregarding simple orders like chewing tobacco in the office," he said, looking up to stare at Hugh. "I could potentially overlook all that if it wasn't for the sloppy staff work and missed deadlines. I could go on."

Was this really happening? Was he really getting reamed out like he was the biggest fuckup in the world by a soldier—using the term loosely—who'd been a desk jockey for over a decade? Hugh had clawed his way through the ranks from private to major, seen combat on multiple tours, been decorated for meritorious service, and yet here he was, at the chow by a man who thought chewing tobacco was a moral failing in a soldier.

But he's right, isn't he? About almost everything. It was suddenly too much. His eyes began to water, and he blinked furiously. *Get a grip.* He couldn't break down here.

Williams settled back in his chair, seemingly oblivious to the struggle occurring across his desk. "At the end of the day, over the last few weeks, you've been an empty uniform. Actually, worse. An empty uniform doesn't get in as many arguments." He ran a hand over his bald head. "Do you have anything to say?"

"I apologize, sir," he said, not trusting his body. *Don't show any weakness.* He sat ramrod straight, wrestling for control of his emotions. "Like we talked about the other week, I'm having trouble sleeping. I'm trying different things, but so far nothing's working."

Williams studied him, then opened an inch-thick green file folder. "Hugh, I've reviewed your file, seen everything you've done, the decorations you've earned," he said. Glancing up, he scrunched his eyebrows in disbelief. "You're saying this is all a lack of sleep?"

He shook his head, trembling at what might come out of his mouth.

"So the Visine two or three times a day, that's normal?" Williams said. "And the weight you've lost? Come on, Hugh.

I wasn't kidding when I said you look terrible. You must have been sleeping poorly for months."

"Since January," he said quietly, the words slipping out.

"That long?" Williams said, eyes widening. "Talk to me, okay? There is clearly something going on, because you are not the guy who showed up here eight months ago."

He nodded silently, eyes focused on a midpoint on the desk. He'd thought he'd been so careful, keeping a grip on things despite his problems, but Williams was right about everything. *Unbelievable.*

Williams sighed. "Hugh, if you don't give me some sort of explanation, I'll have no choice but to use administrative discipline to deal with this," he said. "I'm talking about counselling and probation, recorded warning, maybe even a performance review board. You know where this is going, right? It's potentially career ending."

"I understand, sir." He closed his eyes, fully aware of the administrative measures available to discipline wayward subordinates. He'd just never thought they would be used against him.

"Talk to me."

Opening his eyes slowly, he looked at Williams, who wore an almost pleading expression. His mouth opened, then snapped shut as tears welled in his eyes. Blinking hard, he looked away, hating the growing heat in his face. "I don't know where to start."

"Is everything all right at home?"

"I'm angry all the time," he said, blurting out the first thing that came into his head.

"No kidding," Williams said, his face impressively impassive. "About what?"

He snorted, a hard, disdainful sound. "What doesn't make me angry?" he said. "People, traffic, work, the news, anything."

"Is that why you can't sleep?"

"Partly. I also have nightmares," he said, nodding. Now that he'd started talking, the words gushed forth. "And since I'm so tired, I get angry more easily."

"Are you taking any medication?"

"No."

"Drugs? Alcohol?"

He shook his head, feeling his heart beating in his chest. Was Williams genuinely concerned or looking for something to hammer him with?

"Have you talked to anyone else about this?"

He sniffled. "I was seeing a therapist for a while," he said. "But it seemed to be making things worse, so I stopped." He glanced at Williams, who was fidgeting, his mouth half-open. "And before you ask, no, I'm not thinking of suicide," he said.

"When did you stop seeing the therapist?"

"About a month ago," he said, wiping his eyes.

"Maybe you should try again," Williams said. "Or maybe you should report in to the medical clinic."

He nodded again, mulling over his options.

Williams leaned forward, resting heavily on the desk as if bearing the weight of the world on his shoulders. "Listen, my biggest concern is getting you help. If you need time, let me know, I'll do what I can," he said, clasping his hands in front of him. "That aside, work needs to get done. I could reassign some of your tasks, but that's not sustainable in the long term."

His head snapped up. "I'm taking care of it, sir," he said. "I'm not taking a knee." Of course the bastard was more concerned about his paperwork. It was always the same old line: people were the most important resource, as long as they were getting the job done.

Williams held up a hand. "I didn't mean it like that," he said. "This is about getting you help." He sighed. "Look, we'll leave it for now, give you more time to figure it out. But think about your options, okay?"

He took a deep breath, becoming aware that his hands were balled into tight fists in his lap. *When had that happened?* "There's more," he said, forcing his hands open.

"More?" Williams's eyes opened slightly.

"My wife's pregnant."

"Congratulations," Williams said, his face breaking into a lopsided smile. "That's great news."

"We're losing the baby."

Williams's smile disappeared.

"There's some sort of a procedure she needs. We're just waiting for the appointment."

"I'm sorry," Williams said, looking first at Hugh, then off to his right.

He followed Williams's gaze to a whiteboard hanging on the wall. It had been sectored into four quadrants, with the horizontal axis representing urgency of an issue and the vertical axis representing importance. Within the quadrants were a variety of tasks, scrawled in alternating colors that represented people in the section according to a legend along the bottom of the whiteboard. Hugh's color was green, and most of his tasks were in the important row.

"Let me know when you get the date," Williams said, distraction in his voice.

Was the man already rearranging his tasks?

"Yes, sir," he said, hands clenching back into fists, fingernails digging into his palms. An urge to smash Williams's face into the whiteboard came over him, and for one horrifying yet tantalizing moment, his body inched forward in the seat.

"Let's track this over the next few weeks and go from there," Williams said, looking back at him and closing the file. "And if you ever need anything, don't hesitate to call me."

He nodded, not sure if the offer was genuine or if Williams merely thought it was something he was supposed to say. *Probably the latter.* Either way, it didn't matter; his boss would be the last person he'd call if he needed to talk. More urgently, his body had resumed creeping forward, struggling against his efforts to resist. It was either give in or get out.

"Anything else?" Williams said.

"No, sir," he said through gritted teeth as he strained to keep his body in check.

"All right then," Williams said. "That'll be all."

At a nod from Williams, he rose woodenly to his feet, standing awkwardly for a moment before reaching for the door. Pulling the handle, he paused briefly and looked back at his boss, who'd already gone back to contemplating the whiteboard. He could cover the distance in one step, grab his boss at the base of the skull, and drive him up and into the whiteboard in one fluid motion. *How easy it would be.* Wrenching himself away, Hugh turned and left before Williams could say anything more that might erase his remaining free will in the matter.

⛉ ⛉ ⛉

Hugh stood on the front porch. Almost as soon as he'd turned off the truck, Elizabeth had appeared in the front doorway, arms wrapped protectively across her chest.

"The D and C is Thursday."

Stepping closer, he enveloped her in his arms and rested his chin on her head, which nestled perfectly into the hollow of his neck. He willed himself to relax, to forget about Williams and work and everything else. She needed him, and that was all that mattered. "Nothing sooner? That's three days from now."

She shook her head, rolling it back and forth against him.

Cupping the small of her back, he reached up and buried his other hand in her lush blonde locks, holding on to her like she was his only anchor in a turbulent world. "Thursday it is then."

She mumbled a reply, the words lost against his shoulder, and he relaxed his grip, letting her pull slightly away.

"I need to get out of here," she said, staring into his chest. "Can we go out for supper?"

"You're not going to yoga?"

She shook her head. "I don't feel well."

She must have really been feeling bad; Elizabeth never missed a class if she could help it. "Let's go," he said, gazing into her eyes.

She smiled, a half-hearted spreading of the lips that tore at his heart. He helped her into the truck and closed the door behind her, then got in himself. He backed out of the driveway, then headed down the road.

"Did you talk to your boss?" she said.

He nodded, placing his hand on her knee. "I let him know we're waiting for an appointment."

She smiled again, a little wider this time. Placing her hand on top of his, she gently stroked his fingers. "How did your day go?"

"Shitty."

"That bad, huh?"

He glanced over. Her eyebrows were raised, but her expression was blank as she stared at their clasped hands. Any other time, she would have chided him good-naturedly for swearing. In the five years they'd been married, he could count on one hand how many times he'd sworn around her. He could be a beast at work, but Elizabeth deserved better.

"I got counselled for performance today," he said, forcing a lightness into his voice that he hoped belied the fact he'd almost cried all the way home.

"I'm sorry," she said, meeting his eyes. "What did you tell him?"

"That I was having trouble sleeping, feeling angry," he said, shifting his gaze to the road.

"Did you tell him about the PTSD?"

He said nothing, instead checking over his shoulder for traffic before merging onto a main road. "Not exactly," he said finally. "But I think he got the point." Or maybe Williams had only heard what had been important to him: that he'd be short one employee.

"I'm sorry, honey. I wish there was something I could do," she said, bringing his hand to her mouth and kissing it. "Did he understand?"

He swallowed, blinking rapidly as his eyes suddenly grew moist. What would he do without her? If only he could support her as well as she supported him. "He was pretty concerned with how work would get done," he said, giving her what he hoped was a brave look, then turning back to the road.

A car darted in front, forcing him to step quickly on the brakes. He jerked forward, seat belt locking up. White streaks appeared on his knuckles as his hand tightened on the steering wheel.

"He told me to go talk to someone."

"You told him about Dr. Taylor?"

He did a mirror check. *What's with all the idiots on the road?* "I stopped seeing Taylor about a month ago."

"You did?"

Ahead, the traffic light changed from green to yellow, and the car he was following suddenly stopped.

"Were you planning on telling me?" Her leg tensed under his hand.

His lips tightened. "Seeing him wasn't helping," he said. "So I decided to stop." *Did that sound as lame as it felt?*

"It takes time," she said, exasperation in her voice. "These things can't be dealt with overnight."

"I know that," he said, withdrawing his hand from her leg. "But things were only getting worse. Talking to him was a waste of time."

"Did you get in an argument with him?"

He clenched his jaw and stared at the road.

"You did, didn't you?" She looked out the passenger window.

She didn't understand. "He was pushing my buttons."

"It's called therapy, Hugh," she said, her voice lashing him. "Sometimes that's what it does."

"How can he help when he doesn't even know what I do?"

"He could learn," she said, urgency in her voice. "You need to go back."

He glanced over, jaw set. "I'm not going back," he said. What didn't she get? "I'm done with psychologists and arm-chair generals. I can do this on my own."

"How?"

He kept driving, tendons standing out in his neck.

"How?"

He mumbled under his breath.

"What?"

"I'll figure something out," he said, the words clipped.

"Do you know how ridiculous that sounds?" she said. "I can't believe we're even talking about this."

A surge of anger tore through him, and he glared at her. "I'm done. Let it go," he said, spitting out the words. "I'll take care—"

She pointed to the front. "Look out!"

He snapped his eyes back to the road, then stomped on the brakes.

The truck skidded, barely missing the car in front, which had stopped for another red light. A noxious smell of burning rubber wafted into the cab.

"Learn to drive, you fucking asshole," he said, smacking the steering wheel. "What is it with these fucking idiots?"

After a few moments, the light turned green, and they drove on in silence. Minutes later, they pulled into the restaurant's parking lot.

"Let me out here," she said abruptly.

"Let me park first," he said quietly. Why did he always ruin everything?

"I said let me out."

His ears burned at the steel in her voice. Pressing softly on the brakes, he eased the truck to a stop. "I'll park and meet you out front."

"I think it's best if you don't come in," she said, opening the door and stepping down to the curb.

"Honey," he said, unable to look at her.

"Please go."

He flinched as if she'd slapped him. Turning to her, he held out his hand. "I'm sorry, I—"

"Save it," she said, head held high. "I don't want your excuses. You think you're so strong, but all you seem capable of doing is thinking about yourself. I'd rather be alone." A single tear ran from her eye, but her tone remained firm. "I'll take a taxi home." She closed the door, then strode toward the restaurant, not looking back.

"Liz, wait," he said, grabbing the door handle. He had to go after her. A honk from behind drew his attention, a car trying to get past. "Give me a fucking minute." Putting the truck in gear, he stomped on the accelerator, roaring forward and stopping at the entrance to the restaurant. He rolled down the passenger window and leaned across the seat. "Liz," he called.

She ignored him, entering the restaurant as if he didn't exist.

What now? Behind him, the same car was honking again.

"All right, all right," he said, glaring in the rearview mirror. Should he go after her? *Why won't that idiot lay off his horn?* He couldn't think. "Fuck this." Slamming the truck into drive, he floored the gas pedal and squealed out of the parking lot.

❧ ❧ ❧

It was Thursday morning before Hugh convinced Elizabeth to let him accompany her to the D and C. Even then, it was only through a small shift in her silence from ice-cold to begrudgingly chilly that he realized she'd relented. Getting the day off had been easy; Williams hadn't even blinked an eye in approving the request. The toughest part had been everyone handling him with kid gloves around the office. Some coworkers had made a point of telling him everything would be all right; others simply avoided talking to him or making eye contact, like he wasn't there. But the ones that bothered him most were those who used to joke around and now treated him seriously. Even Roach was being less of an asshole.

They parked and entered the hospital, finding two seats in the waiting area. The minutes ticked by slowly. Finally Elizabeth's name was called. She stood and hugged him, then disappeared with a middle-aged female nurse down a sterile white hallway. He sat again, the lights bright against his tired eyes, staring at a magazine, outwardly composed while he read the same page over and over. Finally, a half hour or so later, the same nurse who'd accompanied Elizabeth reappeared.

"Mr. Dégaré?"

His head snapped up. "Yes," he said, the magazine forgotten.

"The procedure is finished."

He stood and strode over to the nurse. "How is she?"

The nurse smiled politely, her matronly face suggesting she dealt with this situation every day. "She's fine, just resting."

"Can I see her?"

The nurse's eyebrows contracted. "We're going to keep her under observation for a little while longer, then you can see her. We'll send someone to get you, okay?"

"Sure," he said, nodding.

So it was over. A sigh of relief escaped him, and for a moment, his heart rate decreased to something approaching normal. Still, the minutes crawled by until a different nurse came to escort him to a simple recovery room. Inside, Elizabeth lay in bed, head propped against two thin white pillows. Against the room's barrenness, she seemed forlorn, her hair a sickly yellow under the harsh lights. His heart ached.

He sat down beside the bed and took her hand in his own. After a few seconds, she squeezed his hand and lifted her head to look at him, a frail smile on her face. Smiling back, he raised her hand to his forehead and closed his eyes, wishing they were anywhere but here. Yet for all the sterility of the room, he was strangely relaxed, as if the world had narrowed to only himself and Elizabeth, the warmth of her skin on his brow a poignant reminder of his love for her. Only the squeaking of shoes on linoleum broke the silence as hospital workers passed in the hallway. He didn't know how long they sat there, but eventually the footsteps came more frequently, occasionally pausing outside the room.

He stirred and began to rise from the chair. "I'll ask for some more time."

As he turned, she tugged on his hand, pulling him back. "It's okay," she said in a faint voice. "I'm ready to go."

"Are you sure? We can take as long as you like."

She didn't answer, only gave a slight nod. Throwing back the covers, she rolled around until her feet tumbled over the side of the bed, then shifted forward, testing her legs. He stooped beside her, offering a shoulder, yet even with his support, her legs were wobbly as a newborn foal's.

"I need to sit," she said, leaning heavily on him. Carefully, she lowered herself back onto the mattress, perched precariously while he struggled with the controls to lower the bed to a more comfortable height. "I don't think I can walk."

He held her hand. "We can stay longer."

She shook her head. "I want to go. Can you help me?"

"Of course."

After helping her get dressed, he gently transferred her into the wheelchair that had been brought into the room. Once settled, he rolled her slowly down the corridor, unable to forget how light she'd been in his arms. When had she gotten so frail? It was like there was some poison in her life leaching away her strength. *Maybe it's me.* His throat tightened.

He took her home and made supper, which she left mostly untouched. When she'd finished eating, he brewed a tea for her, which she sipped in silence while he cleaned up. After her tea, he helped her upstairs, then disappeared to his workshop while she took a shower. It had been a while since he'd had the urge to putter around the garage, but despite his best efforts to strip a chair to be stained, he made no progress. No matter how hard he tried to focus, visions of Elizabeth's frail body lying in the hospital bed kept returning to him.

After an hour or so, he gave up, returning inside to extinguish the lights and lock up. It was early still when he went upstairs, not even nine o'clock, yet she was already in bed, sheets pulled to her nose. He showered quickly, then joined her in bed, pressing his chest against her back and wrapping his arms around her. Her breathing was deep and steady, and he was on the verge of releasing her to roll onto his back when she spoke.

"Thank you."

He started. "For what?"

"For being there today." Her voice was calm, dispassionate. "I couldn't have done it without you."

"I'm sorry, honey," he said. "I know how much you wanted this." Maybe if he'd wanted it more, this wouldn't have happened.

She didn't reply, and he was about to speak again when she answered. "Maybe it's for the best," she said, her detached voice unnerving him.

This was not the Elizabeth he knew.

"We can always try again later. Once all this is done."

Could they, though? Silken strands of her hair brushed against his face, tickling his nose. In the overwhelming silence, he shuddered, his buried emotions revolting.

Lifting her head, she peered over her shoulder, trying to see him in the room's semidarkness. "What is it?"

He shuddered again. "It's my fault," he said, voice breaking.

Her body tensed ever so slightly in his arms. "What do you mean?"

"It's my fault this happened," he said, tears worming out from between clenched eyelids. "I did something, stressed you with my temper tantrums, and I caused this to happen."

She laid her head back on the pillow, cupping his hand with one of her own. "No, you didn't," she said. "Maybe a different sort of miscarriage, but not this one. This one was flawed from the start."

He sniffled. "I still feel like it's my fault."

"Why?"

"I didn't want it." He'd finally said what he felt.

She lifted his arm off her and rolled over to face him. When he moved to place his hand on her side, she caught it in midair, lowering it onto the bed between them. "Why was that?"

He hesitated, mouth half-open. Could he keep going? What choice did he have? "I was scared what might happen," he said. "I can't be a dad."

"What do you mean?"

He flopped onto his back, crossing his hands on his chest and staring at the ceiling. The words came faster, gushing from wherever he'd bottled them up. "I'm a mess. What kind of father would I be?" he said, biting his lip when the answer sprang to mind. *The kind whose children walk on eggshells.* He forced himself to keep going. "This is karma, payback for all the shitty things I've done. Maybe I gave off some sort of negative energy that poisoned the pregnancy, I don't know."

She reached up and caressed his cheek. "You didn't sabotage our baby," she said gently. "You're a good man."

"I'm not," he said, pulling away her hand. "You've read my journals. You know what I've done. For Christ's sake, I've killed children. How could I have ever thought I'd deserve to have one of my own?"

She replaced her hand on his cheek. "You need to forgive yourself."

"I can't," he said, his voice hoarse. "The only thing I'm good at is hurting people and destroying things." And he was doing it still, stashing Daryl's weapons in the basement, knowing it would terrify and infuriate her if she found out. Whom would he hurt next? Warm tears ran along his cheeks, trickling down his neck and dampening the pillow.

"This wasn't your fault," she said, running her fingers through his shortly cropped hair. "It's just one of those things." She rested her chin on his chest and stared at him, her eyes intense in the dark. "But you do need help."

The pores on his skin prickled with the sheer matter-of-factness with which she'd spoken. As she mulled over her next words, he held his breath, hanging on what she'd say.

"You've seen and done some terrible things, I know," she said, her eyes holding his gaze. "But even still, you've let me down the past month. I needed you and you weren't there." She took a deep breath. "But I forgive you. Now you need to forgive yourself and get on with your life."

He turned his head to escape her stare.

"You're a wreck, honey," she said, pulling on his chin until he faced her. "I worry about you all the time. Sometimes I think I'll come home and find you gone or . . . worse."

He should tell her about the guns. She had a right to know. He rose up off the mattress. "Liz—"

"Shhh," she said, placing a finger on his lips. "Just listen. I'm scared for you, for us. Your anger, it's . . . I don't know what you're going to do anymore. Sometimes it's like you're a complete stranger." She glanced down, staring blankly at his chest. "We can't go on like this."

"I know." How could he have pretended otherwise? "What if I can't forgive myself?"

She sighed and traced the line of his jaw with one finger. "Then you'll have to choose."

He stiffened. "Between what?"

"Between the past and the future."

What would it be? He closed his eyes, scrunching them as tight as they would go. "I choose you."

"Then get help," she said, nuzzling against him. "I'm here for you. We're family, and family sticks together."

"Thank you," he said, swallowing. He wrapped an arm around her, pulling her tight. "How can you stay with me through all this?"

"Because I don't give up on things," she said, resting her head on his chest. "And because you're my knight in shining armor. Even if it is a little tarnished."

He pressed his lips together in the dark, straining against the tears. *Enough crying.* He'd chosen her, his future, and that was a good thing. He stroked her arm where it lay on his chest and waited for sleep to take him. Now that he'd confronted the truth, would tonight be the night he finally slept?

It was not. Hours later, he lay awake, the familiar anxiety in his chest all the more frustrating for having been so close. Beside him, Elizabeth softly snored, at first endearing, but increasingly grating the longer it went on and the more envious he became that she slept and he couldn't.

This wasn't working; he needed to break the routine. If he couldn't sleep, he'd do something until he grew tired. Moving slowly to avoid waking Elizabeth, he extracted himself from under her arm and eased out of the sheets. Donning some jogging pants and a T-shirt, he bent over the bed and kissed her on the cheek, then whispered in her ear, "You deserve better."

She stirred and mumbled something unintelligible, then smacked her lips and resumed snoring.

Tucking the sheets up under her chin, he smiled in envy. "I'll make this right." With a final caress of her hair, he left to make sure the front door was locked, at one with the darkness as he padded through the night.

CHAPTER 15

It took two weeks before Hugh mustered enough courage to report to the National Defence Medical Centre for morning sick call. The night before was like a ritual. First, he soaked his beret and shaped it on his head, wearing it while he completed other preparations so it could form as it dried. Next, he ironed and starched his shirt, then methodically aligned his name tag, medals, and qualification badges as per dress regulations, pinning and repinning accoutrements until they were perfectly dressed off. With the iron still hot, he pressed a pair of pants, then used brass polish to shine his belt buckle. When the clothes were finished and hanging in the closet, he pulled out his shoe polish and worked his oxfords until his reflection gleamed in their glassy finish. Lastly, he set the alarm, not that he needed it to wake up, but to cue him for when to start getting ready.

When the morning came, he went into the bathroom and shaved, meticulously clipping every last piece of stubble before showering. Then he dressed, tending to every detail of his uniform, from gathering the loose material of his shirt at the sides of his waist to hide wrinkles to making sure the cap badge on his beret was directly above his left eye. Finally, he was good to go. He kissed Elizabeth good-bye, then drove to the medical clinic, arriving as it opened.

As with most things military, the medical clinic had a specific way to do things. First, he waited in a line to register his vehicle in the parking lot. Then, he waited to register with his care delivery unit, which told him to wait until a physician's assistant could do an initial screening. After the screening, he waited to speak with a doctor, finally getting called to an examination room after about ninety minutes.

The doctor was a tall, lanky man who could only have recently finished medical school, by his youthful face and the lack of any ribbons on his uniform. He asked the now-familiar questions.

"Are you having problems sleeping?"

"Yes."

"Nightmares?"

"Yes, recurring ones."

"Intense emotions? Anger?"

"Yes, I'm often angry."

"What about sadness?"

"Yes, but not as much."

"How about alcohol, do you drink?"

"Not much."

"Medication? Drugs?"

"No."

"Even to help sleep?"

"No."

"Have you thought of suicide?"

"No."

"Have you thought of hurting others?"

"No." An internal voice mocked him. "Sometimes."

With each answer, the doctor checked something on a notepad. When the questions were done, Hugh sat in silence while the doctor wrote on several smaller pieces of paper, which were held up in turn.

"This is a sick chit to excuse you from work for the next thirty days," the doctor said, handing him the first piece of paper. "It's only a temporary measure until we can schedule a more detailed operational trauma assessment."

The words came staccato quick, and Hugh struggled to process the information.

"When will that be?"

"Ideally within a couple of weeks, max four," the doctor said, already writing on the next piece of paper. "This is direction to make a follow-up appointment with the front desk for two weeks from now. It's not a specific assessment, more like a checkup in the event you haven't received your trauma assessment yet."

Hugh pondered the scrawled writing on the second piece of paper. "Will someone call me?"

The doctor didn't glance up from the third piece of paper he was writing on. "To schedule the operational trauma assessment? Yes. Make sure to leave your details at the front desk. And last, here you go." He held out a third piece of paper. "This is a prescription for an antidepressant and a sleeping aid. The pharmacy's on the third floor."

It was like drinking from a fire hose. "All right," he said, glancing between the pieces of paper in his hand.

"Good luck," the doctor said, then left, closing the door to the examination room behind him.

His head was spinning. *What now?* He wandered the hallways for several minutes before finding the pharmacy, where he waited in yet another line to get his prescriptions filled. When all was said and done, three hours after he'd arrived at the hospital, he was back outside, standing on the sidewalk with a bag of medication in one hand and an appointment reminder card tucked in his wallet. And just like that, he was officially walking wounded.

He returned to his truck, where he sat aimlessly, considering his options. Go home? Somewhere else? As a minimum, he should probably let his boss know he wouldn't be at work for the next month, maybe even longer. Besides, then he could pick up some of his personal effects. An hour later, he was sitting in Lieutenant Colonel Williams's office.

"I'm glad you're getting help, Hugh," Williams said from the other side of his desk.

"You are?" he said, fidgeting in his chair. "I thought you might be upset at the time off."

Williams frowned. "No, no, it's good you're taking some time. Get this taken care of, then come back better than ever."

He nodded dumbly, not sure how to respond. His stomach was queasy—things were happening so fast.

"Did the doctor mention the Joint Personnel Support Unit?"

He shook his head. "I don't think so, sir."

Williams leaned forward, bracing his elbows on the desk and speaking in a conspiratorial tone. "The JPSU could be a good fit, especially if you'll be off for an extended period," he said. "It's specifically designed as a holding organization to let injured members focus one hundred percent on their recovery."

He nodded. He'd heard about the JPSU through a series of mental health updates over the past year, but he hadn't paid much attention.

"It works like this," Williams said, holding out his hands to explain. "The JPSU has a section called the Integrated Personnel Support Centre made up of different support platoons. Their job is to provide you administrative support and get you access to health care services while you recover. When you're ready to come back to work, in any capacity, they help coordinate a return-to-work plan. Bottom line, you'd go into a support platoon, they'd assist your recovery, then help you ease back into the swing of things when you're ready."

Why did it seem like Williams was selling him a car? "What happens to my position here?"

His boss averted his gaze for a moment, then looked back. Was he deflecting? "We'd fill your position with somebody else," Williams said. "It helps us get on with work without having to burden share around the section while a member is off. It's really win-win, Hugh. I wouldn't worry about it."

"So you'd backfill me?" he said. It seemed to make sense— was he missing something?

"That's right," Williams said. "While you focus on recovering, we'd get another warm body in to do your job."

A warm body? Is that all he was? "What about contact with the chain of command? Would you keep in touch?" It sounded like they were washing their hands of him, in which case, in only weeks it would be like he'd never been there.

"We'd stay in contact as much as possible, Hugh, but you know as well as I do that it gets tricky," Williams said. "I mean, ten years ago, people with PTSD didn't talk to their chains of command for months at a time, it just wasn't done." Williams interlocked his fingers and placed his hands on top of his head. "Of course, everyone knows that wasn't the way to do things, but I'm still not sure how much we can actually talk to you. Besides, you'd technically belong to another organization, so you can see where it gets complicated." He waved a hand in dismissal. "But we can figure all that out, the important thing is your recovery."

"Of course," he said. Why was Williams pushing the JPSU so hard? "I just thought that treatment of PTSD was best handled as far forward as possible, keeping contact with the chain of command," he said quietly. "Obviously that's not totally possible for me, it just seems like . . ."

"Like what?"

He shrugged. "Like I'm being shuffled off to be someone else's problem."

"Of course not," Williams said, hunkering over his desk. "This isn't some sort of punishment. It's about getting you the best help possible."

And about getting your work done. "Okay," he said.

Williams rubbed his bald head. "Now, don't let me hold you up anymore. I appreciate you telling me what's going on. Call me if there's anything you need, okay?"

"Yes, sir," he said, standing up. He paused, then thrust out a hand. "Thanks."

"Don't mention it," Williams said, taking Hugh's hand in his own. "I'll be in touch."

Sure you will. He released Williams's hand and turned, reaching for the doorknob.

Back in his cubicle, he spread an olive-drab duffel bag on the desk and numbly began packing the few personal items he kept at work. Vaguely aware of people walking by, he opened the small closet and removed his dark-green formal tunic, slowly tracing a finger over the rack of medals pinned above the left breast pocket. Medals for the former Yugoslavia, including one with a bronze oak leaf for the Mention in Dispatches he'd received after a firefight with the Croats, as well as the medals for Afghanistan. Then there was the Medal of Military Valour, awarded after the incident with the psyops team. Beneath the medals were his commendations, one from the chief of the defense staff after the tour in '09, as well as a unit commendation from '02. His jump wings and a winged burning torch, his Pathfinder Badge, rounded out his tunic, a cloth-and-metal résumé that would make any soldier proud. How had he ever earned so many? And what good did it do now?

He stuffed the tunic into the duffel bag, covering it with a pair of dark-green pants, several mint-green shirts, and a tin of shoe polish wrapped in a stained rag. With the closet empty, he silently eased the door shut, then stood for a moment with his hand resting on the closed door, as if paying his respects.

That done, he turned to his desk, picking up a folding picture frame. On the left side was a picture of himself supposedly in jail, hands gripping two black bars with his face scrunched up in a silent growl. His face looked younger, the crow's-feet at his eyes there on purpose instead of ingrained, like now. Above his head hung a sign reading, WORLD'S MOST DANGEROUS ANIMAL. The same bars and sign appeared on the right side of the frame, only this time Elizabeth was behind the bars, her cutesy attempt at fierceness bringing a smile to his face. They'd taken it at the Calgary Zoo six years ago, just before he'd proposed. Would they ever be happy like that again?

"You got everything?"

He jumped, dropping the picture frame.

"Shit, sorry," Roach said. "Just wanted to see if you needed a hand." He glanced up, his lips tight. Was that a smile? "I thought I could do inventory for you, make sure you've got everything." The smile disappeared, and he glanced away. "That was supposed to be a joke."

"Thanks," Hugh said, stooping to pick up the picture frame, running his hands over it and finding it intact. Straightening, he wrapped the black frame in one of the shirts and placed it carefully into the duffel bag. "I got it."

When was the last time he'd inventoried someone's personal effects? Seven years ago, the guy who got crushed in the turret when his armored vehicle flipped. *Such a stupid way to go.* Still, the soldier had been one of his—why couldn't he remember the name?—and he had helped account for the possessions before shipping them home. Piece by piece, he and another soldier had documented every item, tallying most while surreptitiously making others disappear, the porn magazines and the lace panties from a mistress. Everything had gone into packing Tri-Walls, the sum of a man's life captured in two rigid plastic boxes. Roach had a point; this wasn't so different. He just wasn't dead.

"What did you call this thing again?" Roach held the black club that had been on his desk.

He sighed. "A shillelagh. It was a—"

"I know, a gift from a friend," Roach said quietly, turning the wooden cudgel to inspect it from a different angle. With a hand at each end, he carefully held it out.

Gaze locked on Roach, he warily took the club and placed it in the duffel bag. What was with Roach? Whatever it was, he wanted no part.

"So, do you need anything?" The words sounded awkward, as if it were the first time Roach had asked that particular question. Maybe it was.

It was suddenly too much. "What the fuck do you care, Bill?" After everything the man had said, did he really think he could drop a few platitudes and everything would be good to go?

Roach shuffled in place. "I just . . . some of us heard . . ."

"It's PTSD, Bill. I've got PTSD," he said, placing his hands on his hips. "That thing you don't believe in?"

"I don't. Didn't, I guess," Roach said, staring intensely at his feet. "But, I've been thinking a lot about it." He looked up, meeting Hugh's glare. "I don't think you'd make something up."

"Unbelievable," he said, shaking his head. "So what's this? Your coming-to-Jesus moment?"

Roach's face bloomed scarlet. "I wanted to offer my condolences."

"Condolences?" he scoffed. "You know I'm not dead, right?"

"It's not . . . it's not like that."

"What's it like then?"

Roach's shoulders slumped. "I didn't realize things were as bad as they were," he said, dropping his eyes and speaking to the floor. "I wanted to say I was sorry, for what I said."

"Well, halle-fucking-lujah," he said, raising his hands to the air in mock celebration. He really was fucked up if Bill Roach pitied him. "Glad I could help you with that. Anything else you need?"

"No," Roach said. For a moment, he seemed ready to say more, and then he blinked several times and looked away. "Take care." Turning slowly, he retreated from the cubicle.

He raised a hand and massaged the bridge of his nose. "Bill," he said to the man's back. "Thank you."

Roach paused mid-step and looked over his shoulder. "You're not alone, Hugh."

His half-hearted effort to return Roach's smile didn't reach his eyes. *Sure I am.* As Roach walked away, he scanned the cubicle one last time, then zipped the duffel bag closed and threw it over his shoulder.

When he stepped into the hallway, his heart raced, nearly off the charts. There were sixty-seven steps to the elevator—he'd counted them one boring day a few months ago—but today they seemed like a mile.

Would he ever return? Sweat trickled down his back as he passed people in the hallway, some mumbling good-byes while simultaneously avoiding his eyes, others offering sympathetic smiles. He gave brief nods in return, not trusting himself to speak. *Don't run.* Body shaking, he finally made it to the elevators, taking one to the main floor and practically running through the revolving security door until he was outside, gasping fresh air as he crossed the Mackenzie King Bridge.

He closed his eyes, inhaled deeply. The world hadn't ended. Life kept going. Didn't the mass of people swarming around him like he was an orange traffic pylon prove it? They were oblivious to anything but their own concerns. So why was he struggling for air? Exhaling between clenched teeth, he willed himself to move, to reach the parking garage that housed his truck.

At home, he tossed the duffel bag on the floor and stood aimlessly in the living room. Elizabeth was at work, so he had the house to himself, for better or worse. It was the first time he'd had a chance to think.

What the hell had happened? In only a few hours, he'd gone from fully functioning soldier to someone with only the promise of a medical appointment in a couple of weeks. What was he supposed to do all day? He threw on a ratty T-shirt and a pair of sweatpants emblazoned with a military emblem, then flopped on the couch.

He was still there, watching television, when Elizabeth got home around four thirty.

"How did it go?" she asked, sitting beside him. When he didn't answer, she picked up the remote control and turned off the television. "Honey?"

He blinked several times before looking at her. "Sorry, I must have zoned out there."

"What are you watching?"

Had he been watching television? "I don't know . . . something about cars?"

A patient smile broke across her face. "What did the doctor say?"

He stared at the now-black television screen, her words barely registering. His heart thumped in his ears, and he couldn't seem to fill his lungs.

"Hugh? What did they say?"

It was real, this was happening. He no longer had a job. His eyes flitted around the room, never staying in one place. "I'm off for thirty days," he said, voice trembling. "I've got a checkup in two weeks, and I'm supposed to have a follow-up assessment sometime in the next month."

Reaching out, she cupped his chin and tenderly turned his head to face her. "Calm down."

He inhaled deeply. "They gave me some drugs for the insomnia and anxiety."

Leaning closer, she rested her head on his chest, her hair cascading across his shoulder. "It was the right thing to do," she said, hugging him despite the awkward angle. "I know it wasn't easy."

He closed his eyes, lowering his head until his nose became buried in her hair, the reassuring scent of her shampoo slowing his pulse, at least a bit. "I stopped in at work."

"And?"

"I cleared out my stuff," he said, forcing out the words. Hot tears pooled in his eyes, burning trails down his cheeks. What else could he say? That he didn't know if he'd have a job to go back to? How ashamed he'd been to face everyone? A single sob escaped him, racking his body and forcing him to clench shut his eyes. He couldn't breathe. His chest was tight, and he couldn't breathe, oh God, his mouth was open but no air was coming in. *Please, God, no.* He was choking.

"Shhh," she said, lifting her head and holding his face in her palms, her eyes red with tears of her own. Her voice penetrated the blood rushing to his ears, gave him something to focus on. "Calm down, it's all right." Snaking a hand behind his neck, she gently cradled his head to her shoulder. "I love you."

With the warmth of her body against his face, he finally succeeded in drawing a torturous breath, the smell of her body helping him draw another, then another, until his breathing gave way to sobs.

❧ ❧ ❧

The following morning, he rose at his normal time and was halfway through shaving before realizing he had nowhere to go. He stood stupidly at the sink, mesmerized by the shaving-cream-covered face in the mirror. Whose eyes were those? They were dull, not sharp like they should be. Was that the medication already?

He could have stood there all morning, but his body took over, completing his morning routine like some semi-aware robot. When he was ready, he went downstairs and sat at the kitchen table, drinking coffee until Elizabeth left for work. And so began one of the longest weeks of his life.

Each minute seemed like an hour. He didn't have work to aggravate him, which also meant he had nothing to do. He tried running and working out, but he tired quickly and had trouble getting motivated. The medication might have been helping, but he wasn't sure. He didn't get angry as much, nor did he seem to be sleeping any better. Worse, near the end of the first week, he began fighting bouts of nausea. It was during one of these spells that he pulled out Daryl's AR-15, running through drills to take his mind off his roiling stomach. It helped, some-what, made him feel like a soldier for at least a few minutes.

A week after he'd started medical leave, Elizabeth came home from the gym to find him cleaning Daryl's P226 Sig Sauer. He was on the couch in the living room, the pistol disassem-bled into numerous parts arrayed on the coffee table before him, along with a large Tupperware container filled with rags and cleaning tools.

"What are you doing?" she said, standing at the edge of the living room with her gym bag over a shoulder. Since the D and C, she'd been going to the gym with a vengeance, sometimes twice a day.

He didn't respond, focusing instead on rotating the lower part of the pistol in front of his face so he could get a better view. His other hand held a dental pick, which he periodically used to scrape away built-up pieces of carbon.

"Honey?"

"I'm cleaning a pistol," he said flatly, dragging the pick along the inside of the magazine housing.

She shifted her weight, sending a creak through the floor. "Whose pistol?"

"Daryl's," he said, trading the pick for a stained rag, which he used to wipe down the piece in his hands.

"Why do you have it?"

He glanced at her, then back to his work. "He wanted me to take it." Draping the rag over one knee, he began picking up other pieces of the pistol and assembling them together.

"I don't want a gun in the house," she said, folding her arms across her chest. "You know that. Please tell—"

"Guns."

She hesitated, blinking while her mouth continued to silently move. "What?"

"Guns," he said, concentrating on the now-almost-reassembled pistol. "There's more than one."

"No, this is not okay," she said, storming toward the coffee table. She dropped her bag and reached for the Tupperware container. "You need to take that gun . . . guns . . . back to Daryl. Right now."

"Don't touch that." He placed a hand on the transparent plastic container, pressing it to the table.

"You know how I feel about guns," she said, voice rising as she straightened. "How could you bring guns into this house without telling me? How long have you had them?"

He set the pistol on the table, picked up the rag, and wiped his hands. While he worked, the tendons in his lower jaw clenched and unclenched.

"Look at me," she said, waving a hand in front of his face. "Why didn't you tell me?"

The acrid smell of chlorine filled his nose. He frowned. "Were you swimming?"

"Don't change the subject."

"You haven't swum since your car accident," he said. "Didn't you say you'd never swim again?" It shouldn't have bothered him, but for some reason, it did.

"What does it matter?" she said.

"I have to answer your questions and you don't answer mine?"

"Of all the . . . ," she said, throwing a hand in the air. "Yes. I swam today. I swam yesterday and the day before that. Now why didn't you tell me about Daryl's guns and why you brought them into my house?"

"Because I knew you'd react like this," he said, springing to his feet and throwing the rag on the table. "You don't even know why Daryl wanted me to take them."

"I don't care," she said, hands out to her sides as if to stabilize herself. "You need to give them back." She picked up the Tupperware container in one hand, then reached for the pistol with the other.

Lunging across the table, he snatched the pistol before she could reach it. Brow furrowed, he stepped toward her, the pistol held between them with its muzzle pointed at the ceiling. "He was going to kill himself."

Her face went pale. "He wouldn't," she said, shaking her head.

"He was," he said, tendons sticking out of his neck. "He asked me to take his guns so he couldn't. And you want me to give them back?" He stepped closer.

Stumbling back, she continued shaking her head. "You didn't have to take them," she said. "He could have given them to the police."

"I'm his friend," he roared, drawing out each word. "What was I supposed to do? Leave him with this?" He waved the pistol in the air, the barrel passing inches from her nose.

"What about me?" she yelled back. "For once, why don't you think of me before yourself?" She flailed at the pistol. "Get that out of my face."

He stopped walking and glared at her, nostrils flaring. The urge to lash out was taking over. "You think I'm selfish?" he said. "Fair enough." He stooped, grabbed a magazine from the coffee table, and slammed it into the pistol. He needed to get out of here. "I'll leave."

Holding the pistol at waist level, he pulled the upper receiver to the rear with his left hand, then released it, letting the slide ram forward with a metallic thunk. Whirling on his heel, he stormed toward the front door.

"Where are you going?" she said. When he didn't stop, she chased after him, grasping for his shoulder. "Wait."

"Leave me alone," he yelled, shaking off her hand. He was in the foyer now, stuffing his feet into boots and jamming the pistol into the waistband of his pants.

"Don't go," she said, her voice piercing his ears. "I'll call the police." From somewhere she'd pulled her phone, holding it beside her head as if she would throw it at him.

He looked up sharply. "Do it. See what happens." With a snarl, he jerked open the door.

Elizabeth ran, following him onto the front porch. "Stop!"

In response came the throaty rumble of the truck's engine as it roared to life; then he was backing out of the driveway onto the road. With a high-pitched squeal, he tore off.

Hours passed before he returned. He entered the living room, where a single table lamp cast dim shadows over Elizabeth asleep on the couch, phone cradled in her lap.

He stood for a minute, watching, deadened to the events of the day. How had their relationship come to this? Slowly, he freed the pistol from the waistband of his pants and placed it on the coffee table, then sat down beside her, his weight shifting the cushions.

With a gasp, she lurched upright, tearstained eyes blinking in the dim light. When her eyes settled on him, she sank into the couch, breath returning to normal. "You need help," she said, curling her legs to her chest. "Not next week. Right now. Tonight."

He scanned the room as if trying to get his bearings, then shook his head and brought a hand to his forehead. "I know," he said, his voice hoarse.

"Call the doctor," she said. "Get them to move up your appointment, or call the emergency line. But do something." She stayed completely still while she spoke, as if unwilling to spook him.

He leaned forward, picked up the pistol, and held it in front of his face, turning it back and forth, staring at it as if mesmerized. Then he muttered and tossed it back on the coffee table, where it landed with a heavy clatter.

She started, a squeak escaping her lips. "You're scaring me."

"I'm sorry," he said, resting his elbows on his knees and burying his face in his hands. "For what it's worth, I'm scaring myself, too. And as much as that's true, I can't stand the thought of talking to more people I don't know." His shoulders heaved. "Always starting over, covering the same shit."

She reached out tentatively, placing a hand on his shoulder. He tensed, and she recoiled, pulling back, but he reached for her, taking her hand and resting it against his forehead. After a moment, she slid closer, her eyes alert even as she let him hold her hand.

"What about Dr. Taylor?"

He sighed, then massaged the bridge of his nose. "Maybe," he said. "Maybe he's my best hope." He yawned and lowered his head onto her shoulder, wishing for sleep.

Maybe Dr. Taylor was also his last hope.

CHAPTER 16

"Welcome back, Hugh," Dr. Taylor said, his unruly hair and graying beard exactly as Hugh remembered. The only thing different was the short-sleeve collared shirt, a concession to the summer heat. "Why don't you tell me how you've been?"

So much had changed. He'd put on weight, maybe twenty pounds or so if the tightness of his pants was any sign. It wasn't muscle, either—he hadn't seen the inside of a gym in over a month. Though the bags under his eyes had stopped growing, he still looked hollow-eyed and exhausted.

Taking a deep breath, he launched into a narration of the past month. The psychologist listened raptly, grunting acknowledgment while taking notes. The words came fast, but so did a sinking sensation that he was telling someone else's story. Who was this crazy man he'd become? When he got to his trip to the clinic, he paused, waiting to see Dr. Taylor's response.

Sure enough, the therapist's pen stopped, hovering over his notebook. "Which medications were you prescribed?"

He tried to recall the names. "There's a couple," he said. "Lunesta and trazo . . . trazo-something."

"Trazodone."

He nodded. "That's it."

"An antidepressant and a sleep aid," Taylor said, scrunching his lips in thought. "Well, that should cover you for the triad of depression, anxiety, and insomnia. How have they been working?"

He shrugged. "A bit, maybe. I think they're just starting to kick in," he said. "Some of the side effects are wicked."

"Like what?"

"I've been feeling like shit. Nausea, dizziness, headaches, the whole nine yards."

Dr. Taylor nodded, his brow furrowing. "How long have you been taking them?"

He shrugged again. "Two weeks." Where had the time gone?

"All right," Dr. Taylor said, lowering his pen. "Stay with them, even with the side effects. It may be necessary to adjust the dosages, maybe even the types, but for now, give them time." This said, the therapist settled into his chair. Looking directly at Hugh, he smiled broadly. "Please don't take this the wrong way, but I'm very happy to see you again."

"I'm not sure how I feel about that," he said, a smile tugging at the corners of his mouth. It was hard not to like Dr. Taylor's polite authenticity.

"I was sorry about how our sessions ended. I blundered, an innocent mistake done in ignorance. I've thought a lot about that meeting, and I accept how what I said would have insulted you, and for that, I'd like to apologize."

What could he say? No matter how he'd thought this would go, Dr. Taylor apologizing hadn't crossed his mind. "I appreciate that," he said in a throaty mumble.

"I can see you might be a bit hesitant toward me, Hugh. It's understandable and completely natural. But please know that I really am glad to see you. Not because it means you've still got an issue, but because I thought I had missed my chance to help you."

He stared at his feet, unwilling to meet Dr. Taylor's eyes, lest he lose control. "Well, I'd be lying if I said I'd never insulted anybody," Hugh said awkwardly. He glanced up, a lopsided smile on his face. "We don't have to hug, do we?"

"I think we can forego that," Dr. Taylor said, smiling in return. "Now, let's get to work, shall we?"

Hugh's smile grew bigger in spite of himself. It was hard to stay upset with Dr. Taylor.

Removing his glasses, Dr. Taylor massaged the bridge of his nose. "Have you been keeping your journal?"

He nodded, and for the remainder of the session, they discussed various journal entries, both new and old. Before he knew it, the session was nearing its end.

"We made good progress today," Dr. Taylor said, folding his notebook and placing it beside him.

"When can I see you again?" Hugh asked, standing and shaking his stiff legs.

Dr. Taylor thought for a second. "You can have your weekly spot back, if you'd like."

He nodded. "Sounds good." Dr. Taylor beside him, he moved toward the door. At the threshold, he paused, turning to the therapist. "Thanks for understanding. I know this is probably hard for you, too. I appreciate it."

Dr. Taylor shook his head. "Please don't mention it," he said. "*Nemo mortalium omnibus horis sapit.* Even the wisest people make mistakes." A twinkle appeared in his eye, and he cocked his head. "Which reminds me of one last question.

Have you given any more thought to the examples of Achilles and Odysseus?"

His heart sank. "A bit," he said. It was a lie—he'd thought about it a lot. "I want to be like Odysseus, but it's hard." But that wasn't really true, either, was it? "But honestly, Achilles was always more appealing." What self-respecting soldier would say otherwise?

"A start," Dr. Taylor said, clapping him on the shoulder. "We'll talk about it next time."

"Sure," he said, his body numb. He turned, opened the door, and exited, stopping briefly to make another appointment with the receptionist. As he left, Dr. Taylor's question stuck with him. Knowing what a struggle it was to keep it together from minute to minute, how could anyone not think that going out in a blaze of glory would be better?

❧ ❧ ❧

Hugh lay in bed, waiting for Elizabeth to doze off. It wouldn't take long, considering she'd swum in the morning and hit the gym in the afternoon. He knew he should care more, should do something as his wife shrank before his eyes from her incessant exercising. But what could he do? His eyes were open, adjusting to the blackness while he took deep, steady breaths, trying to calm himself even while every instinct screamed for him to move. Straining to hear in the thick dark, he periodically tensed then relaxed different parts of his body.

Rain raked the bedroom windows, buffeted by a strong wind that periodically shook the house. As he lay poised to react, the only other noise was the sound of his heart, beating restlessly in his throat.

Like every other night, he couldn't have explained what specific threat had him worked up, only that there was one.

There had to be, because as soon as the lights went out, his fight-or-flight response kicked into overdrive, a visceral urge to get up, to move. From years of sleepless nights spent under the stars with tactical gear on and weapons in hand, he'd learned to trust this instinct. Tonight was no different.

To keep his mind occupied, he mentally rehearsed the routine. It was still relatively new—he'd only started since Elizabeth's D and C—but he was muddling toward something that worked. At least, something that contained his unwanted memories long enough to help him sleep, if nothing else.

He hadn't been entirely honest with Dr. Taylor. Even with the medication, every night was a challenge. Part of him wondered how long he could keep this up, how long he could function on a few hours of sleep a night. The thought was quickly silenced—far easier to deal with symptoms of insomnia than his suppressed memories. He forced his attention back to the task at hand.

First, he'd arm himself. Then, he'd check the alarm. Those things done, he'd walk the perimeter. Tonight he'd start the walk around in the basement and work his way up, floor by floor. Tomorrow would be different. Changing the routine was important, he'd learned that lesson on his basic patrolling course. And from experience, his nerves would never settle if he thought he was becoming predictable.

Beside him, Elizabeth's breath caught lightly in her throat in a soft snore. He counted to one hundred in his head, thankful for something to break his train of thought. Elizabeth wasn't a light sleeper, but he didn't want to face her questions should she wake to find him ghosting around the house. He couldn't even answer his own questions about what he was doing, only that he needed to do it, had needed to since the first time. It just felt right.

When he reached one hundred, he delicately raised the covers and slipped out of bed. From the top drawer, he pulled the Sig Sauer pistol, as well as a small camping headlamp, which he looped around his forehead. Geared up, he tiptoed out of the bedroom.

He gripped the pistol in both hands while he descended to the main floor, elbows bent to keep the weapon tucked protectively against his chest. At the landing, he padded into the mudroom, where the light of the alarm panel gleamed angrily. In the darkness, the red tint reflected eerily off the ceramic floor and wooden cupboards, strangely reassuring with its implications of security. He knew, intellectually of course, that he'd set the alarm before going upstairs, but even so, the tightness in his chest eased at confirming the alarm was activated.

Reaching up, he flicked on his headlamp, and red light flooded the small room, throwing shadows off the jackets on the coatrack. He cocked the hammer of the pistol, pulled back the slide, and looked into the chamber. The metallic reflection of a jacketed hollow-point bullet gleamed in the dim light. *Good.* Letting the slide go forward, he then depressed the pistol's decock lever to bring the hammer forward. Satisfied, he reached up and turned out the headlamp, then started the patrol.

The sweep through the basement was uneventful, and he noted nothing out of the ordinary. And yet, the hard lump in his stomach remained, like someone, or something, was watching him. When the basement was done, he swept the main floor, finding it similarly secure. He spent several minutes at the front door, studying the street through one of the sidelights, tucking himself far enough back into the foyer that anyone outside would be unlikely to catch sight of him. The street appeared empty and quiet.

He finished the patrol by creeping upstairs to check the spare rooms. Only after physically verifying every possible access point and place where someone could hide did his breathing start to settle. Still, he knew from the way his pulse was racing that it would be some time before he could sleep. Returning to the main floor, he settled into a chair in the living room.

For several minutes, he simply sat in the dark, doing nothing. Another patrol lesson he'd always practiced was the listening watch, five or ten minutes of dead silence after major movements to listen if anyone had been following. In the dark quiet, he marveled how long this drill had seemed to take when he'd been learning, time slowing to a standstill just so he could demonstrate knowledge of patrol procedure. Yet here, where his life depended on it, every sense tingled in anticipation and time flew by. Only when his heart stopped throbbing in his ears did he relax and check his watch. Nearly twenty minutes had gone by.

He set the pistol down on the coffee table, ensuring it was within arm's reach, then reclined in the chair and willed himself to drift off. At first, nothing. His body was still revved up, like he'd just run a marathon, but gradually, slumber stole over him. As his control wavered, his mind wandered.

Unbidden, an image sprang into his mind, and he jerked forward. Too slow, the sight of the young girl from the vehicle checkpoint was seared to the inside of his eyelids. He blinked repeatedly, unable to rid himself of the image of her knee-length dress, covered in blood, or the flecks of brain and bone that had painted the rear window of the car in which she'd been shot.

He leaned forward and grabbed the pistol off the table. Would it ever end? After a minute, he settled back into the chair, bringing the pistol up until the cold metal of the slide rested against his forehead, like a child seeking comfort from a cherished stuffed animal. The hard raised points of the rear sights dug into his brow, and he took refuge in the pain, concentrating every last thought on the single, overriding stimulus.

Alone in the dark, he closed his eyes. All his future nights seemed to stretch out ahead in an unending punishment. Would his memories always haunt his sleep? He couldn't bear those sights even one more time, let alone every night into eternity. Numb inside, he opened his eyes and inhaled deeply. The hard smell of gun oil filled his nostrils. Perhaps there was a way out of this living nightmare.

He let the barrel of the pistol trace a line down his forehead, along his nose, until it rested on his chin. He opened his mouth and slid the barrel between his teeth, coldness pressing against his lips. The hard metal barrel pushed indifferently on his teeth, unyielding to his discomfort. Wouldn't this solve everything?

He brought his left hand to the pistol, his wedding band making a metallic tap as it touched the hand grip, the sound piercing the still dark. He thought of Elizabeth, and his cheeks grew hot. *Not like this.*

Gagging, he pulled the pistol from his mouth and leaned forward, resting his elbows heavily on his knees. He was a good soldier, wasn't he? Like Achilles. And good soldiers never gave up, they never quit. He'd beaten everything else he'd faced in life, he'd beat this, too. If not for himself, then for her. After all, she deserved much more than this ignoble end to their marriage.

Grimacing, he rose from the chair, steeling himself to walk the perimeter again. Maybe this time it would be enough to calm him.

Hugh pulled into the parking lot outside Dr. Taylor's office and found an open spot near a barber shop and a liquor store. He reached for his door when the ringing of his cell phone interrupted him. Pulling the device from his pocket, he checked the number, not recognizing the caller. Should he answer? His appointment was in five minutes.

"Hello?" he said, his free hand tightening around the steering wheel.

"Hugh?"

A woman's voice, vaguely familiar. "Yes."

"It's Laura."

Of course, it was definitely her voice. He eased his hand off the steering wheel. "Hi, Laura. How are you?"

"Are you driving?"

Strange question. "No, I just parked."

"Good," Laura said, her tone clipped. "Elizabeth said you were going to a meeting, and I didn't want to catch you on the road."

"You spoke with Elizabeth?" Goose bumps broke out on his arms.

"A couple of minutes ago," she said. "I was looking for you."

"I'm just getting out of my truck now." He glanced out the window and across the parking lot to Dr. Taylor's office building. He should go; he was going to be late. *Stop.* It was irrational, he could talk to Laura for a minute or two. He smiled at himself in the rearview mirror and forced a positive tone into his voice. "What can I do for you?"

"It's Daryl."

"Okay," he said, staring through the windshield at a man entering the liquor store. Was she calling to tell him they'd split up? "What about him?"

"Hugh, I'm sorry, there's no easy way to say this."

"He's dead." The words escaped his mouth of their own accord.

"Yes."

She may as well have reached through the phone and punched him in the solar plexus. *But you don't sound sorry.* What a terrible thought. He scrunched his face together, forcing himself to concentrate. "How?"

Silence from the other end of the connection, then finally an answer. "Does it matter?"

"He killed himself, right?" The continuing silence answered his question. *Of course he did.* "How did he do it?" Was that really important? Sure it was; it was the only thing that was important.

Silence again, then Laura answered, her voice husky. "There'll be time for that later."

"Tell me." What if he could have stopped it?

"It can wait."

"It can't," he said, wanting to scream. "I need to know." He'd taken Daryl's guns, what else could he have done?

Only the sound of Laura's breathing came through the phone.

"He was my friend," he said through clenched teeth. "Tell me."

"I can't—"

"Please," he said. How desperate he sounded, a grown man pleading like a baby. "Tell me."

"He hung himself," she said. Sighing, she continued. "In the basement. With an extension cord. I found him this morning."

"Okay." So that was that. He closed his eyes, pictured Daryl hanging from the ceiling of his specially crafted room, face blue with his tongue lolling out of his mouth. "I'm sorry."

"Thank you."

Someone else was talking with his voice, continuing to talk to Laura even as he listened to himself. "Is there anything I can do?"

"No, I'm fine." Her voice was surprisingly strong, as if there were no way she could have found her husband dangling from the basement rafters mere hours before. "I just knew you'd want to know."

"I appreciate it." Where were these words coming from? His best friend had killed himself, and he appreciated being told about it?

"As you can imagine, I don't have details for the funeral yet, but it will probably be sometime next week here in Kingston. I'll keep you informed."

She'd keep him informed? "Thanks, Laura." Was she planning a funeral or a dinner party?

"I have to go, Hugh, I have more calls to make," she said. "I'll talk to you soon, okay?"

"Okay," he said.

"Good-bye, Hugh," she said, and before he could respond, the connection went dead.

Sluggishly, he let the phone drop from his ear. "Good-bye," he said to himself. Then the phone was tumbling from his hand, clattering off the steering wheel onto the floor. Both hands came to the top of the steering wheel, where he stared at them, stared at his watch, a Casio Pathfinder with built-in compass, altimeter, and barometer. It told him it was five minutes past fifteen hundred hours on Wednesday, the fifteenth day of the sixth month. The blocky digital numbers ascended dispassionately, adding second after second, minute after minute, until he couldn't stand to look at them.

Slowly, he lowered his forehead onto the backs of his hands and screamed, a primal, guttural yell that left his ears ringing and his throat raw. He yelled until all that would come out was a strangled croak, and then he beat his hand on the seat beside him, throwing hammer fist after hammer fist into the seat cushions.

After a while, he stopped. He sat with his hands in his lap, utterly spent, an empty husk. Lethargically, he glanced at the dashboard clock. He was late for his appointment. It didn't matter now, though. He wasn't going.

A voice deep inside urged him to reconsider, told him that seeing Dr. Taylor might be the only thing that could stop him from doing something stupid. Now was when he needed therapy most.

But he'd had lots of experience suppressing this voice, and it was easily silenced.

He searched for his phone, eventually finding the device after bumping it with his foot. Picking it up, he stared dumbly at the screen, then dialed Elizabeth's number.

"Are you okay?" she said as soon as she answered.

"I'm fine," he said, his voice sore in his ragged throat.

"Laura told me," she said. "I told her not to call you, to let me tell you after your appointment." The phone did nothing to hide her trembling voice.

"Well, she told me."

Her words came from across a chasm, a conversation between two other people. "You told me and I didn't believe you." She sniffled. "I'm sorry."

Her words were a knife in the gut. "It's okay," he said. "I'll be home soon." Why had he thought anything had changed? His situation wasn't getting better, only worse.

"Aren't you going to your appointment?"

"I missed it."

"Only by a couple of minutes. You could still—"

"No," he said. "I'm coming home." There was no way he could face this with Dr. Taylor, not now, maybe not ever. It would destroy him. "I'll see you soon."

"Let me come get you."

"With what? You don't have a car."

"I'll take a taxi and drive your truck home."

He clenched shut his eyes. "It's all right." He didn't deserve her. His imagined vision of Daryl hanging from the rafters returned. "I'm fine to drive home."

"Be safe, honey."

"Good-bye," he said and hung up. In his mind, the image of Daryl opened his eyes and winked. Gasping, he lurched forward, one hand gripping the steering wheel as he tried to blink away the image. What had possessed him to think of that?

He stared out the windshield, focusing on anything to take his mind off the image of Daryl. On the curb to his front, a red-haired woman in black yoga pants and a gray halter top was exiting the liquor store, a brown bag in hand. She stopped and pulled out a cigarette, balancing the bag under an armpit while she lit up. What a shitty world.

The next thing he knew, he was buying a bottle of rye—the cheap stuff, Daryl's favorite. He got back in his truck, opened the bottle, and put it to his mouth, taking a long pull.

After a couple of swallows, he gagged. He tore the bottle away from his mouth and grimaced at the burning taste. Before long, the heat worked its way down his throat and into his body, relaxing him like an old friend who'd been gone too long. He raised the bottle again, intending to drain it then and there, when some reptilian part of his brain took over, the instinct for self-preservation asserting itself. Capping the bottle, he placed it between his legs and started the truck.

Elizabeth met him at the door, standing on the front step as he walked up with the bottle in a brown paper bag that crinkled as he walked. Her red eyes stared first at him, then at the bag. When she looked back to him, any sympathy that might have been in her face had disappeared. "Don't do this."

His answer was to take a pull from the bottle. He didn't want to stop; he wanted to drink himself into oblivion, until the pain went away. "You can't stop me." He stood in front of her and took another swig.

She slapped him, knocking the bottle from his mouth and sending rye spraying. His head turned to the side, and he closed his eyes, waiting for the next slap. What did he care anyways? The sting paled in comparison to the dead ache inside. She could slap him all night if she wanted.

Instead, she yanked the bottle from his hand. Blinking his eyes open, he caught a flash of her back disappearing into the house, heading for the powder room just visible through the open front door.

Roaring, he leaped after her, bounding up the steps. As she entered the bathroom, he stretched out, thrusting his hand into the rapidly closing gap only to have the door smash shut with a muffled thud on his palm, trapping it against the jamb. The door shuddered open, and on instinct, he retracted his arm, clutching it to his chest like a wounded wing.

Free from obstructions, Elizabeth slammed the door shut and locked it. Seconds later, he heard liquid being poured down the drain. How could she? He howled in frustration, beating on the door with his uninjured hand until long after sounds ceased to come from the bathroom.

When his voice gave out, he turned, leaned his back against the door, and slumped to the floor. Resting his head back, he closed his eyes. He was so tired, but the fury still burned through him, consuming him. He was a prisoner in his own body. The rye would have helped; he could've drunk himself unconscious and at least gotten a few hours of respite, but now,

now he'd have to face the emptiness head-on. How could she do that to him? He tried to yell again, but all that came out was a croak.

Eventually the anger seeped away, replaced with a coldness that was somehow worse. How long had he sat there? He couldn't tell, didn't really care. He clenched shut his eyes, and Daryl's blue face appeared again, wearing a mocking smile. He began to cry.

From the other side of the door came Elizabeth's voice, near his level on the floor. She must have been crouched in almost the same position as he. "I couldn't let you do it," she said. A few seconds later, she went on. "Is it safe to come out?"

What did he expect? What could he say? He'd given her reason to be scared, hadn't he? He brought his knees to his chest and hugged his legs, letting his head drop until it rested on his forearms.

"Honey?" There was something in her voice, not fear exactly, but certainly concern.

"It's okay," he said in a raspy voice. "I'm done."

The door cracked open, and he flinched, his torso straightening briefly, then falling backward into the open door frame. He caught himself, then scooted over on his bum and propped his back against the wall. Only then did he look up. Elizabeth stood in the door frame, clutching the empty bottle before her. Shame bloomed hot in his cheeks, and he lowered his head onto his arms.

"I had to," she said. "I'm sorry."

"I know," he said, the words hollow to his ears. "You did the right thing." It was true; he knew it in his brain, probably in the same part that knew chewing tobacco was unhealthy. And just as he chewed regardless, this knowledge would do nothing to stop the soul-searing fury within.

She shuffled into the hallway and sank down beside him, one hand settling on his arm while her head came to rest on his shoulder. "Will you be all right?"

The pain in her voice only made him hate himself more. "I don't know," he said.

He'd gone through this before, with Mitchell, but it seemed different now, more personal somehow. He and Daryl had been fighting a common enemy, and Hugh had let his friend go off on his own, without support. Was this how Achilles had felt at the death of Patroclus? Right before he'd slaughtered half the Trojan army and desecrated Hector's body? He shivered. "I don't know."

CHAPTER 17

Hugh came to a stop outside Daryl and Laura's house and stared. The building looked more run-down than before, the porch railing now hanging almost completely off. It oozed hopelessness, worse than many Afghani hovels he'd seen. He clenched the steering wheel, trying to psych himself up. Strange to think almost a week had gone by since Daryl died.

So what was he doing here, looking to repeat the last time he'd spoken with Laura? He should go check into the hotel that Elizabeth had insisted he book so he wouldn't have to drive back to Ottawa between the visitation today and the funeral tomorrow. Besides, Laura undoubtedly had tons to do, and he'd see her later that afternoon anyways.

But Laura was a friend, and Hugh told himself he owed it to Daryl to make this effort; it was the right thing to do. With a deep breath, he walked to the front door and rang the doorbell. Seconds later, Laura appeared, her flaming-red hair hidden beneath a black bandanna. He attempted a smile, and they hugged awkwardly.

The small foyer was cramped with brown cardboard moving boxes, stacked two to three high. Against another wall were even more boxes, still folded and leaning in ranks four or five deep.

"Don't mind the mess," she said, disappearing into the house.

He took off his shoes and followed her into the living room, taking in the unhung pictures and decorations leaning against the walls. "I take it you're moving?"

"I am," she said. "We only moved to Kingston because he thought being near his family would help him deal with getting out of the military. But if anything, it only made things worse." She paused and surveyed the room, hands on her hips. "I need a fresh start, somewhere else."

"Daryl," he said softly, picking up a plaque from an open box with the word *disposal* written on the side in bold black letters. When he'd been here before, the plaque had hung in Daryl's man cave, proudly stating he'd finished his basic reconnaissance course. Hugh had been right there beside him. "Daryl thought it would help his recovery."

Laura stared at him, her lips tightening. "Can I get you something?"

He glanced over, pulled from his reverie. "Whatever you have."

"Excuse me a minute." Wiping her hands on her pants, she vanished into the kitchen, returning minutes later with two glasses full of a pale-yellow liquid. "Here's some lemonade."

He looked for somewhere to sit amid the boxes and packing paraphernalia, eventually settling for what must have been Daryl's worn chair. While he sat, Laura began emptying a china cabinet, methodically removing plates, wrapping them in brown paper, and placing them into a box.

How to proceed? He sipped his lemonade, watching Laura and collecting his thoughts. Talking about death was never easy, and she certainly wasn't making it any easier. "It's good, thanks." He grimaced. *Smooth.*

"Sure," Laura murmured. Another plate into the box.

He fidgeted, then sat forward. "Laura," he said, adopting the formal voice he'd used when offering condolences at work. "I wanted to say how sorry I am for your loss. If you need anything, just let me know." It sounded so hollow.

Laura shook her head. "Nice of you to offer, but it's all in hand," she said, her manner almost brusque. Was she humming?

"And you're okay?" he said, wincing. Sure she was okay; she'd only found her husband hanging from the rafters a week ago. "I mean, do you have someone to talk to? If you needed to?"

She paused, a wineglass half covered in wrapping paper in her hands. As she stared at the glass, she bit her lip lightly, then looked up at him. "Hugh, can we be honest with each other?"

He nodded, eyebrows furrowed. Weren't they already being honest?

She knelt beside the box, placing her hands on her thighs. "I know I'm supposed to be the grieving widow mourning her recently deceased husband, but all I've really felt over the past week is relief."

He choked on a sip of lemonade. "Maybe you're in shock," he said, setting down the glass. "Denial's the first stage of grief." At least that's what Dr. Taylor had said.

Her gaze lowered, a thoughtful expression on her face. Slowly, she resumed wrapping the wineglass as she spoke. "Hugh, I realized a long time ago that the man I fell in love with, the man I once knew, was gone. The man you've seen these past few months, that wasn't him."

"You're talking about Daryl," he said, floundering over the words. "And whatever happened recently, you loved him, at one time anyways."

With the wineglass fully wrapped, she paused and looked at him, one eyebrow raised. "Of course, and part of me still does," she said. "But the man I loved died long ago, and I did my grieving already." She turned back to the box, placing the glass inside. "You might hate me for saying this, but another part of me is glad he's dead. At least now it's over."

His mouth dropped. "How can you say that? This isn't some guy we're talking about, it was Daryl. My friend, your husband." He grabbed his knees to still his shaking hands. "I could have stopped him."

"That's touching, Hugh," she said, her face calmly composed. "But open your eyes. He couldn't move beyond his problems, couldn't face his fears and get on with life." She closed the lid of the cardboard box and reached for a roll of packing tape. "And he didn't even have it all that bad. Lots of people get by with two prosthetic legs."

"You don't know what he went through," he said. How could she be so heartless? "You don't know what it's like to not be able to do something you've always wanted to do."

"Actually, I do," she said, eyes suddenly spitting fire as she glared at him. "You think I didn't have dreams? Things I wanted to do? But I couldn't accomplish much, because he couldn't get past his self-pity." She closed her eyes, took a deep breath, and regained her composure. Wrapping another wineglass, she went on. "In the end, everyone has a choice. He chose to wallow in his problems instead of facing them. Lots of other soldiers had it worse, men with brain injuries, but they're handling it better. All he could do was be bitter and hate." She paused, resting her hands on the lip of the box. "He was a coward and proved it by taking a coward's way out."

His cheeks burned as if she'd slapped him. She was right, though, in a way, wasn't she? Until a few weeks ago, he might've even agreed that suicide was the weak way out. "So you just throw it all away?" he said, the words barely louder than a whisper. "It's just . . . it's sad."

"I don't need your sympathy," she said in a calm, detached tone. "As I said, I did my grieving long ago. There was nothing you could have done."

He had to say something, keep talking, or he'd explode. "The last time I saw him, he said you two were going to split up," he said. "Trial separation or something like that."

Laura brought a hand to her lip and turned her face away. After a few seconds of silence, she spoke. "He threatened to kill himself if I left. He was very persuasive when he wanted to be," she said, her voice barely carrying across the room. "In the end, he was more afraid of being alone than anything else."

"I didn't know," he said. "I'm sorry, we don't have to talk about it."

"It's all right, I want to," she said, wiping one eye. "I stayed, for a few weeks. Then one night I woke up and he had me by the back of my neck, pushing my face into the pillow, calling me a whore and a slut. I thought he was going to kill me." Reaching up, she tucked a stray strand of red hair back under her bandanna. "I got away, hid in the bathroom for the rest of the night until he passed out." She folded her arms over her chest and looked at him. "I left after that. I never spoke to him again."

He looked at his hands, twisting his wedding ring on his finger. What bothered him more—what Daryl had done? Or that both of them had caused their wives to cower in the bathroom? He drained his lemonade, hoping it would settle his suddenly queasy stomach.

Across the room, Laura dragged the back of a hand across her eyes.

"I should go," he said, not knowing what else to say. "You've got a lot to do."

She nodded in return, then canted her head to one side like she'd remembered something. "Just a minute," she said, walking down the hallway leading toward her bedroom. When she returned, she had a book, which she held out to him. "He would have wanted you to have this."

Reaching out tentatively, he took it, a simple black soft-cover book held closed with an elastic band. "What is it?"

"A journal he kept," she said, looking at the book with something akin to aversion. "Ramblings for the most part."

He unfastened the elastic band and thumbed to the first page, finding a photo of Daryl's basic training course. From over twenty years ago, a young Daryl sporting a crew cut stared up from the picture, a relic from another era in his olive-drab camouflage uniform. "I can't believe he would've kept something like this." The only pictures he'd ever seen Daryl keep had been of guns or girls.

"He kept all his photos, but the journal is relatively new," she said, eyes locked on the book. "He lived in the past so much, I guess it helped him on some level." She turned and walked back to the china cabinet, standing with her back to him. "You should have it, if anyone should. But you might not recognize the person who's writing in there." She crossed her arms. "I thought about destroying it."

"You did?" he said, glancing up. "Why?"

"He had a lot of hate in him, especially near the end." She met his gaze briefly, then looked away. "You don't have to take it, if you don't want to. It might be better if you didn't."

What was she frightened of? He turned back to the journal, remembering his recent conversations with Daryl. The journal could hardly be worse, could it? He thumbed through a few more pages, until the silence grew heavy. Looking up, he realized Laura was staring at him.

"Maybe you need to let the past go, too," she said.

"He was my friend," he said quietly, eyes pulled inexorably back to the book. Maybe she was right. What good could come from more of Daryl's rants? But if he really had been Daryl's friend, how could he turn it down? He'd already let him down enough by not stopping his suicide. "If you think he would've wanted me to have it, I should take it." Then why did it feel like his chest was in a vise? "Besides, it's one less thing for you to have to deal with." He stood. "I should go."

She walked with him to the door, standing beside him in the foyer as he put on his shoes.

"If you reconsider about needing anything, let me know," he said, straightening and facing her. Then he smacked his head. "Shit, I totally forgot. I've still got his guns."

"Keep them."

"What?"

"I want those guns even less than that journal," she said, her voice firm. "Keep them."

"I never wanted them, either," he said, not meeting her eyes. "I thought I was doing him a favor, but I guess not." Tears suddenly welled up in his eyes, and he clenched them shut. Maybe if he'd done more, Daryl would still be alive. A touch on his arm startled him, and he blinked open his eyes.

"Don't blame yourself," Laura said softly. "You couldn't have done anything to stop him."

"I don't know what to say," he said, shifting his weight awkwardly. Finally, he held out his hand. "Thank you?"

A small smile appeared on Laura's face. She gave him a hug and a peck on one cheek. "You always were a good man," she said, then pulled back. "The best." Grasping his shoulders, she gazed into his eyes, fixing him in place. "I see the same thing that happened with Daryl happening with you. But for some reason, you worry me more." She palmed his cheek, tenderly lowering his face so he looked directly in her eyes. "You're a better man than my husband was. I hope that doesn't mean you just have farther to fall."

⩒ ⩒ ⩒

Hugh entered his hotel room, hunched over as if the overnight bag slung from his shoulder weighed a hundred pounds. Belly flopping onto the bed, he grabbed the remote and flicked through channels, wanting only to numb his brain into submission.

Today could have gone worse. *How?* Maybe if Laura had told him she'd killed Daryl and was going to kill him, too. He smiled grimly. That might have still been preferable to how the conversation had actually played out.

Even with the television chattering senselessly, his mind raced, replaying Laura's words. Sighing, he stood, dug the journal out of his bag, and sat back down to read.

The book was roughly organized, with entries at random places separated only by simple headings noting the dates and times of the entries. He found himself squinting at the pages— the writing was little better than a five-year-old's. Was that what Laura had meant when she'd said he wouldn't recognize the words?

Thinking of her made his stomach churn—what she'd said bothered him. He'd known Daryl was troubled, but obviously not how badly. Letting the journal drop to his lap, his gaze fell on the small bar fridge tucked under the television stand. He walked over to it and retrieved a miniature bottle of whiskey.

Cracking the seal, he upended the bottle into his mouth, draining it in several long swallows. Grimacing, he put the back of a hand to his mouth. After a few seconds, the burning in his throat eased, as did the sickness he'd had at the thought of Laura. Better, but it wouldn't be enough.

After his stomach settled, he did a quick inventory of the fridge. There were five or six miniature bottles, which, at this rate, wouldn't go very far. Hadn't Daryl said that Kingston had a dial-a-bottle service?

Searching the Internet on his phone, he soon found a site and ordered a twenty-sixer of rye for delivery. As an after-thought, he phoned room service and ordered a hamburger. Satisfied, he pulled out another miniature bottle—rum this time—and sat down at the small desk with the journal open to the beginning.

The first entry had been written less than eighteen months ago, accompanied by a photo of Daryl's recruit course glued to the page. A quick flick through the journal's pages revealed numerous additional clippings and photos Daryl must have saved from throughout his career. He whistled. He couldn't even remember Daryl taking a picture, much less keeping them.

Returning to the beginning, he followed the chicken-scratch writing describing the trials and tribulations of basic training: inspections, push-ups, yelling, and a helpful course mate. He'd heard this story many times, could almost picture Daryl tell-ing how he'd almost gotten kicked out for repeatedly failing dress inspections until the intervention of Recruit Dégaré. He smiled. Dress and deportment had never been Daryl's strong suit, but he'd been hell on wheels in the field.

A pattern emerged, at least in the early entries, all of which described various courses Daryl had taken or units he'd been part of. In most cases, the entries were paired with a group photo, with circles drawn around various people. Interspersed among the entries was a mélange of career mementos, a cap badge taped haphazardly to a page or various certificates folded between the pages.

A knock at the door startled him. Heart pounding, he poked his head into the hallway, only to find room service with his supper. Just in time. He'd already started his third mini bottle on an empty stomach. He wolfed down the burger and was halfway through the fries when there was another knock at the door, which proved that the dial-a-bottle service was as reliable as Daryl had said. After fetching some ice from a machine in the hall, he poured himself a drink and picked up the journal once more.

About halfway through, around the time of Daryl's first deployment to Afghanistan, the entries took a different turn, veering away from general reminiscing to become opinionated rants. Some of the tirades he'd heard before, such as how people claimed to be upset with the treatment of veterans, yet did nothing to fix it. Other entries were more rambling, filled with vitriolic antigovernment diatribes and disgust for veterans' programs, in some cases even attacking veterans themselves as hypocritical whiners. The later entries even referred to conspiracy theories, how big businesses owned the government and ran roughshod over a flaccid populace.

He shook his head. So this was what Laura had been talking about. Sprinkled in with these criticisms were answers, of sorts, stream-of-consciousness examinations into what could spark citizens to action to fix things. While Daryl had said on the range that he hadn't wanted to incite violence, that sentiment wasn't consistent with his writings, at least as captured in positive assessments of lone-wolf attacks or acts of sabotage as potential catalysts.

Hugh remembered on the range when they'd been gathering up the zombie targets and Daryl had said most citizens were sheeple, so naive they probably thought zombies posed a greater threat than real-life risks, like terrorism. Hugh had asked what it would take to change the situation.

"People need to realize that rights and freedoms are earned, not an entitlement," Daryl had said. "They have to work for that shit. Problem is, most people take 'em for granted. They'd never risk fighting for 'em, and they sure as hell wouldn't fight for the rights of someone they didn't know, like a veteran. It'd be too much inconvenience."

"What's obtained too easily is valued too lightly," Hugh said. "That type of idea?"

Daryl spat. "Maybe. All I know is people are so comfortable they'd never consider that how a country treats its veterans might be a sign of how citizens in general are viewed."

"Which is?"

"Like lambs to the slaughter, brother," Daryl said, smiling grimly. "Think about it. If the country treats someone who's ready to lay their life on the line like garbage, imagine how it feels about someone whose only contribution to the greater good is paying taxes." He shrugged. "The only way people will ever understand that is if they're treated openly like the state treats them behind closed doors."

The journal went further. The answer, of course, was fear. Fear was the motivator that would get citizens to act. If governments were supposed to be afraid of their citizens and not the other way around, then citizens had to be afraid of something even worse, something that would happen to them before they'd hold the government to account. Until then, nothing would change.

Moreover, the threat of "badness" alone wasn't enough. It had to be real fear, a dismembering attack on their perception of safety. In effect, people would only accept that something like the treatment of veterans impacted their daily lives if there was a demonstrable link to their personal security. In other words, if getting shot in the face by a disgruntled veteran was a real threat, people might start paying attention.

He closed the journal and refilled his glass. Leaning back, he rubbed his aching eyes. Why was he reading these phony-baloney ramblings? There were too many inconsistencies. Why had Daryl said that civil action was the better option when he'd apparently believed only violence could reliably transform the status quo? It was too much.

"I want my life back," Hugh said aloud, head hanging over the back of the chair.

Closing his eyes, he sipped his whiskey and envisioned Daryl in the room with him. There he was, in the chair near the window, clad in his old dress uniform with his face a light blue-gray. His tie was loose around his bull-like neck, revealing a horizontal contusion paralleling his jawline.

"Not looking so good, brother."

"Go to hell," Daryl said, his voice gravelly.

He gasped, snapping forward and spilling whiskey onto his lap. The chair was empty. It had been so real. He drained the rest of his drink and refilled his glass, hand shaking as he held the bottle, now half-empty. When he closed his eyes once more, Daryl appeared again, laughing silently at some joke.

"I can't believe I'm pretending you're here," Hugh said. Was he really talking to his dead friend? "As if you'd have any advice for me anyways."

"Your mistake is thinking you can beat PTSD with the current policies," Daryl said, speaking around a bloated black tongue that fought to poke out of his mouth. "You can't."

"Tell me something I don't know," he said in frustration.

"That's outside my control."

"No shit," Daryl said, pulling a cigarette from thin air and lighting it, contentedly puffing two streams of smoke out his nostrils. "And they'll never change unless somebody holds the government's feet to the fire."

"So what?" he said, shaking his head. He tried to will the phantasm away.

"So, who's not doing their job?" Daryl whispered, his macabre image fading.

He blurted out the first thought that came to him. "The people."

"Ahhhhh," Daryl said, his voice full of satisfaction, like a mentor seeing their pupil achieve enlightenment. "And what do we do with people who don't do their job?"

"We hold them accountable," Hugh said, eyes opening. Blinking, he looked across the room, but Daryl's chair was empty. He held up a hand in exasperation. "I get it, this is the same old shit. It still doesn't answer why you said violence wasn't the answer when you obviously thought it was."

Whatever the answer, it was official; he was well and truly on the crazy train. Still, why had Daryl told him one thing and written another? Aside from the man's positive qualities, he'd also been a shit magnet, always making trouble. It was entirely possible he'd simply been stirring up shit.

He raised his glass, holding it to his lips as he spoke. "Everyone always dismissed you," he said, drinking in the oaky aroma. "Good thing you didn't try something. People would have written you off as a malcontent."

Maybe that was it; Daryl hadn't wanted to be typecast. Again, so what? He knocked back his drink, pondering the question. For someone to be taken seriously, they'd need operational experience, ideally some decorations, both of which Daryl had in spades. Also, a spotless record, which Daryl definitely didn't have. Being an officer wouldn't hurt, either.

The glass lowered from his lips, forgotten. "Someone like me." Sitting forward, he glanced at the empty chair, cursing himself for an idiot. Was he really taking advice from his embittered dead friend? He'd definitely had too much to drink.

He stood up, stumbling slightly, and got undressed. Naked, he pulled aside the bed's covers and lay down. The television was still on, volume turned low. With his eyes closed, it wasn't long before the room began to spin. Willing himself to focus, he concentrated on voices emanating from the television. One even sounded like Daryl.

"If you did something, people would notice," the voice said.

His stomach suddenly heaved, and he staggered into the bathroom, barely making it before spewing the undigested remains of his supper into the toilet.

❱ ❱ ❱

Hugh stood outside the church where Daryl's funeral service was being held, shielding his eyes with a hand. The church's steeple swooned in and out of focus, perhaps because he had to squint in the bright sun, but more likely from his hangover. *Please let there be air conditioning.*

The oppressive humidity made the air thick, and he rolled his shoulders to gain some circulation in his clingy suit. He headed toward the church's entrance. If he could keep it together for the next couple of hours, it would be a miracle. As he neared the doors, two men standing outside turned to him.

"Hugh?" the taller of the two said. A diagonal scar cut through the man's right eyebrow in what should have been a distinguishing feature. In this case, the scar was overshadowed by a lazy eye, which stared at a point beside Hugh.

"Steve?" he said, stopping in midstride. He peered closer at the two men, their uniformly short hair and near-identical clothing choices—collared polo shirts and khaki chinos without belts—marking them as either serving or ex-military. On closer inspection, the second man was even wearing his issued oxford shoes. "Rick?"

"Good to see you," Rick said, sticking out a pudgy hand. "How the hell are you?"

"I'm all right," he said slowly, uncertain what to say. "You?"

Steve Patterson and Ricardo Lofthaus, Rick, had served with him in battalion, deploying together to Afghanistan in 2002, although in different companies. He couldn't remember when he'd last crossed paths with either of them—at least six years if not more.

"Good," Rick said. With sweat beading across his entire face, Rick looked like he was melting. Even the ends of his handlebar mustache were drooping. "Where are you working?"

"I'm in Ottawa," Hugh said, face stolid. "National Defence Headquarters." His stomach tightened at omitting that he was on sick leave, but he didn't want to discuss it. He'd never been all that close with either man; they'd loosely had the same circle of friends, as would be expected of young grunts from the same battalion, but there'd been a limit since they were in different companies. Still, if memory served, both of them had been huge gossips.

"Sorry to hear that," Rick said. "I'm posted here in Kingston at the peacekeeping school."

"How do you like it?"

Rick nodded and raised his eyebrows. "It's great. They'll have to pry me out of here."

He turned to the man with the lazy eye. "How about you, Steve?"

"I'm in Petawawa, working in battalion."

"That's great," he said. "Glad you guys could come." *For Daryl anyways.*

"Yeah, what a tragedy," Rick said, shaking his portly head. "Another suicide. When's it going to stop?"

"Each one is one too many," Steve said quietly.

He nodded in what he hoped was agreement, keeping an eye on Steve. Something about that guy had always rubbed him the wrong way, but maybe his hangover was making him sensitive.

"We were just laughing about how Daryl started smoking so he could stop chewing," Rick said, looking at Hugh. A smile crept onto his face, looking like it belonged. "In fact, didn't you guys try quitting at the same time?"

Despite himself, Hugh returned the smile. "I tried Copenhagen because it tasted so bad, and Daryl started smoking," he said, reaching into his suit jacket to pull out his tin of tobacco. "Didn't work so well for either of us."

Rick burst out in an infectious laugh. Steve chuckled. Several people filing into the church threw questioning looks as they walked past. By the time Rick had stopped laughing, Hugh and the two other men were the only ones outside.

Rick glanced around, then shrugged. "Guess we should head in."

Hugh followed Rick and Steve through the doors and into the nave. The large, open room was surprisingly bright and warm, with large windows running along the elongated walls. He sat alongside the other two men in a cedar pew three rows from the front. Shortly after they sat down, silence fell over the room.

He peered over his shoulder. A minister in long black robes strode solemnly up the aisle, his concentrated blackness contrasting powerfully against the lightness of the room. Laura walked a few steps behind, thick red hair cascading around her face. She was wearing a black pencil dress a shade too short for a funeral. In her hands, she clutched a small metal urn.

Rick leaned across Steve. "I thought Daryl wanted to be buried," he said in a loud whisper.

"I thought so, too," Hugh replied, mostly to himself. They'd talked about it a few times, one of those discussions soldiers had. Daryl had always been firm; he'd spent so much time in a trench, spending eternity underground would be like going home. His brow furrowed. What was Laura doing? She hadn't even mentioned anything at the visitation the day before. And wouldn't it be normal to wait until after the funeral? As the minister moved to the pulpit, he pushed the thought from his head.

"Blessed are those who mourn, for they will be comforted," the minister said, his deep baritone resonating throughout the space.

His jaw muscles clenched and released, clenched and released. This was supposed to comfort him? Knowing he could have stopped his friend from killing himself? He shook his head, trying to concentrate.

"We have come here today to remember our brother Daryl before God, to give thanks for his life, and to commend Daryl to God, our merciful redeemer and—"

A fist dug into his ribs, and he jumped. Beside him, Rick was pointing at a pamphlet Steve held in his hands.

"Is anyone giving a eulogy?" Rick asked.

He scanned the program. No eulogy. *What the fuck?* Daryl deserved better.

"—your mercy turn the darkness of death into the dawn of new life, and the sorrow of parting into the joy of heaven—"

This was a load of shit. Daryl would be rolling over in his coffin if he could, except, oh wait, he'd been cremated, not buried like he'd wanted. A vein throbbed along the side of his head, and he reached up to massage his temples. *Pay attention.*

Movement to his right drew his gaze, Laura making her way to the front. Shit, was it the reading already? He'd barely caught a single word so far. As she neared the pulpit, the minister backed away, making room. Looking down at the dais, Laura smoothed a piece of paper, then took a breath and began speaking.

"'To every thing there is a season, and a time to every purpose under the heaven.'"

Holy fuck. He closed his eyes. Not this reading.

"'A time to be born, and a time to die; a time to plant—'"

The last time he'd heard this, he'd been standing on a ramp at the Kandahar Airfield, shoulder to shoulder with hundreds of other soldiers as the sun baked them into the tarmac, all watching a coffin draped with a dusty Canadian flag being carried into the back of a pale-gray CC-130 Hercules. The disconsolate harmonies of bagpipes had accompanied the coffin, capturing the malaise of a fallen comrade like no words could. Far better than this reading.

"'—a time to mourn, and a time to dance; A time to—'"

The speaker had been a military padre who'd deployed with the battalion, a fat piece of shit who hadn't known the first thing about the infantry or even being a soldier. Instead of magazines full of bullets, the padre had carried licorice in the pouches of her load-bearing vest, which she handed out to the soldiers on her rounds.

"'—A time to get, and a time to lose; a time—'"

Before the ramp ceremony, she'd come around the lines to offer comfort, which none of the troops wanted, at least from her. He'd spoken to her, partly because he'd felt sorry for her, only to be given the advice that when she was sad, she liked to sew. He'd been speechless.

"'—away; A time to rend, and a time to sew; a time—'"

"How many soldiers like to fucking sew?"

Laura paused, eyes darting in his direction. Had he spoken aloud? *Shit.* His face grew hot as she continued speaking, her words no longer registering. He barely noticed her taking her seat or the minister moving back to the pulpit.

"Let us pray."

He bowed his head, hands folded in his lap. *Keep it together.*

"Merciful Father and lord of all life, we thank You now for all Daryl's life, for every memory of love and joy, for every good deed done by Daryl, and every sorrow shared with us."

Merciful? So it was merciful to allow a man to dedicate his life to his country, then let him die by his own hand in some dingy basement? Or was that supposed to be sharing in Daryl's sorrows?

"Father, the death of Daryl brings an emptiness into our lives. We are separated from him and feel broken and disturbed."

Sweat rolled down his back, but despite the heat, goose bumps were popping on his arms. How much longer could he sit here? Thankfully, the minister appeared to be nearing the end.

"May God give you His comfort and His peace, His light and His joy, in this world and the next."

So it was peace Daryl had found? While the blood had slowly been cut off to his brain, he'd found peace at last? Or had he wished he'd done more? Had he felt pain at the end?

He squinted up at a window where the sun struck him square in the face. Pressing his lips together, he forced his eyes open, reminded of yet another ramp ceremony he'd attended in Afghanistan, where the sun had blinded him as he'd listened to yet another speech commending a dead brother to the unknown. Tears welled in his eyes.

The dead man had been an American, a soldier who'd been catching a ride between forward operating bases with a Canadian platoon only to be killed in a vehicle ambush en route. Hugh hadn't known anything about the soldier, had only gone to the ramp ceremony to show support, noticing with interest the battle-hardened Special Forces officer who'd spoken.

"Pain strengthens the soldier's heart."

He'd been captivated from the opening words, the officer being the only person who'd ever been so up-front about death. Death wasn't simply one of those things; it was the biggest suck of all. Death was loss, and any self-respecting soldier hated to lose.

"Pain strengthens the soldier's heart."

But soldiers didn't have to meekly accept their fate. Out of all the motivators, pain was one of the best, especially considering all the terrible things that were part and parcel of a soldier's job. War was hell, and real soldiers knew how to weaponize their pain to fight back.

"Pain strengthens the soldier's heart."

Daryl had been a real soldier, and so was he.

Another jolt in his ribs drew his attention back to the proceedings. The minister had ceased talking and was walking to the head of the aisle. Shaking his head, he glanced at Steve, who was retracting his elbow from Hugh's side.

"Is it done?" he asked.

Steve nodded. "You all right? You were zoned out there, staring at the ceiling and mumbling."

"I'm fine," he said.

Laura had retrieved the urn and was taking position behind the minister. When she was ready, the minister led the way down the aisle. As they filed out, people in each subsequent pew rose and followed, maintaining a respectful distance behind Laura.

After the congregation passed his pew, he rose and followed the mass of people outside, bringing a hand up to shield his eyes as he exited into the bright sunshine. In front of the

church, Laura got into a car, which drove away. He turned to
Steve and Rick.

"I guess that's that," he said. What had just happened?

"Definitely short and sweet," Rick said, shaking his head.
"Never thought I'd be wishing for a longer service."

"No kidding," he said, then checked his watch. Time to get
going. "You guys know the directions?"

Steve and Rick nodded. After shaking their hands, he made
his way to his truck, then drove to the memorial gardens for
the interment. He linked up with Steve and Rick on the edge
of the parking lot, walking with them along a crushed-gravel
pathway.

"Does this seem a bit fake?" Rick said, gesturing around.

"The gardens?" Steve asked.

"No, this whole service. It's like she's going through the
motions," Rick said, frowning.

Following behind, footsteps crunching along the crushed
gravel lining the path, he said nothing. Laura had loved Daryl;
she'd said as much yesterday. Still, Rick had a point. Daryl
hadn't been big on formality, but he'd recognized the importance of ceremony.

Up ahead, the path widened into a poured-concrete landing with what looked like a row of lockers in the center, beside
which stood Laura and the minister. A bronze plaque leaned
against the bottom row of lockers, upon which he could just
make out Daryl's name. As people formed a semicircle around
the lockers, he followed Steve and Rick onto one of the wings,
coming to a stop with his hands clasped behind his back.

When the last straggler had joined the circle, the minister
began speaking. "Into the freedom of wind and sunshine, we
let you go. Into the—"

Rick nudged Hugh. "This is where she's putting him? These
look like the type of lockers you'd find in a bus station."

Daryl had loved being outdoors; she could have placed him at the base of one of the dozens of trees that populated the grounds. But this, jammed into a safe-deposit box, would have been the last thing he'd have wanted.

In front, the minister droned on. "Into the wind's breath and the hands—"

Rick was shaking his head. "It's disrespectful, is what it is."

He glared at Laura, the blood rushing to his head and drowning out the speech. Whatever else he'd been, Daryl had been a good friend. She could have told him any time yesterday that she was cremating him, but she hadn't. Why? And what could he do now?

He almost missed Laura placing Daryl's urn into a locker. After setting the urn inside, she stepped back, and the minister put a hand on her shoulder, then led her off. Once she was out of the way, people began moving forward individually to the niche where Daryl's urn had been placed, standing quietly, then departing. At the edge of the concrete pad, he waited with Rick and Steve until it was their turn.

"That cold bitch," Rick said, speaking loudly enough to cause several heads to turn toward him. "She doesn't give a shit he's dead."

"Looks that way," Hugh muttered. She had to know this wasn't what Daryl would have wanted.

Steve nodded to the lockers. "Here she comes."

He turned, instinctively stepping aside to make room for Laura.

"Thank you, all of you, for coming," she said, pausing a few feet from the group.

Rick extended his arm to shake Laura's hand. "The least we could do," he said, voice dripping with fake sincerity. "I'd have been happy to do more if you'd asked, maybe done a reading or something."

Dropping Rick's hand, she turned to Hugh. "You did more than enough just by coming," she said. "He would've wanted to keep this as minimal as possible."

"Are you sure?" Hugh said, nodding toward the row of lockers where Daryl's urn sat. "I thought he wanted to be buried."

"He didn't."

He gestured around him. "At least you could've picked a nicer spot. Closer to nature," he said. "Not in some storage locker."

"It's called a columbarium," she said, a thin smile on her face. "And I didn't want him to feel alone."

His heart leaped into his throat. He wanted to yell at her, call her out as a heartless bitch. Daryl would've probably loved it, but disrupting the ceremony wouldn't do anything now. Body shaking, he swallowed his rage, pushing it deep inside where it could simmer. "I'm sure he'd appreciate the thought."

"I'm sure," she said, contemplating him for a moment before looking away. "Gentlemen, again, thank you for coming." With a final nod, she moved off, stopping to speak with others among the crowd.

"Jesus H. Christ," Rick said, whistling. "I changed my mind. She's actually glad he's dead."

"Funerals always bring out the worst in people," Steve said, shuffling his feet uncomfortably. "Daryl could be an asshole sometimes, but he still served his country proudly."

"Damn right he did," he said, hands balled into fists. He should have said something. Daryl would have done as much for him.

"We'd better pay our respects," Rick said, turning to face the niche. Without waiting for a response, he walked up, came to attention, and snapped his right hand to the corner of his right eye in a crisp salute.

Steve followed, standing beside Rick and making the sign of the cross on his forehead and shoulders. His lips moved in silence, and then he stepped off. When he had gone, Hugh approached the urn.

Standing in front of the columbarium, he drew a deep breath, then reached out to place a hand beside the niche where Daryl's urn rested. Leaning against the concrete column, he hung his head. "I'm sorry," he whispered, a tear running down his cheek. "I let you down." Images of Daryl played through his head, mostly the memory of Daryl asking him to take his guns. "I should have done more."

Blinking away tears, he backed up. After a couple of steps, he set his jaw, puffed out his chest, and came to attention, remaining rigid for several seconds before slowly raising his right arm in a salute, holding it for several seconds. With a snap of his jacket sleeve, he dropped his arm, then whirled on his heels and walked to where Rick and Steve stood on the path leading back to the parking lot.

"Let's get out of here," Rick said. "You guys want a drink? I know a place close by where we could toast a few to Daryl's memory."

He nodded. But as he followed Rick and Steve, the idea lost its appeal. It wasn't like they were all best buds. Rick was all right, but to be perfectly honest, Steve had always creeped him out, always trying too hard to be sincere and friendly, like a religious freak. Besides, the only people he could stand these days were Elizabeth, Daryl, and Dr. Taylor, and Daryl was dead.

By the time he reached the parking lot, he'd decided to return to the hotel, maybe even drive back to Ottawa. "Listen, guys—"

Rick turned. "You're not backing out, are you?"

He shrugged, hands in his pockets. "I'm not sure it's the best idea. I'm tired."

"Come on," Rick said, holding his hands out. "Don't disappoint Daryl. You know he'd have done the same for you."

It was true, of course. Daryl would have drunk all night to his memory, with whoever was around. Hugh paused. "All right, I'll see you there."

As he watched Rick and Steve head to their cars, Hugh wondered if the tightness in his chest might be wrong. It had been a while since he'd been off work; maybe being around soldiers—real soldiers, not desk jockeys—would be good. Hell, maybe he could even throw out a few of his recent thoughts without having to worry about it coming back on him. Shaking his head, he went to find his truck.

After a twenty-minute drive, he was striding through Kingston's Hub, a central area of bars and restaurants catering to university students, military personnel, and even the families of convicts imprisoned in one of two major penitentiaries in and around the city. Normally packed during the school year, the streets of the Hub were dead on a Thursday night at the start of summer, much to his relief.

He arrived at the pub where Rick had said to meet and found them seated at a rickety table with a piece of paper jammed under a leg. He walked over and sat down, his shoes squeaking across the scuffed floor. "Nice place."

Rick smiled, picked up a pitcher of beer, and filled an empty pint glass, then shoved it across the table. "Nothing fancy," he said. "But the price is right."

"Daryl's kind of place," Steve said.

"To Daryl," Rick said, raising his glass in the air.

"To Daryl," Hugh and Steve said in unison, raising their glasses in salute before clinking them together and taking long mouthfuls.

"Can you believe that funeral?" Rick said, wiping his mouth as a waitress came by with a plate of nachos.

Steve reached for a tortilla chip, working it free from layers of hardened cheese. "It wasn't much," he said, finally extracting the chip and stuffing it into his mouth. "But it did the trick. What else is important?"

Rick leaned forward, resting his meaty forearms on the wobbly table and spilling beer from Steve's glass. "What else is important? How about showing some respect?"

"Was it really that bad?" Steve said, shaking beer off his hand.

"Are you serious?" Rick said. "Daryl was a hero, he should have been buried in the national military cemetery up in Ottawa, never mind cremated against his wishes and left in some grubby locker. And why wasn't there an honor guard or a bugler?" He threw back the rest of his beer, then refilled his glass. "And how about that wife of his? You know what I heard?"

Steve shook his head.

"What?" Hugh asked when it became apparent Rick was waiting for a response.

"A friend of mine with the Kingston police told me that when they showed up to tell her the news, she took one look at them and said, 'Let me guess, Daryl's dead.' They didn't even get a chance to say anything. Can you believe that? Like she expected it or something."

He closed his eyes. "That's not true," he said. Rick's habit of exaggerating had evidently not diminished over time. "She's the one who found him."

"How do you know?" Steve said.

"She told me."

"Maybe so," Rick said, his face impassive. "But she obviously didn't give a fuck. How else do you explain today?"

He sighed. "I don't know," he said. "She told me they'd been having problems."

"All I can say is if you don't stand behind the troops, feel free to stand in front of 'em."

He chuckled. Rick could be full of shit, but every now and then, he made some good points. Like Daryl deserving better.

Rick took another long draught, then emptied the pitcher between the glasses. "Hey, who's up for some shots?"

"I don't know, it's early," Steve said.

"Come on, for Daryl," Rick said, scanning the room for a server. "A little nectar of the gods is just what the doctor ordered."

Hugh stared into his half-empty glass. This was a bad idea. Still, hadn't the gods given Achilles nectar after his best friend, Patroclus, had been killed? Had Dr. Taylor told him that? He couldn't remember, but it couldn't be a coincidence. He held up a finger. "Okay, one round."

"That's what I like to hear," Rick said. "One round at a time." He flagged down a waitress and ordered three shots of dark rum and another pitcher of beer.

When the drinks arrived, he raised his shot glass in silence, then solemnly tipped the contents into his mouth. As the slightly warm rum burned down his throat, he grimaced, recalling something else Dr. Taylor had said. Achilles had only received the nectar after embracing the inevitability of his own death.

He met Rick's eyes and made a circle in the air with a finger. "Another round."

Yeah, one round at a time.

CHAPTER 18

Hugh blinked his eyes open. Pounding filled his brain, making it impossible to think. Everything was throbbing. Why couldn't he focus? He brought a hand up and rubbed his eyes, discovered he was lying facedown on carpet. No wonder his face burned. Raising his head, he peered around through bleary eyes. Where was he?

With a Herculean effort, he braced himself on the floor and lifted himself to a semi-push-up position, knees still on the ground. Exhaling, he pushed into a full kneel, his stomach revolting at moving from horizontal to vertical. He hunched over, hands on his bare knees. Wait a second, where were his pants? He had his shirt, but his pants were AWOL. His stomach churned once more, and suddenly his pants didn't matter, not throwing up was the important thing. When the queasiness passed, he looked around again.

His feet were in a door frame, on the other side of which was a bathroom. Taking several short breaths, he lurched to his feet, bracing himself against the wall. Toiletries cluttered the bathroom counter, his own by the look of them. So he was in his hotel room, better and better. How long had he been lying here?

His stomach heaved again, and he staggered into the bathroom, leaning heavily on the countertop. Battling the fog in his head, he searched for the toilet, catching a glimpse of a haggard image in the mirror, its worn-down face covered in black dust. *What the . . . ?*

Bringing a hand up, he wiped his chin, pulling it away to find his palm covered in small black flecks. On instinct, he smelled his palm, recoiling when the overpowering stink of Copenhagen assaulted him. Gagging, he jerked his hand away and collapsed over the toilet, hugging it as he vomited.

When he stood, his stomach marginally stabilized, the pounding in his head had diminished. Except the noise was still happening. Stumbling into the foyer, the thumping grew louder. Like a misguided homing missile, he zeroed in on the sound until he stood in front of the door to the hallway. How long had it been going on?

Reaching up, he fumbled with the latch, and the pounding thankfully stopped. As the chain was about to fall, he paused. *Better check first.* He stooped, pressing an eye to the peephole. Something moved in the hall, drawing away from the door until Steve's face came into view. *Shit.*

"What do you want?" he said, cringing as his voice reverberated off the door.

"Hugh?" Steve said, putting his face back to the peep hole. "You all right?"

"I'm fi—" he said, stifling another gag. "What are you doing here?"

Steve pulled back from the door, his face fuzzy through the distorted perspective of the peephole. "I wanted to make sure you made checkout," he said. "And I brought breakfast."

Hugh glanced at his watch. Ten o'clock—checkout was in an hour. "Shit." He should tell Steve to go away; the last thing he wanted to do was talk to anyone. Still, the guy had checked on him; the least he could do was be somewhat gracious.

He fiddled with the chain, and then opened the door. Steve had a brown paper bag in one hand and a cardboard tray holding two paper cups in the other. Annoyingly, aside from some light stubble and reddish eyes, the man looked none the worse for wear.

Steve whistled. "You look terrible," he said. His eyes flicked down. "Where are your pants?"

On instinct, he looked down also, triggering a brief bout of dizziness. Right. His pants were still missing. "They're in here. Somewhere," he said, leaning on the wall.

"Can I come in?"

He nodded, shuffling aside. Steve came into the room and set the bag and tray down by the television, then pulled out one of the drinks and cracked the brown plastic top.

While Steve sipped his drink—coffee by the smell—Hugh entered the bathroom and ran water in the sink. Passing a face cloth under the tap, he squeezed it, then pressed it to his face, the cold dampness fresh on his skin. "How did you know I was here?" he said, voice muffled by the face cloth.

"I brought you back last night." From the main room came the rustling of curtains being opened. "You were pretty messed up."

He traded the face cloth for a hand towel, speaking as he dried his face. "I think I still am."

"I brought breakfast if you want it."

He grunted, his stomach roiling. "Not sure food is the best idea." Or maybe the greasy odor wafting from other room might help. *Worth a try.* He found Steve sitting in a chair by the window, sipping coffee.

"You reconsider?" Steve asked.

He nodded, hesitantly, then reached into the bag and removed a squarish lump. He unwrapped it and took a tentative bite, letting his body warm up to the idea. When the first few bites stayed down, he sat on the foot of the bed and began taking larger bites.

He glanced at Steve, who was staring off and periodically sipping his coffee. *What's your deal?* When the first sandwich was done, Hugh dug into the bag and pulled out another. "Thanks," he said. "I almost feel like a person again." He took a bite, then continued speaking, mouth full. "You said you got me back here last night?"

Steve nodded, crossing his legs and shifting so his body faced away from Hugh. "You don't remember?"

"No," he said, grabbing the remaining cup of coffee. "Don't remember much. What happened to Rick?"

"I got him a taxi," Steve said. "He was a little more coherent than you."

Staring at Steve, he swallowed the remains of the breakfast sandwich and washed it down with some coffee. He spied his wayward tin of Copenhagen, upended on the bedside table. Cursing at the wasted tobacco, he reached across the bed and scraped together a mouthful from the pile splayed across the tabletop. The direct approach with Steve would probably be best. "So what's bothering you?" Hugh asked, scooping the accumulated tobacco into his palm.

Steve coughed. "Just glad you're all right."

"Steve, I might have been born at night, but it wasn't last night," he said, jamming the dip into his bottom lip and tamping it into position with his tongue. His mouth filling with saliva, he scanned the room, spying an empty glass on the bedside table. "No offense." He grabbed the glass and held it in his lap.

"None taken," Steve said, face contorted in a thin smile. "Like I said, I wanted to make sure you were all right."

"I'm fine," he said, spitting. A long tendril of drool hung from his mouth, stubbornly refusing to disconnect until he wiped it away.

"That's disgusting," Steve said, shuddering.

He smiled. "It's always like that after a night of drinking." He straightened his face. *Enough small talk.* "Why are you really here?" The combination of food, caffeine, and nicotine had gone a long way, but now he just wanted to get out of this shitty town.

Steve abruptly stood, turning to peer out the window. "What do you remember from last night?"

This again? Looking into his lap, he racked his brain. "I remember having shots at that place we started, then getting kicked out and going to another place." He winced. "I remember tequila shots. Not much after that." He squinted at Steve. "Wait a sec, you were drinking all night, too, I remember that. How come you're not hungover?"

Steve's sheepish face peeked over his shoulder, his lazy eye skewing toward the bathroom. "I started drinking water while you guys kept doing shots."

He shook his head, trying to recall. It was possible.

Turning around, Steve sat back down, leaning forward with his elbows braced on his knees. "So you don't remember the things you were saying last night?"

"No," Hugh said, raising the glass and spitting into it. Where was this going? "Are you going to let me in on the big secret? Because if you're not, I should hit the road."

Steve chewed on his thumbnail, his face pensive. "All that stuff about Daryl's journal, you don't remember any of that?"

A tingle ran up his spine, but he shook his head. *Careful.* "I might have talked about the journal, I don't know. Laura gave it to me. Take a look if you want." He nodded to where the book lay on the desk.

Steve glanced over, then got up, grabbed the journal, and sat back down. Cracking it open, he began thumbing through the pages.

While Steve read, Hugh searched for his pants, finding them tucked between the bed and the wall. While he put them on, he stole glances at Steve, who was buried in the book. "Why are you so interested in that thing?"

Instead of answering, Steve kept leafing through pages. The furrow between his eyebrows deepened the more he read.

"Hey, I asked you a question."

Steve's eyes flicked up over the top of the journal, then back down. He sighed, then lowered the journal and met Hugh's gaze. "Last night. You said Daryl was onto something."

"So what?" His stomach suddenly complained, as if breakfast was revolting.

Steve looked away. "We were talking about treatment of veterans. You said Daryl wanted to attack civilians to make a point, that civilians were sheep or something like that."

"Sheeple," he said quietly. Snippets of conversation played through his head, vaguely matching what Steve was describing.

"Sheeple, that's it," Steve said, one eye darting back to Hugh, the other one focusing beside him. "You said Daryl was right, but he chickened out." He leaned forward. "You said you could do it, finish what he couldn't. What did you mean by that?"

"I was drunk," he said in a quiet voice. Had he really said that? Hell, he didn't even know if he really believed it, so why would he have said it? He realized Steve was expecting some sort of response. "I'd never do that."

Steve sighed again as if the weight of the world were on his shoulders, then replaced the journal on the desk. He stood and ran a hand through his thinning hair. "You weren't totally honest about what you're doing."

"I was," he said, body tensing. "I work in Defence Headquarters."

"I'm talking about you being on sick leave."

Another pang in his stomach. "How do you know that?"

Steve shook his head. "People talk, Hugh, and it's a small military, you know that," he said. "I'm worried. About you. About what you might do."

He closed his eyes. *Christ.* Was he seriously listening to this right now? "I'm going through a rough patch, that's all. You shouldn't take everything I say to heart. Whatever I said, I was just bitching. That's what soldiers do." He opened his eyes to find Steve facing him, slowly edging closer.

"Guys going through a rough patch don't talk about attacking civies," he said, reaching out to lay his hands on Hugh's shoulders. "And when those guys have PTSD, it gets serious."

Familiar tendrils of rage lashed through him. This was Steve talking—the man who'd faked so many medical problems he'd earned the label of sick parade commando. He rose from the bed, dimly aware of his heart beating in his throat. "Who the fuck do you think you are?"

Steve stepped back, mouth agape. "I'm just trying to help—"

"You're not," he said, snarling. "I don't know what you're up to, but it sure as hell isn't helping."

"That's not fair," Steve said, shielding his body with his hands as he backed away. "I know what it's like to be down on your luck—"

He drove a finger into Steve's chest. "You're talking out of your ass. You have no idea what I'm going through," he said, spittle flying into Steve's face. "You've never even finished a tour, never mind multiple deployments to the world's worst shitholes. And you were always safe in the rear, cozying up to whatever boss you could find. So don't tell me what going through a rough patch is like."

"Well, it wasn't me who was blabbing about shooting civies last night," Steve said, chin thrust out as if daring Hugh to hit him.

Hugh spat in the glass, then slammed it down on the desk, sending black, tarry spit over the sides. "First of all, we're soldiers—at least I am—and if I was talking about shooting people last night, well, that's what I do for a living. If you were half the soldier you claimed to be, you'd know that. Close with and destroy? That's not just a pretty motto. Maybe when you've done some real soldiering you can judge me for what you think I said. Until then, keep your fucking ideas to yourself."

Steve's shoulders rose nearly to his ears, as if to say he couldn't help himself. "I'm just trying to help."

"I don't need your help."

Steve stared at Hugh for a few moments, and then his face hardened. "I should have known better." He made for the door, pausing halfway to spin and face Hugh. "You and Daryl are two peas in a pod. Too stupid to ask for help."

Hugh spoke through clenched teeth. "Just too stupid to talk to self-interested fucks like you."

"I ought to report you," Steve said. "How would you like that?"

"Go ahead, maybe it'll shorten the wait time for an appointment," he said, fists forming at his sides. "Besides, it would give me an excuse to beat the living shit out of you. Or did you not consider the potential consequences of taunting a guy with PTSD?" He took two predatory steps toward the door, closing the distance in an instant. Part of him wished Steve would take the bait.

Face suddenly pale, Steve fumbled for the door handle. Turning to exit, he paused, briefly, then looked over his shoulder, mouth open as if to say something. Meeting Hugh's eyes, he closed his mouth with a snap, turned, and walked out.

Hugh strode to the door, slamming it shut and latching the chain before stomping to the bed and sitting down. Leaning forward, he held his head in his hands, rocking back and forth, his body shaking while he racked his brain, trying to recall what he'd said last night. Try as he might, the adrenaline hammering through his veins made it impossible to focus.

Besides, he couldn't deny it; intimidating Steve had felt good, really good, as if he could diminish his own pain by taking it out on someone else. Maybe standing up for himself a little more was what he needed to do. Was that what Daryl had been getting at? He closed his eyes and buried his face in his hands.

CHAPTER 19

Hugh sat bare chested on the floor of his unfinished basement, the room tinged gray as light filtered through the windows off the concrete floor. It was cooler here, a welcome respite from summer's heat, but it also felt better down here for other reasons, too. Maybe it was the Spartan decor, or the cave-like environment. Whatever it was, it seemed to be the only place he felt like himself.

The stairs creaked behind him, and he looked up from the tablet in his lap. Elizabeth. It had been a week since Daryl's funeral, and in that time, they'd been like two specters haunting the same abandoned house.

She started down the stairs, then stopped. "Can we talk?"

"We can," he said, setting the tablet beside him.

The stairs creaked again. "Do I have to talk to your back?"

He sighed and dropped his head, gaze flitting to the tablet's screen, where he'd been scanning the news. Another suicide, this time a master corporal with three tours in Afghanistan, found dead in the barracks at Canadian Forces Base Edmonton. Daryl's suicide two weeks prior had received no media attention, but this one promised to get lots of coverage since the member's family was claiming he'd been battling the military for years for help fighting PTSD. The media was lapping it up.

He turned off the device, then glanced over to Daryl's journal, the covers splayed open. Underneath the journal was the P226 Sig Sauer pistol. His eyes lingered for a moment, and then he pushed himself up and turned to face his wife.

Her eyes were puffy, and her hair hung limply. The ridges of her cheekbones jutted out, creating a look of gauntness that might have shocked him if he hadn't been so numb inside.

"What are you doing down here?" she said, crossing her arms over her chest.

"Keeping cool."

She sniffled, then wiped one eye. "Why won't you talk to me?" she said, stepping off the bottom step.

"We're talking right now."

She tittered, a nervous laugh that made it sound like she was actually about to cry. "This isn't talking," she said. "This is me speaking and you being the ice man."

He watched her through his peripheral vision, not taking in specific details, but noticing every movement she made. His senses were heightened now, continually dialed in like he was on patrol all the time. Good thing he'd stopped taking his medication after getting back from Kingston.

She slowly raised a hand to his cheek. "What happened at Daryl's funeral?"

Now that she was close, he focused on her, plucking her hand off his cheek. "I said good-bye to my friend." He held her arm in front of him, staring at her, then abruptly released her. Spinning on his heel, he sank to the ground and pulled his legs back into the cross-legged position he'd been sitting in when she'd come downstairs.

"Why are you so different? I don't even know who you are since the funeral."

He reached for his tablet, tapping in his password to unlock the device.

Her voice came from above and behind him; she hadn't moved. "Do you even care how I'm doing?" she said. "You just lock yourself away down here."

He did care for her, didn't he? But things seemed to be falling away from him.

She circled him and sat down opposite him, sticking her face in his own. "What do you do down here all day?" Her voice was desperate.

His eyes darted to the black book on the floor beside him, then returned to the tablet. "I stay connected."

"To who? To what? By surfing the Internet?" she said, her eyes widening. "Or by reading this stupid diary?" She reached for the journal.

His hand shot out, pressing the journal into the floor. A slight scraping of metal on bare concrete came from the pistol underneath. Had she heard? He looked up, but her eyes were unreadable. A hot flash seared through his head. "What do you care?"

She stared at him, body trembling. "Why won't you return Dr. Taylor's calls?"

He turned back to the tablet, leaving his hand on the journal. "The military will assign me a therapist." Did that sound as hollow to her as it did to him? The truth was, he didn't really care either way.

"The same military that blew off your initial assessment?" she said, an incredulous tone in her voice as she shook her head. "It's been a month, and you haven't seen anyone."

"The case load is too high. The clinic explained that when they rescheduled the appointment."

"You're falling through the cracks," she said heatedly, sticking her face into his. "Call your boss, get him involved. Do something."

He flinched away. "He won't do anything." Couldn't she see that?

"But you're dying down here," Elizabeth said, her bottom lip quivering. "Have you seen yourself?"

"You should talk," he snapped, glaring at her. *Enough.*

She drew back, mouth shaped into a perfect O. "Excuse me?"

He scowled. "Don't look like that. You think your obsession with working out is healthy?"

"I can't do this anymore," she said, her voice so quiet he could barely hear. Pushing herself to her feet, she wiped the seat of her pants. "If you don't care our marriage is falling apart, why should I?" She clutched her arms to her chest and moved back to the stairs.

"Where are you going?" he called after her.

Her voice came from the foot of the stairs. "I need a break," she said. "I'm going to my parents."

Great, just great. "What about Canada Day?" he said, speaking over his shoulder.

Her footsteps paused. "Seriously?" she said. "What about it?"

"It's in three days," he said. "I thought we were going downtown." He'd even booked a room in the Laurier.

"Are you for real?" she said. "After what we just talked about, you still think we're going to Canada Day?" She shook her head. "Go by yourself if it's so important to you." The stairs creaked as she set foot on the bottom step.

Springing up, he dropped the tablet to the floor and strode after her. "What's your problem? I thought you'd be there for me."

"Be there for you?" She paused, one hand on the bannister. "You think I'm not there for you?"

"Did I stutter?"

She closed her eyes. "I had a test yesterday," she said, her voice catching. "My hormone levels aren't returning to normal."

He stopped in midstride. Had she told him that? Maybe, he couldn't remember.

She wiped an eye with the back of one hand. "I might have cancer." Dropping her hand, she met his gaze, staring at him like he was an insect. "And if I remember right, you said you'd be there for me."

Blackness oozed from his heart as he shifted his weight from foot to foot. "I'm sorry."

"Are you?" she said, her voice lashing him. "Because from what I can see, the only person you feel sorry for is yourself."

How dare she? "What the fuck do you want me to do?" he said, rage pulsing through him.

"I want you to try," she said. "Show me even one sign you're trying."

"I am." He looked away, hands clenched into fists. "It's not easy, you know."

She scoffed, and the embers of his anger lit, fanned into something that threatened to consume him. "You always used to tell me how important your job was, how you were making the world a better place. Remember what you'd say every time you got another task?"

He looked down. "More duty, more honor."

"That's right. And all those times you were gone on exercise or deployed and I cried myself to sleep, I always repeated that to myself. More duty, more honor. I thought you were such a hero." She sniffed. "But I see the truth now."

"Stop."

"There's always something more important you have to do. You don't care about us, but what you don't see is the military doesn't care about you. They'll use you and throw you away when they're done because you were wrong. It's not more honor, it's just more duty."

"Stop." Whatever was coming, it would send him over the edge.

"You've bought into their message completely, and it's going to cost you everything, and for what? The world's no better because of anything you did. You're just a chump."

He threw his hands up and roared, turning and slamming a palm into an exposed steel support beam. She couldn't talk to him that way, not after everything he'd sacrificed.

"Get out," he said between gritted teeth.

"I want my husband back," she said, softly, the words cutting him to the bone.

He turned to her, seething. "That man is gone," he bellowed, body shaking. "Get out!"

She flinched, as if he'd physically struck her, staring at him with an intensity that rooted him to the ground. The silence that followed filled the basement with an almost physical presence, and he screamed, a primal yell of agony and rage. When he finished, she said nothing, merely looked at him, then slowly ascended the stairs.

Screaming again, he stomped over to where Daryl's journal lay on the floor and savagely kicked it. The book flew across the room and into a wall. Clippings sprayed from it like feathers from a bird hit by buckshot. His kick caught the pistol also, sending it skittering across the floor.

The front door slammed with a muffled thud. He closed his eyes, tried to control his breathing, counted, everything he'd been taught. It was useless. Red fire filled his head, fueling his anger like an accelerant, and he screamed again. The fury filled him, like he was going supernova. If it didn't stop . . .

He smashed his forehead into a wall stud, the resultant ringing in his head driving his wrath to new levels. He tore at a nearby wall, ripping open the plastic vapor barrier and clawing at the blue insulation underneath. When he grew short of breath, he cast about, the pistol lying on the concrete floor catching his attention. Gasping, he picked it up, walked to the middle of the basement, and sat down.

Still breathing heavily, he swung his head from side to side, the tattoo of St. Michael finally catching his eye. The frown on the archangel's face, something he'd always told himself was the burden of responsibility, now seemed to be an expression of disappointment, as if Hugh had failed some test.

"You were my guardian," Hugh said, the words coming out in a snarl. With his free hand, he began scratching the tattoo, sinking his nails into the shield until his skin became raw and moist. The face of the angel remained impassive.

Closing his eyes, he raised the pistol and placed the rear sights against his forehead. He inhaled deeply, then exhaled. Once. Twice. Eyes clenched tight, he lowered the pistol and depressed the magazine-release button, letting the loaded magazine fall out. With a metallic clang, it clattered onto the concrete, the top bullet popping out and tumbling across the floor.

He pulled back the slide with his left hand, then engaged the takedown lever, locking the action to the rear. Still breathing deeply, he continued stripping the weapon by feel, laying each piece on the floor in front of him from left to right. When the pistol was disassembled, he paused. One . . . two . . . three . . . all the way to ten, then picked up the frame and reassembled the pistol.

How many times did he take the pistol apart and put it back together? He couldn't tell, but by the time the rage had run its course, the last remnants of sunlight trickled in through the windows. Shaking his head, he stood and turned on a light, and the room filled with the weak yellow glow of two uncovered bulbs jutting from the ceiling. He was thirsty.

Fetching a bottle of whiskey from a stash under the stairs, he broke the seal and sipped, his cracked lips burning at the touch of alcohol. He retrieved his tablet and resumed his place on the floor, relishing the solid coldness of the concrete. Before turning on his tablet, he put in a dip, washing down the saliva with another belt from the bottle. He grimaced slightly, then entered his password and brought up the news.

It was the same story about the suicide in Edmonton. Why did he do this to himself? He took another swig, the heat in his throat the only warmth in his body. The rage lingered inside like some lurking menace, threatening to obliterate the tenuous control he'd established, so he drank again, scrolling through the comments section of the story.

"This guy was obviously mentally weak," Mike123 wrote. "No doubt made worse by the coddling that new recruits get. Canadian Forces need to bring back the tough-love training of the seventies and eighties to sort this out."

He clenched his jaw so tight his teeth hurt. He skipped to the next comment.

"Only news because it's a soldier. Suicide rate for soldiers is less than the country. Stop glorifying war."

His hands tightened on the tablet, sending little ripples across the screen. He should look away; reading more would only make him angrier. But he couldn't stop.

"What, was crappy old Canada too much for him? This guy must have been messed up if he could handle Afghanistan, then kill himself once he got back home. Good thing he did it before Canada Day."

The room went red. Roaring, he lifted the tablet, smashing it across his forehead, then tossing it aside as his yell morphed from rage to pain. A drop of blood trickled down the bridge of his nose, falling between his crossed legs. Impotent with fury, needing an escape valve, he turned his fists on himself, beating his head until spots appeared in his vision. He snatched up the bottle and hurled it against the wall, sending shards of glass spraying. Finally, he bent down, picked up the pistol, and jammed it into the waistband of his pants.

He paced like a caged animal. *Someone needs to pay.* A crunching under his foot caused him to stop and glance down, discovering his tablet, a spiderweb of cracks across the screen. Through the maelstrom of white lines, a green text box had popped up.

Bending over, grunting as the butt of the pistol dug into his stomach, he picked up the device and squinted, trying to see through the cracks. It was a calendar reminder for the reservation at the Château Laurier. *Go alone, how could she say that?* His heart quickening, he unlocked the device and opened his e-mail, searching for the confirmation.

After several minutes, he found the e-mail confirming his reservation for June 30 and July 1. He'd requested a room overlooking Major's Hill Park so they could see the Canada Day festivities. Had they given him one? He slumped to the floor.

As he sat, the pistol jabbed him again, so he pulled it out, holding it before his face. She thought he was a chump, did she? Gently, he placed the pistol down and turned to the tablet.

The device barely registered his finger dragging atop the screen, but eventually he opened a new window and started a search for Canada Day activities. Within seconds, he'd found a schedule for downtown Ottawa, including Parliament Hill, Confederation Park, and Major's Hill Park. His chest tightened.

Activities in Major's Hill Park started at ten in the morning and ran until ten forty-five at night, with many shows performing at a large temporary stage set up in the north end of the park. Great weather was expected—upward of thirty degrees Celsius—and the website was already advising people to plan for large crowds. By all rights, the entire downtown core would be packed from midmorning until late in the evening.

He let the tablet settle onto his lap and closed his eyes. The rage that had burned so brightly on reading the comments of the suicide story had died in intensity, but the coals remained, waiting to be fanned up. With Elizabeth gone, a part of him had been burned away. He had nothing else, no anchor, nothing holding him back. He opened his eyes and beheld the pistol on the floor in a new light.

Turning back to the tablet, he opened the reservation e-mail, then fumbled around for his phone. He dialed the hotel.

"Good evening. Château Laurier. How may I help you?"

He faltered. Surely the voice on the other end of the line would see through him, like the blinded cyclops had seen through Odysseus. But what exactly was he planning? He didn't know, only knew that he had nothing left to lose. "My name is Hugh Dégaré," he said. "I'd like to confirm a reservation for the thirtieth and the first, please." His heart raced even though it was a completely legitimate reason to call.

There was a brief pause at the other end of the line, broken only by the distant clicking of fingers on a keyboard. Then the receptionist answered. "Yes, sir, we've got you for the night of the thirtieth and the first. Check-in is at three p.m."

"Fantastic," he said, blood racing.

"Will there be anything else?"

He paused again, should he say anything? "Do you know if the room overlooks Major's Hill Park?"

More silence. "It does, sir. Were you planning on taking in the festivities?"

"Absolutely," he said. "I'm sure it'll be a blast."

"We look forward to having you stay with us. Have a good night."

The phone went dead. He pulled the receiver from his ear and stared at it. "I'm looking forward to it as well." Placing the phone on the counter in the darkened kitchen, he turned and went back downstairs. There was a lot to do to get ready.

CHAPTER 20

Hugh paused in the Château Laurier's parking lot, adjusting the golf bag slung from his left shoulder. In his right hand, he carried his olive-drab duffle bag, its weight straining against his fingers. On the verge of entering the hotel, an invisible force field held him back.

Was he really going through with this? It wasn't too late to turn around and go back to his truck, break out of the whirl-pool that was dragging him under. Nobody would be the wiser.

He shook his head. *No.* He'd come too far already. Besides, if not this, there'd be something else. There was no safe haven for him; he was between Charybdis and Scylla.

He entered the hotel, his boots clacking on the sandy-colored marble, the noise reverberating along the hall. It reminded him of the clickers worn on military parade boots, of resoluteness and purpose. At the thought, he subconsciously puffed out his chest and straightened his back.

The Adam Room was on his left, windows covered by white curtains that hid its sky-blue walls, white pillars, and chandeliers, like something transplanted from a French palace.

He kept walking, moving through the hotel's reading lounge, a room with a starkly different motif and wood paneling. The notes of a piano drifted from the lounge, its melodies echoing melancholic in the high-ceilinged room.

Skirting the lounge into the main lobby, he spied the reception desk. He beelined past several plush red chairs arranged around four large blue couches, then passed under an arch at least twice his height to join the rear of a line.

He shuffled in place, partly from impatience, partly from a churning in his stomach, like he needed to go to the bathroom. It was a familiar feeling, one he normally got at the onset of a mission. It was the call to action, a good sign; at least it had been in the past. When the person ahead of him moved off and the newly free receptionist smiled at him, he nodded in return. Hoisting his bags, he stepped toward the dark granite desk.

"Good afternoon, bonjour," the receptionist said, her dark hair pulled back into a tight bun. "How can I help you? *Puis-je vous aider?*"

"Dégaré," he said, lowering his bags, his left hand resting protectively on the golf clubs.

A polite smile broke the girl's face. "*Un moment s'il vous plaît,*" she said, turning to her computer. "*Je vais vérifier votre réservation.*"

He stammered before spitting out a response. "I'm staying today and tomorrow."

When the girl glanced at him, her smile tightened, though whether she was embarrassed or apologetic from mistaking him for French Canadian was anybody's guess. "In town for Canada Day, sir?"

"I live here, actually," he said. "We wanted to stay downtown to avoid the traffic."

"We, sir?" she said, eyes darting around the lobby. "Will you need extra room keys?"

His heart skipped. *Keep it together.* "I'm the only one checking in," he said, tugging on his collar. Why hadn't he worn something else? He'd been trying to blend in with what he thought guests at the Laurier would wear, choosing a pair of tan chinos and a tailored long-sleeve shirt. The garments now clung to his sweating body like a straitjacket. "My wife couldn't make it."

The girl tilted her head. "*Désolé,*" she said, presenting him with a small folio containing the swipe cards to his room. "Here are your keys."

"Thank you," he said, plucking the folio from her hand. He stooped to hoist his bags, then turned, searching for the elevators. If he remembered right, they were directly to his front, past the grand staircase with its black-and-gold railing. A glimpse of movement to his left caught his attention, and he whirled, clutching the golf bag closer.

A young bellhop stopped in midstride, a quizzical look on his face. He extended a hand. "Sir, can I help with your bags?"

"No, thanks," he said, pulling the clubs over his left shoulder and hoisting the duffel bag in his right hand. "But could you point me to the elevators?"

He moved in the indicated direction. A set of elevator doors was already open, so he entered and reached for the button to close the doors. At least he'd have the car to himself.

The doors were almost shut when a man's hand jutted between them. There was a brief struggle as the man's arm pushed against the doors, and then they relented, opening enough for the man to board. He smiled as he stepped in.

"You take your life in your hands with these old elevators," he said, chuckling. The man was at least a head shorter than Hugh and probably twice as wide, a body type Daryl would have described as a beached whale. He nodded at the bag on Hugh's shoulder. "Hoping to shoot a few rounds?"

Hugh nodded, adrenaline shooting through his veins. "Something like that."

"You picked a great time, if you ask me," the man said. "Downtown will be packed, so the courses should be empty."

"I'm counting on it."

The man continued to stare at the bag slung from Hugh's shoulder. "New set of clubs?"

"The bag is new," he said, smiling. "The clubs are old ones, but good ones."

The man breathed in, as if satisfied. "Nothing like a reliable set of clubs. They boost your confidence just holding them."

"I know exactly what you mean."

The elevator lurched to a stop, followed by the ringing of a bell. It was the floor below where Hugh was staying. As the doors opened, the man smiled again, then exited. Seconds later, he arrived at his own floor.

A trickle of sweat rolled down his forehead as he shouldered his bags and stepped out of the elevator. Searching for his bearings, he found a sign indicating the direction of his room and walked briskly down the hall, eyes flitting between the numbers on the doors. Finally, he found it. The first part of his plan, the infiltration, was almost over. He slid one of the keys into the slot, opened the door, and entered. Once inside, he set down his bags, turned, and latched the door. The room was similar to the one he'd stayed in with Elizabeth, only smaller. Yet despite the similarities, this room felt sterile, almost sepulchral in contrast to the luxury and warmth he remembered from earlier in the year. Was it the room? Or that Elizabeth wasn't with him?

He pressed his lips together. It didn't need to be cozy; this was no vacation. Indeed, the only thing that mattered was the room's view. He moved to inspect the window.

He parted the thick drapes and pressed his face to the glass. Beneath him lay the full length of Major's Hill Park, with the northern end of the park—the part farthest from the hotel—in particularly good relief. In the afternoon summer light, it seemed closer than he'd remembered, probably under three hundred yards. Well within range.

The trees were a pleasant surprise. Although there were a lot—all in summer bloom—they didn't obscure the ground like they could have. Instead, only small portions of the park were covered from sight, mostly in the dogleg northwest corner. The park's open areas, including the far end, where a large covered stage had been erected, were all in clear view. In fact, practically the entire length of the park was observable. All in all, a lucky break.

He imagined what it would look like tomorrow, full of people like fish crammed in a barrel. He nodded, then went to his bags. First things first.

As he walked, he mentally rehearsed his next steps. It was just after five o'clock, and his stomach was growling. He'd go out for food—which would allow him to walk the ground in the park—then return to the hotel to complete his preparations. But before leaving, he needed to take a few precautions.

He reflected on his conversation in the elevator while running a hand over the hard gray shell that served as a cover for the golf club bag. He hadn't lied; he'd only bought the bag yesterday. Even the comment about the clubs being old wasn't a lie, not really. Releasing the cover's clips, he removed the protective hood and set it on the floor. Then he reached inside, grabbed the pistol grip of the AR-15, and pulled it out, cradling it in his arms.

Turning the rifle left and right in his hands, he inspected every inch of its jet-black surface, searching for any damage. There was none. Satisfied, he replaced the rifle in the bag's main compartment and knelt to unzip a side pouch, from which he pulled the Sig Sauer P226. After another quick inspection, he determined that it, too, had escaped any damage. Now he just needed to secure them.

A knock on the door caused his head to jerk up, and he fumbled the pistol, nearly dropping it. His heart leaped into his throat as a muffled voice called from the hallway.

Shit! His words caught in his throat as he jammed the pistol into the bag's side pocket. Grating came from the area of the doorknob—a key being inserted into the slot—and he groped for the pocket's zipper. *Don't panic.* But he couldn't help it. He stood hurriedly and shoved the golf club bag into a nearby closet, shutting the door at the same time the door to his room opened and a maid entered.

When the maid saw him, she stopped short, eyes opening wide. "I'm so sorry, sir, excuse me. The room was supposed to be empty."

He held up a hand, the other one resting on the closet door. "It's okay," he said, affecting a nonchalant air even as a flush burned up his face.

The maid backed out. "I'm very sorry, sir. Is there anything you need while I'm here?"

He shook his head, unable to speak.

"Have a good night, sir, and sorry again," she said, smiling as she shut the door.

He reached up and massaged his temples. His chest was tight, painfully so, and he focused on his breathing, imagining that even now, the maid was on her way to inform hotel security. Heart racing, he stood in the doorway where the maid had been, turned, and examined the closet. Nothing was visible from that angle; he was being stupid. A bite to eat and some fresh air would settle him down. Besides, what would happen, would happen.

He tossed his duffel bag onto the bed and opened it, removing a baseball hat. Returning to the closet, he secured the hood, then gently jimmied the bag into a corner of the closet. Next, he perched the hat precariously on top of the bag, carefully aligning the brim with one of the horizontal lines of trim.

He stepped back to inspect his work, nodding after a few seconds. If anybody meddled with the bag, the hat would fall, and if that happened, it was virtually impossible they'd replace the hat in the same position. He couldn't be too careful; the maid was a case in point.

Shutting the closet, he grabbed a room key and exited, hanging a Do Not Disturb sign from the knob on his way out. He returned to the room twice to ensure everything was as he'd left it, but finally he made it out of the hotel. Darting around several cars near the doors, he descended the front steps and melted into the throng of people along Rideau Street. A breeze funneled down the street, still warm, but circulating enough air to make his shirt less sticky. He turned left and headed toward the ByWard Market.

He got a hamburger and fries at a fast-food place, washing down the meal without tasting it. Still hiccupping from eating so fast, he headed for Major's Hill Park, feeling for his Copenhagen as he walked, only to find an almost-empty tin. That wouldn't do.

There was a smoke shop in the heart of the market, but the thought of going there sent shivers up his spine. It wasn't simply the crowd, it was the chance of seeing someone he knew, even if he did have a perfectly fine reason for being downtown. Someone who knew him would ask where Elizabeth was or why he looked like shit, questions to which he had no good answers. Still, no chew was a nonstarter.

On the way, his senses worked overtime, noting everything ahead, above, and behind him. Several souped-up sports cars cruised the street on a loop while a group of bikers congregated on the open patio of one of the many restaurants, ten or fifteen street-racing motorcycles lined up outside. Women in flowing sundresses lined the sidewalks, followed by groups of peacocking young men. It was the ByWard Market in its summer glory, vibrant with laughter and the smells of fine dining spilling from patios and people mingling in the streets.

But for him, this sensory assault only made it more difficult to scan and assess the crowd for threats. He matched his gait to the people walking leisurely around him, using the forced slowness to watch invisibly as people enjoyed their evening, oblivious to nearly everything around them. There was a time he might have driven circuits through the market himself or admired the fit of a sundress. Now, he could barely suppress the urge to run. It was ironic, really; he no longer fit in to the very society he'd thought he'd been protecting.

He purchased two tins of Copenhagen at the smoke shop, topping up the wad in his mouth before leaving. Once outside, he resumed angling toward Major's Hill Park. His gait quickened, the urge to hasten growing more irresistible the longer he was gone from the safety of his room.

At Sussex Drive, he dashed across the street near the south end of the American embassy, then entered Major's Hill Park from the southeast. The air was cooler here, imbued with an aroma he hadn't experienced in some time, one he'd never smelled this early in the year. He didn't know what it was exactly—had always thought it was harvest dust kicked up by combines—but to him it meant summer changing to fall, the beginning of a season's end. The smell had always comforted him, and he closed his eyes and inhaled deeply, basking in the fragrance. It was right. Everything was right.

With a last breath, he opened his eyes and took in his surroundings. He was standing on a wooded path, but even here most of the park was visible. Glancing south at the Laurier, rising above the skyline like a medieval castle, he tried to visualize the view from his room. Some areas would be concealed, but by and large, he'd be able to see almost everything.

He moved to the center of the park and looked north to the outdoor stage, behind which stood the tall, blue-glassed walls of the National Gallery. Turning around, he found himself pointed almost directly at where his room was located in the Laurier's east wing. He smiled. How did the old saying go? *Time spent on reconnaissance is seldom wasted.*

The urge to return to the hotel was getting stronger, but he needed to walk the rest of the ground, see it for himself. What if he was missing something? He moved across the grass in the direction of the stage, paralleling a row of stately maple trees and flower beds bordering the park. The trees would offer some concealment, but concealment wasn't the same as cover. Leaves weren't much of a barrier.

He and Elizabeth had wanted to walk this route in February, but the snow had been too deep. His footsteps faltered at the memory. What would she think about what he was doing? He hardened his heart and continued walking. She'd walked out on him, not the other way around.

But the thought persisted, combining with the now barely contained need to return to his room. He stopped and turned. Behind him, sunlight lit the northern face of the Château Laurier like a postcard. Across the Rideau Canal, the Houses of Parliament cast long shadows, the structures themselves shrouded in darkness. In the orange light of the dying sun, the metallic green roofs were rust stained, blood colored.

She'd have loved it. Shaking his head, he checked his watch. With a last look, he hurried along, and ten minutes later, he was in his room. He headed straight for the closet, yanked open the door, and inspected the golf club bag. The hat's brim was still aligned with the horizontal line. *Good.* He exhaled, the tension that had been building in his body all night easing. He lugged the bag into the room.

Pulling out the AR-15, he placed it carefully on a spare blanket on the bed, then took out the pistol, several rifle and pistol magazines, and, lastly, a shoebox-sized container with his gun cleaning kit. He popped the lid off the plastic container and took out wire brushes, pull rods, cotton pads, rags, and oil, even dental picks for scraping carbon in hard-to-reach areas. Every tool had its place, and he laid them out in careful order from left to right, like a surgeon readying an operating room. Elizabeth had never understood that this was like meditation for him.

The thought of her made him pause, empty container in hand. The more he tried to suppress it, the more her face kept coming back. There was so much she didn't understand. He needed to explain it to her.

Abruptly standing, he rummaged in his duffel bag until he found Daryl's journal. As he removed the book, his hand brushed against the round firmness of a bottle. Bottle and journal in hand, he sat down at the room's desk. Unscrewing the cap, he raised the bottle to his lips and drank.

He opened the journal to one of Daryl's last entries, staring at words that seemed like so many scribbles. Had it really come to this? Now that he'd sat down, it was so real. He took another drink—longer this time—and slouched in the chair.

How would she ever understand what had brought him to this moment? What he was planning went against everything that had ever been important to him. Concepts that had been drilled into him for over twenty years—honor, duty, integrity— was he really going to callously throw those values aside? As if the greater part of his life had meant nothing? And how would he be remembered, after breaking what he'd always told her was a sacred trust?

"We, reposing especial trust and confidence in your loyalty, courage, and integrity . . . ," he said, reciting the introduction from his commissioning script, the document that made him an officer. He drank from the bottle again, like it was water. He'd spent hours poring over his commissioning scroll, awed by the responsibility it conferred. And here he was, about to throw it all away. He might as well wipe his ass with his scroll—there'd probably be more honor in that than in what he was planning.

But could honor help him sleep? Could courage help him forget? No, integrity could no more stop his hands from shaking than duty could help him bear the sight of the little girl he'd helped to kill. And weren't all those values predicated on trust between society and the military? So what happened when that trust broke down, when society forfeited its obligation to take care of those who would lay down their lives for the greater good?

"What goes around, comes around," he said, taking another swig, gagging, then forcing the bottle back to his lips. Amber liquid trickled from the corner of his mouth. Lowering the bottle, he belched.

He turned back to the journal, smoothed down a page, then wrote the date and time. At the next fresh line, he placed the nib of the pen, then hesitated, unsure how to proceed. Five seconds passed, ten. Words streamed through his head, pithy statements railing against the system or standing up for veterans. It was all so hollow, even his own justifications, how he had no other choice. Sighing, he drew his hand back, the pen hovering inches above the paper.

What did it all mean anyways? Had his best years been spent helping corrupt motherfuckers retain power in some godforsaken country on the other side of the world so his own country's selfish government could play partisan politics with the dregs of his miserable life? Where could he even find the words to express the rage, the sense of betrayal? It was visceral, primeval, something that had to be experienced, not explained.

He drank. Maybe he should close the book, stop this self-flagellation. But as the thought entered his mind, the pen touched the page as if guided by someone else's hand.

I'm so alone.

He carefully set down the pen beside the journal and read the words, the ink so fresh it glistened. When he was done, he read it again, and again, as if the words would disappear. What more could he say? There was nothing else, at least nothing he could explain in words.

But was that so strange? The communication he was best at was the language of death and destruction. Instead of words and sentences, he used grenades and bullets, rounds tumbling through flesh and bone in place of grammar and syntax. It was his profession—how many times had he told her that?—the only thing he'd ever been good at. She'd been the only truly good thing to happen to him, and he'd destroyed that, too. Now, in his time of need, he'd been cast out, human refuse.

He'd had a deal with the country, a bargain. He'd led a life like no other, an adrenaline junkie's dream of parachuting, rappelling, and, the biggest hit of all, armed combat. In return, he'd done the country's dirty work, knowing he'd be taken care of when all was said and done. But it hadn't worked out that way, had it?

"I did my part," he said, eyes watering. It had been so easy when it was only training. Even Bosnia hadn't been that bad— it wasn't like he'd committed atrocities; he just hadn't been able to stop them.

"I did my part." But nobody had told him how bad his part could get. Recruiting posters didn't show pictures of friends with the tops of their heads missing from the force of their helmets being blown off in explosions. And mission briefings didn't mention the women and children that would die because they were in the wrong place at the wrong time.

There was so much more he could say, but what would it add? He stood up, slowly, uncertain on his feet, the chair tipping over backward. Leaning on the table, he took another swig, then threw the bottle against the wall. "I did my part," he yelled. The bottle hit with a crack, splashing whiskey like thin paint splattering the wall. So be it. He would deal with the pain through the only language he knew. Violence.

With a start, he picked the pen up and wrote again.

Forgive me, Elizabeth.

He set down the pen and shut the journal. On wobbly legs, he teetered to his duffel bag and jammed the journal into the bottom, then stood, staring dumbly at the weapons on the bed. How could he clean them like this?

Spying the still-intact bottle on the floor, he staggered toward it. Halfway there, he tripped, so he crawled the remainder of the way, then drained the last drop into his mouth, the remnants of his supper rising in his throat.

What would she think now? He couldn't even do this right.

The thought of her caused a lump in his throat, and he braced himself on the floor, struggling to his feet, only to trip halfway there. Stumbling forward, he fell and struck his head against the back of a chair. He crumpled in a heap, blackness interspersed with sparkling dots spreading across his vision. As darkness took him, the words of her father came back, unbidden. The man had been right; the best thing he could do was get out of her life.

CHAPTER 21

An incessant buzzing dragged Hugh back to consciousness. As he worked his way to a sitting position, he tried to pinpoint the noise. *The alarm clock.* How long had it been since he'd woken to one of those? Steadying himself against the wall, he struggled to his feet, then stumbled to the bed, fumbling for the snooze button, finally turning it off.

His head was throbbing. Reaching up to massage his temple, he flinched at the touch. *Christ.* Groaning, the noise rough in his ash-dry mouth, he ran his tongue around his gums, trying to remove the fuzz inside his lips. No use.

His eyes popped open. Shit—what time was it? He jerked his head back to the alarm clock: just after eight thirty. He exhaled, not even realizing he'd been holding his breath, and sank onto the bed. *What a night.*

Something hard brushed against his thigh. Reaching down, he found a piece of his cleaning kit, a pull rod that had moved when he sat down. Now that he noticed it, his entire cleaning kit and the guns themselves were all where he'd left them. He still had so much to do.

He stood and glanced at the window, wincing at the bright sunlight sneaking into the room around the edges of the curtains, like a mini eclipse. On shaky legs, he moved to the window and threw open the curtains, squinting at the park below. People were already there, not many, but enough to suggest that it would be packed by midafternoon, especially if the weather held. Still, he could count heads later. For now, he needed some food.

Returning to the bed, he packed away the guns and cleaning supplies he'd laid out so carefully, placing everything exactly how it had been the last time he'd left. Before leaving, he scanned the room for any telltales. Except for the faint odor of gun oil in the air, everything looked the same. Hedging against a maid visiting while he was out, he opened the window, placed the hat carefully in position on top of the bag, then checked that the Do Not Disturb sign hung from the doorknob before stepping into the hallway. Minutes later, he was walking down Rideau Street in search of a fast-food restaurant.

The street was already crowded, most people sporting red clothes of some sort in deference to the national colors. They pressed in on him, crowding him; he couldn't avoid them. His heart pounding in his throat, he forgot all about trying to blend in and marched as purposefully as he could, ignoring the puzzled stares that followed whenever he flinched from human touch. He needed to finish this task as quickly as possible.

The line in the restaurant was painfully slow, and by the time he was on his way back to the hotel, takeout meals in hand, it was already nine thirty. Thankfully, he made it back without incident, letting himself into his room and ensuring the Do Not Disturb sign was still in place. Locking the door behind him, he placed the food on the desk and inspected the room. All clear.

Taking a seat by the window, he pulled out a breakfast sandwich and began eating. He surfed the Internet on his tablet, peering through the cracked screen. The schedule for Major's Hill Park showed one or two activities starting at ten o'clock—any minute now—but most events wouldn't get under way until later. Bottom line, by one o'clock, the park should be at its fullest, and it would stay that way through much of the afternoon. He still had lots of time.

His hand shifted to the tablet's off button when he noticed the icon indicating he had unread e-mail. Curious, he opened his inbox and found a message from Elizabeth, with no subject line. His stomach tightened, and his finger hovered over the message as he fought with himself. What should he do? The best thing would be to delete it. Too much had happened.

But what if there's a chance? A chance of what? Her coming back to him? There wasn't. She'd made that clear. Clenching his jaw, he deleted the message without reading it, turned off the tablet, and put it in his duffel bag. His path was set.

He pulled out the weapons and cleaning kit, laying everything back on the bed. Once everything was arranged in order, he picked up the AR-15 and performed a safety check, then used his thumbnail to pry out the rear takedown pin. After the pin was out, he tipped the upper receiver, revealing the guts of the weapon. Working steadily, he began field stripping the rifle, laying down the component pieces left to right on the comforter. His breathing was deep and rhythmic as he worked, fully immersed in the weapon.

When the rifle was disassembled, he held up the upper receiver and peered down the barrel, savoring the scent of gun oil on metal. The barrel was almost spotless, with only a few specks of dirt marring the tiny spiral pattern of the barrel's rifling. Even the chamber only had a few flecks of carbon.

The rifle really only needed a good oiling, but he had expected nothing less; Daryl had always taken care of his weapons.

After cleaning and oiling the upper receiver, he turned his attention to the lower receiver, with similar efficiency. When everything was scraped, wiped, and oiled, he reassembled the weapon, the room silent save for his breathing and the cold, metallic sound of gun parts moving together.

When the rifle was assembled, he pulled the charging handle to the rear, engaged the safety lever, and squeezed the trigger. Nothing, exactly what should have happened. Switching the safety to fire, he squeezed the trigger again. This time, there was a sharp crack as the hammer fell forward. Again, exactly what he'd expected. He carried out the rest of the performance check with a smile, confident the weapon was performing properly. When he was done, he set the rifle down and picked up the Sig Sauer.

Cleaning the pistol went quicker—it was much smaller, after all—although he still took his time. The longer he worked, the more his heart beat at a regular pace. When he laid the freshly scrubbed handgun on the bed forty minutes later and started packing his cleaning kit, it was like coming out of a trance. Most importantly, the weapons would work; of that he was sure.

From inside a pouch of the golf club bag, he withdrew several magazines, three each for the AR-15 and the P226. Reaching back into the same pouch, he grabbed two boxes of ammunition and started loading bullets. When the magazines were full, he set them on the floor, placed the guns beside them, then replaced the golf club bag in the closet. Now for the room.

He ripped off the comforter and sheets and threw them into a corner. Next, he lifted the mattress and dragged it toward the door, staggering under a deadweight that bowed and bent in his arms. The room's foyer was too narrow to place the mattress on its long side, so he wedged it in front of the door on its narrow end. Grabbing a chair, he braced it behind the mattress, then stepped back to inspect. *Sloppy.* It definitely wouldn't stop an entry team, but it would buy some time, which is all he needed.

The box spring followed, and he leaned it against the wall where the foyer opened to the main room, creating a quasi-chicane in tandem with the mattress. The box spring itself wouldn't stop anyone, but the frame might absorb the shock of a flash grenade thrown around the mattress, perhaps gaining more time to resist an assault. Still, he had no illusions how this would finish; a police entry team would take him down in no time.

In a way, it was liberating. He'd planned numerous operations, both in training and on deployment. Many people thought getting into an area was the hardest part. In truth, getting out was harder. Going in, a force had the element of surprise, at least if it was a good plan. Getting out, the enemy knew exactly where to look. Sometimes, planning for a viable exfiltration forced teams to accept suboptimal attacks in order to ensure they could get out after. The beauty of the current plan was there was no escape.

With the makeshift obstacles in place, it was time to set up a firing position. Although he'd already confirmed the sight lines from the window, a great view didn't necessarily translate to an ideal spot. For starters, the firing angle was a bit oblique. That meant he'd either have to be close to the window—as in skylining himself in it—or shoot from an elevated platform tucked back into the room. Hanging out the window with a rifle was clearly a nonstarter, so he'd have to improvise something else.

Dumping the room's television in a corner, he lugged the cabinet upon which the television had been sitting into the middle of the room. *Good, but not great.* The cabinet alone wouldn't be tall enough. At this short distance, the small difference between the gun's barrel and the scope was magnified, and he'd be liable to shoot into the bottom of the window frame if he wasn't careful. But it had potential, especially if he could get it higher.

After some thought, he spread the spare comforter on the cabinet and perched a dresser drawer on top. When it was built, he rested his elbows on the drawer, mimicking a supported shooting position, and shifted back and forth, testing for movement. It seemed stable. Last, he placed a pillow on top of everything to create a cushioned platform for his elbows to rest on.

The window itself was the last thing to prepare. Stepping closer, he undid the latch and pulled. The pane moved on rails and opened into the room, but a small metal bar at the base prevented it from opening more than a couple of inches. Good thing he'd stayed here before.

Turning to his duffel bag, he grabbed a pair of bolt cutters and severed the tiny restraining bar, then slid the window fully open. Before stepping away, he replaced the thin privacy curtain. It was flimsy enough to see through, so it could stay in place until the last moment, giving him a modicum of concealment from outside. Hell, he could probably even shoot through it. One more thing to lessen the signature.

Everything in place, he moved into the center of the room and looked around. The setup wasn't perfect, but it would work. He checked his watch for what seemed like the hundredth time—almost quarter to one. *Not much longer.*

He absently munched a cold hash brown while scrutinizing the room. It was good work, the best he could do in the time available. He swallowed a lump of food and winced at a cramp in his stomach.

When the feeling passed, he returned to the weapons, picking up the pistol and tucking it into the top of his cargo pants at the small of his back. He picked up the AR-15 magazines next, visually inspecting the rounds and testing the strength of the springs by pushing on the top bullet with a thumb. *All good.* Grabbing the AR-15, he seated a clip in the magazine housing and pulled the charging lever, chambering a bullet. Thumbing the safety lever, he set the rifle on top of his makeshift firing position, then arrayed the other two magazines within easy reach.

He bent down to pick up the pistol magazines, sticking two in a pocket of his cargo pants and keeping the last one in his hand. Drawing the Sig Sauer, he seated the remaining clip and jammed it home, his hands coming together with a solid click. He pulled back the slide and released it, then carefully performed a press check to ensure a bullet was in the chamber. It was. Breathing deeply, he thumbed the decock lever to ease tension on the hammer, then replaced the pistol at the small of his back.

He started to check his watch again when pain shot through his stomach, like it was on fire. Doubled over, he staggered into the bathroom, falling to his knees in front of the toilet. Raising the lid, he stuck his face into the bowl and dry heaved. Nothing. He jammed a finger down his throat and vomited, partially chewed food tinged with greenish bile and a surprising amount of redness spewing from his mouth.

When everything was out, he lurched to his feet, wiping his mouth with a hand. He flushed and hurried into the main room.

From the bedside table, he grabbed his Copenhagen, putting a large wad into his mouth and stuffing the tin into a pocket of his cargo pants. *Ready.* He checked his watch: almost one o'clock, time to get into position. He moved to the window, taking care to stand to one side, then gently pulled the privacy curtain aside with a finger.

The park was almost overflowing, the large crowd ebbing and flowing like so many crawling ants, the movement almost hypnotic. For a moment, his task was forgotten and he watched, mouth hanging open. It was wondrous, like watching a single living organism.

Among the mostly red-and-white-clad people moved several police officers, easy to pick out in their dark uniforms as they strode purposefully through the mass of bodies. His breathing grew faster, so he took a deep breath. *Calm down. Focus.* Steeling himself, he stepped away from the window, picked up the AR-15, and got into position on top of the cabinet, hunching into a supported firing stance and putting his eye to the scope.

Everything looked less real, like a television show. A momentary pang gripped his chest as he remembered he'd neglected to zero the scope to his eye relief, but he dismissed the thought as quickly as it came. It didn't matter. There were so many people he could throw bullets out the window and hit somebody.

He kept scanning, part of him reveling in the unseen power he wielded over the unsuspecting lives playing out mere hundreds of yards away. On one side of the park, a couple was having what looked like a passive-aggressive fight, both of them studiously ignoring each other, the man wearing a scowl. Behind them, a young man was picking pockets, working his way through the crowd as smoothly as a shark in the ocean.

Pulling his eye from the scope, he wiped his sweating brow, then bent back over the weapon. Where should he make the first engagement? The center of the park—force everyone to the outside? Maybe on the edges, force them to the center. How would they react?

His stomach revolted again, and he turned away from the scope to press his mouth against his shoulder. Clenching his eyes, he bit himself, relishing the physical pain. His heart beat so loudly it filled his ears, buffeting him like a tiny boat in a raging hurricane. *God, let this end soon.*

When the sickness passed, he lifted his head, rubbed his eyes, and turned back to the rifle, training the sight picture near the stage. *What the fuck?* He gasped, jerking away from the scope as if he could unsee the woman who'd been in the crosshairs. It couldn't be. Slowly, the weapon shaking in his hands, he took up his sight picture again.

Had that been Elizabeth? *Near the stage?* It took a few seconds, but he found the woman again. She certainly looked like Elizabeth, blonde hair almost hurting his eyes as it caught the sun. Still, the woman in the scope seemed different, as if she'd never smiled in her life, her morose expression out of place among the sea of revelers around her. It might even have been that look that had caught his eye, or maybe it was the aimless way she floated around, like she had lost something.

His vision blurred, and he raised his head, warm moistness flooding his eyes. Had he thought he'd felt pain before? Nothing like this. A moan escaped his throat as he wiped away tears, rubbing his eyes so hard spots appeared in his vision. He had to make sure. Blinking his eyes open, he inhaled, exhaled, controlling his breathing, then lowered his eye once more to the scope.

In the time he'd been looking away, the woman had moved on. He swung the rifle back and forth, trying to locate her. *Where was she?* Maybe he'd been wrong. Suddenly, she was there, closer to the stage than before, her back to him, perhaps why he'd missed her. It was her all right, weaving through the crowd with a gymnast's grace, heading for the northern edge of the park. Before reaching the street, she sat on a bench, staring impassively back in his direction.

Raising his head, he rubbed his eyes. Why was she here? She'd come back for him, that had to be the reason. Then why hadn't she come to the hotel? *Idiot.* She didn't know; he hadn't told her he'd booked the room. He laid the AR-15 down on the cabinet, turned, and paced across the room.

What to do? It was a sign, it had to be, a final chance at redemption. He snorted. Amid the chaos of his surroundings, the thought was preposterous. His snort turned into laughter, ringing peals that racked his body until he spied Daryl's journal. He couldn't back out now. Daryl had been right; a message had to be sent. And he'd already come too far.

Besides, Elizabeth's dad was right; she'd be better off without him. Looking around at the ruins of his room was proof enough of that. The laughter died on his lips. The best he could do now was ensure she'd be all right. There'd be a stampede when he started, and he didn't want to drive a flood of people toward her.

Returning to the firing position, he pressed the rifle's butt into his shoulder and trained the scope on the bench where Elizabeth still sat, almost unchanged and oblivious to the battle raging within him.

"I love you," he whispered, trying to engrave her image on his brain. Drawing a shuddering breath, he scanned her immediate vicinity, confirming there were fewer people in that area of the park than anywhere else. She'd be okay. Exhaling in several bursts, he drifted the scope away, moving to the center of the park, a good place to start.

A group of five people stood in a semicircle, and he randomly dropped the crosshairs on one of them, a man probably in his mid-forties, balding, slightly overweight. The man wore a red Canada T-shirt and tan cargo shorts. Were the other people the man's friends? Family? He shook his head. *Stupid.*

He concentrated on his breathing, inhaling deeply through his nose, holding it, slowly pushing the air out through half-closed lips, holding it again for several seconds with half a breath in his lungs, then releasing the remainder in one quick blast. Then repeat, like he'd been trained. After several cycles, he synchronized the crosshairs, moving the point of aim up and down in time with his breathing, up on the inhale, slowly falling on the exhale, steady on the pauses. Repeat.

His pulse thudded through his body, even in his fingertips, sending minute shivers through the rifle every time it beat, his body transferring the rhythm to the rifle cradled in his arms. With each cycle of breath, he struggled to maintain control, relaxing into the weapon tucked securely at his shoulder.

On the next breath, he slowly clenched his right hand at the start of the exhale, his index finger tightening on the trigger. With half a breath left, he paused, willing the sights to become steady, all exterior influences removed. The rifle trembled ever so slightly; then he was drowning for oxygen, unable to hold position any longer. With a gasp, he let off the trigger and sucked in air, pulling away from the scope. It was now or never.

He took a quick, deep breath and forced it out in a rush, then took another. Clenching his jaw, he put his eye back to the scope and found his target in the same spot. Another deep breath, then it was hissing out between his lips as he took the slack out of the trigger. At the halfway point, he held his breath, settling the crosshairs. Elizabeth's face flashed through his mind, and with a groan, he pushed the thought from his head and jerked the trigger.

CHAPTER 22

Hugh's ears rang from the force of the concussion in the small room. He held the trigger after the first shot, had to consciously relax his hand; then he was squeezing again, and again. The third shot came easier, as did each one after it, each one passing harmlessly over the crowd and into the Ottawa River. He was unable to stop until he was squeezing and nothing was happening except the dead feel of the trigger under his finger.

Canting the AR-15 on its side, he stared through the ejection port cover into the empty chamber, almost in wonderment at the bolt carrier stuck to the rear. Out of bullets. Instinctively, he depressed the magazine-release button, and the empty clip slid free, bouncing off the cabinet and clattering to the ground. Lowering the rifle, he stared out the window.

In the park beneath, people were frozen, heads swiveling everywhere as they searched for the origin of the sounds that still echoed through the downtown core. When the first person ran, propelled by some primordial urge to flee the park, the panic caught like a contagion. The crowd pulsed and surged in all directions at once.

He picked up the rifle and observed the chaos through the scope, catching a fleeting glimpse of the overweight balding man in the Canada T-shirt.

"Live to fight another day," he said, keeping the crosshairs trained on the fleeing man, the group he'd been standing with nowhere to be seen. Within seconds, the park's center had emptied.

Why had he changed his point of aim? Were those warning shots he'd fired any less of a crime than if he had sent the bald man's brain tissue and skull pieces soaring into the air? For that matter, why hadn't he packed everything up and slunk away, disappeared with nobody the wiser?

All he knew was that in the end, he couldn't do it, but he'd still had to do something. In a way, he was like the park he now watched, insides roiling, impossible to contain, yet possessing small pockets of calm that fought to control the beast, direct the aggression in a harmless direction. In the park, these small pockets were invariably centered on police officers, bulwarks against humanity's base instincts for survival, whereas his calm centered on something else, something found in the only other oasis of stillness amid the churning mass of people.

Elizabeth.

Peering through the scope, he found her where he'd last seen her, standing behind the bench where she'd been sitting. Her gaze was locked in his direction, and he could have sworn she was looking right at him. In that instant, her using the bench as a protective wedge against the exodus of people, he loved her more than ever. He had to see her, hold her.

He scanned the crowd one last time, picking out the police, who were having difficulty establishing control over the chaos. Some had weapons drawn, some didn't, but their efforts were uncoordinated, adding as much to the confusion as they attempted to solve. He could easily slip into the park and find Elizabeth, see her once more, explain everything.

Hands trembling, he did a safety check on the AR-15, stood, and dropped it on the bed. His right arm numb, he was breathing fast, almost hyperventilating. He'd been so close to the edge, and having stared into a dark, bottomless pit, he'd never wanted to live as badly as he did right now. He had to redeem himself. He had to reach her.

Turning on his heel, he sprang for the door, clawing the makeshift obstacles out of the way. Stumbling over the mattress, he jerked open the door and ran into the hallway. As he sprinted toward the stairwell, heads poked out of doors, just as quickly disappearing at the sight of him, like a game of Whac-A-Mole. Within seconds, he was at the stairwell, ripping open the door and careening headlong down the narrow steps, oblivious of the danger.

Barging his way into the crowded lobby, he weaved a path through the mob toward the front exit, where a bellhop held up his hands to stop him. Shoving the man aside, he darted through the doors and ran around the side of the building toward the park.

Once he was outside, the wave of people threatened to carry him away. Banged about like flotsam, he made slow progress, clinging to his desire to see Elizabeth like a life preserver. Around him, the roar of the crowd mingled with the shouted directions of police officers, creating a numbing hum of noise that blended with the ringing in his ears.

By the time he reached the center of the park, the crowd had thinned out, although many people lingered on the edges, partly concealed in the trees. Across the mostly clear park, he caught his first glimpse of her, halfway between him and the stage. Their eyes locked, and he paused, briefly, before resuming his movement toward her.

"Stop where you are!"

He slowed to a walk, chilled despite the heat. Ahead, Elizabeth's eyes flickered to his right, where the voice had come from, her face pale. He glanced over his right shoulder, at two uniformed police officers standing on the edge of the park, almost forty yards away. One was waving people back to the Laurier; the other was focused on Hugh, pistol drawn and pointing roughly around his feet.

"Drop the weapon!" the policeman pointing the pistol yelled, his voice breaking.

What? What weapon? He furrowed his brow and looked around. The guns were back in the room, so what the hell was the man talking about? *Is he talking to me?* He slowly side-stepped nearer to Elizabeth, now rooted to the ground, keeping his hands at chest height.

"I said stop!"

Turning slowly to face the officer, he slowly brought his hands to his sides, palms open and facing the front. A hard pang of panic blossomed in his stomach.

"Freeze!" The police officer took two quick steps, spread his feet, and bent his knees into a shooting stance, at the same time raising his pistol until it pointed directly at Hugh's chest.

He froze, goose bumps on his arms. "Calm down," he said, meeting the policeman's eyes and struggling to keep his voice from trembling. "Take it easy." He glanced at Elizabeth, now parallel to him, her hands at her mouth. What was she staring at? Twisting to look behind him, he stopped as something hard jabbed him in the small of his back.

The Sig Sauer. Christ, he'd forgotten it. His mouth went dry. He looked back to the policemen, eyes rolling in his head. What had he been thinking? Too late now, he needed to concentrate on getting out of this.

The officer with the pistol advanced methodically toward him, perhaps thirty yards away and closing the distance with slow, purposeful steps. Hugh's gaze darted everywhere, searching for options.

His immediate vicinity was empty, but several people hid in the trees behind him, directly in line with the angle of the policeman's advance. The cop was still a bit far to risk shooting with a pistol—especially with innocent bystanders in the line of fire—but in a few more seconds, he might decide it was worth the risk. He had to act now.

He locked eyes with Elizabeth. He could make it; even if the cop tried a shot, he'd probably miss under these conditions. *Stupid.* What was he thinking? It was too dangerous. Even still, the urge to run became so strong he stepped in her direction, then again, the cop screaming at him to freeze, until she shook her head, her hands covering her mouth. He stopped.

She was right. He'd fought enough, now he needed to listen. It was the only way he'd make it home. Turning back to the officer, he held up his hands.

"It's all right," he said, willing the officer to meet his gaze, projecting his compliance like a spear and broadcasting that he'd heard and understood. "I'll do everything you say." Was this cop even old enough to shave? *Concentrate.*

The officer stopped about twenty yards away and squared off, pistol brandished before him. At this distance, the pistol's barrel had become a black hole that threatened to drain away his life, faster than he could hope to avoid.

"Get on the ground," the cop said. He was sweating, the whites of his eyes showing around his pupils.

Hugh nodded, flexed his knees.

"Get on the fucking ground!" another voice yelled. It was the second policeman, the one who'd been directing people to the Laurier, running up to join his partner.

The first policeman flinched, glancing beside him while his pistol wavered wildly to his front.

He tensed, crouching lower as every sense dialed in to the two policemen to his front. *Not like this.* "Don't shoot," he said, reaching for the ground.

The first officer looked back at him. "Freeze!"

"Shut your fucking mouth!" the second police officer yelled. "Get on the ground!"

He cringed, eyes drawn inexorably to the second officer. *He's going to shoot.* It was a fact, the man's wide eyes told him the officer wasn't all there. He was on blackout drive and wouldn't remember a thing when this was all over.

His only chance was the first officer, to whom he now looked. "Don't let your partner shoot me," he said, adding a silent prayer. *Please, God, make him listen. I'm not a threat!*

"I said freeze," the first officer said. His hands were shaking.

He nodded. He couldn't stay like this for long; his bent legs were already trembling as the muscles seized up. He took a deep breath. "I'm going to get on the ground. My legs—"

"Shut the fuck up!" the second cop yelled, striding closer and thrusting the pistol at him.

He flinched backward. "My legs are seizing up," he said, raising his hands as if to ward off a shot. "I'm going to lie down. I won't try for the pistol." He stared at the first cop.

The young officer nodded warily at him. "Okay, slowly."

The second cop glanced furiously at his partner, then back at Hugh.

"Don't shoot, all right?" he said, tears welling in his eyes. *Don't let me go out like this.* "I'm not a threat. I'm getting on the ground, all right?"

The first officer stared at him, his eyes flickering to his partner. He nodded again, slowly.

His eyes flitted between the officers, the aggressive face of the second cop turning his insides rotten. But what other choice did he have? "Okay, here I go. Don't shoot."

Eyes glued to the officers, he slowly moved, lowering himself gently to the grass until he knelt on his right knee. He was going to make it, the soft grass was so close. And at least he was in the middle of the park and wouldn't have to lie on the hot pavement. The thought sent a crazy urge to laugh through him, and he clenched his lips tight, then reached behind with his left foot, hands moving to the ground.

His foot caught on something.

Then he was stumbling, arms flailing as he wobbled and lost balance, teetering toward the ground. As he fell, his arms instinctively reached out to break his fall.

Fire spat from the second officer's pistol, blinding him, searing his eyes seconds before he was bowled over as effortlessly as if he'd been kneeling in front of a train. He came to rest on his back.

His ears rang, snuffing out noise as if he were floating in water, ears submerged. Above him, the sky was an impossibly deep blue, so deep it seemed endless, an inverted chasm. He swallowed, the sound unnaturally loud inside his head. There was so much saliva in his mouth; he was drowning. He swallowed again, but the fluid came back as quickly as he got rid of it. Why were his hands wet? Was he sweating that badly? He tried to roll over and sit up, but his legs wouldn't work.

"Stay with me." The voice was faint, as if from across the park.

Were they talking to him? He opened his mouth to respond, choked, tried turning his head to spit, but couldn't. His mouth was full, he was gagging on warm, thick liquid that bubbled from the corners of his mouth, running through the stubble on his cheek and down his neck. Someone moved his head, lifting it up, and then Elizabeth's face was above his, hair hanging down to enclose the two of them in a golden cocoon.

Tears streamed from her eyes. "Don't leave me."

I won't. I'm home now.

He'd been gone a long time, but he was back now, and that was what mattered. He'd done terrible things to get here, but so had Odysseus, so had everybody who made this journey. It was all right. The important thing was that he'd made it, he'd finally made it.

I love you. Did she know that? Why couldn't he speak? He had to tell her. Did she know how sorry he was?

Hands appeared on her shoulders, pulling her from him. She screamed, flinging off the hands to throw herself protectively across his chest.

He reached for her, but his arms, they wouldn't move. Why was it so cold? He shouldn't be cold. He fought to hold on, closing his eyes and taking a torturous, bubbling breath that made him cough in desperate drowning hacks, each one weaker than the last.

He was tired. Blackness spread across his eyes, and he blinked to clear his vision, blinked again, then left his eyes closed. God, he was tired. But not tired enough to stop panic from gripping him in a vise as arms wrapped around his neck, his dream come to life. *Not the little girl.*

"Don't leave me," a woman said, her voice penetrating the fog that was enveloping him. "I missed you."

No, no, no, no, no. Using all his effort, he opened his eyes, praying to see her. *Elizabeth?* Through failing eyes, her face was barely visible, blue eyes blurring to brown, blonde hair merging to black. And her voice sounded different, distorted, almost foreign, although he could still make out the words as her lips moved.

"I love you."

He'd gotten it all wrong, everything. But he understood now. His battle was over, and he was ready to face his judgment.

He attempted a smile, drawing forth another bout of coughing, weaker this time. It was too much. *I'm sorry.* He closed his eyes, resting his head against the hard concrete. *I love you, too.*

Someone took his hand and clasped it against their chest. "You're not alone."

For the first time in his life, he knew that to be true. As the darkness covering his eyes gave way to blinding light, Hugh Dégaré slowly sank into the welcoming, unmindful embrace of the abyss.

TEASER CHAPTER

Jihadi Bride

For the second time in his life, Erik Petersson was at war.

Perched on the pedals of his banana-yellow hardtail bike with his butt hovering over the saddle, he pushed the thought from his head. A rock garden was coming up, and he needed to concentrate. Knees and elbows bent, he coasted on the hardscrabble trail and scanned for the best line through the upcoming obstacle, tuning out the branchless lower trunks of towering pines whipping past.

That night, as always after riding, he'd lie in bed with eyes closed and relive the trees zipping by, so vivid he'd inadvertently flinch while sections of trail slalomed through his mind. But right now, rattling over exposed tree roots riddling the track, only the ride mattered.

Which was, after all, why he was here, loosening tightly coiled internal springs.

This second war was different. There were no uniforms. There was nobody shooting at him. There was no dirt or sweat or blood or cowering in a concrete bunker from wayward rockets or a whole host of other things he associated with war. Biggest of all, while he might technically still be a soldier, he wasn't in the army anymore.

Mud sprayed his legs as he splashed through a puddle, sideswiping a partially submerged rock that wrenched the handlebars under his grip. He should've missed that one, but it had been a while, so he had an excuse. With the other rider opening up distance, he might need it.

He needed less time hunting people, more time in the saddle, which was another thing different about this war. Indeed, this war made up for everything he'd experienced the first time he'd been at war with a whole host of different features, at least for him.

Such as time to go trail riding, even if it was a rare occurrence.

The black handlebar bag shifted side to side between the grips. It should be tighter, his phone and wallet were in there. Where would he be without his phone? Where would anyone be? Phones were critical to this war, modern-day rifles that enabled the conflict to be fought virtually, as much as or more than in the physical domain.

But that was only part of it, the proverbial tip of the iceberg.

This war had Twitter, Facebook, and YouTube. This war also had overtime and statutory holidays and Starbucks. In this war, he never left home, never deployed to a combat zone despite being on duty twenty-four hours a day, seven days a week. At times, this second war was so different he forgot he was even at war.

Times like those, the similarities eventually brought him back.

The crowded bush gave way to a field of bulrushes under a clear sky. He rode onto a boardwalk barely wide enough for two people to walk abreast and blinked to clear the sweat dripping into his eyes, then pedaled faster.

Competition, at least, was one thing that would always be the same.

This war was still a struggle between opposing forces. There were tactics and strategies that adapted and evolved. There were still people trying to kill each other, even if they employed old-school methods like sawing off heads, crucifixion, and burning alive. There were politics (of course!) and there were also contradictory reports and false reports and reports that arrived too late and exaggerated reports and, his personal favorite, circular reports. And because people were still needed to sift through all those reports, this war still had long periods of boredom broken up by bursts of intense excitement.

Sometimes, though, like in the previous month, he'd link two pieces of information together and enable the team to stop the virus gripping the country from metastasizing. Times like that made him feel like doctors must feel after removing a brain tumor; it didn't get much better. Even with all the sacrifices he'd made—probably because of them—coming through in the breach was direct feedback that he was protecting his loved ones.

Like Arielle.

Speaking of which, he spared a glance at his watch. Time to head back.

"Hey, Jordan," he called at the rider ahead. "Let's turn around."

Jordan pumped the brakes and skidded to a stop. "What?" he asked, pulling his water bottle from its clip on the down tube.

He eased to a stop beside the younger man. "I've got to head back," he said. "I'm on *World of Warcraft* in an hour."

"Can you hear the words coming out of your mouth?" Jordan said, spitting water onto the ground. "You're like fifty years old. You know that's too old to be playing video games, right?"

"I'm forty-five," he said, then shrugged. "Besides, I don't play for me. It lets me keep in touch with Arielle."

"You know you could go for coffee, right? Like normal fathers and daughters?" Jordan said, angling his bike to face the opposite direction.

"Tough when we're not in the same city. And I adapt to what she likes," he said, the banter coming easily. "Unlike your relationship with the spawn from your three divorces."

"Touché," Jordan said, smiling. "Do you at least have a cool character? Some ginormous ogre to compensate for your puny five-foot-five frame?"

"Five nine," he said without hesitation. "And no, my character's pretty pathetic. If I wasn't in Arielle's guild, I'd get my ass handed to me every time."

Jordan chuckled. "At least you're honest," he said, then sighed in mock resignation. "Okay, Lord Farquad, let's go. You take the lead."

He hopped the bike around and then leaned into the pedals, moving back onto the boardwalk. Going slower on the return trip, his thoughts wandered to Arielle. Gaming online with her was great, but they didn't connect very often. He needed to make more effort to get to Montreal. Hell, it was less than two hours door to door from his place in Ottawa.

"You think Stephanie would be interested in a night of playing *World of Warcraft*?" Jordan called from behind, yelling over the rattling of the bikes.

"Fuck you," he said over his shoulder, cheeks heating up.

"Yeah, you're right," Jordan said. "She doesn't like men with goatees. Or tattoos."

"Work's too busy," he said, sparing a glance at the faint shadow of a black devil on his forearm. Still there even after five laser removal sessions. Grunting, he returned to the scree-covered hill that was kicking his ass.

"Another good point." From the closeness of his voice, Jordan must have been hugging his rear wheel. "I'm sure she'll be all over you once you catch that asshole radicalizing people in Quebec. That shit's like Spanish fly to the ladies."

Laughter sprayed from his mouth, forcing him to dab a foot onto the ground to avoid spilling. Rolling to a stop, he smiled back at Jordan, shoulders heaving. "What's wrong with you?"

"What? Why are we stopping?" Jordan said, a mock frown on his face. "I thought you had to nerd out?"

"I'm not asking Stephanie out," he said, shaking his head. "And al-Kanadi is real. All I need—" Ringing came from the black bag on his handlebars. "You'll see," he said, unzipping the bag and removing his phone. The number was familiar, although Arielle shouldn't have been calling already. They weren't supposed to be online for another forty minutes.

He glanced at Jordan. "It's Arielle," he said. "It shouldn't be long."

Jordan nodded up the trail. "I'll keep going. I'll go slow so you can catch up, old man."

"Right behind you," he said, bringing the phone to his ear.

"Stephanie. *Warcraft*. Genius," Jordan called out as he rode off. "Start a blog."

"Asshole."

"Dad?" Arielle said, her voice lifting up in confusion.

His heart jumped into his throat. "Sorry, sweetie, not you. I'm talking to Jordan."

Silence from the other end of the line.

"Arielle?"

"I'm here."

His shoulders relaxed. "I'm in the woods, thought I lost you for a second," he said. "What's going on? Are we still on for noon? I know how we can get the secret—"

"Dad . . ."

He stopped. "Arielle?"

A deep breath, then, "I can't make it."

"What do you mean?" he said, switching the phone between ears. "I thought we had a date."

More silence.

"Sweetie? Is everything okay?" Under the dense canopy overhead, the air where he'd stopped was suddenly thick, the branches choking off both sunlight and the fresh breeze. "Talk to—"

"I love you."

"I love you, too," he said, skin prickling. "What's wrong?"

"I'm not going to be able to see you for a while," she said.

"What are you talking about? Did something happen at school?"

"I'm not at school."

"You're not . . ." He squinted. "Where are you?"

Another deep breath. "Oslo."

"Oslo . . ." *Oslo, Norway?*

"I don't have much time. My flight's in a couple of minutes."

"Wait, what?" he said, brow furrowed. "Flight to where? Why are you in Oslo?"

"I want you to know that I don't disown you," she said, her voice wavering. "We're supposed to—that's part of it—supposed to erase our previous lives. But I still love you. I know you always meant well, and I pray for you."

She prays for me? He juggled the phone in his sweaty hand, missing part of her next words.

"—to Turkey," she said.

"What? What about Turkey?"

"We're flying to Turkey," she said. "We're meeting someone there who'll take us into Syria."

His mouth opened and closed without making a sound, what Jordan would have called blowing fish kisses if he'd been around to see. *Syria?*

"Dad?"

His heart jackhammered inside chest, trying to escape. *Syria?*

"Are you there?"

"I'm here," he said, the voice babbling out of his mouth not his own. "Sweetie, stop. Don't do this. Whatever yo—"

"I have to," she said, the steel in her voice evocative of when she was three years old and refusing to get ready for bed in any other order besides brushing her teeth *then* brushing her hair. The image filled his mind, rendering him speechless again. She was his little girl; how could she be going to Syria? He opened his mouth to force out something, anything—even a moan would be progress—but his throat constricted, choking off the words.

She continued, seemingly oblivious. "I have to do this, it's an obligation."

"Not for you," he said, as if explaining to a child how her argument didn't logically make sense. "You're not even Muslim."

More silence. "I converted four months ago," she said finally, her voice barely audible.

Four months? He staggered, as if her words were buffeting him. *Keep her talking.* Blinking, he rallied his strength. "Is it school?" he said, unbuckling the strap under his chin and removing his helmet.

She paused. "No . . . yes . . ."

"Sweetie—"

"It's not just school, it's everything," she said, louder now. "I can't live like this anymore, and Naomi says it'll be better there."

"Who's Naomi?" he said, cocking his head to the side.

"I met her at school," she said. "She introduced me."

"To who?" he said, free hand running through his short brown hair. He shook his head. "No, no, no. Do you know how dangerous this is?" *What is she thinking?* "What are you even going to do there?"

"There's lots we can do," she said, defensiveness creeping into her tone. "We can tend the wounded in hospitals, treat orphans. So many people have been hurt by this war—"

"Sure, but that's not the whole story," he said, pleading through suddenly moist eyes. "You can't even walk around without being covered up."

"That's my choice."

"Okay, but do it here, in Canada," he said, then wiped his mouth. He needed to try another tactic. "Listen, stay where you are. I'll meet you. We'll come home together. You can leave school, we'll—"

"I have to go. My flight's boarding."

His heart pounded in his ears, the rapid thumping drowning out his thoughts. "I'll call ahead to stop you. The police will pick you up in Turkey."

"There's not enough time," she said. "You know that."

He checked his watch, a lump forming in his stomach. How long could the flight be, four hours? Five, max? *Shit.* She was probably right—so what now? He blinked rapidly, looking wildly around. "Come home." *Think!* His free hand fingered a plain metal ring worn around a leather cord on his neck. Damn it, he couldn't lose his daughter as well.

"I love you."

"Arielle," he said, staring at the sky. Was this really happening? This could be the last time he'd ever talk to her. He closed his eyes as a single tear trickled down his cheek.

"Dad . . ."

"I'll find you," he said. "I'll bring you home."

Another voice sounded through the line, a girl's urgent voice, the words muffled.

"Send me a message when you make it through," he said, numbness spreading through his body. "You probably won't be able to call, but sending a text should be safe."

Silence.

What else? "Don't go with anybody you don't trust," he said, then shook his head. *Stupid.* What kind of advice was that? Well, what did he expect—his job was to catch people fleeing to Syria, not to coach them through the process. "Please be careful."

"I will. I promise," she said. "Bye."

"Arielle—" he said. Then the line went dead. He stood there, eyes unfocused, with the phone held loosely beside his ear. "I love you."

He lowered the phone, staring at the screen only to be scornfully informed that the call had ended. Hand shaking, he returned the device to the handlebar bag, then simply stood, rooted to the ground.

His daughter was going to Syria.

Images of black flags, masked men, and blindfolded prisoners with sawtooth knives held to their throats flashed through his mind in quick succession. Eyes rolling in his head, he gasped for breath, the thick woods suddenly suffocating him. His hand gravitated back to the ring hanging from his neck, his eyes closing as his fingers touched the warm metal.

He had to stop her. What was he doing standing here?

Snatching his helmet from the ground and jamming it onto his head, he hopped onto the bike and began to pedal as if the jihadist terrorist hordes—his foe in the second war of his life— were nipping at his heels.

ACKNOWLEDGMENTS

I am indebted to so many people who helped make this book a reality. Gloria Kempton, who gave me the initial guidance and confidence that I could tell this story. Terri Valentine, whose patience, insight, and honesty were a huge part in not only bringing this story to fruition, but helping me learn about the craft of writing (of which I have a lot left to learn).

A number of beta readers sacrificed their time and energy to give me feedback and improve the story; Jeff Peck, Tiffany Fraser, Jerry and Margaret Smith, thank you so much. And of course, Ryan Clow; not only were your suggestions incredibly perceptive, but this project gave me the chance to reconnect with you.

From a crowdfunding perspective, I don't even know where to start. Even though the book includes a list of grand patrons, every person who contributed to a preorder deserves thanks for entrusting me with this project. Of particular note is the crew at Canadian Forces Morale and Welfare Services, including Nancy Branco and Brieanne White. Also, my family, on both my and my wife's side, was so very supportive; I know the crowdfunding wouldn't have succeeded without your efforts. Thank you.

I'd also like to thank the team at Inkshares for creating and stewarding such a wonderful business venture, including Thad Woodman, Jeremy Thomas, and Adam Jack Gomolin. Elena Stofle provided wonderful support during the crowd-funding campaign, and Angela Melamud, Matt Kaye, and Avalon Marissa Radys all played a big part in bringing this to completion. Emily Zach and Devon Fredericksen from Girl Friday Productions were outstanding in guiding the editorial and design process and truly made me feel like part of a team. Shannon O'Neill, the developmental editor, not only helped to dramatically improve the story, but basically put on a writ-ing clinic for me, which was a wonderful opportunity. Laura Petrella, the copyeditor, continued this process, and the story has benefitted greatly from her attention to detail. Also, Alban Fischer, who created an iconic cover. I consider myself truly fortunate to have worked with such an outstanding team.

A few last people deserve specific mention. Mike Day, per-haps one of the most gifted and inspirational military leaders of his generation and whom I had the honor of serving with and for, thank you for the support as I took my off-ramp. I hope this story makes up for my decision in some small way.

My wife, Tabatha, undoubtedly my biggest believer and fan. I could not have done this without your support and sac-rifices. Thank you.

Last, but certainly not least, I could not have written this book without the experiences and opportunities I've enjoyed while serving in the Canadian Armed Forces. If there was ever any doubt in the maxim that "Humans are more import-ant than hardware," let it be put to rest immediately, for the Canadian Forces is nothing without the wonderful and inspir-ing people who serve, in whatever capacity. This story is not mine, it's theirs; I'm simply the conduit. I hope I've lived up to your expectations.

FNV

ABOUT THE AUTHOR

Photo © 2016 Robin Spencer of Spencer Studio

Alastair Luft is a lieutenant colonel in the Canadian Army with twenty years of service in the Princess Patricia's Canadian Light Infantry. Luft graduated from the Royal Military College of Canada with a BA in politics and economics. He lives in Ottawa with his wife and two daughters, and except for his multiple tours of duty around the world, he has spent the greater part of his life in eastern Ontario. *The Battle Within* is his first novel.

PATRONS PAGE

INKSHARES

 Inkshares is a crowdfunded book publisher. We democratize publishing by having readers select the books we publish—we edit, design, print, distribute, and market any book that meets a preorder threshold.

Interested in making a book idea come to life? Visit inkshares.com to find new book projects or start your own.